Innocent Traitor

Innocent Traitor

ALISON WEIR

HUTCHINSON
LONDON

First published by Hutchinson in 2006

3 5 7 9 10 8 6 4 2

Copyright © Alison Weir 2006

Alison Weir has asserted her right under the Copyright,
Designs and Patents Act 1988 to be identified as the author of this work

Hutchinson
The Random House Group Limited
20 Vauxhall Bridge Road, London SW1V 2SA

Random House Australia (Pty) Limited
20 Alfred Street, Milsons Point, Sydney
New South Wales 2061, Australia

Random House New Zealand Limited
18 Poland Road, Glenfield
Auckland 10, New Zealand

Random House (Pty) Limited
Isle of Houghton, Corner of Boundary Road & Carse O'Gowrie
Houghton 2198, South Africa

The Random House Group Limited Reg. No. 954009

www.randomhouse.co.uk

A CIP catalogue record for this book is available from the British Library

The Random House Group Limited supports The Forest Stewardship Council (FSC),
the leading international forest certification organisation. All our titles that are printed
on Greenpeace approved FSC certified paper carry the FSC logo.
Our paper procurement policy can be found at www.rbooks.co.uk/environment

Mixed Sources
Product group from well-managed
forests and other controlled sources
www.fsc.org Cert no. TT-COC-2139
© 1996 Forest Stewardship Council

FSC

Typeset by
Palimpsest Book Production Limited, Polmont, Stirlingshire

Printed and bound in the UK by CPI Mackays, Chatham ME5 8TD

ISBN 9780091936761 (Trade Paperback)

This book
is dedicated to
my dear mother
and to Jim
who has been a father to me.

It is also dedicated
to Samuel Marston
to mark his first birthday.

Acknowledgements

I should like to express my warmest gratitude to my agent, Julian Alexander, and my editorial director at Hutchinson, Anthony Whittome, for their tremendous encouragement, support and creative suggestions, all of which have sustained me during the writing of this book. I should also like to thank Kirsty Fowkes for her creative input, Mandy Greenfield and Jane Selley for their extraordinary attention to detail, and the other members of the team at Random House – Kate Elton, Sue Freestone, James Nightingale, Richard Ogle and Neil Bradford – who have all helped in different ways to put the book together and inspire and spur its author.

I wish also to express my profound appreciation of the constant assistance of my husband Rankin, without whose selfless and loving support this project would never have come to fruition.

Thank you all.

Alison Weir
February 2006

The Royal House of Tudor in the Sixteenth Century

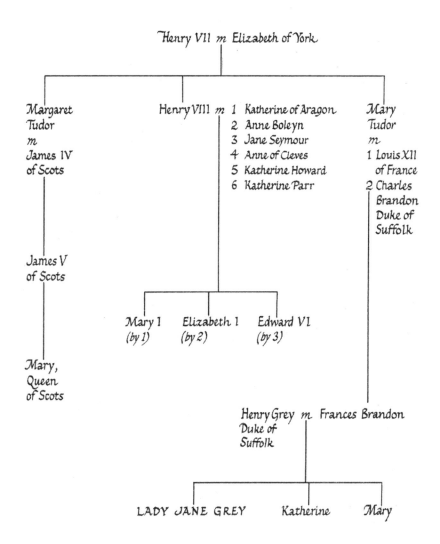

Henry VII *m* Elizabeth of York

Margaret Tudor *m* James IV of Scots

Henry VIII *m*
1 Katherine of Aragon
2 Anne Boleyn
3 Jane Seymour
4 Anne of Cleves
5 Katherine Howard
6 Katherine Parr

Mary Tudor *m*
1 Louis XII of France
2 Charles Brandon Duke of Suffolk

James V of Scots

Mary 1 (by 1)   Elizabeth 1 (by 2)   Edward VI (by 3)

Mary, Queen of Scots

Henry Grey *m* Frances Brandon
Duke of Suffolk

LADY JANE GREY   Katherine   Mary

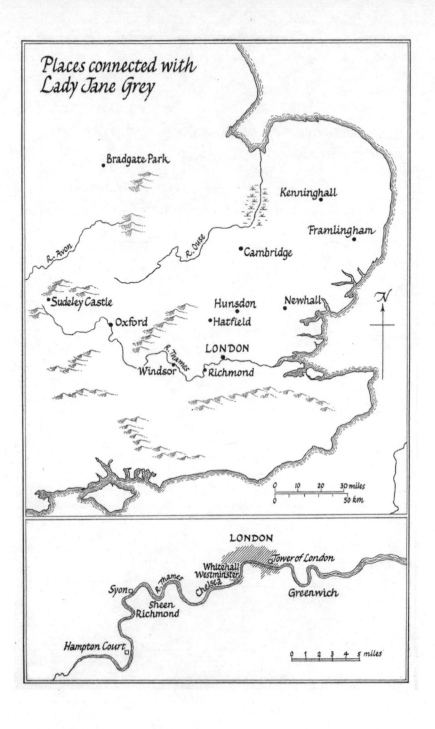

Places connected with
Lady Jane Grey

'If my faults deserve punishment, my youth at least, and my imprudence, were worthy of excuse. God and posterity will show me more favour.'

Written by Lady Jane Grey in the Tower of London, February 1554

Prologue

14th November 1553

It is over. My trial has ended, and I am now back in the Tower of London, this place that was once my palace and is now my prison.

I am sitting on my bed, my fingers feverishly creasing the crewel-work on the coverlet. The fire has been lit and crackles merrily in the hearth, but I am shivering. I am now a condemned traitor, and all I can hear in my head are the sonorous words of the Lord President, sentencing me to be burned or beheaded at the Queen's pleasure.

These are terrible words that every human being must tremble to hear, but especially terrible to me, who has spent only sixteen summers upon this Earth. I am to die when I have hardly begun to live. That is appalling enough, yet it is not just the dying that I fear, but the manner of it. Suddenly I am hideously aware of the leaping flames in the grate, the prickle of gooseflesh on my neck, and am sickened by the normally comforting smell of wood-smoke. I want to scream. I am rocking in misery, hearing those words again and again, and unable to believe that they were really said to me.

Not my will, but Thine, O Lord. And the Queen's, of course. I admit freely that I have offended grievously and deserved death for what I have done, but that my heart and will were bent to it, I shall truthfully protest to my last breath. *My last breath.* Oh, God.

Yet she said that she believed me. The Queen did accept my explanation, and she told me – I remember it well, as a drowning sailor clutches at driftwood – that this sentence would be but a formality. She was clearly angry with me, but she was also pleased to say that my youth excuses much. She must know that the plot was not of my making, and that I was the instrument of others' treasonous ambitions.

Dare I believe her? I have her promise, her royal promise, the word of a queen. I must hold fast to that when the panic threatens, as it does now, here in this tidy and peaceful room filled with homely things. I must believe in that promise, I must.

I lie down on my bed, gazing up unseeing at the wooden tester. I try to pray, but the old familiar words will not come. I realise that I am exhausted and drained of energy, my emotions shattered like shards of ice. All I want is to sleep and thus obliterate this horror for a time. But sleep eludes me, no matter how desperately I court it. Instead, for the thousandth time, I go over in my head how I came to be in this place. And in my tormented reverie I hear voices, clamouring to be heard, all speaking at once. I know them all. They have all played a part in shaping my destiny.

Frances Brandon, Marchioness of Dorset

Bradgate Hall, Leicestershire, October 1537

My travail begins as I am enjoying a walk in the garden. There is a sudden flood of liquid from my womb, and then, as my maid runs for cloths and assistance, a dull pain that shifts from the small of my back to the pit of my stomach. Soon, they are all clustering around me, the midwives and the women, helping me through the great doorway of the manor house and up the oaken stairs, stripping me of my fine clothing and replacing it with a voluminous birthing smock of bleached linen, finely embroidered at the neck and wrists. Now I am made to lie upon my bed, and they are pressing a goblet of sweet wine to my lips. I don't really want it, but I take a few sips to please them. My two chief ladies sit beside me, my gossips, whose job it is to while away the tedious hours of labour with distracting chatter. Their task is to keep me cheerful and to offer encouragement when the pains grow stronger.

And they do grow stronger. Less than an hour passes before the dull ache that accompanies each pang becomes a knife-like thrust, vicious and relentless. Yet I can bear it. I have the blood of kings in my veins, and that emboldens me to lie mute, resisting the mounting screams. Soon, God willing, I will hold my son in my arms. My son, who must not die early like the others, those tiny infants who lie beneath the flagstones of the parish church. Neither lived long enough even to sit or crawl. I do not account myself a sentimental person, indeed, I know that many think me too strong and hard-willed for a woman – a virago, my husband once said, during one of our many quarrels. But hidden within my heart there is a raw place reserved for those two lost babies.

Yet it is natural that this third pregnancy has often led me to revisit this secret place, to disturb and probe it gently, testing to see if past tragedies still have the power to hurt. I know I should forbid myself such weakness. I am King Henry's niece. My mother was a princess of England and Queen of France. I must face the pain of my loss as I do my labour – with royal dignity, refusing to indulge any further in morbid fancies, which, I am assured by the midwives, could well be harmful to the child I carry. One must try to be positive, and I am nothing if not an optimist. This time, I feel it in my bones, God will give us the son and heir we so desperately desire.

Another hour passes. There is little respite between each contraction, but the pain is still bearable.

'Cry out if you need to, my lady,' says the midwife comfortingly, as the women fuss round me with candles and basins of water. I wish they would all go away and leave me in peace. I wish they would let some fresh air into this foetid, stuffy chamber. Even though it is day, the room is dark, for the windows have been covered with tapestries and painted cloths.

'We must not risk the babe catching any chills from draughts, my lady,' the midwife warned me when she ordered this to be done. Then she personally inspected the tapestries to ensure there was nothing depicted in them that could frighten the child.

'Make up the fire!' she instructs her acolytes, as I lie here grappling with my pains. I groan; it's hot enough in here already, and I am sweating like a pig. But, of course, she is aware of that. At her nod, a damp cloth is laid on my brow. It does little to relieve my discomfort, though, for the sheets are wet with perspiration.

I stifle another groan.

'You can cry out, Madam,' the midwife says again. But I don't. I would not make such an exhibition of myself. Truly, it's the indignity of it all that bothers me the most, conscious as I am of my birth and my rank. Lying here like an animal straining to drop its cub, I'm no different from any common jade who gives birth. There's nothing exalted about it. I know it's blasphemy to say this, but God was more than unfair when He created woman. Men get all the pleasure, while we poor ladies are left to bear the pain. And if Henry thinks that, after this, I'm going to . . .

Something's happening. Dear God, what's going on? Sweet Jesus, when is this going to end?

The midwife draws back the covers, then pulls up my shift to expose my swollen, straining body, as I lie on the bed, knees flexed, thighs parted, and thrusts expert fingers inside me. She nods her head in a satisfied way.

'If I'm not mistaken, this young lad is now in something of a hurry,' she tells my anxiously hovering ladies.

'Ready now!' she crows triumphantly. 'Now push, my lady, push!'

I gather all my strength, breathe deeply and exhale with a great effort, knowing that an end is in sight. I can feel the child coming! I ram my chin into my chest again and push as I am instructed, hard. And the miracle happens. In a rush of blood and mucus, I feel a small wet form slithering from me. Another push, and it is delivered into the midwife's waiting hands, to be quickly wrapped in a rich cloth of damask. I glimpse its face, which resembles a wrinkled peach. I hear the mewling cry that tells me it lives.

'A beautiful daughter, my lady,' announces the midwife uncertainly. 'Healthy and vigorous.'

I should be joyful, thanking God for the safe arrival of a lusty child. Instead, my spirits plummet. All this – for nothing.

Queen Jane Seymour

Hampton Court Palace, Surrey, October 1537

It has begun, this labour that I, the King my husband and all England have so eagerly awaited. It began with a show of blood, then the anxious midwives hurried me into bed, fearful in case anything should go wrong. Indeed, every precaution has been taken to guard against mishap. Since early summer, when the babe first fluttered in my womb and I appeared in public with my gown unlaced, prayers have been offered up throughout the land for my safe delivery. My husband engaged the best physicians and midwives, and paid handsomely to have the soothsayers predict the infant's sex: all promised confidently that it would be a boy, an heir to the throne of England. Henry insisted that I be spared all state appearances, and I have spent these past months resting in opulent idleness, my every whim and craving gratified. He even sent to Calais for the quails I so strongly fancied. I ate so many I sickened of them.

Most pregnant women, I am told, sink into a pleasant state of euphoria as their precious burden grows heavier, as if Nature is deliberately affording them a short respite before the ordeal that lies ahead and the responsibilities of motherhood that follow it. But I have enjoyed no such comforting sense of well-being or elation at the glorious prospect facing me, God willing. My constant companion is fear. Fear of the pain of labour. Fear of what will happen to me if I bear a girl or a dead child, as my two unfortunate predecessors did. Fear of my husband, who, for all his devotion and care for me, is still a man before whom even strong men tremble. How he could ever have settled his affections on such a poor, plain thing as I is beyond my limited comprehension. My women, when they dare mention the subject, whisper that he loves me because I am the very antithesis of Anne Boleyn, that black-eyed witch who kept him at bay for seven years with promises of undreamed-of carnal adventures and lusty sons, yet failed him in both respects once he had moved Heaven and Earth to put the crown on her head. I cannot think about what he did to Anne Boleyn. For even though she was found guilty of betraying him with five men, one her own brother, it is horrifying to know that a man is capable of cutting off the head of a woman he has held in his arms and once loved to distraction. And it is even more horrifying when that man is my husband.

So I live in fear. Just now I am terrified of the plague, which rages in London so virulently that the King has given orders that no one from the city may approach the court. Confined to my chamber for the past six weeks, as is the custom for English queens, with only women to wait on me and the imminent birthing to brood on, I am prey to all kinds of terrors, so in a way it is a relief now to have something real upon which to focus my anxieties.

Henry is not here. He has gone hunting, as is his wont and passion, although he has given me his word that he will not ride more than sixty miles from here. I would be touched by his concern, had I not learned that it was his council that advised him not to stray further from me at this time. But I am glad, all the same, that he has gone. He would be just one more thing to worry about. His obsessive and pathetic need for this child to be a boy is more than I can cope with.

It is now afternoon, and my pains are recurring with daunting intensity, even though the midwife tells me that it will be some hours yet before the child can be born. I pray God that this ordeal may soon be over, and that He will send me a happy hour, for I do not think I can stand much more of this.

Hampton Court Palace, 12th October 1537

It has been three days and three nights now, and I am at the end of my feeble strength. Nothing in my life has prepared me for this agony. Not all the prayers, processions and intercessions that are taking place in London, by the King's order, can help me, for I am beyond help. There is just me and the pain. I have forgotten why I am here. I know only that if I scream loudly enough, someone will have to take the pain away.

Once, I heard the hastily summoned physicians whispering, asking each other if they should save mother or child. Even then, I was beyond caring, for all I had heard one of them suggesting that the infant be cut from my body. It did not matter, so long as the pain ceased. But that was hours, years ago, and still I am suffering. They have not carried out their dreadful threat.

Now it is night. I am barely aware of the darkness outside the mullioned window. They have pulled aside the curtain to let some air into the foetid room, which is heavy with the stink of my labour. The doctors and the women huddle around my bed in a frantic conclave. I am ready to give up the ghost, but they will not let me.

The midwife presses a handkerchief to my nose. It smells of pepper, and makes me sneeze violently. All of a sudden, the pangs begin again, stronger and stronger, consuming me with their ferocity. I lack even the power to scream, my mouth opening wide in a silent grimace. Something is happening, there is change in the rhythm of my body and an overpowering compulsion to bear down, to push. They are urging me to push, begging me. And as I push, making one last supreme effort, I am pushing the pain away; I am in charge of my own destiny. Then there is a violent wrenching: I feel as if I am being riven in half.

'A healthy, fair prince, your Majesty!' cries the midwife in jubilation. But I feel nothing. All I want is to sleep.

Frances Brandon, Marchioness of Dorset

Bradgate Hall, October 1537

Shouts from the courtyard below herald the return of the hunting party and wake me from slumber. It is late evening already. I must have slept for hours. My husband is here.

Beside the bed stands the heavy oak cradle carved with the Dorset crest, two unicorns ermined and hooped with gold, all painted in bright colours; within it lies my baby, now tightly swaddled and slumbering soundly. Beyond, seated in the glow of a candle and the dancing firelight, sits the nurse, Mrs Ellen, stitching a seam on a tiny silk bonnet. I close my eyes again as I hear footsteps approaching. I would give anything to avoid having to tell Henry, my lord, that I have failed him yet again.

But he already knows. The expression on his face as he enters the room tells me that. He is a man easily overruled in many matters, but this is one that touches his pride, and his nobility.

'A girl,' he says brusquely, 'and all to do again. Why God

8

should not favour us is beyond me. We go to Mass regularly, we give out charity by the dollop, we lead a Christian life. What more can we do?'

I ease myself up, profoundly grateful that I have not suffered tearing during the birth. Lying flat on my back sets me at an immediate disadvantage. Even so, Henry is looming over me like a stiff caricature of outraged manhood.

'The child is healthy, at least,' I say coldly, 'and with God's grace, a brother shall follow her. I know my duty.' And you, my lord, the son of a mere marquess, need not remind me, the daughter of a queen, where that duty lies.

I can see in his eyes that, despite himself, he admires my dignity and resolve. Even now, exhausted as I am in my childbed, I know he desires me and finds me alluring, even though I am not beautiful in the conventional sense. He likes my auburn hair – Tudor hair, he calls it, and I suspect that is part of the attraction. He thinks my lips are sensual, he admires my dark brows, my tilted nose, my determined chin. Even after bearing three children in four years, my twenty-year-old body, large-breasted and wide-hipped, still has the power to arouse him, especially with those breasts made more voluptuous by pregnancy. But he is not thinking now of the lusty delights in which I am usually so willing a partner. Instead, Henry looks at his little scrap of a daughter and has to smile, for she looks so like her royal great-uncle, the King: she has the same red-gold hair, determined little mouth and blue-green eyes, which, for all that she is but new-born, are regarding him with what seems to be uncommon intelligence.

I am surprised to see the saturnine, finely chiselled features form themselves into a grin.

'A pretty wench,' I venture.

He nods, straightening, a calculating light in his eyes. 'Indeed. We shall make her a brilliant marriage, to bring glory on our house. And in the meantime, Frances, we shall make merry getting her a brother. As soon as you are recovered, of course.'

'Of course,' I agree. 'As I said, I know my duty.'

'One can always combine duty with pleasure,' he smirks. The worst moment has passed. Both of us are making light of our terrible disappointment.

*

Our as-yet-unnamed daughter – we are arguing, because Henry wants Katherine after his mother, and I want Frances, or Jane, for the Queen – is a week old today. She is a good baby, taking her feeds with vigour from the wet-nurse, and sleeping regularly already. She rarely cries. I, on the other hand, am restless and uncomfortable, enduring the ache of engorged breasts, and the leaking of milk through the bindings applied to them by the midwife, who says that it should dry up in a few days. That's not soon enough for me.

Today it is crisp and cold, but bright. By late afternoon, the sky framed by my window is suffused with the golden light of the setting sun. Below this vast sky lie the fertile acres of the Bradgate estate, stretching far away into the distance. I am sitting in a chair, gazing out upon the sparkling lake and the wilderness beyond it. In the distance I can glimpse the thatched roofs of cottages.

I like this place. I am aware that there are those who think I married beneath me, but there are many compensations, not the least of which is a virile and like-minded husband, who shares my hopes and ambitions. And then there is this house, this mellowed, turreted red-brick mansion with its courtyard and gatehouse, its rooms richly furnished in the latest fashion, and its patchwork of gardens and arbours, in which it is a delight to take the air.

Suddenly, I want to be outdoors. I was never one to sit at home reading or embroidering, which most girls of my rank are encouraged to do. For me, walking, riding and hunting are essential. And I have had enough of this wretched, stuffy bedchamber.

'My cloak!' I snap. I will defy Madam Midwife and go out, just for a short walk. With one maid in attendance, I brave the stairs and then, with increasing boldness, sweep out of the house, hoping that the midwife is watching disapprovingly from a window. Not that she would have dared to try and stop me.

I thank God as I cross the outer court that I have suffered no injuries from the birth. I have known women left in great and lasting discomfort. But I am strong. I feel almost myself again.

I am walking now in the shadow of the great gatehouse. At

either end of the range facing me stand two lofty towers, built by Henry's father, the second Marquess of Dorset. They make the Hall look imposing. Passing through the gatehouse, I turn away from the tiltyard on my left, and enter a door in a wall on my right, which leads to a pretty garden where roses normally flower in summer. I sit for a while on a stone seat, enjoying the sharp autumn sunshine that lends a roseate glow to the red bricks of the wall and the manor house beyond.

I am not left for long to enjoy my escape. Not five minutes have passed before I hear a horse's hooves galloping along the approach that leads to Bradgate. Its rider wears green and white livery: the royal Tudor colours. Whatever news he brings will be important, that much is certain. I rise to my feet and hastily retrace my steps to the house, where I find that my lord has already summoned our household to assemble in the great hall.

'This is news of great moment, Frances,' he tells me. 'All must hear it.'

We sit together on the dais, as the hastily convened ranks of ladies, gentlemen, household officers, grooms, pages, chamber attendants, kitchen staff and servitors part to allow the King's messenger to approach us. The vast hall, with its great oak-beamed roof and tapestried walls, is a-hum with expectancy; everyone, from the stiff-necked chamberlain to the lowliest pot-boy, cranes forward to hear.

The mud-spattered rider drops to one knee before us. Although his words are meant for both of us, it is to me that he defers – me, the King's own niece.

'Good news, my lord and lady,' he cries. 'The Queen is brought to bed of a fair prince, and all London – nay, all England – rejoices! His Majesty sends to tell you this joyous news, and also to have word, Madam, of how you do yourself. He bids you come to court with my lord here as soon as you have recovered from your confinement.'

I sink to my knees on the rushes, thanking God for this news that the kingdom has been eagerly awaiting for nigh on thirty years. After two disastrous marriages, and a cataclysmic quarrel with the Pope, my uncle, King Henry VIII, at last has a son and heir. The Tudor succession is assured, and the country is finally free from the threat of civil war. This is wonderful, but for me, beneath my outward jubilation there is a desperate sense of disappointment, of having been cheated of my own son, a son who was desired just as fervently as this prince has been, and not just because my lord needs an heir to inherit this title. Deep in my heart – and, no doubt, in Henry's too – has long lain the unspoken, treasonous hope that Fate might ultimately cheat the King of a male heir and so pave the way for a son of mine to inherit the throne. For my mother, Mary Tudor, daughter to Henry VII and younger sister of his Majesty, not only bequeathed me her royal blood, but also a claim to the very crown itself. Yet these desires must stay buried deep, for it is dangerous even to think of such things. The King has an heir, and we must rejoice.

'God be praised!' I exclaim fervently, noticing with gratification that everyone else present has followed my example and knelt. 'I shall write to the King's Majesty at once and send our heartiest congratulations, along with a suitable christening gift for the Prince. What is he to be called?'

'Edward, Madam, because he was born on the Eve of St Edward the Confessor.' A fitting name, since St Edward had once been King of England. I should have liked to call my own son Edward.

'And how does the Queen, my good aunt?' I inquire, inwardly wondering why Jane Seymour, that pale witless milksop, should have been favoured by the Almighty with a son, while I deliver a useless girl.

'She is well, my lady, and they say that, even after a long and dangerous travail, she was soon sitting up and writing letters announcing the glad tidings. The christening has already taken place. The King's daughter, the Lady Mary, was godmother, and the godfathers are the Archbishop of Canterbury and the Dukes of Norfolk and Suffolk. His Majesty, I can assure you, is the happiest man alive.'

We dismiss the messenger, sending him to the kitchens for refreshment, and bid our servants return to their duties. As we leave the hall for our private chambers, the air is abuzz with excited comments about the momentous tidings. But as we mount the stairs together, Henry and I say nothing to each other of the matter. I cannot quite take it in, this news that the former Mistress Seymour, that prim-mouthed, two-faced trollop, has accomplished what the grand princess Katherine of Aragon and that great whore Anne Boleyn both failed to achieve: she has borne the King a healthy son. How I envy her: she has presented her husband with a male heir, and so has ensured her future security and position as both wife and queen, as well as her place in my uncle's affections. And I am furious at the injustice of it. Why can I bear only sickly brats and girls?

And then the answer comes to me, quick as a flash of lightning. Maybe God sent our daughter for a reason, to bring a different kind of glory upon the House of Dorset. It seems to me that His will could not be plainer.

'So, his Highness at last has a son,' I say. 'And that son will one day, before many years are past, need a wife.'

Henry regards me with a calculating look that tells me he understands my meaning perfectly.

'Yes.' I smile. 'I think you get my drift. There could be no more fit mate for the noble Prince Edward, don't you agree, husband?'

Of course he agrees. He is as ambitious as I am. His desire for advancement and greatness is cruder than mine, but then, given our relative positions in life, that should not surprise me. I was born into the royal House; Henry has had to claw his way up the ladder of opportunity. I should remember, of course, that his great-grandmother, Elizabeth Wydeville, a renowned beauty in her day, once snared herself a king, no less: King Edward IV, my great-grandfather. My husband takes after this grasping lady. He did not scruple to dump his previous well-born betrothed to make a more dazzling marriage with me, the King's niece. And since then he has not ceased to scheme with me for the advancement of our House. Now, it seems, the very throne itself is within our sights.

'I see it clearly,' he says. 'You know that such a course would be fraught with dangers. The King is a proud man, ambitious for his dynasty. He will likely look abroad for a glittering foreign marriage for the Prince, one that will cement an advantageous alliance or win him new territory. He is a suspicious man too; were he to get wind of our scheme, he would think we look for a dead man's shoes. I need not remind you, Frances, that it is treason to predict the death of the King. We would have to go very carefully.'

'I do not doubt we could bring it off,' I tell him. 'Or are you too fearful? I need to know you are with me in this, Henry.'

'Of course,' he replies, admiration in his eyes. 'Do you not think I would rejoice to see my daughter a queen? And with your courage and my caution, I do not doubt we shall play all our cards well.' Already the idea seems less outrageous. In fact, it makes perfect sense. Princes nowadays do not always marry foreign princesses: look at Elizabeth Wydeville, Anne Boleyn and Jane Seymour. None was of royal birth. But our tiny daughter has one great advantage over those exalted ladies: she is of sound stock. Tudor blood runs in her veins.

Henry smiles his satisfaction, and plants a light kiss on my lips.

'You have done better than you think, my lady,' he says gently. 'And when you attend upon the Queen, you must keep your eyes and ears open, as I shall when I go to court, for we may be certain that the King's Highness will soon be casting his eye around for suitable brides for his son.'

My mind is now teeming with possibilities. All sense of disappointment has vanished.

Pausing to open the door to our apartments, Henry looks back.

'I think you are right, Frances. We should call this child Jane, in honour of the Queen. The Lady Jane Grey. It has a right royal ring to it!'

Mrs Ellen

Bradgate Hall, December 1537

Not three weeks after my little Lady Jane's birth, we heard that the Queen had died. We had the details from the sweating and travel-stained messenger who had raced here to bring us the sad news. For seven days, he told our shocked household, she had lain ill, struck down with childbed fever on the day after the Prince's christening. People at court were saying that those in attendance on her had over-indulged her fancy for too-rich food, and since the King could deny nothing to the mother of his son, she was given everything she asked for, however unwise.

'But there was a time when we thought she would recover,' went on the messenger. 'After her confessor had administered the last rites, she seemed better. She even sat up in bed and conversed with his Majesty, who was greatly relieved. And he was able to gladden her heart with the news that, while she was ill, he had created her brother, Sir Edward Seymour, Earl of Hertford. That evening, however, she suffered a relapse and lay delirious on her bed. The King was distraught, and ordered the bishops to lead the clergy in a solemn procession through London to St Paul's Cathedral, where they offered prayers of supplication, beseeching Our Lord to spare the Queen's life. But there was no improvement.'

The man paused. My lord and lady waited, impassive, for him to go on, but some of his listeners were plainly fighting back tears. The Queen had enjoyed great popularity with the commons of England, who had hated Nan Bullen, that ill-starred witch who had magicked the King into loving her. And the thought of that poor motherless little Prince was enough to tug the strings of any heart . . .

'The King,' the messenger continued, 'cancelled his plans to go hunting and remained at Hampton Court, since he could not bear to leave his wife in such a piteous condition. Then there was a slight improvement, and it was all round the court that the doctors had said to his Majesty that, if the Queen could last the night, they were in good hope that she might live. But that evening, the King was urgently summoned to her bedside, where he remained until the end, weeping and willing her not to die. We were all truly amazed that he, who is famous for his horror of illness and death, did not stir from his place. And truly, he has taken her passing in a most Christian manner, and is minded to be both father and mother to the little Prince.'

The tears were streaming down my cheeks by then. I have

never had children of my own, and carry the title 'Mrs' only as a courtesy of my status as nurse, but I have ever had a soft spot for the little ones, and I could not bear to think of that poor little boy, wrapped in cloth of gold and lying in his vast decorated cradle, surrounded by pomp and luxury, yet deprived of the one thing that is vital to any child, a mother's love. Even a prince may be pitied.

By contrast, my lady has taken the tragic news impassively. I watched her as she stood there listening to the messenger, straight-backed and dignified in her crimson velvet. To look at her, you'd never think she herself was not long out of her childbed, for she's as slender as before, and as energetic. Back in the saddle within a fortnight, she was. Of course, she's said all the right things about the poor Queen, but it only goes skin deep. She never had much time or sympathy for her. Still, what can you expect from a woman who's handed her own infant to the wet-nurse and barely taken a peek at her since? Oh, I know that the aristocracy are different, and that they consider it unnatural for a mother to rear her own child – I remember all the fuss when Nan Bullen wanted to breastfeed the Lady Elizabeth – but I've been employed as head nurse in three noble households now, and I've seen enough to know that most mothers love their babies and want to spend time with them. It's the men who have imposed these harsh rules, insisting on wet-nurses and rockers and the like, and I know why. It's so that the milk dries up, and then they can breed more sons on their wives. And of course it would never do to have a mother get too attached to a child who is going to be sent away to be educated, or be married off at an early age. It's a terrible world we live in, to be sure. But I doubt Lady Dorset would share that view.

Later, I happened to be in the kitchen. It's my duty, as nurse to the Lady Jane, to oversee the preparation of food for the nursery and to ensure that the proper standard of hygiene is maintained. They are hot, noisy places, these great kitchens at Bradgate, but, coming from yeoman stock – my father sold his small farm and set up a successful merchant business in London – I feel at home here, bustling about in the bakehouse, the pantry, the larders, the buttery and the servants' hall, chattering and joking with William Yates, the master cook, and his legion of underlings and servitors. Here there are no airs and graces, just hard work and good comradeship, even if tempers do get a bit strained in the steam and the heat from the roaring cooking fires. The kitchens in any noble household are also the place where those who work learn the most about the lords and ladies who employ them, for servants are prone to relieving the tedium of their duties by gossiping about their betters, who are an endless source of fascination to them, and even by sharing information that should have been kept strictly private. In fact, I sometimes think that we servants know more about the lives of Lord and Lady Dorset than they do themselves!

On this day the messenger, by now the merrier for several beakers of ale, became very confidential with Master Yates, and I overheard the most astonishing thing.

'There's a rumour,' he was saying, 'that Master Secretary Cromwell is worried that the Prince might die in infancy, as so many do, and that he has already urged his Majesty to marry again for the sake of his people and his kingdom.'

'And do you think the King will agree?' asked Master Yates.

'The word is that he has already,' was the reply, 'and with the Queen not yet in her grave.'

Perhaps, I thought, his Highness was thinking of that motherless infant . . . I sincerely hoped so.

Two months have passed since then, and there has been no more talk of the King remarrying. Perhaps, after all, it was just a rumour. But Prince Edward, we hear, is thriving, which gives great satisfaction to the Marquess and Marchioness.

'He has been given his own household,' says my lady during her daily visit to the nursery, which takes place just before dinner every morning, and affords her the opportunity to inspect her baby in its cradle and to give the staff instructions or reprimands, as her mood takes her. Yesterday she was complaining about Mrs Mallory, the wet-nurse I engaged, who apparently gave offence by failing to curtsey when the Marchioness entered the room. Last week the table had not been polished to her satisfaction. But today she is disposed to be talkative. And since I run this nursery, she will condescend to converse with me on matters that are within my remit, even if they do concern the King.

'His Highness has issued the strictest instructions for the cleaning of the Prince's rooms,' she tells me. 'The walls and floors are to be washed down three times a day, so that the place is kept wholesome and free from infection. And all visitors are carefully checked in case they carry some deadly illness. When the Prince is weaned, his food will be assayed for poison.'

She gives me one of her looks. I never know what my lady is thinking. Does she wish me to do the same in my own nursery? Or is she amazed at the King's fastidiousness? She is a very taxing mistress, and I cannot ever be certain that I give satisfaction. Yet my little Lady Jane is flourishing under my care. How could she not be – I love her as much as if she were my own, and would gladly lay down my life for her, if needs must. Which is more than one can say for her own mother, who barely seems to notice her.

'The King has appointed Lady Margaret Bryan as Lady Governess to the Prince,' continues the Marchioness. 'She was nurse to the Lady Elizabeth, and will have charge of Prince Edward until he is six and commences his education. My lord says that the King visits his son frequently, and delights in his progress. He even involves himself in the smallest details of the nursery. He approves the baby clothes chosen for the Prince, he has appointed the right age for weaning him, and suggested remedies for teething troubles.'

Thank God I don't have him or Lord Dorset poking their noses in here. Such matters are far better left to women. But of course, my lady would not see it that way. For her, the King her uncle is a paragon. She is so proud of him. In my humble opinion, which I take care to keep to myself, he is a monster. That's treason, of course, but no less true for all that. Any man who can cut off an innocent wife's head is a monster. I have no good opinion of Nan Bullen, but anyone with any sense could have guessed she was innocent, whatever else she was. They just made an occasion to get rid of her because she saw him for what he was and wasn't very good at keeping her mouth shut. Five men indeed! Living the life she did, with people always around her, she'd have been lucky to smuggle one man into her bedchamber. Only a fool would take such a risk and she was no fool. I shudder when I think of what happened to her. They say she was very brave at the end. What must it be like to face the executioner, knowing yourself to be innocent of any crime?

My life at Bradgate is one unending routine, but I heartily enjoy it nonetheless. Our nursery, which is housed in the tower of the east wing, flourishes on a rather humbler scale than Prince Edward's, but it is clean and warm, and my little Lady is the pride and joy of all who serve her – that is myself, Mrs Mallory, two rockers and two serving girls. Already she has gummy smiles for us, her willing slaves. When I see her tiny heart-shaped face peeping out from under the covers, my own captive heart melts. She is a very forward child with a merry countenance and docile temperament. God be praised, she now sleeps through the night and does not trouble the wet-nurse.

Some would reckon me greatly privileged to be employed in a household such as this. Bradgate Hall has such a dramatic setting: it lies on the edge of Charnwood Forest, and is enfolded on all sides by a rugged landscape with sweeping hills, granite cliffs and rocky outcrops. Red deer roam its chases and deer parks, and buzzards and peregrines keep grim vigil from their high eyries.

The mansion is a fine one, built in the early years of this King's reign by the present Marquess's father, and improved more recently. It is famed far and wide for its riches and luxury; no effort has been spared to emphasise the Dorsets' wealth and status. The great hall alone is eighty feet in length. Rich tapestries line the walls, cupboards groan under the weight of gold and silver plate, and jewel-coloured armorial glass glitters in the tall windows. My lord and lady keep a large, bustling household, and the tables in the hall are laid each day for no fewer than two hundred persons. Extra places are always set, for the Dorsets like entertaining, and there are always guests of quality with their retinues; moreover, the laws of hospitality demand that any passing traveller be given food and shelter.

When guests are present, the Marquess and Marchioness sit in exalted state at the high table on the dais, while those of us of lesser rank are seated, according to our degree, at the lower trestles set along the entire length of the hall. During meals, musicians play to us from the gallery, and a veritable army of servitors marches in with course after course of dishes that have been prepared in the teeming, sweltering kitchens that lie beyond the richly carved screens.

On the rare occasions when they do not have company, the Dorsets' meals are served in their summer or winter parlours in the east wing, but always with great ceremony. My lady is very conscious of her royal blood.

It's a privileged existence and I suppose I am lucky to enjoy it, coming from such an ordinary background, but it's not what I came here seeking. I came because my vocation in life is to care for children. And now for one child in particular.

Yes, it's all very grand and impressive, the life at Bradgate, but there are uneasy undercurrents here. I do not like the Dorsets very much. My lady is proud and her heart seems cold; I know she is far above me in rank, but – and I've said it before – a mother is a mother, and I don't think it's natural to show so little affection towards your own babe. And Lord Dorset, he's a man with an eye mainly to his own advancement, and she is entirely behind him. In fact, I think she is the driving force in the marriage. There's a ruthlessness about them both. If I was not so attached to their daughter, I might think of leaving. But my heart is now utterly devoted to that sweet child, so that is no longer an option for me.

Bradgate Hall, December 1539

My little Lady is now two years old, and since she was born has lived almost entirely in the three tower rooms that comprise her nursery. On the top floor is her bedchamber, on the middle floor the room I share with the nursery maids, and on the ground floor a great chamber with a wainscot and mullioned windows. The furniture in these rooms is much older and more worn than the pieces in the private apartments, and there is little of it. Lady Jane sleeps in an oak tester bed with ancient painted hangings. Her infant prayers are lisped at a prayer desk within the window embrasure, her clothes and linen are folded in a huge chest by the wall, and her meals are taken at a plain trestle table spread with a white cloth, she seated – like the rest of us – upon a stool. The food is simple – boiled meats, boiled fish, boiled vegetables, and the inevitable daily rations of bread, ale and pottage – and her mother has ordered that she is to eat it all up, every morsel.

As soon as the dear child had hauled herself to her feet and was walking, she was provided with a circular wooden walker on wheels and allowed to set off at speed, gurgling and whooping with laughter, along the tapestried long gallery that runs the whole length of the east wing.

'Watch me, Nellen!' she cries in glee, as she rattles along the wooden floor, cap dangling by its strings, red curls flying, cheeks rosy with effort. She has her own spaniel pup, and is allowed to play with the cook's daughter, Meg, a mischievous three-year-old. One day, Jane has the misfortune to clatter at full speed into her mother, as she and Meg come screaming with merriment along the gallery. Lady Dorset, who has brought some guests to view the family portraits that are displayed there, is furious, and lands a stinging slap on Jane's innocent cheek. The child registers surprise, then shock, before bursting into loud wails. I swoop on her, pulling her none too gently out of her walker, and carry her off, mumbling my excuses, terrified in case my lady's anger provokes her to further severity.

'There, sweeting,' I murmur, back in the nursery, as I bathe her poor inflamed cheek. 'All better now.' The baby lip stops quivering, the tears dry on the tender skin.

My lord is never so harsh. On the rare days when inclement weather keeps him indoors, away from his interminable hunting, he will spend the odd hour with his daughter in the gallery.

'Catch!' he cries, throwing a cloth ball to her. Sometimes he lets her chase him in her wheeled contraption, she shrieking with laughter. Such occasions are rare, though, for the Dorsets are not people to allow rain, or even hail and snow, to interfere with their sport and they are usually to be found outdoors, on horseback and surrounded by hordes of retainers and excited, yapping dogs. Jane, who spends most of her life in the nursery or the gardens, has therefore seen very little of her parents during her infancy – far less than any other child I have had charge of.

Lady Dorset's visits to the nursery, although regular, are brisk and brief.

'Make her stop sucking her thumb,' she will order. Or, when Jane was teething, 'If she persists in that grizzling, she is to have no supper.' Jane has never been a difficult child and needs little chiding, but my lady seems determined to constrain her to a state of perfection such as few human beings have ever attained. Whenever she is in her mother's presence, Jane is expected to stand still, remain silent, and behave in a dutiful manner with head bent and eyes lowered respectfully. If she is spoken to, she must answer meekly and clearly. My lady will brook no disobedience, and when little Jane displays some infant frailty, such as fidgeting in her place, or giggling when her dog piddles on the floor, the resultant smack is swift and sharp.

The most painful incident, for Jane and for me too, occurred on the day when Jane, after the manner of many two-year-olds, bit young Meg during a scrap, and Meg's father mentioned it to the Marchioness, who sent for us at once.

'Mrs Ellen, I do not wish to hear that my daughter is behaving like a savage,' she said coldly.

'No, Madam,' I replied, hoping that that would be an end to the matter. 'I am sorry, Madam. It will not happen again.'

'You may be sure of that,' she answered grimly. 'Jane, come here.'

Hearing the angry tone in her mother's voice, the child hid her face in my skirts, but Lady Dorset pulled her away, hauled her over her knee, tore up her petticoats and administered a sound spanking that had Jane yelling in fear and pain. It was all I could do to stand there and watch, clenching my fists behind me to prevent myself from snatching her from her mother's clutches. Then my lady stood her down.

'If I ever hear that you have bitten anyone ever again, you will be beaten more severely,' she said sternly, wagging a finger. Jane said nothing, just sobbed and sobbed. Poor child, she is too young to understand what her mother was saying.

'Take her away, Mrs Ellen,' Lady Dorset commanded. 'I do not wish to set eyes on that naughty girl again today.'

I fled, angry that I had lifted no finger to spare Jane such punishment.

Perhaps the Marchioness has never developed any natural bond of closeness with her child because the poor babe was not the boy she had hoped for – even though my lady is barely three-and-twenty, and more children will surely follow. But she has never shown Jane any open affection, nor, I am sure, does she question whether she has given the child cause to love her. Of course, it is the natural duty of a child to love and honour its parents, but my lady does not appear to see that there are two sides to the bargain, and I fear that, if there is any lack of love, she will blame Jane.

Naturally, I do my best to protect Jane from her mother's severity.

'When your lady mother comes to the nursery today, Poppet,' I tell her, 'you must curtsey and wait to be spoken to. Stand up straight, and don't stare, because it's rude.' This is as much as most people expect from a two-year-old, but Lady Dorset sets impossibly high standards.

There comes a day when my lady arrives later than usual, just as Jane's dinner is being put in front of her. The Marchioness seats herself at table, her eagle eye on the child. Jane takes a mouthful of fish.

'Don't like this,' she mumbles with her mouth full.

'We must not despise what God gives us,' says her mother. 'Eat it up.'

Jane looks at her mournfully, and begins pushing the food around the plate with her spoon.

'Eat it!' commands my lady.

Jane shakes her head, her big blue eyes brimming with tears.

'How dare you defy me!' cries Lady Dorset. 'Eat your dinner, or I will beat you.'

Jane starts wailing loudly. I decide to risk the lash of my lady's tongue.

'Madam,' I say, 'let me try to persuade her.'

'Persuade her? She must do as she is told. You are too soft with her, Mrs Ellen.' She turns to the sobbing child. 'Come here.'

'My lady,' I intervene, 'please allow her to calm down. She cannot eat while she is in this state.'

'She has defied me and must be punished,' hisses her lady-ship. 'And you should know better than to contradict your betters. Remember your position in this household.' Rising, she grabs Jane by the upper arms, her angry fingers pinching the tender flesh, and pulls her from the chair.

'You will not disobey me!' she warns, shaking her. 'You will ask my pardon and then you will eat your dinner. Is that understood?'

Jane is gulping in fear, and beyond words.

'Answer me!' Lady Dorset bellows, and when Jane remains mute and trembling, she slaps her on the cheek, twice. The child screams, and I make to go to her, but a scowl from my lady stops me dead in my tracks. I dare not provoke her further, for to do so might lead to my dismissal, and that would never do. Loving Jane as if she were my own flesh and blood, the prospect of being parted from her is unbearable to me, as is the thought of what her existence would be like without the protection of her doting nurse, for her mother's harshness towards her seems to increase daily.

I watch in silent misery, knowing myself powerless, as the Marchioness dumps her squealing daughter back on the chair, hands her the spoon, and orders her: 'Eat!'

And Jane does eat, her fish salted with the tears that are streaming down her face. Later, when Lady Dorset has gone, she is very sick, and spends most of the afternoon asleep in my arms, exhausted by distress and nausea.

'Jane's education,' my lady announces, 'will be as good, if not better, than that afforded to the King's daughters, the Lady Mary and the Lady Elizabeth. She will be made familiar with the classical works of the ancients, as well as history, mathematics, theology and the scriptures. She will learn the languages that are advantageous to her future role in life. At the same time, we shall engage dancing and music masters. You yourself, Mrs Ellen, can teach her embroidery. We must not neglect the traditional feminine arts. And Jane must be schooled in the ways of the court. She must be taught perfect manners, how to dress like a princess, and how to carry herself like one. The importance of her high birth must be drummed into her. She is born to great things.'

It all seems a shade too burdensome for such a tiny little girl. Looking at Jane's pointed, heart-shaped face, with its freckled nose and earnest, dark-browed eyes, I wonder if she will grow up to be a beauty. That is not a requirement of the greatest importance in marriages of state, but it helps. I've heard that the King, in his search for a foreign bride, has insisted that he see her first before committing himself.

Lady Dorset is determined to help Nature along.

'Something must be done about those freckles, Mrs Ellen,' she demands. 'We must search out a remedy.' We've already tried several lotions and pastes, but nothing has worked so far.

'Her good feature is her hair,' declares my lady. 'It's the same Tudor red as the King's.' Yet she complains that Jane's is frizzy and unruly, and it is true that it does not submit happily to being scraped back under a cap. In my humble opinion, it should be left to fall free, a wavy cloud of auburn flying in the wind. But my lady would never agree.

'Jane is very small for her age,' she says. 'She's too skinny. It gives her the appearance of being delicate, which she most certainly is not.' She has good cause to know this, for it has been made abundantly clear, on the occasions when the Marchioness has had cause to pull Jane over her knee and chastise her protesting, wriggling body, that this child is strong and healthy. She is also highly intelligent, and much advanced for her age, but although my lady values erudition in girls, she sees Jane's precocity as undue forwardness, which must be discouraged.

'A clever maiden is no great asset in the marriage market,' she declares. 'We must cultivate sufficient modesty to overcome this handicap.'

'Indeed,' I agree, but unlike Lady Dorset, I shall not be too rigorous. She is right that it does not become a maid to be too saucy and forward, but I have no desire to break Jane's spirit.

Lord Dorset paid one of his rare visits to the nursery today. Like most fathers, he has little to do with his daughter. He pats her on the head, calls her his 'winning little filly', and makes his escape. He is quite happy to leave the rule of her upbringing wholly to his wife, until such time as Jane reaches marriageable age, when she is between twelve and fourteen. Then he will no doubt suddenly find her most interesting for the advantages that she can bring him through a nuptial alliance. I pray God that he thinks also of her welfare and happiness when it comes to choosing a husband.

Bradgate Hall, 1540

'The acquisition of virtue,' my lady tells me, 'is as much the product of education as of upbringing.' Jane is not yet three, but already her mother has given her a horn book to hang around her neck on a ribbon. On its smooth wooden surface is written, in beautiful black script, the alphabet, simple numbers and the Lord's Prayer, and Jane is expected, with my help, to learn them all. I think myself fortunate that my father had me tutored in letters, so that I can help her with her lessons.

Every day, we sit together and I go through them with her, repeating everything over and over again so that, when the summons comes from Lady Dorset at five o'clock, the child will be able to recite her lesson without making any mistakes, because if she does, her mother will certainly deliver a stinging slap. It has happened before, for much lesser crimes. Today, we are late. We hurry along the gallery to the winter parlour, where my lady is waiting, Jane's little legs running at twice the pace of mine in order to keep up. We are late because I made her go over her lesson just one more time, so that she will be word-perfect for her mother. As we enter the chamber, Jane is clutching her horn-book, and holds it before her as she reads aloud, her tiny finger tracing the letters carved into the smooth wooden surface. Lady Dorset nods and dismisses us. She cannot find anything to criticise; nor does she offer any praise.

Young as she is, Jane is already well-grounded in religion. Outwardly, the Dorsets conform to the Catholic doctrines authorised by the King after he had made himself Supreme Head of the Church of England, but privately – and I must speak carefully here – I believe that they, like many other people, have secret sympathies with those who wish to reform the Church, and even, I suspect, with those who promote the teachings of Martin Luther and his Protestant followers. Luther dared to attack the very sacraments of the Church, and in England today it is very dangerous to express such heretical views. People are burned at the stake for doing so. The King is a great one for tradition in matters of religion, for all he has broken with the

Pope – or the Bishop of Rome, as we have had to call him since our gracious sovereign took his place as Head of the English Church.

Jane has been taken to Mass since her infancy, and is now familiar with the Latin rubric of the service, although I doubt she understands much of what it means. She has been taught to revere Our Lady, the Blessed Virgin Mary, and to pray to the saints to intercede for herself and others. She has even had explained to her the miracle of the Mass, wherein the Host, at the moment of elevation by the priest, becomes the very body and blood of Our Lord Jesus. Like all little children, she accepts these teachings without question, and has conceived a proper and dutiful love for her Creator. I believe she is set to become a very devout little person.

'The King's Grace,' announces my lady jubilantly, on a cold January day, 'has married the Lady Anne of Cleves at Greenwich. I am summoned to court to pay my duty to the new Queen, and am honoured in being appointed one of the great ladies of her household.'

That very afternoon, the whole household gathers in the courtyard to watch as, nobly attired in a splendid gown of red velvet, and swathed in furs, she climbs into her coach, ready to depart for the south. Lined up behind are two chariots for her ladies-in-waiting, her maids and two pages.

'How beautiful my lady is!' Jane whispers in awe. 'I want to look just like her when I grow up.'

'You will, my little beauty, you will,' I assure her, patting her head.

'Farewell,' says Lady Dorset to the assembled throng, as the chamberlain hands her a basket of refreshments for the journey, and a fur rug to keep her warm.

Lord Dorset is ready with the stirrup-cup, which he hands to his wife. She takes it, then leans forward and kisses him on the lips. He murmurs something I do not catch, and they smile. Then my lady remembers she has a child.

'Be a good girl, Jane,' she says.

'Goodbye, my lady,' answers Jane.

'And God keep you,' I whisper.

'God keep you,' she repeats. The Marchioness nods her approval, then she is away, the coach trundling out of the courtyard. Beside me, Jane stands waving decorously to her mother until the vehicle is through the gatehouse and out of sight. There is no answering wave.

During my lady's absence, Lord Dorset bestirs himself to spend some time with his daughter. He quickly gets bored with hearing her read, so he decides to teach her to ride.

'I'll make a huntress of her before long, Mrs Ellen,' he promises.

I follow the pair of them to the stables. In the end stall, ready saddled, is a plump dappled pony, the dearest little creature imaginable, and ideally suited to a novice rider.

'Her name is Phoebe,' my lord says, beaming.

Jane extends a tentative hand and pats the pony's mane and nose.

'Beautiful Phoebe!' she exclaims.

My lord lifts Jane on the pony's back, and she sits there gripping the reins, a big smile on her face. As we watch, a groom takes the bridle and leads the pony into the courtyard, where he walks it round and round to enable Jane to get used to the motion of its gait. The child is in her element.

'Watch me, Sir!' she cries to her father as she passes us, red curls bouncing and skirt spread wide across the animal's flank.

'Well done!' calls Lord Dorset. 'She's doing well,' he says to me.

'If I may be so bold, my lord, you should let her ride regularly,' I venture.

'A capital idea, Mrs Ellen!' he replies. 'She shall ride each afternoon, for the space of an hour. I will see to it.'

And see to it he does. Unless the weather is very foul, Jane is out there daily on her pony, being put through her paces, learning to trot and jump, and to keep a straight back in the saddle. She loves it, and it is pleasing to see how well she and Phoebe accord together. The riding lessons also give Lord Dorset an opportunity to get to know his daughter better, and it is gratifying to see him praise her for her prowess.

'Why, it's Diana the Huntress!' he smiles, as Jane emerges in her new miniature riding habit and feathered bonnet, which he himself ordered for her. 'Today, daughter, you can come out riding with me.'

'Oh, Sir,' I say, alarmed, 'I beg of you, take care. The countryside around her is dangerous. The rocks and cliffs...'

'Stop fretting, Mrs Ellen, the child will be safe with me. Won't you, Jane?' And he trots off on his mighty steed, leading Jane by the bridle. Sure enough, they are back two hours later, she rosy-cheeked and exhilarated, he jubilant, smiling down at her. Then I catch the pained look that briefly shadows his eyes, and I know for a certainty that he is regretting, probably for the thousandth time, that his little girl is not a boy.

My lady is gone a month before we hear any word from her, but news from court travels fast, even to these remote parts, and gossip is rife within the household. I am obliged to remind the servants and the nurserymaids to hold their tongues in Lady Jane's presence, yet I am sure the child has picked up something of what is going on. After all, we were chattering very excitedly about the new Queen's arrival a few weeks ago, and now we do not mention her.

Everybody in the household, if not in the whole of England, has heard by now that the King's fourth marriage is going the way of the other three, and if his Majesty were an ordinary man, doubtless they would be laughing at his lack of success in the matrimonial stakes. There is much chatter and speculation – a lot of it bawdy – about what has gone wrong this time, when he's barely been wed five minutes, but I do my best to ensure that Jane hears none of it. To be truthful, I do not know much myself – nobody does, really – and it is not until Lady Dorset returns that I learn a little more of the strange goings-on at court.

It is now March, and my lady is home. As her coach clatters into the courtyard, its leather curtains tied back, my lord summons the household to attend on her and receive her. But when the Marchioness dismounts from the coach to greet her husband, regal in a velvet cloak over a damask gown trimmed with furs and a bejewelled French hood, I notice that she looks pale and ill, while Lord Dorset is showing himself uncommonly solicitous in his welcome. As she raises her arms to embrace him, her cloak falls aside, and immediately it becomes clear why she looks unwell. Jane notices the change and shrinks fearfully into my skirts; later, when we are back in the nursery, she asks, 'What has happened to my mother, Nurse? Why does she look so fat?'

'Bless me, what a bright child it is!' I smile at the nursemaid. Jane stands mute, urgent to know more.

'Your lady mother is with child again,' I tell her. 'That is all. There's nothing to worry about. God willing, you will have a baby brother soon, to become Marquess of Dorset after your father.'

Jane takes this in wide-eyed.

'Why can't I be Marquess of Dorset?' she asks.

I laugh at that. The very idea! 'But Jane, you are a maid, and maids do not become marquesses. So we must pray that your lady mother has a baby boy.'

Jane thinks about this. 'That's not fair.'

'Oh, you are old-fashioned!' I answer, chuckling. 'It is God's will. We females are the weaker sex, and only men are fitted to rule. That is why you cannot be a marquess, and why you have to obey your father in all things.'

Jane seems to accept this. Forward as she is, she is still a very young child, and usually accepts unquestioningly what I tell her. She is more concerned about what is happening to her mother, bless her. If only the Marchioness deserved such devotion.

'When will the baby come?' Jane whispers.

'By the look of her, sweetheart, the baby will come in high summer.' That can mean little to the child – she has as yet no sound concept of time. 'You must pray for your mother every day, and ask God to send her a happy hour and a lusty boy.'

'I will,' Jane says fervently. Then, unexpectedly, she looks me straight in the eye and asks if the Queen is going to have a son too.

I get up abruptly.

'Time for your horn book,' I say.

This afternoon, I found out a lot more about what's been going on at court of late. Jane and I had returned from our usual afternoon walk, and then I settled her to some rather untidy embroidery in her bedchamber, before going downstairs. Then Mrs Zouche, one of my Lady Dorset's women, came by with a jug of wine, and asked me if I'd like to share it while we both got on with our mending. Mrs Zouche is chamber-woman to my lady, and tends to her wardrobe. There is always something to be sewn, and today she was mending a tear in one of my lady's court gowns.

There we were, Mrs Zouche and I, sitting by the nursery fire, getting very confidential. Mrs Zouche has been at court with my lady, and we passed a very pleasant hour discussing the latest gossip.

'I'm delighted to be back here, I can tell you,' she declared. 'Four months at court is as much as any body can stand. All those great lords and ladies, jostling for place. And the back-biting – you wouldn't believe! Then I was on the go from start to finish, making sure her upstairs was well turned-out with all those changes of clothes she insists on. Mind you, I did get to see the King a lot. Never seen a man wearing so many jewels. But the size of him... He's put on even more weight since I last saw him.'

'Did you see the Queen?' I wanted to know.

'No, not sight nor sound of her.' She lowered her voice. 'She's been sent to Richmond. It looks like he's trying to get rid of her.'

'But why?' I ask.

'It was all round the court the day after the wedding,' said Mrs Zouche. 'The King made no secret of the fact that he had no liking for her. No one could remember him saying such things about any of his other wives, even Anne Boleyn.'

'What did he say?' I asked avidly, biting off my thread and shaking out Jane's mended chemise.

'When Master Cromwell asked him how well he liked the Queen, his Majesty said he now liked her a lot worse than before. She was not fair, like Queen Jane, and she had evil smells about her. Worse still, he said he took her to be no maid. He told Master Cromwell that he had felt her breasts and other parts, and believed other men had known her, and this being so, he had neither the will nor the courage to consummate the marriage.'

I gasped at such brutal candour. 'Is it true, do you think? What he says of her?'

Mrs Zouche shook her head and took a sip of wine. 'No one believes it, if only because the Queen is patently so innocent, and appears to think there is nothing amiss. Lady Rutland told my lady in my hearing that she and the other ladies-in-waiting were amazed when her Majesty praised the King for his solicitude. The Queen said that, when he came to bed, he always kissed her, took her hand and bade her, "Good night sweetheart." And then, every morning, he kissed her and said, "Farewell, darling." Lady Rutland and the others could not believe their ears, for the Queen seemed to expect no more than this. Then Lady Edgecombe said she thought her Grace was still a maid, but Queen Anne said no, how could she be when she slept every night with the King? The ladies told her there must be more than that, if she is to present us with a duke of York. But the Queen wished to hear no more, and said she received as much of his Majesty's attention as she wished.'

I laughed. 'Can any woman be so ignorant? Perhaps she's no fool.'

'I think she did say it in all innocence. But now she is left all alone at Richmond Palace, whilst the court is elsewhere. It must be obvious even to her that he is neglecting her. There is even talk that he will put her away like he did Queen Katherine. It is also said' – and here Mrs Zouche lowered her voice still further – 'that his eyes have lighted upon another.'

'Who?' I asked, surprised, refilling our beakers. Is yet another poor woman to be burdened – in some ways literally – with the favour of the King?

'The Duke of Norfolk's niece, Katherine Howard. A very little girl, only about fifteen, but pretty enough to stir an old man's loins. It seems the Catholic party are pushing her forward in order to crush the influence of the reformers, who have made headway since the King decided to marry this Protestant Queen.'

'Will he really think of marrying her, this little girl?'

'Most people think so. His Majesty will have his way, as ever. But do not divulge a word of what I have told you to anyone here. My lady would have a fit if she heard me gossiping like this. She will not brook any disrespect to her kin, especially the King.'

I assured my friend of my discretion, and then our talk moved on to other matters. Suddenly, there was a scratching noise outside in the stairwell, and getting up to investigate, for we thought it might be a mouse, I noticed that the door was slightly ajar. Opening it, I found young Jane kneeling there, clearly surprised in the act of eavesdropping.

'You bad girl!' I scolded, my anger spurred by concern about what she might have overheard, rather than indignation at her naughtiness. 'You will go to bed right now, and stay there for the rest of the day.' Jane's lower lip trembled, and she turned without a word and went up the stairs. I looked at Mrs Zouche.

'I hope to God she didn't hear all that,' I said.

'Or that she doesn't repeat it,' replied Mrs Zouche. 'My lady would kill me if she found out I'd been saying such things in the Lady Jane's hearing.'

Chastened by the thought, we turned our talk to other, less contentious matters.

Later in the evening, I look in on Jane. She is wide awake, and in her eyes I can detect both surprise and puzzlement.

'I've come to say goodnight,' I tell her. 'Would you like a drink, Jane?'

She sits up in bed, still looking at me in that disturbing way, and again I wonder just how much she overheard this afternoon. Her next words confirm my worst fears.

'Why does the Queen smell, Nurse? And why did the King feel her all over? That's horrid. If I were Queen, I should not allow it. Can the King send her away because she smells bad?'

I sit down beside her on the bed.

'You should not have been listening, child. But since you were, and you heard things that were not fit for a little girl's ears, I shall do my best to explain. The King does not like the Queen, I hear. Perhaps she does smell. If so, it's because she doesn't wash very often. And it may be that the King will send her away, but it won't be because she smells bad. He will have to find a good reason for it, and because he's the King, he will.'

That seems to satisfy Jane. Fortunately, being so young a child, her mind is soon concentrated on something else. She asks me no more about the matter, and I congratulate myself on having deflected her more embarrassing questions.

'Now, Jane,' I tell her, 'we must never say anything bad about the King, whom God has sent to rule over us; it is wrong to do so, and we might be punished for it. You must promise that you will not repeat what you have heard today, to anyone. Will you do that?'

'I will,' she says solemnly. 'I promise.'

'Then goodnight,' I say, tucking her in and kissing her. 'God bless you.'

It is midsummer, and my lady is close to her time, when we hear that the King has had his marriage to Anne of Cleves annulled; and for her eager compliance – which I hear he found rather unflattering – she has been rewarded with fine palaces and a handsome annuity, as well as the dubious privilege of being able to call herself his Majesty's dearest sister. Next thing we hear is that, within a month of the marriage being dissolved, our besotted monarch has married Katherine Howard, whose buxom charms he cannot refrain from caressing, even in public.

I try to explain what has happened to Jane, as we sit in the garden making daisy chains.

"You see, Poppet, the King's marriage to the Lady Anne was not a proper marriage, and therefore the Archbishop of Canterbury has said they are free to part and can marry other people." I omit, of course, to say what a proper marriage is, and desist from making any reference to the Lady Anne's personal hygiene and his Majesty interfering with her person. But Jane's mind is keen.

'Couldn't the Archbishop of Canterbury have made the Lady Anne wash?' she asks solemnly, which makes me rock with laughter. My, my. The things this little maid utters! She's a sweet pip with the sharpness of the lemons that come to the kitchens from Spain, and she never ceases to amaze me.

Lady Dorset did not return to court to wait upon the new Queen because she was great with child. Instead, she has been bustling about the house, rearranging rooms here, or ordering new furnishings there, and driving us all to distraction with a constant stream of instructions.

'It's the nesting instinct,' observes Mrs Zouche. 'She'll be brought to bed shortly, you mark my words.'

Despite the upheaval in the house, I love this time of year, when summer holds sway. It is cool indoors, with all the casements open, and the rooms smell sweet, scented with the fragrance of the fresh rushes on the floors. No longer do the great fires roar up the chimneys; instead, the hearths are decorated with great displays of flowers. The gardens are full of colour, alive with growing things, and there is the promise of a good harvest to come.

With very little fuss, Lady Dorset bears another daughter. Her labour lasted through the night, and gave her little trouble.

I take Jane to see her new sister on the day after the birth. We find her lying in the cradle by their mother's bed.

'Her name is Katherine, for the Queen,' says the Marchioness. It must be plain to Jane that her mother looks tired and disagreeable, due, no doubt, to the disappointment of not having borne a son. Nevertheless, this new infant is very beautiful, lacking altogether the crumpled appearance of most tiny babies. She is fair, with enormous blue eyes and a sweet, angelic-looking face. Jane clearly thinks she is wonderful, and seeks to cheer her mother.

'She's better than any boy,' she announces, but the effect is not what she had anticipated.

'Take her away,' snaps my lady, 'for she talks a lot of nonsense.' I hurriedly usher Jane out of the room.

'It's alright,' I soothe, seeing her dismay. 'You meant well. Your lady mother is just tired and not herself. Now come upstairs, and we'll get on with sewing that pretty nightgown for Lady Katherine. And perhaps I can find some marchpane comfits in my coffer.' Thus consoled, Jane begins to skip happily along the passage, then remembers that a well-bred girl such as herself should comport herself with decorum, and slows her step, continuing at a more stately pace. My heart aches for her: so toward, and yet so young. And so unloved by those who should care for her most.

Lady Jane Grey

Bradgate Hall, October 1541

Today I am four years old. Mrs Ellen wakes me up at six o'clock, and bids me to my prayers. I kneel at my prie-Dieu and ask God to make me a dutiful, virtuous child and to bless my parents, but all the time I keep thinking of the day that is to come, and what my lord and lady have ordained for me. Now that I am a great big girl, I am to take my meals with them at the high table in the great hall. This is a very grown-up thing, but it is also very frightening, because there are so many rules of courtesy I have to remember that I am sure I shall forget some of them, and so make my lady mother very wrathful. She is often angry with me, even though I try my best to be good, but Mrs Ellen has told me lots of times what I must and must not do. I must not speak during the meal, unless anyone speaks to me. I must never, never yawn, belch, pick my nose, wipe my fingers on the tablecloth or, worst of all, let go a fart. And I must above all remember that each meal is like the Last Supper, so I must eat with as goodly manners as if I were in the company of Our Blessed Lord Himself.

All these things I think I can remember, but there are more. Lots of dishes are served at table, but a child must not commit the sin of gluttony, and I am not supposed to choose more than two or three at a time. Eating too much rich food, Mrs Ellen says, overheats the blood. And if I get a tummy ache from doing so, I must sit quiet in my chair and not make a fuss.

I have been dancing up and down at my devotions, and cannot eat my breakfast because of nervousness, so Mrs Ellen stops tending to Katherine and tells me to leave it, as it is time to prepare myself for my great day. I stand still, stretching out my arms, as she dresses me in lots and lots of fine clothes - far too many for this warm day, I say.

'But it is the custom, Jane. You must be properly attired to attend upon your parents. They have guests at table, and you must dress as beseems your rank. A lady does not complain, even if she is hot and uncomfortable.'

First, Mrs Ellen puts on me a long-sleeved cambric smock with cuffs embroidered in gold. Then I am made to breathe in as she laces the stiff bodice with a pointed front that flattens my tummy. On top of that goes the kirtle, an undergown of smooth creamy silk, and over that a green velvet gown with a tight stomacher, a low square neck that gapes on me, a big wide skirt, open at the front, and a long train. It has full, wide sleeves, and I have to hold out my arms so that Mrs Ellen can hang a pair of fur oversleeves on top of them. Now she is fastening the clasp of the jewelled girdle, with its hanging pomander, at my waist. She brushes my long hair and plaits it, rolling the plaits into a knot at the back of my head. Then she puts on a coif of satin and cloth of silver, and on top of that, a round French hood with a black veil. Last come the jewels: a pearl drop on a chain at my neck, to match the pearl trim on the gown, a brooch on my breast, and three rings.

I look at myself in the mirror. I am dressed exactly the same as my mother or any other great lady, and I look like a little woman. Then I remember with some dismay that I have to behave like one. In the tight, heavy gown, it won't be difficult, for I can hardly move. I couldn't possibly run about in it, and I will have to be careful not to trip up over my train. Fortunately, I've had lots of lessons in walking with a train. And to keep my hood safely on the back of my head, I must keep my chin up.

My mother chose all these clothes for me. She said she wanted me to look splendid, and to do justice to my House. I don't quite understand what she meant, though I will do my best. But I hate these hot, heavy clothes, and wish I didn't have to wear them. How will I eat when I can hardly breathe? How will I eat anyway, when I am so nervous about dining in the hall? Oh, how I wish I was wearing my ordinary plain gown and kerchief, running around the apple orchard with Meg, the cook's daughter!

Meg is here now to see me dressed up.

'You look beautiful, Jane,' she says.

'I'm uncomfortable,' I complain. I would I could be like Meg, and not have to have lessons, and be free to run about the fields instead with my hair flying loose, stealing apples from the orchard or paddling in the stream. But I am always being made to behave like a young lady. Meg is so lucky. Her mother might beat her when she's naughty, but she cuddles her a lot to make up for it, and she often gives her little treats – warm tarts from the oven, or pretty ribbons, or – once – a sweet little kitten. I wish my lady mother was kind like that.

'That's a lovely dress,' Meg says, looking at it longingly; I am guessing that she would like to change places with me, and I should like to tell her that it's much more fun being her any day.

'Run along now, Meg,' says Mrs Ellen. 'Oh, and take those dishes to the kitchen for me, please, if you would.' Meg leaves, carrying the plates.

Mrs Ellen is looking me up and down. I can't tell if she likes what she sees or not.

'You look fit now to face the world, and your mother,' she tells me, and takes me and Katherine downstairs to greet our parents. We do this every morning, and I don't always enjoy it because sometimes my mother scolds me for things I have done or not done. More often than not, she will find fault with me for some small thing, a strand of hair out of place, or a grubby fingernail, and she might give me a sharp pinch or tap, and tell Mrs Ellen off for being soft with me.

At other times my parents are getting ready to go hunting or receive important visitors, and they don't really seem to want me or Katherine getting in the way. Their chamber reeks of dogs, because the creatures are always at their heels. It's a sickly, sour smell, and I can't bear it, which is a shame, because I love this cheerful room, with the jolly blaze in its great stone fire-place, the brightly-coloured hangings, the polished furniture and the portraits of my kinsfolk that I find so fascinating, especially the one of my great-uncle the King, which was painted when he was a young and handsome prince.

We curtsey and stand, heads bowed, to receive our parents' blessing.

'Good morning,' says my lady.

'Goo morning,' replies Katherine in her baby voice, and holds up her chubby hands. 'Cawwy! Cawwy!'

'Not now, sweeting,' smiles my lady. 'You must stand up straight like a good girl.'

'Good morning, my lord, my lady,' I say, trying to hide my fear of my mother, and watching her closely. She is a beautiful woman, with copper brown hair and fair skin, and today she is wearing a gown and hood like mine, but in dark green velvet edged with pearls, and a tiny jewelled book hangs from her girdle. In her rich robes, she looks like a queen — an ice queen, cold and distant.

'Jane.' Her voice is cool, and there is the usual note of reproof. 'Come here.' She looks me up and down sternly, and nods at Mrs Ellen.

'She will do,' she says.

Towards Katherine, my lady shows more kindness. She kisses her on her head, ruffling the fluffy fair curls, and helps her make her shaky, giggling way across the carpet. Katherine can do no wrong. It's always me who gets into trouble.

But today, I think, I am in my mother's good books, and I relax a little when she beckons me to stand before her and gives me a big book with a red leather binding. When I open it, I find it to be full of brightly-coloured pictures, lots of them shiny with gold paint.

'It has stories and prayers from Holy Scripture, for your edification,' says my lord father, although I'm not sure what he means. 'It once belonged to your grandmother, and I hope that very soon, Jane, you will be able to read the Latin words for yourself.'

'Thank you, my lady, thank you, Sir,' I say, as prettily as I can. I am thrilled by their rare kindness, and with their gift. There are not many books in the house, so I have never seen such beautiful pictures, and I am looking forward mightily to looking at them all and making up stories of my own about them. And I want to learn my letters more quickly than ever, so that I can find out what the real stories are.

It's time to go back to the nursery now. My mother is dismissing me.

'Look that you behave at table at dinner!' she orders.

'Yes, Madam,' I reply. I return upstairs clutching my precious gift.

*

It is ten to eleven, and Mrs Ellen is bidding me wash my hands and tidy myself. She leads me down the great staircase once more, to the hall, where a serving man shows me to my place, which is at the high table on the dais, below the great gold salt, as befits a mere child. I stand behind my stool until my parents are seated in their high carved chairs, then the whole company sits down and our household chaplain says grace in Latin.

In front of me is a silver charger, a knife and fork (which I know well how to use), a goblet of fine glass from a place called Venice, a little bowl of salt, and a damask napkin folded around a small manchet loaf. There are fresh herbs and flowers scattered along the tablecloth, and some silver finger bowls for washing our hands of grease. A servitor unfolds my napkin, which he kisses and lays across my lap. He then does the same for the old lord, one of our neighbours, who is sitting next to me. On my other side is Mrs Zouche, who smiles kindly at me but does not say anything. Most of the people in the hall do not seem to have noticed that I am here.

Suddenly, there is a fanfare of trumpets as the first course is carried in. There are lots of dishes that look and smell heavenly – we never have anything like this in the nursery, where the food is always plain. I choose some roast pork with a herb crust and raisin and cream stuffing, which is lovely, and from the next course I ask for a piece of carp and fig pie. While I am tucking in, my servitor keeps refilling my goblet with wine, which I am not at all used to without water, but I have added lots of salt to my food and got very thirsty, so I swallow great gulps of it. Before long, my head is feeling very funny, and I badly want to go to the privy.

There is no one to help me. Everyone is talking and eating, and the noise is so loud that they are shouting to make themselves heard. Mrs Ellen is nowhere to be seen.

What should I do? Panic races through me. Will I get into trouble if I leave the table to go to the privy? No one else has done so. Is it against the rules of courtesy? I cross my legs tightly and look urgently at Mrs Zouche, but she just smiles at me again and turns away.

I can't hold out for much longer. I feel like crying. How terrible it will be if I wet myself in public. I cannot bear the thought of such shame and disgrace, or the punishment it will earn me.

Suddenly, the whole company rises to its feet. I am startled. What is happening now? The surprise takes my mind off my discomfort for a moment, and I slide off my stool and stand up as well, though my head is scarcely above the table. The servitors are marching into the hall in a great procession, bearing with them, on its vast gold platter, a huge joint of fragrant, steaming meat. The old gentleman next to me sees my bewilderment and bends down.

'It is the sirloin of beef! The most favoured of English meats. We always stand to salute the sirloin, you know. It is a very old tradition.'

I am bursting, but suddenly I see what I should do. I slide my feet apart beneath my heavy skirts and, as quietly and slowly as I can, relieve myself onto the rushes on the floor. Then I sit down, hoping that no one will notice the puddle that my skirts are hiding. Or, if they do, I pray they will think that one of the dogs did it, for there are many of them in the hall, begging for scraps or lying under the tables.

The relief is great; at last I can relax, and my fall from grace is not noticed. I gobble warden pears in red wine and nibble on marchpane cake. The steward orders the plates to be cleared and the spiced wine called hippocras to be served with wafers. I hardly have room for these, and my head is still muzzy when I stand for the final grace. My mother beckons.

I make my way giddily behind the guests and curtsey to her, praying she will not notice my burning cheeks, or discover my transgression.

'You may go now, Jane,' she says. 'Mrs Ellen is taking you for a walk in the park, and then you will continue with your embroidery until it is time for supper. Afterwards, you must practise your dance steps for a while before bedtime.'

'Yes, Madam,' I whisper, dipping another bob. But I notice now that there is a nasty, telltale smell from my skirt-hem and train, and so does she. She frowns. Quickly, she bends down and pinches the velvet between her thumb and forefinger, then sniffs her hand. I hang my head in shame. I dare not look at my lady. I know she is furious.

Mrs Ellen is hovering in the background. The guests are

chattering happily; they have no idea what is happening.

My mother beckons the nurse.

'Take this child, wash her and change her clothes,' she says, very low, 'then bring her to me in the great chamber, where I will teach her some manners.'

Mrs Ellen takes me by the hand. I follow her up the stairs and burst into tears. As she changes me, I tell her what happened.

'Did you not think to crave leave to withdraw?' asks my nurse, sharp.

'I thought I would get into trouble,' I weep.

'Well, you're in far more trouble now. And I too, I dare say. Now, you'll do. We had best go and face the music.'

In the great chamber my mother is waiting, straight-backed, frowning and forbidding.

'Fortunately, Jane, your shame has not been exposed in front of the guests,' she tells me, her voice cold. 'But really, you should know better, a great girl of your age. Why did you not excuse yourself?'

Of course, my mother could never understand that I am so scared of her that I would put up with much to escape her displeasure. And she has forgotten that it is my birthday, and my first time at the high table. All that matters is that I should have known better.

'You have behaved very badly,' she is saying, 'and it is my duty to correct such behaviour.'

I stand before her, trembling, Mrs Ellen behind me.

'Prepare her,' commands my lady, reaching for her riding crop.

Mrs Ellen looks unhappy as she leads me to a bench, bends me over it and lifts my skirts.

'Jane, you have conducted yourself in a disgraceful manner,' my mother tells me. 'I am shocked that a young lady of your age should do such a thing in company. In future, I hope you will remember your manners and your position in this house-hold. I trust that this will serve to reinforce that remembrance.'

I hear the whip swish through the air, then feel it lash the soft flesh of my bottom. I bite my lip, trying so hard not to cry, knowing in some strange way that to do so would please my mother. But as I wince under the fourth stroke, the tears burst through my screwed-up eyelids and I start wailing uncontrollably.

'Stand up,' orders my lady. 'Tidy yourself. Now, what have you to say?'

'I am sorry, Madam,' I sob. 'Please forgive me.'

'Pray to God for forgiveness,' she answers. 'Now go.'

Bradgate Hall, February 1542

Something awful has happened. I know it because I have heard hushed whispers in the household. People stop talking when I enter the room, and I can guess that whatever they are talking about is unpleasant.

Soon, I learn what it is. I am repeating the alphabet to Mrs Ellen when my mother comes into the nursery. We curtsey, then stay standing until my lady has sat down in the high-backed chair by the fire. Katherine is crawling around the room, babbling to herself, happily ignorant of the tension in the air.

'I am sure you have heard about the Queen,' my lady says to Mrs Ellen, 'but there is fresh news, and the child may as well hear it, since it is an object lesson in what can happen to a woman who falls from virtue. Anyway, she is bound to find out sooner or later.'

Mrs Ellen looks at me unhappily. I realise she already knows something of what my mother is talking about. I fear I am going to hear something terrible. Over by the windowsill, Katherine is reaching up for a cloth ball, crooning to herself, lost in her own small world.

'There has been a lot of gossip, and wild rumours multiply daily,' my mother begins, 'but let me give you the truth, as I have it from my lord. Last November, after his Majesty and Queen Katherine returned from their progress in the north, certain accusations were made by mean persons concerning the conduct of the Queen, and an inquiry was made to discover if they were true. Unfortunately, they were. It seems that her Grace was corrupted by her music master before she was even twelve years old, and that she later lived with her cousin, Francis Dereham, as if she were his wife. This all took place while she was being brought up in the household of her grand-mother, the Duchess of Norfolk. Apparently, the servants testified. They had seen her naked in bed with Dereham in the maids' dormitory.'

I am astonished. What does 'corrupted' mean? And why would the Queen want to be naked in bed with her cousin? How immodest of her! No wonder she is in trouble.

My mother looks at me and frowns.

'Pay attention, Jane. This is a lesson you must learn. You are four years old and big enough to understand. As if it were not bad enough that the Queen was unfit to marry his Majesty, she continued her immoral life after her marriage to the King, engaging Dereham as her secretary. Then, when she had apparently tired of him, she began a secret liaison with another cousin, Thomas Culpeper, a Gentleman of the King's Privy Chamber. His Majesty was very fond of Thomas, which makes his conduct all the more disgraceful. With the connivance of that dreadful Lady Rochford – you remember, George Boleyn's wife, who gave evidence that her husband had sinned with his sister, Queen Anne – the Queen arranged to meet Culpeper in her chamber at night, even on the progress. On one occasion, the King came to her door, expecting to lie with his wife, and was kept waiting while Culpeper made a hasty escape down the back stairs. Another time, Lady Rochford kept watch while the Queen received Culpeper in the privy!'

In the privy? I am shocked. I know beyond question now that the Queen is a very naughty lady who deserves to be punished. I would never let anyone come into the privy while I was using it. How rude!

'That is disgusting behaviour, my lady,' murmurs Mrs Ellen. 'It is scandalous that she should have so dishonoured the King's Highness!'

'Indeed,' says my mother grimly. 'When his Majesty was informed by his councillors of the truth of the allegations, he broke down and wept before them, then called for a sword to slay her whom he had dearly loved. My lord was there, and he wrote to say it was a pitiful sight to see one of the King's courage brought so low. The upshot was that the Queen was placed under arrest at Hampton Court. She was in a terrible state, weeping and wailing, and once she managed to break past her guards and run towards the chapel, where the King was attending Mass, hoping to soften his heart by a personal appeal. She probably thought that her charms could save her. But she was caught and dragged back, screaming, before she could reach him.'

'She is very young,' Mrs Ellen says.

'Yes,' agrees my lady. 'scarce seventeen. But old enough to know right from wrong.'

'Yet by all accounts, Madam, she was never taught virtuous behaviour. I have heard that her grandmother neglected her, and now you tell me that she was led astray by her music master when she was but a child. Yes, she has committed a grievous wrong, but is there no one to take pity on her? The poor girl must be in misery, remembering the dreadful fate that befell her cousin, Anne Boleyn.'

I have heard Anne Boleyn's name mentioned before, but only in whispers or corners, and I do not know who she was, or what happened to her that was so dreadful. I would love to interrupt and ask about her, but I dare not chance a rebuke – or worse – from my mother.

'Of course she remembered,' my lady is saying, 'and that accounted for her wildness and weeping under questioning. And of course she denied it all, but the sworn testimony of the witnesses was enough to prove that she lied.'

'Have they tried her?' Mrs Ellen asks sadly.

'No. The King had her banished to Syon Abbey, and she stayed there over Christmas.'

'I heard as much,' Mrs Ellen nods. 'Is she still there?'

'No.' My lady pauses. 'A week ago, Parliament passed an Act of Attainder declaring her a traitor and depriving her of her life and all her titles and possessions. Last Friday, although she resisted frantically, she was taken by barge to the Tower of London, and there, on Monday, her head was taken off by the executioner.'

I gasp. This is horrible, horrible, worse than the nastiest nightmare. Her head was taken off. How? And why? She had been very naughty, but surely not naughty enough to have her head taken off. I feel sick. Would there have been a lot of blood. I hate blood. When I cut my finger it bled a lot, and hurt too. It must hurt an awful lot to have your head cut off. Much more than cutting your finger. So there must be lots more blood. And what happens to you when your head is cut off? You must be dead.

I am shaking with the horror of it. I am also crying, although I do not realise it. Mrs Ellen, whose face looks very white, kneels down beside me and holds me close to her. She looks up at my mother.

'She is too young to understand, my lady! It is too much for her to take in.'

My mother looks at me as I stand sobbing. There is no softness in her as she stands there in her gorgeous furred gown and bejewelled hood. She has been angered by the Queen's affront to her blood.

'Jane,' she says sternly, 'you have been born into a family of the royal House. People in our position lead public lives. We have power, rank and wealth, but we also have duties and obligations, and as women of this family, we must be above reproach. If a noblewoman or queen sins as Queen Katherine has done, she sets her husband's very inheritance, his titles, lands and riches, at risk. In this case, the succession to the throne itself has been disparaged, for if the Queen had borne a child to one of those traitors she sinned with, she could easily have passed it off as the King's, and that could have led to a bastard of base blood sitting on the throne of England. A wife must keep faithful to her husband, and adultery in an aristocratic woman is a vile crime, and is rightly punishable by death.'

I do not know what adultery means, but I know what death is. As soon as I was old enough to ask what the tombs in the church were for, it was explained to me. The chaplain told me that, when God decides that a person's time on Earth has ended, He summons them before His dreadful judgement seat. If they have been good, He sends them to Heaven, where they may dwell for ever in bliss with Our Lord Jesus, the Blessed Virgin and all the saints and angels. But if they have been wicked, they are sent to Hell, to suffer for all eternity. The chaplain has told me all about what awaits sinners in Hell, and I know it is true, because in one of the churches in Leicester there is a horrid wall painting that I dare not look at for fear of seeing the cruel devils tearing the flesh of the damned with their pitchforks. Mrs Ellen says I must not think about that picture, and that my sins are not so bad as to deserve eternal damnation, and if I am a good girl, and say my prayers and keep the Commandments, and receive absolution for my sins, I will go straight to Heaven.

Mrs Ellen told me that most people die of illness or old age, or a mishap, like Sam the thatcher who fell off his ladder and broke his neck. She told me that brave soldiers die in wars, and that for most people death is just like going to sleep; but surely no one could be deliberately killed by having their head taken off, especially when they hadn't done very much to deserve it.

It was the King, my great-uncle, who had ordered that the Queen must be killed. Kings can do whatever they like – I know that. I have also been taught that they are above ordinary people and must be obeyed. I have never met the King, but I have heard many tales of him, and his portrait hangs in the great hall. He is a big man, a giant in his gorgeous clothes, with a fat tummy and a red beard, standing with his hand on his hip and his legs apart. He looks very frightening, grimacing out of the picture, as I imagine an ogre might look. Perhaps he is an ogre. He had the Queen's head taken off. But perhaps he is sad now, and wishing he hadn't done it.

I am feeling a bit better now, although I still want to ask lots of questions, because there is much that I yet don't understand. But my mother is preparing to depart.

'I leave it to you how much you elaborate to the child,' she is saying to Mrs Ellen as she pauses by the door, 'but for the love of God, bid her be discreet. If ever she should go to court, we don't want her disgracing us with embarrassing remarks.'

When she has gone, Mrs Ellen starts tidying the room, putting my toys away before supper. I sit on the floor with Katherine, helping her to dress her cloth Polly doll, all the while thinking of the terrible death of the Queen.

'Let's put Polly to bed,' pipes Katherine, getting up and toddling towards the miniature cradle standing in the corner. She tenderly lays down the doll and covers her up, very tightly.

'Not over her face.' I force a smile. 'She can't breathe.'

'Bedtime for you too, Katherine,' says Mrs Ellen. The nursery maid leads a protesting Katherine up the stairs.

Mrs Ellen closes the toy chest, smoothes her apron, seats herself in her chair by the fire and takes up her mending.

'You must not dwell on what has happened to the Queen, Jane,' she tells me.

'It's horrible,' I answer.

'Horrible, but necessary, I dare say. She had been very silly and very wicked. She must have known the risks she was taking.'

'But what had she done wrong?'

Mrs Ellen folds Katherine's tiny smock, the tear in it hardly visible now. Her stitches are so minute you can hardly see them.

'Come here, child, and stand at my knee.' She beckons, and I go to her, resting my hands on the soft holland cloth of her apron.

'Mrs Ellen, how did they cut off the Queen's head?' I am bursting to know, yet fearful of the answer.

'With an axe, Jane.'

'Like the axe Perkin cuts the logs with?'

'Like that, but bigger and sharper.'

'Did it hurt?'

'I'm sure she didn't know anything about it. It's a very quick death.'

I pause. I want to ask another question, but I know it's not polite to talk about naked people.

'Why was the Queen in bed with her cousin?' I venture at last.

'I expect because she considered herself to be his wife. Married people are allowed to sleep in the same bed.'

'But she was married to the King. You can't be married to two people at once, can you?'

'No. But I have heard that Dereham said she had promised in front of others to marry him, and people consider that to be as good as a marriage itself. The Queen insisted she had never done so, but she must have been lying, for folk heard Dereham call her "wife", while she called him "husband".'

There is still something I do not understand.

'But why did they go to bed together' – I feel my cheeks going red – 'without any clothes on?'

Mrs Ellen does not answer at once. She thinks for a bit, then says, 'Listen, child, God decrees that, when a man and woman marry, one of their duties is to have children. It is a sin to have children outside marriage, so marriage has been ordained by God so that children can be born and brought up in a godly manner, and have a father and mother. Do you understand?'

I nod.

'Good. The Scriptures tell us that God made men and women differently. Their bodies are different. The husband plants a seed from his body inside his wife. Inside the tiny seed is a complete person, and it grows inside its mother's womb, which is in her tummy. It stays there for nine months, then it is born. Now, to plant that seed, the husband and wife have to take their clothes off, otherwise it would be difficult.'

'Don't they mind?' I ask, my face afire.

'Not at all. God has made it a pleasant business, although He has ordained that it be lawful only in holy wedlock. Now the Queen was unfaithful to the King because she received seed from other men. Thus she committed a terrible crime. She endangered the blood royal. That is treason, and the punishment is always death.'

I remember something.

'Did Anne Boleyn have her head chopped off too?'

'Mercy me, how sharp you are!' cries Mrs Ellen. 'Yes, she did, my dear, and for much the same thing, but it must not be spoken of. It was a dreadful business, and a matter of too-great grief to his Majesty and your parents.'

'But who was Anne Boleyn?' I ask.

'She was the King's second wife, the mother of the Lady Elizabeth, your cousin.'

I have heard a lot about my cousin Elizabeth. She is four years older than me and lives in her own palace with a lot of servants. She hardly ever goes to court because she is busy at her lessons. She is an uncommonly clever girl, my mother says.

'The Lady Elizabeth must be very sad about her mother's head being cut off,' I say. 'Is the King a kind father to her?'

Mrs Ellen pats my hand.

'At first, I heard, he could not bear the sight of her. She was only two when her mother died, and she was left in the care of her governess. When she grew out of her clothes, there was no money to buy new ones, and Master Secretary Cromwell did not like to trouble the King. But then Queen Jane took pity on the poor motherless child, and brought her back to court, and her other stepmothers were also kindly towards her, and to the Lady Mary too, the King's daughter by the first Queen Katherine. Now the Lady Elizabeth is well received at court whenever she visits there. She never speaks about her mother, it is said. Perhaps it is best that way. And she adores her father the King. But Jane, you must remember, these matters must never be spoken of outside this room, do you heed me?'

'I heed you, Mrs Ellen,' I say, all solemn.

In the small hours of the night, I wake up screaming, bringing Mrs Ellen rushing in, all frowsty from bed and carrying a lighted candle.

'There now,' she soothes, cradling me in her arms, 'it was just a bad dream.'

It had been a very bad dream indeed. It had been so real that I woke up expecting to see the Queen's headless body, with blood streaming from its ragged neck, stumble blindly through my door.

Frances Brandon, Marchioness of Dorset

Hampton Court Palace, July 1543

There is a great throng in the holyday closet leading to the chapel royal, and it is unpleasantly hot. Here we all are in our damasks and velvets, perspiring profusely and marvelling at my royal uncle's irrepressible optimism. For today, His Majesty is marrying his sixth wife.

Standing beside my lord at the front, I press a handkerchief to my nose to blot out the stink of sweat. Only a foot or so away from us stands the King, resplendent in cloth of gold, and the woman he is taking in holy matrimony – Katherine Parr, Lady Latimer. The nuptials are being conducted by that toady, Archbishop Cranmer, and among the guests are the highest in the land.

The new Queen is no giddy girl like Katherine Howard, but a mature woman of thirty-one, russet-haired and comely, yet no beauty. Good seat on a horse, though, and an old friend of mine, being but five years older than I. Her two previous husbands were old men, to whom she bore no children, so she is well qualified to look after my ailing uncle. Whether he will get sons on her is another matter. The whisper goes that he is now so infirm with his huge bulk and diseased legs that he is no longer capable of getting a filly in foal, for all that he still goes out of his way to act the stallion, with his magnificent suits and thrusting codpieces, larger than any other man's. But what he really desires, I suspect, is the soothing companionship that only a woman can give him. A nurse in his twilight years. And in Katherine Parr, with her quiet, kindly ways and her famously erudite mind, I believe he will find what he seeks.

It is well known at court, however, that Lady Latimer has not always displayed such gravity. Last year, after Lord Latimer died, she fell in love with the Lord High Admiral, Sir Thomas Seymour, younger brother of the late Queen Jane. These Seymours, upon whom I am now bestowing a gracious smile, are an ambitious, upstart breed. The eldest brother, Edward, Lord Hertford, has risen to power sheerly by virtue of his sister bearing the King a son, and he is now one of the most powerful men in the kingdom. And I make no doubt he will retain that eminence, being uncle to the future King.

The ambitious Sir Thomas is plainly jealous of his brother. He resents his power and influence, and makes no secret of his opinion that Lord Hertford, who is noted for his high ideals and penny-pinching ways, should do more to advance his younger brother. But the truth is that Sir Thomas, for all his dark good looks and persuasive charm, is a volatile, untrustworthy schemer, plainly unfitted for high office at court. Lord Hertford knows it, and the King knows it. Nonetheless, the young buck is seen as a goodly fellow, and he has been appointed Lord High Admiral so that his impulsive, adventurous spirit may be put to good use.

Sir Thomas was not in love with Lady Latimer, we all knew that, but he had certainly realised that she was a rich widow with a good reputation, who would make a desirable wife for any aspiring nobleman. It was also obvious that she was ripe for the picking. And no doubt he thought that, after being married to two old men, she would appreciate having a lusty young one in her bed.

It was only two months ago, when Kate – or rather, the Queen, as I must shortly call her – and I were sitting in her lodgings at court, that she told me herself how she had fallen so wildly for Thomas Seymour.

'I had to fight him off – he would barely take no for an answer, Frances,' she confided. 'And I . . . well, I wanted him. What woman wouldn't? He's so handsome and charming. But when he realised I wasn't going to let him have his way with me, he spoke of marriage. Oh, Frances, you can't imagine how happy I was. After two old greybeards, to whom I was nurse rather than wife, I was to have a young and virile husband. And then the King made known his interest, and Tom told me he had no choice but to withdraw. Soon afterwards, he was sent abroad on a timely diplomatic mission, and then his Majesty began to press his suit in earnest.'

He's no fool, my uncle. Unlike Kate, poor, virtuous matron, who was beguiled by the blandishments of a self-seeking scoundrel.

'When the King proposed marriage to me,' Kate went on, 'I was reluctant to accept. I did not want the burden of queenship. Truly, I feared it. With respect, Frances, for I know he is your uncle, his Majesty has not had a happy matrimonial career.'

'You speak truth there. But it has not all been his fault.'

'No, no,' she hastily agreed. 'But revere him as I do, as my sovereign lord, I did not love him as I love – loved – Tom. God forgive me, but when the King asked me to marry him, I told him I would rather be his mistress than his wife.'

Her reluctance was understandable. The position of queen consort in this realm has indeed become fraught with hazards. It is now high treason for a woman with a dubious past to marry the King without first declaring that she has led an impure life. And once she is married to him, she must take care that, like Caesar's wife, she remains above suspicion. With two of my uncle's wives having gone to the block already, there are few ladies at court who would aspire to the honour of becoming his queen.

Yet here Kate is, standing by my uncle, receiving the congratulations of their guests, and merrily clasping his hand as he leads the way from the chapel, he staggering manfully on his ulcerated legs, broad and magnificent in his gem-encrusted short gown and feathered bonnet, with Katherine, a diminutive figure in crimson damask, leaning on his arm. In the privy chamber, where the wedding banquet is laid out ready, bride and groom are smiling broadly, in high good humour, extending their hands to be kissed as the lords and ladies, like so many peacocks, bob up and down before them.

'My Lady Dorset, we are pleased to welcome you,' says the new Queen, as I rise from my curtsey. 'I should be grateful if you would attend me tomorrow. I have need of ladies like yourself in my household.'

'I feel highly honoured, your Majesty,' I say, as my husband looks on approvingly.

'Frances will have you well organised, Kate,' chimes in the King, smiling. 'Quite a formidable lady, my niece!' He grins at me as he says this, and I laugh.

'Your Majesty is too unkind,' I retort. I have a great affection for my uncle, whose character is in so many ways like my own. I know that many people are terrified of him, but he has always been kind to me, and I believe that, because I deal with him directly and approach him in the right way, I bring out the best in him. I can remember him as he was in the years before he was soured by constant matrimonial trials and his fears for the succession, and I can still detect something of that golden, athletic younger man beneath the layers of flesh and the puffy, ruined face.

The King invites us to accompany him on the hunt tomorrow, then moves off with his bride to circulate among the other guests. I suddenly find myself next to Anne of Cleves – still smelling a trifle high – who greets me in her deep guttural English and glances humorously in the direction of the royal couple.

'A fine burden Madam Katherine has taken upon herself!' she murmurs.

'I'm sure she will cope,' I say, tart. 'His Majesty thinks very highly of her.'

'As he did of the late Queen, and most of the ones before her,' retorts Anne. 'Excepting, of course, myself.' She smiles. 'But I am not complaining. And I am delighted that my dear brother has found happiness at last.' It is an open secret that Madam of Cleves was not exactly displeased at being so unceremoniously dumped by the King. She did very well out of it financially, and now leads a comfortable life that is mercifully free from court intrigue. And she kept her head!

I smile back stiffly. I do not much like this German princess with her penetrating observations. Really, she should consider well that she is speaking to the King's own niece. But Anne suddenly grasps my arm.

'I hope I have not offended you,' she states shrewdly. 'I assure you, his Majesty has been very good to me, most generous. I am happy to be his dear sister and to stay in this lovely England.'

I incline my head and move on, reflecting that my uncle had not exaggerated – the woman smelt awful. Do they never change their body linen in Cleves?

I join my husband, who is deep in conversation with my cousins, the Lady Mary and the Lady Margaret Douglas, who is a bridesmaid to the Queen.

'I am sure you are pleased to see your father the King so happily settled,' Henry says to Mary, as I take up my position at his side.

'It is a blessing after what happened with the others,' she replies, peering at him intensely with short-sighted eyes. Mary, at twenty-seven, is a year older than I am; but where I am strong and healthy, she is a tiny, thin woman, plagued by ill-health, imagined or chronic, and whatever bloom she once had has long since dulled, blasted by tragedy and disappointment. Today, she is wearing a tawny gown of figured corded damask, its white lawn undersleeves banded with crimson velvet. Her frizzy red hair is parted severely under her French hood, and her thin fingers are fiddling anxiously with the gold prayer book that is attached by a ribbon to her girdle.

I feel a certain pity for Mary, but I can't help being irritated by her. She's had a hard life, and it is true that the King treated her with great severity when he put away Katherine of Aragon, but then the wretched girl had been so stubborn, refusing to acknowledge that her mother's marriage had been unlawful.

One does not defy the King thus and get away with it, and my uncle kept her apart from her mother to teach her obedience. He would not let Mary visit Katherine, even when the old Queen was dying. Instead, Mary was proclaimed a bastard, the fruit of an incestuous union, and sent to wait on her half-sister Elizabeth, Anne Boleyn's child, who had just been born. What surprised us all was that Mary, who had been thwarted of marriage and motherhood by her debased status, quickly developed a touching affection for Elizabeth. And she was very kind to her when Elizabeth, in her turn, was declared base-born after Anne Boleyn's fall. It is astonishing that, despite their mothers being deadly rivals, these two sisters have so much in common and are evidently devoted to each other. Furthermore, both are deeply fond of their brother Edward.

Neither of the King's younger children is here today. Prince Edward, now five years old, is at Havering, and the Lady Elizabeth is at Hatfield. They are missing a merry occasion, but then I suppose that, as ever, his Majesty is fearful of them catching some contagion through over-much contact with the court.

As I load my plate with gilded marchpane and candied oranges from the buffet, the consort of musicians in the corner begins playing a stately pavane. But no one is dancing. Instead, there is a babel of chatter, as goblets are replenished and the courtiers circulate, regrouping as their fancy takes them. The King sits on his chair of estate, his new Queen on a stool to his right, and beckons favoured courtiers in turn to converse with them. From time to time, he takes his bride's hand, raises it to his lips and kisses it, his blue eyes narrowing playfully in lust. For all his infirmity, there is still much of the old Adam left in my uncle, and I make no doubt that he will hasten Kate away to bed as soon as he may.

I watch this touching by-play out of the corner of my eye, as Henry and I discuss the events of the day with the Earl of Hertford, brother to the late Queen Jane. Then I am rudely jolted back to the world of politics by his lordship venturing into more contentious matters.

'You heard about the treaty, Dorset?'

'Treaty?' Henry looks nonplussed.

'Then you'd better keep this under your bonnet,' Hertford

says, lowering his voice and leaning forward so that we can hear him. 'His Majesty has just signed a treaty with the Scots providing for the betrothal of the Prince to their little Queen.'

I am truly shaken by this. Last year, the Scottish King, James V, died, leaving as Queen of Scots his infant daughter Mary. I was aware that my uncle had been scheming to marry her to the Prince and so unite England and Scotland under Tudor rule, and when we heard that he had sent envoys to the Scottish Queen Regent in Edinburgh to ask for her daughter's hand, we were appalled, but I never really thought the Scots would agree to it. So this is a bitter blow to my lord and me, who have long cherished the hope that Edward would marry our Jane, and I am hard put to keep the smile on my face.

'Of course,' says Hertford, 'the Scots do not want it, but they do not have the forces to resist. It is feared, though, that the Queen Regent will try to enlist the help of the French in order to break the treaty, but she must surely know that that will mean war.'

'She's a woman,' my lord remarks, 'and women have little judgement in such matters.' I throw him a look, but I know better than to argue with Henry in public. He can be so pig-ignorant and tactless. I might be a woman, but I'll wager I understand more of this matter than he does. Subtlety was never his strong point.

'When is the marriage to take place?' I inquire of Lord Hertford.

'Not for a few years, of course. His Majesty recalls that his brother Arthur died after being married too young. It was thought that over-exertion in the marriage bed killed him. But the King will ask for the Queen of Scots to be brought to court here to be educated.'

'And do you think the Scots will agree to that?' asks my lord.

'They might not have a choice,' answers Hertford grimly.

After he has moved away to join another circle of courtiers, I snatch a quick word with my husband.

'Henry, this is terrible, I know,' I mutter, 'but if we just bide our time, all might yet work out for the best. After all, the Prince is far too young to be properly wed, and there's many a slip betwixt cup and lip.'

My lord nods, squeezing my hand.

'You can console yourself to, my dear, with the sure knowledge that royal marriage negotiations often come to nothing.'

'I shall direct my prayers to that end,' I tell him determinedly.

Lying in bed at night, in our lodgings here at court, I am awake, pondering on the situation. My mind is in turmoil, and I reach across the coverlet for Henry's hand.

'Are you awake, husband?' I whisper, squeezing it.

'Go to sleep, Frances,' he groans, roused from the deep slumber that inevitably follows the slaking of desire.

'No. I can't sleep. I am lying here worrying about that treaty, and hoping that it might even now be possible to make a queen of our daughter.'

'Leave it till the morning,' he mumbles.

'No. Henry, you must listen. If the Prince marries the Queen of Scots, what will become of our Jane? Who shall she marry? There will be no match as great as this.'

Henry rolls over to face me and draws me into his arms. It is comforting to rest my cheek against his hairy chest.

'Stop fretting, sweetheart,' he murmurs. 'All shall be well, I'm sure of it. You'll see.'

His calm complacency irritates me, and I sit up, the better to make my point.

'Henry, we have got to do everything in our power to frustrate the Scottish alliance,' I tell him. 'Now will you listen to me?'

He sighs, and stretches back on the pillow.

'Alright, Frances. I'm listening.'

'You, my lord, must remain at court. You must be a dissident voice amongst those of whom the King takes counsel. You must do your best to convince my royal uncle that the Scots are a perfidious lot who have no intention of marrying their queen to his son and giving up their sovereign independence, and that the path to the altar will almost certainly be paved with blood. Of course, his Majesty might not pay any heed, but it is worth a try. Anything is worth a try.'

'I doubt the King will listen to me,' he says. 'And I was planning to go up to Bradgate for the grease season. These things have a habit of sorting themselves out.'

'You would do better to stay here and help matters along,' I tell him firmly. 'Rushing off hunting indeed, when so much is at stake. There are times when I just don't understand you. I can't influence the King's council – I'm a woman. But you can. And I, for my part, will give some thought to Jane's education. She is intelligent and able enough to benefit from an academic regime like that enjoyed by the Lady Elizabeth. And since the King has had his daughters well tutored, he would surely appreciate a similarly erudite bride for his son. I shall convey Jane to London, and bring her to his Majesty's notice. We must give her every advantage.'

'That might not be to her advantage if this Scottish match falls through,' Henry observes. 'Most men don't want a clever wife.'

'Nonsense! And the match we plan is *not* going to fall through,' I snap. 'It's your duty to make sure of that. I'll do my part. Since you're so concerned about Jane appearing too clever, I shall continue to instil in her the feminine virtues of modesty and obedience. Any streak of wilfulness – and I know that it is there – will be beaten out of her. I shall make her, above all things, biddable and conformable to the will of her future husband. Then she will be fitted not only for the great destiny that will surely be hers, but also for any other that God wills for her, if you fail in your duty.'

'By God, Frances, you expect too much,' Henry growls.

'I'm doing this for all of us,' I say. 'Don't tell me you do not look for the greatness this marriage will confer. You want to see our daughter a queen as much as I do. I'm relying on you, Henry. God helps those who help themselves, and with His grace, we *shall* bring this off, I promise you.'

Lady Jane Grey

Westminster, August 1543

My parents have sent for us, and the rest of the household, to come to London to lodge at Dorset House, our town mansion by Westminster. The house, which is built around a courtyard, is at least a hundred years old, but my lord and lady have refurbished it at great cost. Now the rooms are cosy with linenfold panelling, rich hangings and polished oak furniture, and our family coat of arms is set in glass in the windows. There are gardens round about the house, but they are small compared to those at Bradgate, which is surrounded by beautiful broad sweeps of parkland and rugged cliffs.

Mrs Ellen doesn't like it here very much.

'The air is not as healthy for you children as it is in Leicestershire,' she grumbles. 'And the City of London is dirty, noisy and overcrowded. As for Westminster – think of all the diseases that could breed in these dark, narrow streets. And some of the houses – they're just hovels! No, it's not a place for children, or anyone, come to that.'

I can't see the problem. I like it here in London. There's so much to see and explore, so much happening, and so many new things to experience. For once I favour my mother's views above those of my nurse, for my lady has insisted that we be taken out daily for long walks, so that we shall see the sights.

After living in Bradgate all my life, I find this huge city overwhelming but exciting. I am fascinated by its people, the prosperous merchants and their wives, who ape their betters in their velvets and furs and gold chains; the plump clergymen and priests in their black and white robes and jewelled crucifixes, ever ready to bestow a blessing on a well-dressed child; the street-vendors in their homespun and worsteds, crying their wares, and slipping me a small cake when Mrs Ellen makes her purchases; and the beggars lying in the streets, baring their sores and stumps, crying for alms, and so grateful when I give them a penny. I've lost count of how many fine churches I've seen, how many shops I've looked in, how many fine bolts of material and trinkets I've been shown, and how many streets I've had to fight my way down. I've marvelled at the King's great palace in nearby Whitehall, the ruins of the old Palace of Westminster, which burned down years ago, the beautiful abbey dedicated to St Peter, where all the Kings of England are crowned, and St Paul's Cathedral, the largest building I've ever seen. I've never glimpsed so many wonders in one place.

But today there is to be a special treat. My father is taking us to see the printing works founded by Master William Caxton about seventy years ago. My lord tells us that it used to be near Westminster Abbey, but that after his death, Master Caxton's press was taken over by Master Wynkyn de Worde, and he moved it to premises at The Sun, by St Bride's Church in Fleet Street.

This visit will be of much interest to me, for I have mastered reading and writing, and discovered the pleasure that lies within the pages of a good book. I now know by heart the stories in the Book of Hours that I was given for my fourth birthday. In fact, I read anything I can get my hands on: saints' lives, romances, histories, tales of chivalry, like those of King Arthur, or the travels of Sir John Mandeville. I devour books like gluttons gobble their food.

'Master Caxton,' my lord tells us, as we climb into our barge, 'was the first man to print books in England. He had learned his skill in Germany and Bruges, and we have a great deal to thank him for. Without printing, there would be far fewer books for us all to enjoy.'

Privately, I think that I have never seen my father enjoy a book. With him, it's do as I say, not do as I do.

'Will we see Master Caxton?' pipes up Katherine, as we alight near the house of the Carmelites below Fleet Street and begin walking up the hill.

'Don't be silly,' I rebuke her. She is little, and often stupid. 'Master Caxton would be the oldest man in the world if we did. He died a long time ago, didn't he, my lord?'

My father nods. 'He did indeed. He died when Henry the Seventh, your great-grandfather and the father of our present King, was still on the throne. But others now carry on his work.'

When we enter the printing works, we are received with much bowing by Master Robert Copland, the master printer, who takes us into the main office, which has brick arches set into the walls, and mullioned windows. He shows us the giant wooden presses, which are attached by battens to the ceiling, and demonstrates how they work. He lets us handle small lumps of antimony, the silvery metal that is melted in moulds to make the letters.

'No other metal gives such a sharp casting,' Master Copland

explains. 'But don't put it near your mouths, my ladies – it's poisonous.'

Katherine and I are allowed to put some of the ready-cast letters in place in the galleys, the metal frames on which the text is set out, wiping our inky fingers afterwards.

'All the letters have to be exactly the same size and height,' Master Copland tells us. 'Otherwise, some of them won't show up on the page.'

I notice that my father is looking bored, and when Master Copland takes us into a large room with shelves, on which are stacked hundreds and hundreds of books, my lord is stifling a yawn.

'Most of these were printed by Master Wynkyn,' Master Copland says, as my father's eyes glaze over with boredom. 'He printed no fewer than six hundred titles. We also have here some woodcuts made by that master printer.' He hands us loose sheets of paper on which are printed scenes from *The Golden Legend* and *The Canterbury Tales*. 'And here we have first editions of several of the books printed by Master Caxton himself. Please feel free to take them off the shelf and look at them, my ladies.'

My father is no longer looking bored, I notice. He has found some rather naughty woodcuts showing fat ladies with naked breasts.

'My lord,' says Master Copland, 'I should count myself honoured if you would accept this small token of our esteem. May I present you with this treatise on hunting, *The Master of Game*, which was written by no less a personage than Prince Edward, Duke of York, who was killed at the Battle of Agincourt, more than a century ago.'

My father's smile betrays his genuine delight in the gift, and his words of thanks are warm. Master Copland could not have chosen anything better calculated to give him pleasure, for hunting is my father's chief passion in life.

'Look at this, my lady,' says the printer. A history of Troy, in a beautiful binding, is placed in my hands. 'This is the first book ever printed in England. It is very precious.' There are other first editions, too, *The Game and Play of the Chess*, *The Dictes and Sayings of the Philosophers*, Sir Thomas Malory's *Le Morte d'Arthur*, which I already know and love, and some books by a man called Cicero, which are new to me. Katherine wants to look at them too, but she is only interested in the pictures. Me, I want to read on, to escape into worlds of wonder as yet undiscovered.

Master Copland is watching me, beaming. He takes another volume off the shelf.

'This is for you, my lady,' he smiles, presenting it to me with a bow. 'I can see that you will enjoy it.'

I look at the frontispiece. It is a new copy of *The Golden Legend*. I am in raptures.

'I thank you, Sir,' I say, as my father looks on with approval. 'This will give me much pleasure.'

Katherine is looking a little put out.

'And for my little lady,' continues the master, 'some letters.' He places a box of printing blocks in her hands. She stares at them.

'Your manners, Katherine!' barks my lord.

'I thank you, Sir,' she lisps.

'That's better. Now perhaps you will have some incentive to learn your letters.'

'I hope your lordship will one day do us the honour of bringing the young ladies to visit our shop in Paul's Churchyard,' says Master Copland. 'We have many excellent books on sale there.'

'I will do that, Sir,' says my father, ushering us out of the works. 'Thank you, and good day.' All too soon the visit is over. As we walk back past the White Friars, I clutching my precious book, Katherine is skipping by my side, chattering away. She's three now, and very pretty, with blue eyes and a fair face that is unmarked by freckles. I do wish that Mrs Ellen could find a remedy for my freckles, and that I was pretty like Katherine. Katherine is not like me: she prefers to play with her dolls or ride her hobbyhorse rather than look at books or attend to learning the letters on her horn book. Mrs Ellen gets quite cross with her at times.

'Why can't you be like Jane?' she says. 'Jane's a good girl. She sits still and does her lessons. But you, you scamp, you're a fidget.'

Katherine just smiles. She has such charm. My mother says that some day she'll make some lucky man a very decorative wife. She never says such things about me. In fact, I've been told that, although I must marry to bring honour and profit to our House, I'm too thin and too bookish and too freckled to snare a husband. So I've decided to leave all that to Katherine. I'd prefer to be left alone with my books.

Frances Brandon, Marchioness of Dorset

Westminster, Winter 1543

'There is good news from Scotland!' cries Henry, bursting into my chamber as I sit there checking the accounts with the steward, and shooing the poor man, my startled ladies and our assorted yapping lap-dogs out of the door. 'Listen, Frances. The Scottish Parliament has refused to ratify the treaty. They do not want their kingdom being ruled from Westminster.'

'Blessed be God!' I cry, jubilant, laying down my quill and closing the ledger.

'The King is furious,' my lord says happily, sitting down beside me at the oak trestle and grasping my hands. 'He sees his hopes of a united Britain fading, and says he feels insulted on his son's behalf. He is now determined to teach the Scots a lesson, and has commanded Lord Hertford to muster an army.'

'These are indeed hopeful tidings,' I answer. 'Is it likely that the King will win this war?'

'We won Flodden,' Henry reminds me. 'Slaughtered them. But we were massacred ourselves at Bannockburn. It's in the hands of God. And I would be committing treason if I said I hoped the King will not win.'

'But that is what we both hope, isn't it?' I whisper, smiling. 'Let's hope that God is on our side.'

Henry is rarely to be seen at home these days. He is in constant attendance on the King, not only seeking advancement and preferment, like any of the other noble vultures at court, but also in the hope of picking up any new information about what we call the marriage situation. As for me, I am frequently with the Queen, and have left Mrs Ellen to order my household and children in my absence. I suspect that, under her rule, there will be some laxity and fewer beatings and scoldings than are desirable. Mrs Ellen is a kindly and competent nurse, but she is deplorably soft.

To my sorrow, I have not conceived again. On the few occasions when we do land up in bed together, Henry and I enjoy our couplings, for we have ever been in lust with each other, but it seems that God has closed His ears to our prayers for a son, which is the one thing that my lord desires most. Other men have sons, he says – why not he? But we have to face it: if I do not bear him a son, his title will pass to Jane, or rather to the man she marries. And if our plans come to fruition, our title will be absorbed into the Crown, which means that the noble name of Dorset will fall into abeyance. Henry cannot bear the thought. He wants his dynasty to live on, so we must not give up hope. I comfort myself in the knowledge that I am still only twenty-six, and women have been known to conceive and bear children well into their forties. We must keep on at our prayers – and our less sacred endeavours!

The news from the north is cataclysmic. Lord Hertford's army marched north just before Christmas to begin what people are calling the 'rough wooing' of the Queen of Scots. The King's command was to lay waste the southern parts of Scotland, to sack, burn and subvert the country, sparing neither man, woman nor child. Hertford has obeyed his orders to the letter. Leith, Edinburgh, Melrose, Jedburgh, all were devastated and fired, as our soldiers swept down across the borders to Berwick, leaving a terrible trail of destruction in their wake.

Far from capitulating in the face of such savagery, the Scots have grown ever more resolute, and have formed an alliance with France, with which England has long been at odds. The French declared themselves only too happy to offer asylum to the little Queen, who is half-French through her mother, and she was spirited away across the sea at the dead of night, much to my uncle's fury. He was even less pleased to learn that the Scots had agreed

64

that she should be brought up at the French court as the future bride of the young Dauphin, which has happily, and finally, put paid to his Majesty's plans to marry her to Prince Edward.

We can only express our jubilation in private.

'Now the way is clear for Jane,' Henry declares over a toast to the future. 'But we must bide our time until the right moment. Yet I think that might not be long in coming. His Highness is so offended by the perfidy of the Scots and the French that he may well heartily embrace the idea of an English bride for his son.'

'A bride,' I add, repeating what I have said many times before, 'who has Tudor blood in her veins and is the Prince's own cousin.'

My lord turns to me.

'I think,' he says, 'it is time Jane commenced her education.'

'I entirely agree. And the Queen has graciously agreed to help in the matter of finding a suitable tutor. It would be sensible to take her advice. She has shown great interest in Jane, and you know how assiduous she has been in supervising the education of the Prince and the Lady Elizabeth.'

I am privately relieved that Queen Katherine has offered her assistance in this matter, since although I can read and write adequately, I have no great interest in book-learning, or much understanding of the mysteries of academic disciplines. I was traditionally educated, well drilled in dancing, riding, music-making, embroidery and household management, like nobly born girls used to be before this newfangled craze for teaching them the same subjects as boys. And I am glad of it – I need nothing more. All I've ever really cared for is hunting, hawking, good food and wine, sex, fine clothes and the high life at court.

The Queen, on the other hand, has a reputation as a scholar. She is interested in the new learning and the ancient works of Greece and Rome, and loves nothing more than a debate about religion. Often I have seen her indulge in a friendly argument about some point of doctrine with Archbishop Cranmer, and even with the King when he is in the mood. Yet there are whispers – no more than that – that the Queen, like Cranmer, secretly adheres to the Protestant faith. If that is true, then she is careful to hide the fact, for my good uncle is even more of a strict conservative in such matters than he used to be. Yet she is clever. She takes care, I notice, to denounce the Pope at every opportunity, which she knows will please the King, and she always defers to him whenever an argument looms.

Hence she is admired by him for her virtue and her learning, and she is also very popular with the people. Nevertheless, the Catholic faction at court would throw her to the wolves if they had the chance, for they fear that she favours the reformers and might therefore infect the King with her views, which could lead to even more radical religious changes.

For my part, I wish her well, since I too share those dangerous opinions in secret. Of course, I would never divulge that to her. It would put us both at risk. Henry knows my views, for he is of like mind, but we rarely speak of the matter, even in the privacy of our bedchamber. Walls, you see, have ears, and the penalty for heresy is burning.

Queen Katherine Parr

Hampton Court Palace, 1543

My stepdaughters are with me now.

'Of course you may have them at court,' Henry said, when I begged leave to summon the princesses to us. 'Ask them whenever you like.'

Everyone applauds me for taking them under my protective wing, but it is no hardship, for I am fond of them both. The Lady Mary is but four years younger than me, and despite our religious differences – she is adamant in the old faith, and I think she suspects my true beliefs – we enjoy a firm friendship.

Poor Mary. She is twenty-seven and will never be resigned to spinsterhood, yet she is already aged beyond her years. Of small stature and painfully thin, she has the Tudor red hair, piercing eyes, a blunt nose and a tightly buttoned mouth. She was a sweet, pretty child, the darling of her parents – my mother once waited on Queen Katherine, and I remember her telling me how much she and the King doted upon Mary, but when her father fell for Anne Boleyn, poor Katherine fell from favour, and Mary with her, and now there is little left of Mary's child-hood prettiness – it was destroyed by the sorrows and injus-tices heaped on her from the time she reached the age of eleven. The separation from her mother, her father's stern treatment and Anne Boleyn's malicious and vindictive threats all left her embittered and hypochondriacal.

She has also confided to me that she will be haunted for ever by what she did after the King married Jane Seymour and she thought herself safe at last.

'Queen Jane,' Mary told me in her deep gruff voice, 'wanted me restored to my father's affections and my rightful place at court, but his Majesty was adamant that this would be condi-tional upon my signing a document acknowledging that my mother's marriage was incestuous and unlawful.' There were tears in her eyes as she forced out these words, and my heart dissolved in pity.

'How could I betray my mother's memory thus?' she cried, twisting her hands. 'For three years I constantly refused to recog-nise that concubine, Anne Boleyn, as Queen. But my courage was running out, my health was broken, and so were my spirits. In the end I bowed to the pressure and the threats, and signed, and I've never known a moment's peace since. I cannot forgive myself for what I did in that moment of weakness.'

She was rocking in her misery, and I held her close.

'Now, my Lady Mary, you must not blame yourself,' I murmured. 'An oath taken under duress is no true oath at all. God will surely absolve you for what you did.' She paid me no heed. She pulled back from me, and her eyes were burning with a passion I have rarely seen in them.

'I have my faith,' she declared. 'They cannot take that away from me. It is the faith my mother instilled in me and, in being true to it, I am being true to her. It is my only comfort and solace.'

Having fallen by the wayside that one shattering time, Mary will never again allow herself to compromise on matters of faith or principle, I am sure of that. But Prince Edward is, quite rightly, being raised in the religion of his father and will never turn back to Rome, so I fear that Mary, powerless as she is, is destined to see the old ways, to which she is so devotedly attached, vanish slowly but surely.

Uncomfortable though she is with the new order, Mary is yet kind and generous to a fault. The common people, remembering the affection they had for her mother and the dignity with which she bore her trials, love her, and bring her many touching small gifts – a basket of fruit here, a length of ribbon there. She adores babies and children, and is godmother to many, although sadly, as yet, mother to none. I know that is a source of great grief to her. If only I could persuade my lord the King to find her a husband, I think that marriage would be the making of her.

The Lady Elizabeth is a pert ten-year-old, who seems old in the ways of the world. She is formidably clever and quick-witted, and it gives me great pleasure to oversee her lessons. It was I who, at the King's request, appointed her tutor, William Grindal, who has devised a very comprehensive classical curriculum, in which languages feature prominently. Latin, Greek, French, Spanish, Italian, even Welsh . . . among her many talents, the Lady Elizabeth has a rare gift for languages, and is approaching fluency in most of these, as well as devouring many classical authors.

I was ready to lavish sympathy on Elizabeth, remembering the terrible circumstances in which she lost her mother, but she is not a child for cuddling or cosseting, and if she has any insecurities or fears, she hides them under a self-confident, proud exterior. Yet although she is not the most demonstrative of children, I know she has grown quite fond of me.

'I hope, Madam, that unlike my other stepmothers, you are here to stay,' she announced in her imperious way the other day, as I came upon her at her desk and watched her bent over her books, her quill flying over a sheet of paper. And so, I prayed inwardly, do I. I know that I am embarked upon a perilous sea.

With Prince Edward, who is nearly six, the King has been rather more cautious. The poor child is kept isolated in his spotlessly clean residences, guarded by an army of servants. In my opinion, Henry is being a little over-protective of his son, whose every waking moment is subject to a rigorous routine. I ask as often as I dare if Edward might come to court, but . . .

'Kate,' Henry tells me, holding up my hands to his lips and kissing them, 'I should prefer it if the boy did not come here because of the risk of his catching some infectious disease. He may visit occasionally, but it is my pleasure that he live in the country. Now, if I had other sons . . .'

He regards me archly. There is a great unspoken disappointment between us. I do appreciate that the Prince's life is especially precious, since in him alone lies England's future security and the continuance of the Tudor dynasty. But if only Henry and I could have a son, how different Edward's life would be. And mine. I should not then have to live with the fear that my own position can never be secure.

I would dearly love a child, of either sex, but my womb has never yet quickened with a man's seed. I am thirty-one, still at an age for bearing children, but I often wonder if I am barren. It is hard to tell, for my first husband, the ancient Lord Borough, took me to wife when I was just fourteen, and was very kind to me, but our marriage was never consummated because he did not have the vigour. Lord Latimer was equally kind, but he too was no longer young, and sexual congress between us was infrequent. God must have chosen me to comfort the elderly and give them solace in their infirmity!

Now, for my sins, and not through choice – although I've come to think I've not done too badly after all, for there are many benefits to being Queen, not least the manors and estates that the King has bestowed on me and, most important of all, the opportunity to do some good and make a difference to people – I am the wife of another ageing man, who, although he too is an indulgent and considerate husband, is rarely capable of the act of love. I lie there patiently, legs spread, letting him do what he will with me, as is my duty, and trying not to notice his pathetic flabby rolls of flesh, wasted muscles and putrid leg. (It's my wifely task to dress that leg, and I do it with good grace and as much gentleness as I can muster, trying not to gag at the awful stench of rotting flesh emanating from the ulcerated, suppurating wound. Fortunately, I hide my revulsion well; poor old soul, it's not his fault he has this vile malady, and he is so grateful for my ministrations.)

All too often, however, as we lie in the vast bed with the

arms of England embroidered on tester, pillows and counter-pane, along with the initials H and K, our coming together ends in failure. Henry heaves his great bulk on top of me, so that I can hardly breathe, and presses his member against me, but it is usually only half-aroused, and it is often as much as he can do to accomplish an entry. Then he thrusts desperately, grunting and puffing, before desire withers and he withdraws from the fray, disappointed and ashamed. It is, I realise, utterly humiliating for such a powerful monarch, to whom women had once come running at the crook of a royal finger, to fail in such a manner, and I always endeavour to make light of it.

'You must be tired, my lord,' I whisper, snuggling up to him. 'Or is your leg paining you?'

'Nay, sweetheart, I am over-burdened with the cares of state,' he answers, and then guides my hand to his flaccid penis. Sometimes this strategy works, and then, when it is time for my courses to come upon me, he will innocently inquire of my health with more frequent solicitude than normal. Sadly, I have not as yet had any good news to impart to him.

So there is no second son of the King to bear the customary title Duke of York, and Prince Edward comes but rarely to court. He is an over-solemn little boy, who has now lost his infant chubbiness and become rather lanky, and he has his mother's slanting eyes and pointed chin. Otherwise, he is all Tudor. They have brought him up to be the model of his father, and the last time he visited, I had to hide my smiles at the sight of the imperious little boy strutting around the privy chamber and adopting the regal pose favoured by the King, feet apart, hand on hip, chin high.

'God's blood!' he cried, when his Majesty made a jest, echoing Henry's customary oath, which amused his august parent, but brought his eternally watchful governess, Lady Bryan, running in wrath.

'My Lord Prince, you forget to whom you speak!' she shrilled, as the King suppressed his mirth. 'Do you want poor Barnaby to get a beating?' As she is not allowed to lay a finger on Edward if he transgresses, his whipping boy, Barnaby FitzPatrick, pays the price. Barnaby is of an age with the Prince, and was chosen along with several other young gentlemen to be raised in his household. Edward's punishment is to endure the shame of seeing his friend beaten for something he himself has done.

Once, I catch my husband looking intently at his son's hardening features and red-gold hair.

'He looks very like me, don't you think?' he says.

'Your Majesty must be proud in having sired another such as yourself,' I observe.

'Yet I was more robust, and much bigger, as a child.' His anxiety is palpable.

'My lord, you are chasing demons. The Prince's health has rarely given cause for concern,' I remind him.

'Not since that alarming fever he suffered at the age of four,' he agrees.

'He made a quick recovery, as I remember,' I say. 'And he has grown into a very active little boy.'

'And therein lies the problem,' sighs Henry, watching from the window as Edward and a group of other boys scuffle over a ball. 'I would like to indulge to the full his desire to engage in sporting pursuits – God knows, I did when I was his age – but the truth is, Kate, that I dare not, for fear of accidents. Not while he is the only one.'

We are teetering on the edge of dangerous ground. I deem it best to say nothing, and the moment passes.

'I must constrain him to be more of a spectator than a participant,' Henry continues. 'Which is sad, because he is capable of so much, and he resents the caution imposed on him. He rides well already, but I can only permit him to exercise his skills on the most docile of mounts. He is eager to learn swordsmanship, and there is no avoiding the fact that he must be taught the craft of strategy in war. I know that one day this boy will command both an army and a navy, and that some practical experience is essential, but I have a mortal dread of some mishap befalling him. At the same time, I remain aware that all princes should become proficient in martial exercises. Truly, Kate, I am in a serious dilemma.'

There is no easy answer. I watch the jostling, shrieking group of little boys, and feel a wave of compassion for the red-headed one who must bear such a burden on his slender shoulders.

'There is one thing at least that I can do for him,' Henry is saying. 'He is six now, and has been too long among the women. He must not grow soft and womanish. It is time for him to be given over wholly to the governance of men.'

I am struck with a further pang for the little boy who lost his mother at birth. He has grown into a self-contained child who rarely smiles and is too conscious of his exalted position and the great destiny awaiting him. I resolve to do my best to help choose a kindly and diligent tutor, who will be gentle with the Prince and instil in him a love of learning.

Over the next few weeks several doctors are considered for this coveted post. I am allowed to be present when the King interviews them, and afterwards we discuss their comparative merits.

'What is your opinion, Kate?' Henry asks.

'I think the choice is between two men, Sir. Dr Richard Cox and Dr John Cheke.'

He gives me a suspicious look.

'But both are Cambridge men, Kate, and Cambridge, I fear, is infested with men holding extreme reformist views, or even adhering to the vile tenets of Martin Luther. Do you think there is any danger of Dr Cox or Dr Cheke holding such heretical opinions?'

It is my secret hope, but of course I dare not say so. I suspect that they do; as the King says, Cambridge is notorious for breeding such men.

'I know nothing of such things, Sir, and I have certainly never heard anything ill said about these two excellent doctors. I would not have had them summoned here if I had nourished such concerns.'

'Then I shall rely on your judgement, Kate,' he says, caressing my cheek with a plump, beringed finger.

'Indeed, Sir, I am sure you will not regret it. The scholarly reputations of these two doctors are such that we could not let such an opportunity slip.'

'Exactly my view, Kate!' he agrees. 'I'll engage them both.'

Inwardly, I congratulate myself. But if he were ever to suspect . . . I dare not think of what the consequences would be. I should, of course, plead my ignorance.

We then spend an enjoyable few hours with Dr Cox and Dr

Cheke planning the curriculum that the Prince will follow. It is decided that the emphasis will initially be on reading, writing, mathematics, theology, grammar and astrology. Edward is an intelligent child, and I have no doubt that he will make rapid progress and delight his father. Above all, I am relieved to discover that both his masters prefer to coax children into a love of learning rather than beating it into them.

Secretly I hope that, unbeknown to the King, there might also be another learning process going apace, and that these good doctors will consider it no less than their conscientious duty to open young Edward's mind surreptitiously to the fact that there are more ways to God than that officially sanctioned by the Catholic Church of England.

Lady Jane Grey

Greenwich Palace, October 1544

It's a beautiful, crisp autumn day, and we are sailing along the Thames from Dorset House to Greenwich Palace. The morning sun bathes the City of London in a golden glow, and the spires of a hundred churches point reverently upwards towards Heaven. On the river, the stink of the capital is mercifully diluted, and the City rises imposing and majestic beyond the wide banks. You get the best views of London from the river.

I am going to court to see the Queen herself. I am both brimming with excitement and quaking with trepidation. I fear that my eagle-eyed mother, waiting for us at the palace, will miss no dereliction of manners or deportment.

Mrs Ellen sits with me in the open cabin of my parents' stately barge. We are both fighting losing battles to stay upright on the well-stuffed cushions of Florentine velvet, as the barge sways drunkenly in the strong current. Above us is a wooden canopy hung with blue satin curtains, which are tied back today to enable us to take advantage of the brisk breeze. I would far rather be sitting on one of the oarsmen's benches, trailing my fingers in the water, but I am a marquess's daughter, so it is out of the question.

Mrs Ellen and I are both dressed in our best. She says I look very fine in my court gown of sage-green silk with oversleeves of marten and a matching French hood trimmed with gold braid, but the tautly-laced bodice is cruelly tight and my velvet veil so heavy that it threatens to overbalance my headdress, which I clutch desperately in the wind. My nurse is plainly dressed in good black silk.

For all my discomfort, I am so happy, for the Queen, freed at last from the heavy duty of acting as Regent of England while the King was away fighting the French, has found leisure to advise on my education and has asked my mother to have me brought to court.

We have come five miles down the Thames, and now we see before us the sprawling palace of Greenwich with its steep roofs and its river frontage faced in glowing red brick. It is an awe-inspiring sight. I stare at the great towers, the endless expanse of glittering oriel windows that reflect the sun's brilliance, the sheer mightiness of it all. This is a truly magnificent place.

We alight at the royal stairs. A groom in red livery embroidered with the initials HR escorts us to the privy lodgings. We pass undreamed-of splendours: colourful, fragrant gardens, waterfalls, shady arbours, decorative railings and painted poles bearing heraldic beasts enclosing tamed flowerbeds, magnificent galleries with antique plaster friezes of cherubs and goddesses, fine portraits and framed maps, lofty state rooms rich with Italian tapestries and Turkey carpets – I cannot take it all in, cannot believe there could be such luxury. Everywhere is a riot of jewelled colours, and the heaving mass of courtiers in their sumptuous peacock fabrics press on every side, hoping for a glimpse, a word or – most prized of all – some mark of patronage from the King, my great-uncle.

The palace is a very busy place, crammed with people waiting hopefully in antechambers, or hurrying here and there on important business. There are guards in the green and white Tudor livery at every doorway; pensive or frowning men in long furred gowns and black bonnets, who stand deep in serious conversation and move aside impatiently to let us pass; dark-robed clerics carrying armfuls of parchment scrolls or weighty ledgers; dubious-looking, furtive urchins, who probably have no business to be here; and, occasionally, a fashionably dressed lady sailing haughtily past, maid in tow.

One thing intrigues me as we hasten along behind the groom. I have noticed that, in all the courtyards, someone has painted red crosses at intervals along the walls.

'Why has this been done, Sir?' I ask our guide. He grins.

'Well, my lady, it's been done in the hope that no man would think of pissing on such a holy symbol,' he tells me. I feel my cheeks burn, and wish I had kept my mouth shut, especially since we have now traversed several of the royal apartments and are only a door or so away from the Queen.

A gentleman ushers us into Queen Katherine's presence chamber, where there are more crowds of people waiting to present petitions, beg favours or just gawp at her Majesty in all her glory, should she deign to make an appearance. Pushing through the throng and opening a further door with a flourish, the gentleman informs us that only privileged persons are allowed beyond this room to the privy chamber. How extraordinary it is that I, a humble child, should be honoured above all those gorgeous and important-looking lords and ladies, who are staring jealously at us as we pass.

The great door closes behind us, and at the far end of an airy, flower-adorned apartment stands a red-velvet throne on a dais beneath a fine canopy of estate. There sits Queen Katherine, her ladies standing on either side. I espy my mother among them, tall and haughty in crimson satin slashed with gold. I feel her hawk-like eyes upon me, constraining me to conduct myself with the dignity due to my status. Gravely, eyes cast down, with Mrs Ellen following several paces behind, I advance towards the throne with as much grace as I can muster, then spread my skirts and execute a perfect curtsey, bowing my head demurely.

'Rise, child,' says a kindly, musical voice, and I lift my head to see the Queen smiling at me with great warmth. In truth, I have rarely seen such kind eyes as the ones that are now twinkling in that homely, yet regal face, and I cannot help returning the smile.

'Why, your lady mother has been over-modest in her accounts

of you,' declares the Queen. 'You are a very pretty girl, Jane. Is she not, ladies? And eager to begin your studies, I hear.'

'Yes, your Majesty,' I say. My mother's eyes are boring into me.

'Well then,' continues Katherine Parr, 'you must come and sit by me, and hear the good news I have to impart.' She indicates a stool at her feet, and I gingerly settle myself on it, trying to keep my back straight. The Queen does her best to put me at ease, admiring my gown and stroking my hair and cheek. I did not expect the Queen of England to fuss over me in the same way that only my devoted Mrs Ellen does, and I am not sure how to react, so I sit stiff and unresponsive to her Majesty's caresses, and listen to her speaking of the Lady Elizabeth and Prince Edward, and how well they are progressing at their lessons.

'And now, since you are seven years old and quite a young lady,' she continues, 'it is time for you to begin your proper studies. Your lady mother and I have given much thought to the matter, and I have by good chance found a tutor for you. His name is Dr Harding, and he is from the University of Cambridge, like Dr Cox and Dr Cheke, who both teach the Prince. Dr Harding is an amiable man, and very well learned, and I am sure you will like him.'

I cannot speak my gratitude. The words will not come. I am overwhelmed by the Queen's kindness and care for me. Belatedly, as I open my mouth to thank her, I feel a vicious nudge in my back from my mother's knee. How can she think that I will forget my manners? Does she not realise that I am nervous?

'I am most grateful to your Majesty,' I say in a hurry. But the Queen is looking at my mother with a slight frown. I realise that she has espied that nudge. She turns to me, leans forward and pats my arm.

'Do not be afraid, little one,' she murmurs. 'I am sure you will do very well, and I will watch over your progress. Dr Harding will report personally to me.' So saying, she looks at my mother, and her gaze is no longer so kind.

The Queen calls for refreshments to be served, and leads us into a small adjoining chamber, beautifully panelled in oak, where a cosy fire crackles on the hearth. On the walls are portraits of the King and a lady in a gable hood, and by the fire sit two ladies, who rise as her Highness enters.

'Please be seated,' says the Queen warmly. 'We can dispense with ceremony here. My Lady Mary, may I present to you your cousin, Lady Jane Grey.'

I curtsey before an old, short, stick-thin personage in a gaudy purple satin gown bedecked with jewels and a large rosary. The hair beneath the pearled hood is red and wavy, and her face is blunted with a snub nose and a pursed mouth.

'You are welcome, cousin,' says the Lady Mary. I am surprised by her voice, which is deep, like a man's. I venture a polite smile, but the grey eyes are sad and unresponsive.

'And my Lady Elizabeth,' the Queen is saying, 'meet your younger cousin.'

Elizabeth seems friendly, but she is more like a grown woman than a girl of eleven. She has a pointed chin, a sharp nose and black, piercing eyes that hint of mischief. Her rose-pink gown shows off a slender figure, and her beautiful hands, with their long, tapering fingers, are posed affectedly against her wide skirts. She too has the Tudor red hair, and I am gratified to see that she has a sprinkling of freckles on her hooked nose. I am not the only one cursed with them.

We smile at each other as the Queen picks up Elizabeth's sewing from the chair.

'The Lady Elizabeth has been stitching a cambric shirt for her brother the Prince,' she beams, 'although I have a faint suspicion that she does not much care for needlework.'

Elizabeth laughs. 'Your Majesty is very perceptive! It is a terrible chore to me. I would rather read a history book or be at my translations.'

'But you are so good with your needle,' protests the Queen.

'I told you, I hate it,' declares the Princess.

'You see how wilful she is,' smiles Katherine. I am amazed at the easy familiarity between them. I would never dare jest like that with my mother, or even with Mrs Ellen. Even to hint that I have no liking for my tasks would be considered a crime to be severely punished. I glance at my lady, but she, astonishingly, is laughing along with the rest.

A maid-of-honour enters, bearing wine and comfits. The banter continues.

'Now, Elizabeth, do not be greedy,' says the Queen. 'Our guests should be served first.' Elizabeth pulls a wry face and sits down. Stools are drawn up by the fire, and we help ourselves from the buffet. The Queen seats herself in a high-backed carved chair and bids me sit on the stool next to her. She sips her wine.

'You shall show me how well you read,' she commands, taking a book from a table. It is my favourite: Sir Thomas Malory's tales of King Arthur. The Queen opens it and places it in my hands. Seated upright, taking care still to keep my back straight, I read aloud in a voice that sounds surprisingly steady and clear, doing my best to put expression into the passage.

Engrossed in the story unfolding before me, and concentrating so hard on pronouncing long words correctly, I do not at first notice the door opening, and it is only when everyone present rises to their feet that I realise a splendidly dressed old man has entered the room. He is a very big person, almost as broad as he is tall, and leans heavily on a stick. His coat is of cloth of gold trimmed with fur; his fingers are laden with rings. Everything about him bespeaks magnificence, but I can see the bulge of bandages under his tight white hose.

The ladies sink into deep reverences, skirts billowing, and I realise just that little bit too late that this must be my great-uncle the King, who looks so much older than in his portraits, so I do likewise, praying he has not noticed my tardiness.

'Rise, ladies, be seated,' he commands in a high, imperious voice. 'Well, Kate, you have a merry party here. Who is the young lady who reads so eloquently?'

He beams down at me as he stumps across the room to the chair that the Queen has vacated.

'Sir, this is your very own great-niece, the Lady Jane Grey, daughter of the Marquess and Marchioness of Dorset,' she tells him in her soothing, musical way.

'Then, Frances, I congratulate you on your daughter,' the King says to my mother. 'This is a fine girl you have.' He turns to me. 'How old are you now, Jane?'

'I am seven, Sir,' I tell him, as steadily as I can, for I am abashed to speak to such a great personage.

'You're small for your age,' he observes. I wince inwardly until he adds, 'But pretty for all that.'

'The girls in my husband's family have their growth spurt

78

late, your Majesty,' my mother tells him. My ears prick up – I have never heard this before. 'She is little, but she will grow.'

My uncle chucks me under the chin affectionately.

'She's a true Tudor, and no mistaking it!' he exclaims, and my lady visibly preens with pride. I relax with relief. I have made a good impression on the King, and she must be pleased with me.

His Majesty greets his daughters, raising them from their curtseys and kissing them.

'I see you are kept busy at your needlework, Elizabeth,' he says. She forbears to tell him how much she dislikes it, but smiles sweetly. 'How is your Latin progressing?'

'I am reading Cicero, Sir,' she tells him proudly. 'I have the book here. It is *De Finibus Bonorum et Malorum*. Would your Majesty like me to read a passage?'

The King nods approvingly.

'*Quamquam,*' she begins, '*si plane sic verterem Platonem aut Aristotelem, ut verterunt nostri poetae fabulas, male, credo, mererer de meis civibus, si ad eorum cognitionem divina illa ingenia transferrem, sed id neque feci adhuc nec mihi tamen, ne faciam, interdictum puto.*'

I watch in admiration, wishing I could be as clever as the Lady Elizabeth, and that I could fully understand what she was saying.

The King is pulling a face.

'*Gloriosus inveteratus turdus!*' he retorts, at which everyone begins laughing. Noticing my bewilderment, he leans forward and chucks me again under the chin. 'It means "pompous old thrush",' he tells me, grinning.

'*Bene loqueris,*' says Elizabeth. 'Well said!' And that has us all giggling.

The King turns his attention to the Lady Mary.

'How is your health, daughter?' he inquires.

'I fear I have been plagued by headaches again, Sir,' she tells him.

'You are taking the powders I had made up for you?'

'Yes, Sir. And I am feeling a little better.'

'Excellent. Now perhaps I can cheer you up further.' The King's face grows impish. 'Would you ladies blush to hear a naughty jest? Nothing too coarse, mind you, just a clever joke to put a smile on your faces.'

'By all means, my lord,' the Queen smiles.

The King grows confidential. 'How, then, can you tell if a traitor is well-hung?'

There are bursts of giggles from the women. I can't see the joke, and the Lady Mary's face is a puzzled blank.

'How can you tell?' asks the Queen.

'You can't get your finger between his neck and the rope!' says the King, laughing, sparking more mirth. I smile politely. Mary is frowning slightly.

'I don't understand it,' she says.

'What does well-hung mean? Surely you know, my lady?' asks my mother.

Mary shakes her head.

'I truly believe she hasn't a clue,' smirks his Majesty. 'Let's try you on another, daughter. What is the difference between a husband and a lover?'

'I – I don't know,' replies Mary.

'About four hours!' mutters the King with a smirk, provoking squeals of laughter. I am still lost, and Mary looks no more enlightened.

'I regret that the meaning entirely escapes me, Sir,' she says.

'Then I give up,' he retorts. 'It's a comfort to know that my daughter here is so virtuous that she is innocent of any bawdy language.'

He turns to my lady mother, his expression growing serious again.

'How are the Lady Jane's studies progressing, Frances? Kate here has told me something of them.'

My mother is only too eager to tell him about all the fine plans she is hatching with the Queen for my education, and makes much of the fact that it will be similar to that of Prince Edward and the Lady Elizabeth.

I stand mute, listening, unable to fully believe that I am not only in the presence of the King and Queen, but also witnessing the very easy and amiable relationship between them. The lack of formality, the relaxed atmosphere, and the way the King condescends to joke and laugh with us like any lesser mortal amaze me. It's hard to reconcile this jovial old man with what I have heard about his Majesty in the past; I know that he is not always so merry a companion. My mother once said there are days when his bad leg so pains him that he is like a baited bear, and there are also tales of him boxing the ears of his councillors when they displease him, or losing his temper at any slight impertinence. This is the terrifying monarch who had two of his wives beheaded, yet here he is, before my very eyes, a jolly and caring father sitting with his wife and daughters, discussing domestic matters as any other father would, and drawing the rest of us into this charmed circle to put us at our ease.

All too soon, the idyll is over. The King has a council meeting to attend and bids us a hearty farewell, planting a robust kiss on Queen Katherine's mouth. Soon afterwards, it is time for us to go home, but before I leave, the Queen draws Mrs Ellen aside and begins speaking to her in a low voice. As she does so, I notice her glancing in my mother's direction. My mother is deep in conversation with another lady, and does not notice.

Mrs Ellen looks startled, and briefly shocked, but she quickly recovers herself.

'My lady is most diligent in the matter of the Lady Jane's upbringing, your Majesty,' I think I catch her saying.

'But is she over-harsh?' The Queen's voice is not so subtle. I can hear her clearly. My mother chats on in ignorance that she is being discussed. I pretend to study the portraits on the walls.

'She is strict, Madam, like many parents.'

The Queen is silent for a moment.

'I charge you, nurse, to look to the child,' she commands. 'She is a good girl, but she does not appear to be a happy or confident one. I hope I am mistaken in my suspicions. If so, I beg you to forgive me.'

'I assure your Majesty that I have always done all that I can to ensure the Lady Jane's happiness,' Mrs Ellen says quietly.

'I can well believe it.' The Queen smiles. 'And now you must go, or the tide will be against you.'

'I like the Queen,' I tell my mother, as she walks with us across the sloping gardens to the landing stage where the barge is waiting. 'And his Majesty too.'

My lady is not listening.

'Mrs Ellen, I have noticed that Jane's posture is poor. She stoops too much, and she will get rounded shoulders or a hump if she goes on doing it. I suggest you put her in a corset.'

'With respect, Madam,' replies Mrs Ellen, 'she is too young for a corset.'

'Nonsense!' retorts my lady. 'I had a corset at her age. It was made of leather with iron stays.'

'Oh, no, my lady, please don't make me wear a corset!' I cry. 'I will stand up straight, I promise!'

'Be silent, girl!' hisses my mother.

'Madam, I beg of you to remember that Jane is just a child,' says Mrs Ellen.

'Mrs Ellen, you must remember your position. You set a bad example to the child by defying me. You are too lax with her, too quick to take the easy option. It is my duty, as her mother, to bring her up properly. I should not have to explain myself to you, but I cannot have her appearing at court with a stoop. You will order a corset from my tailor, and see that she wears it. Now, farewell, Jane. Be a good girl.'

I kneel on the grass for her blessing, and then, when she has gone, turn to Mrs Ellen with tears in my eyes.

'It's alright, my lamb,' she says, putting her arm around me. 'I'll order that corset, as your lady mother says. But you make sure you stand up straight in future, then she'll never know you're not wearing it.'

She smiles at me. 'It will be our little secret,' she says.

'Mrs Ellen, I do love you,' I tell her. 'Much more than I love my mother.'

'Mercy, child, what a thing to say! It's your duty to love your mother well.'

'Yes, I know that, but I don't love her as much as I love you,' I say stubbornly.

'You mustn't say such things,' Mrs Ellen reproves. But she looks pleased and happy, all the same.

Later, watching the late-afternoon sunlight reflected in the rippling water as the barge glides back to Dorset House, I wish with all my heart that Queen Katherine might one day take it into her head to invite me back to court. Thinking of her infuses me with a lovely warm glow. I feel as if I truly love her, even after so short an acquaintance. She has a rare kindliness and gentleness about her. I know too that she likes me, and I have a strong feeling that she will look out for me in the future. After all, look what she has done for the King's daughters. She made them a proper family. I should love, one day, to be a member of her household. Nothing would be more congenial than living under the protection of that serene and compassionate lady.

Bradgate Hall, November 1544

And so my education begins in earnest. Dr Harding is a pleasant but firm young man, thin-faced and balding already under his skull cap. He is zealous for learning, and inspires me to be the same. His speciality is languages, and as I am blessed with a good aptitude for foreign tongues, he is teaching me Latin, French, Spanish, Italian and even Greek. I learn quickly, and he is gratified by this and praises me often. My parents receive regular reports on my progress, and they must be satisfied, for they never say anything about them.

Each day a writing master attends the household, and under his tutelage I master the intricacies of the newly fashionable italic script. I read anything and everything – the books I am set, many of them classical works, and others that have been given to me.

Then there is religious instruction.

It's a sunny autumn day, but the fire in the little schoolroom next to the winter parlour is raked up high as usual, and poor Dr Harding is sitting there perspiring in the fur-lined woollen gown and tunic he put on in anticipation of it being colder. But his mind is on other things.

'I have brought something very special to show you, Jane,' he says, 'but if I show it to you, you must promise to keep it a secret between us and not tell anyone you have seen it, because if you do, I would get into serious trouble.'

'I would never tell, Dr Harding,' I promise, eager to see what it is that must be kept secret. He reaches into his scrip and draws out a large book in a fine-tooled leather binding, and opens it to the title page.

'This, Jane, is the Bible in English, newly translated by Master

Coverdale. I think you will derive great pleasure and joy from reading it.'

'Why would you get into trouble for showing it to me?' I ask.

He sighs. 'It is only recently that the King has permitted the English version of the Bible to be read. Now there are English Bibles chained in all the churches, by his Majesty's order, but women are not allowed to read them.'

'Why not?' I ask, a little indignant.

'Only priests or men may interpret the Scriptures,' Dr Harding informs me.

'But I can read this,' I say, pointing to the story of Adam and Eve, 'and I fully understand its meaning.'

'Of course you can, Jane,' soothes Dr Harding. 'But who is to say that the King is wrong?'

He turns to the New Testament.

'I promise you shall read it, Jane, because through study of the Scriptures, we discover the eternal truths. Let us look first at the Gospels.'

We are absorbed in our reading when we hear footsteps. As Mrs Ellen opens the door, Dr Harding hurriedly moves the Bible on to his lap, under the table, and pulls towards us the history book we should have been studying.

'Dinner is ready, Jane,' says Mrs Ellen.

In the afternoon we read some more from St Matthew. This is the first of many enjoyable secret sessions with Master Coverdale's Bible, and I am so grateful to Dr Harding for allowing me the privilege of such instruction. Soon, I am coming to know and love the Scriptures, and gain enormous pleasure and comfort from them.

I am passionate too about music, which is a trait of the Tudor family, but which bypassed my mother. However, because a court lady needs such accomplishments, I receive tuition on the lute, harp and cithern, and can strum many tunes.

'You play with some skill,' my music master tells me. He is old and fat and smells of onions. Sometimes I remember that Katherine Howard, when she was only eleven, engaged in naughty dalliance with her music master, and shudder at the image that conjures up.

'Play for me, Jane,' my mother will say, coming into the schoolroom of an afternoon. She sits listening intently, then she nods and gets up to leave. There is never any praise. It is a great sadness to me that my mother looks for nothing beyond an ability to coax a fashionable tune out of a lute, and that she has no understanding of why I want to do a great deal more than that.

'You spend far too much time at your music,' she complains. 'You should spend more time gaining other accomplishments.' She therefore allocates just a half-hour each day for musical practice, which, for me, is never enough. I know it is useless to complain, so I go behind my lady's back, trying to snatch moments in which to indulge my love of music.

'But my lady, Jane is musically gifted,' says Dr Harding in protest.

'That's as may be,' she retorts, 'but much good it will do her. No woman was ever taken seriously as a composer of music, or as a singer.' And that is that. She will brook no further argument.

One thing that she is particular about is dancing lessons.

'It is essential that a young lady who will one day be an ornament of the court be able to dance,' she says importantly. She is proud of her own grace and skills. And so, each afternoon, with the household consort of musicians playing in the gallery, I practise my steps up and down the great hall, dancing lively brawls, high-stepping galliards or stately pavanes.

With the regular round of prayers, lessons, meals and needle-work, my days are very crowded. Happily, I enjoy the regime that has been ordained for me, and am gratified to be continually occupied. Learning new skills and acquiring knowledge is an exciting adventure, and for the first time I know real happiness.

From time to time, my mother comes home from court. The Queen had need of her there most of the summer, when his Majesty was away fighting in France, but now she is back at Bradgate for a space, and we are all on our mettle.

Today, she has cancelled afternoon lessons.

'One of the chief obligations of a great lady is to dispense charity,' she tells me and Katherine. 'Today I am going to distribute alms to our poorer tenants on the estate, and you girls will benefit from coming with me. It will make you aware of how fortunate you are in life, and teach you your Christian duty.'

Mrs Ellen helps us on with our cloaks and gloves, then puts

on her own outdoor clothes, and we follow my lady across the hall to the kitchen, where several baskets, each covered with a clean cloth, are waiting on the scrubbed trestle. We help to carry the baskets to the waiting coach, and climb in for the short journey.

'This is Widow Carter's cottage,' says my mother, as the coach comes to a standstill outside a mean hovel at the foot of the cliff. 'Her husband was our shepherd, but he died ten years ago. I gave her some work in the laundry, but she's bedridden now.'

She leads the way into the cottage, and I reel from the stench of unwashed flesh, stale urine and frowsty old woman. Katherine hangs back, but my lady grasps her arm firmly and pulls her forward. I am trying not to breathe too deeply.

'We have brought you some food,' my mother says.

The old crone in the dirty bed tries to sit up, mumbling her thanks, but my lady raises her hand.

'I come in Christian charity, Mistress,' she says, 'and I have brought my daughters to profit by my example. May God bless you.'

'Thankee, my lady,' gasps the old woman.

'I'll send one of the maids to help tidy the place,' my mother promises, and places the basket on the table. She sweeps out and we follow gratefully.

The next call is less harrowing, for we are taking some old baby clothes to the coachman's wife, who has just given birth to twins. We admire the babies, who lie sleeping peacefully in the one cradle, and go on to our final destination, a cottage set a little way into the woods. Its inhabitant is a black-haired woman, who seems quite able to look after herself. A pot of stew bubbles on her hearth, and there are dried herbs hanging from the ceiling and a pile of logs in the corner. The place is warm and quite clean.

'A little something for you, Anna,' says my lady, handing over the basket.

'And I've something for thee in return,' says the woman. Her accent is strange, foreign-sounding, and her tone implies something mysterious. She hands my mother a screw of paper, which doesn't look much in return for the provisions she has received.

'Pretty girls they are, my lady,' she says in her odd voice.

'Yes,' says my mother. I notice that Anna is not as deferential as most people are to her, and that my lady does not seem bothered by this. 'Thank you,' she says to the woman, and hurries us out without giving the customary blessing.

'Madam, is that lady ill?' I ask, as the coach trundles homeward.

'No, Jane. But she has done me a service and I must repay it.'

'What did she do?' I ask. Katherine is lifting the leather curtain and peering out at the passing scenery. She is not interested in the strange woman.

'That is none of your business,' says my mother, which leaves me wondering for a little while. But soon we are home and it is time for supper, after which Katherine and I play skittles in the gallery. I have forgotten all about Anna and the mysterious favour she did for my mother.

There is one activity that I loathe, and that is the weekly family hunting party, for which all lessons are cancelled. I am a nervous rider, but every week I am made to follow the chase, hanging on for dear life as the adults, racing forward and further ahead, whoop and halloo from their mounts as the quarry is sighted and takes flight. Later, always, there is the stomach-churning moment when the poor beast is brought down and savagely ripped to death. My lady never fails to snap angrily at me for my lack of enthusiasm and my squeamishness, and wonders aloud for the umpteenth time why I have not inherited my parents' love of bloodsports.

'It must be,' she declares, 'that you are being deliberately undutiful.'

'I am sorry, my lady,' I say, but there is no help for me. I cannot bring myself to love the chase.

There comes a day I shall never forget.

We have just returned from the weekly ordeal of the chase when my father rounds on me impatiently.

'You're far too timid, girl!' he snaps. 'You'll never make a huntress at this rate. No stomach for it, have you?'

I hang my head as he rants on.

'God, why weren't you born a boy?' he growls. I say nothing, but his words grieve me. I know it is a great disappointment to my parents that they have no son.

'Well, by God, Jane, you *will* learn to hunt,' declares my lord. 'I think it's time you were blooded. Yes, we will have you blooded next time.'

'No, please,' I whisper. I know, for I have seen it before, that this is a terrible ritual, and although all of noble blood must endure it, it is horrible, both for the poor beast and for the young person forced to take part. I am certain that I will faint dead away when the dreadful moment comes, for I never could bear to see a dumb creature suffer, and want no part whatsoever in causing it pain.

'I entreat you, Sir. Let me be excused now,' I beg. 'I have an ache in my stomach.' My mother overhears; she is in no mood to be lenient.

'Shut up,' she orders.

'My lord, the child is unwell,' says Mrs Ellen. 'She is sick at the thought of blood,' she adds lamely. But my father merely looks at her as if she is mad.

'This is ridiculous,' he says. 'Of course she will be blooded. And love it, I swear. You are both being foolish to make so much fuss about so little a matter.'

So I am for it. On the appointed day, dinner comes and goes, and afterwards Mrs Ellen helps me change into my russet velvet riding habit with its jaunty plumed bonnet. Shuddering in dreadful anticipation of the ordeal before me, I make my way to the stables with the other riders and mount my dappled mare, White Lady. Then I sip from the proffered stirrup cup, and obediently trot off in the wake of my parents. Soon, we are cantering through the dramatic parkland, with its sweeping hills, rocky crags and splashing streams.

Our quarry today is a beautiful red hind, young and vigorous; she leads us all a merry dance through the chase and into the open countryside beyond. But storm clouds are gathering. The blue winter sky darkens and it begins to rain heavily, drenching us all to the skin in a matter of minutes. My parents and their followers seem unbothered by this, but I am growing colder by the second in my saturated clothes. I could not feel more wretched, especially when I remember what is to come.

At two o'clock, the rain is still falling as the hind is finally brought down and we all dismount onto the muddy ground for the kill. The poor beast lies there in a puddle, wounded in the flank, its belly heaving and its rolling eyes glassy with fear. The huntsmen stand around, restraining the snarling, snapping hounds.

My father places a large knife in my hands. Its blade is of chased steel, long and cruel.

'Jane, yours is the privilege today,' my lord announces. 'See that your hand does not falter.'

I grasp the knife. I have been told that I must plunge it deep into the animal's breast, yet now that the moment has come, I barely have the will or strength to do so. I am shaking so much that I cannot hold the blade steady.

'Look sharp, girl!' barks my mother. Her eyes are glittering with excitement and bloodlust. For her, this is the supreme moment of the chase, and I am spoiling it. 'Get on with it!' she shrieks.

I have no choice. Screwing my eyes tight shut, I raise the knife with both hands, pray vehemently to God to guide me true, and plunge downwards into the yielding, breathing flesh. When I dare to look, I see that the wretched hind is writhing in its death throes, and that there are great spatters of blood on my skirts. I stare in rigid horror as the chief huntsman seizes the knife from my hands and administers the *coup de grâce*, putting the beast out of its misery.

But worse is to follow. A few more slashes of the knife, and the hind's entrails, steaming and bloody in the damp air, are spilling out onto the wet ground.

'Now you shall be blooded, daughter!' my father cries, his voice tense with excitement, as if the killing and the brutality have given him some strange rush of pleasure.

I stand motionless, frozen. I have taken the life of one of God's innocent creatures and I cannot believe that I have done so, that I have been an accomplice in this butchery. I am utterly diminished by my actions. It is one thing to know that this broken hind's carcase before me will provide meat for the table tomorrow, another to know myself responsible for its agony. Yes, it would have died anyway, whoever made an end of it, but I am certain that I shall never forget how it had felt to pierce that living body, knowing that the stroke I dealt would be fatal.

My father roughly shoves me forward and, when I still do not move at his bidding, he pushes me to my knees before the bleeding mess that had only minutes before been a living deer; then, seizing me by the arms from behind, he thrusts my hands into the warm, gaping wounds, draws them out all bloody and smears them across my face.

'There!' he roars triumphantly. 'The Lady Jane is a fully fledged huntress now.' The company breaks into applause, but before I can stop it, the bitter bile has risen into my mouth and I am vomiting on the mud, hot, unbidden tears streaming from my eyes.

My mother angrily swoops on me and pulls me upright.

'Control yourself,' she growls, delivering a stinging slap across my cheek. 'How dare you let us down! Pull yourself together. Can't you see that everyone is looking at you? What sort of un-dutiful behaviour is this? I tell you, girl, it will never do in this world to be so squeamish. God's blood, what am I to do with her?'

'Calm yourself, my dear,' soothes my father, ignoring my distress. 'I have no doubt that Jane will learn useful lessons from this day's work. And if not, and she shows us up again in like manner, she knows what the consequences will be.' Shooting a menacing glare at me, he strides off to where his horse is tethered.

The company remounts and turns for home. Shivering and still blood-spattered, I follow on White Lady, my hands almost frozen to the reins. I console myself in the knowledge that, after the first blooding, there is usually no other. Yet I know too that the weekly hunting expedition will remain a recurring nightmare, and several nights during the following week I wake up screaming in memory of the horror, and the suffering of that poor animal.

Frances Brandon, Marchioness of Dorset

Bradgate Hall, November–December 1544

Henry and I are in bed, and as usual, after the excitement of the hunt, we take our pleasure in each other. My lord is a lusty, vigorous lover, and can sometimes couch a lance two or three times a night, but tonight I am in a disgruntled mood and cannot enjoy it. This is the fault of that stupid child, who made such an exhibition of herself at her blooding today.

I am also brooding on that remark of Henry's about Jane not being a boy. Considering how virile he is, how energetically we couple together in bed, and the measures I have taken to ensure conception, it is surprising that my womb has failed to quicken these past four years and more.

Lying sleepless in the feather bed, my body revealed in its nakedness by the cast-off covers, I notice that I am becoming stout. I have ever had a fondness for rich food and good wines, and now I realise that such self-indulgence has its consequences. By day, good corsetry and tight lacing can disguise a thickening waist, flabby stomach and heavy, drooping breasts. But at night, by candlelight . . .

Peering across the bed, I realise that Henry too is awake, and that those too-pendulous breasts are having their customary effect on him. Perhaps, I reflect, a voluptuous figure is a good thing after all.

But there is no time for thinking. He lunges at me.

This time, our coupling bears fruit. By Christmas, I know that I am to have another child. We are both praying that it will be the longed-for son. Oh, and I must remember to send a Yuletide gift to Anna, the gypsy woman, in gratitude for her charm.

Bradgate Hall, July 1545

I am once more in labour, God help me. This time the pain is far worse than I have ever experienced before, and the midwife is clearly worried. She has even bade Mrs Zouche send for the chaplain, just in case, which is not exactly what I want to hear. In fact, when I am not crying out in my agony – my noble resolve to bear my suffering in silence broke hours ago – I am terrified out of my wits.

Indeed, I am now beyond caring whether I bear a son or daughter, or even whether the babe is dead or alive. My contractions are coming every minute or so, and they are of such deadly severity that I cannot help thrashing about on the bed and fighting off those who would help me, screaming at them to go away. So intense and violent are the pangs that, at their height, I forget that I am giving birth, and use all my ebbing strength to yell.

'Jesus! Jesus help me!' I cry, again and again.

My lord has been summoned from the mews, where apparently he has been soothing his anxiety for me by inspecting a newly acquired pair of falcons. He strides into the birthing chamber, where of course no man has a right to be, but we are now long past such niceties.

'How does my lady?' he asks fearfully, this big man, who is utterly out of place here. I glimpse his face, taut with worry. It is common for women to die in childbed – oh dear God! – and Henry is plainly terrified that he will lose not only his longed-for son and heir, but also his wife and helpmeet, and, perhaps more pertinently, for I know my Henry, his claim to kinship with the King.

'She is not doing very well, my lord,' the midwife says in her country burr. 'The babe is too slow in coming. The head is crowned, but there seems to be some obstruction preventing the rest of the body from being born.'

Henry groans. 'Is there nothing you can do, for the love of God?'

'There is, my lord, but it is a dangerous procedure, and may cost the lives of both my lady and the child.'

'Help me! Help me!' I yell. I feel as if I am being torn apart.

'Is there no other way?' Henry's voice is harsh.

'We can wait upon Nature, my lord, but my lady is weakening by the minute, and time may be running short.'

I scream again. Someone must help me!

'What does this procedure entail?' my lord asks.

For answer, the midwife draws, from her voluminous bag, a long iron rod with a large hook at one end. I catch a brief sight of it and close my eyes in terror. I hear Henry's shocked intake of breath.

'The hook is passed into the womb, Sir, and one tries to pull out the babe.' She pauses. 'It's a last resort, Sir. And it can cause some damage to one or both.'

My lord visibly wrestles with himself for one moment more, then, as I screech out again, he nods.

'Do it,' he orders.

It is over. I lie half-conscious on my bloody, sweat-soaked bed, aware only that my worst agony has ceased and that I can sleep now. I swooned in pain at the moment when they dragged the child from my body, and thus knew no more for a time. At least I am still alive.

I am lying on my back now, knees drawn up, thighs still apart. There is a soreness and aching in my woman's parts, yet it is nothing compared to the torment I have just suffered. At the foot of the bed, the midwife is busy with cloths and a bowl of water, and I feel the soothing comfort of being soaped and clad in clean linen. Presently, my limbs are laid straight and I am rolled from one side to the other so that my bedclothes can be changed. Now, barely half-aware, I am covered by sweet-smelling sheets and blankets, my hair is brushed from my face, and I am left to rest.

It is morning, and I wake, fully restored to my senses. The horrors of yesterday seem to belong to the realm of dreams; but I know that I really did suffer that agony, and am quite resigned to being told that my infant did not survive the ordeal. Yet, turning gingerly on the mattress to get more comfortable, I am astonished to see that the great wooden cradle is there beside my bed. A soft snuffle suggests that there must be something in it. The hour is still very early, and I am entirely alone, so there is no one to ask what sex the baby is.

I have to know. Testing my strength, I raise myself up by inches, a somewhat painful process as I am very sore down below and every movement seems to make it worse. Damn it, I must have torn during the birth, which means that it will take me far longer than usual to recover. My head is swimming with the effort. But before long, gritting my teeth against the pain, I manage to lean across and peer into the cradle.

What I see lying there makes me cry out in shock. My child is a misshapen, deformed hunchback – there is no mistaking the fact. What is almost worse, I soon discover, after the women have come running, is that it is another girl.

We name her Mary, in honour of the Lady Mary, who has kindly consented to be godmother, but I want nothing to do with the child. Not only is she an offence to the eye, but she has likely also put paid to any hopes I have of ever bearing Henry a son. When I shakily rise from my childbed to be churched after ten days of lying-in, and begin to walk slowly around, I realise that something is very wrong inside me. I feel as if my womb is about to slide out of me, or be expelled from my body like some grotesque infant. The physicians tell me there is nothing they can do, and that I will have to live like this, perhaps indefinitely, uncomfortable though it is.

I have not said anything to Henry, although surely he must notice that something is amiss. Lying on my back in the marital bed, I find that doing my duty is not too painful, but the pleasure has gone, and I fear I will never again be able to conceive. Modesty and shame prevent me from telling anyone else of my malady, and I am determined never to discuss the matter with my lord. While he still has hopes of me, I can rule him.

But my temper is now on a shorter fuse than ever before. I know I have always been inclined to sharpness, but I find it impossible to quell the anger I feel at the hand that life has dealt me, I, who should have raised a quiverful of strong sons to delight our old age. Nor have I time or affection to spare for our older daughters, both of whom irritate me unreasonably with their idle prattle and childish concerns, so I snap at them and lash out in resentment more than was my wont.

Everyone puts my evil humour down to the shock I have received and the whims women have when their milk is drying up. The hunchback has been given over to the care of a nurse, who has been told in no uncertain terms to keep her out of my sight. I will not have her brought up with her sisters, or afforded an education like theirs. We will keep her close hidden here at Bradgate, so that the world at large may not discover how God has cursed us.

Greenwich Palace, September 1545

I have returned to my duties at court. The Queen has guessed we have suffered some dread misfortune, and is driving me mad with her unlooked-for sympathy. I politely rebuff her well-meant overtures, but I cannot help being withdrawn and bitter. She has even noticed that I walk and sit with some discomfort, but she is fortunately too well bred to persist in her solicitous inquiries after my health. She has also observed that I am less patient than usual with my subordinates in her household, and gently reproved me for it.

Much more gratifying than this cloying concern is the fact that, of late, she has taken to questioning me closely about Jane's welfare and education, and seems more than ordinarily interested in the child.

'I should be pleased if you would summon Jane to court to stay with us for a time,' she bids me. 'I long to hear for myself how she is progressing with her lessons.' This is a signal honour, and an opportunity not to be missed to bring Jane once more to the attention of the King. Who knows what might come of it? Perhaps Jane is already singled out for special favour.

I must stress to her that much hangs upon her good behaviour at court. She must do everything in her power to please the Queen, and if by chance she should meet with the King, she is to impress him – if possible – by her mien, her decorum and her learning.

My lord is most gratified to hear of her Majesty's kind invitation. He and I spend a fraught evening drilling into Jane instructions as to what she must and must not do at court. Fortunately, she is well grounded in courtesy, but we are determined to ensure that she misses no chance to get herself noticed.

Of course, the ignorant chit does not seem to appreciate the significance of this visit, although I suppose we can hardly blame her for that, since she is unaware of our great plans for her future. Like all girls of her rank, she has been told that her father will one day arrange an advantageous marriage for her, although naturally we have forborne to name the one who we pray will be her prospective bridegroom.

It does not escape me, however, that there is a slightly mutinous look on Jane's face when we have finished reciting our commandments. Plainly, she resents being instructed in her duty. That must be stopped.

'Look at the Queen like that, and she will dismiss you at once, I make no doubt!' I thunder. 'God's blood, will the child never learn humility?'

'Heed your mother, Jane,' Henry says wearily, clearly not wishing to become any more involved than is strictly necessary. He has given up a whole evening's gambling to deliver this lecture, and is impatient to be gone.

'I will do my best, Sir,' Jane replies, but I begin to mistrust her meekness.

Lady Jane Grey

Windsor Castle, Autumn 1545

Windsor is a very old castle, too draughty for habitation in the winter, but in the warmer months it is a fine residence. The Queen is fond of taking her ladies for picnics in the Great Park, and as we sit on the grass beneath a fluttering gay silken canopy, she tells us tales of Herne the Hunter, whose ghostly presence is said to haunt the woods here. This is the third afternoon this week that we have come to this place – her Majesty wants to make the most of the last warm days of the year.

Most mornings see me closeted with her for an hour in her private chamber, our two heads bent over my copy-books and translations. Her Majesty is kind to praise my work.

'I'm impressed to see you so advanced for your years, Jane,' she has said more than once. 'Rest assured, I shall do all in my power to bring your talents to ripe fruition.' I bask in this unaccustomed approval.

The Lady Mary is also in attendance on the Queen, although the Lady Elizabeth, having quarrelled most impertinently with her father the King, has been sent away to repent her disrespect. I know the Queen is concerned about her, for his Highness's anger shows no sign of abating.

I am sorry not to have the company of the spirited Lady Elizabeth, because the Lady Mary is nowhere near as entertaining a companion. She is as old as my mother, and talks endlessly of the Virgin Mary, the blessed saints and God's will. Her disapproval of the King's religious reforms is plain, although she dare not criticise openly. It seems to me that she is living in the past, and I pity her, since it is futile. Everyone knows that the Pope in Rome is no better than the Antichrist, and the Lady Mary is foolish to think differently. As my lady mother says, you cannot put the clock back.

It is odd because the Lady Mary behaves in many ways like a nun, yet when evening comes she loves to sing, play and dance, and her clothes are of the richest fabrics. She affects bright colours and a profusion of jewellery, and looks like a princess to me. But one evening, I heard a lord mutter behind me, 'She looks like an overdressed, overstuffed doll.' And when gentlemen are present she is always awkward and blushing in their company. Yet she makes no secret of her great desire to be married and have children; she loves children inordinately, and is godmother to many, including my poor baby sister. Of course, at twenty-nine, the Lady Mary is an old maid, and far too old to be married. Nor will the King allow it, I am certain, since although her bastard status has debased her value in the marriage market, my mother says he will not consider any husband of less than royal rank, and there are no takers. Of course, a woman must have a husband, so her future looks bleak.

The Lady Mary therefore lavishes love and presents upon her younger siblings and her godchildren, and on me too, now that I am come within her circle. She says I am pretty, a gifted child, an accomplished child, and strokes my cheek. I feel sorry for her, but I am stiff and ill-at-ease in her company. I cannot warm to her, although I wish it could be otherwise.

*

One evening, the Queen summons me, and takes from a drawer a printed book, bound in the finest tooled leather. On the title page is written *Prayers and Meditations, collected out of Holy Works by the Most Gracious and Virtuous Princess, Katherine, Queen of England.*

'You wrote this, Madam?' I breathe in wonder.

'I did,' she smiles. 'And his Majesty approved it.'

I look at her in awe. That a woman should have written a book, much less have it printed for everyone to read, is astounding.

'This is a marvel,' I declare.

'It was a labour of love,' says she, 'and if it brings some small comfort to God-fearing souls, then I shall be content.'

The King enters the chamber, and although I am used to seeing him now, I am still abashed and tremulous in his presence. As we sink into curtseys, I notice that he does not look well today; in fact his countenance is grey, although he seems cheerful enough.

'No ceremony, Kate. I see you are showing our great-niece your book.'

'I am, Sir.'

'And what do you make of it, Jane?'

'I think it is a wonder, your Majesty, that a woman could be such a clerk as to write a book.'

'Oh, her Highness doesn't just write books,' he retorts with a twinkle, 'she debates the points with me beforehand, then steals my arguments! Indeed, I am sorely beset. It is wearying to have a doctor for a wife.'

Queen Katherine laughs.

'It is because I would not presume to boast greater knowledge than your Majesty,' she protests. 'I merely desire to test my arguments against one who is a far better theologian than I.'

'Hmm,' sniffs the King, settling back into his chair. 'You are a flatterer.'

The Queen sits down on the opposite side of the fire. I stand there, unsure as to whether I am welcome to stay.

'Sit down, sit down,' says his Majesty, waving me to a stool.

'Would you like Jane to play for you, Sir?' asks the Queen. 'She shows great promise.'

'Aye. Fetch the lute from over there, child. What will you play?'

Aware of the honour being done me, I falter, 'Whatever pleases your Majesty.'

'Play what you know best.'

I seat myself, thinking rapidly. Then inspiration comes. I begin to strum, and as I start to sing, the King joins in with a high tenor voice:

'As the holly groweth green, and never changeth hue,
So am I, e'er hath been, unto my lady true.
Green groweth the holly, so doth the ivy,
Though winter blasts blow never so high, green
    groweth the holly.'

As the song finishes, the Queen claps her hands. 'Bravo, both of you! That was well sung and played.'

'You like that song, Jane?' asks the King.

'I like it very well, Sir.'

'And do you know who wrote it?'

'I believe it was yourself, your Majesty.'

'Zounds!' he exclaims. 'Now I will never know your true opinion of it.'

'Oh, but it is a superb composition, your Majesty!' I cry.

He smiles, well pleased at my sincerity. Then suddenly the smile fades and his broad face turns an alarming shade of purple. His hands start flailing about, clutching at his throat, and he crumples forward in his chair, emitting strangled little sounds.

The Queen flies to his side, her face fraught with consternation. She grabs his shoulders and tries to raise him upright.

'Sweet Heaven!' she gasps. 'Jane, help me.'

I leap to assist, putting all my weight beneath one of his shoulders, but the King is so heavy and bulky that we cannot shift him sufficiently to see his face in the light or check his breathing. What if he dies? I ask myself, and perhaps the Queen is thinking this too, she looks so frightened. But he is not dead, he is groaning helplessly, so I run to the guards outside the door. Soon my great-uncle is being carried to his bed, and the doctors are summoned.

I can see that the Queen is greatly worried, but she maintains her composure and asks me to play something soothing while we wait to hear the physicians' verdict. I am still strumming when they come to tell her that his Majesty has had a seizure, but is now conscious and able to take some physic. He has been bled to expel the evil humours from his body, and his urine has been satisfactorily tested. He is now, they declare, in the hands of God, and if he rests and partakes of a simple diet, he might well make a good recovery.

All the court entertainments are cancelled, and the Queen finds that her calming presence is constantly required at her husband's bedside. Ill, bored and frustrated, he needs her diverting company. There is nothing for it – I must return home. While I am relieved that my great-uncle is recovering from his alarming malady, I cannot help grieving that my happy idyll with the kind Queen is at an end, at least for the present.

I realise that I hate and dread the prospect of going home.

Frances Brandon, Marchioness of Dorset

Bradgate Hall, Winter 1545-6

The King's recovery has been slow. On Christmas Eve, he was still confined to his chamber, and the Yuletide season – usually the occasion for lavish feasting and merrymaking at court for twelve festive days – was set to be a very quiet affair. The Queen dismissed her married ladies to their homes, and that is how I came to be back here at Bradgate, where we now keep Christmas.

I am worried about the Queen, and voice my concerns to Henry late one evening as we share a cup of spiced wine in our chamber.

'She sits with the King and ventures to dispute with him on religious matters,' I tell him. 'Some of the things she says are quite controversial, but his Highness does not seem to notice. She says he enjoys these disputes, for they keep his mind lively. But I have heard talk that the Catholic faction at court, especially

Bishop Gardiner and Lord Chancellor Wriothesley, have expressed concern that the Queen is openly infecting the King with heretical views.'

'And is she?'

I nod, and lower my voice. 'I fear so. She is often in the company of my good stepmother, the Duchess of Suffolk, and the Seymour brothers – did you know Tom Seymour was back at court?'

'She's not so foolish as to dally with him?' says Henry, incredulous.

'Oh, no. But you may guess for yourself what kind of opinions they hold. Rabid reformists, if not Protestants, one and all. And there are others of her ladies, in particular my Lady Dudley and my Lady Lane, who bring in certain books, which are kept in a locked cupboard in the Queen's closet. Sometimes she and those two ladies read them privily. Of course, none of us would betray her – as both you and she know, I'm sympathetic to her views – but she takes a fearful risk.'

My lord looks alarmed. 'I'm all for reform too, and I think that much of what Luther preached made sense. I'm also heartened to see that the Seymours have influence over the Prince. Mark me, when the King dies, things will change, and probably for the better. But that's in the future. What I'm concerned about is the present. If the Catholic faction moves against the Queen, others will fall with her, or at least come under suspicion. Look to yourself, Frances. Don't go near those books. If anyone asks, you know nothing about them.'

'I'm not a fool,' I say tartly.

By February the King has recovered somewhat, and I am back at court, where there is a further alarm in store.

My good stepmother, the young Duchess of Suffolk, comes flustered one day to the Queen's apartments, plainly in a state of great anxiety.

'Your Majesty, there is evil talk. The woman, Anne Askew, who is in the Tower accused of heresy, has named you in a signed confession.'

'Sweet Jesu!' Katherine rises to her feet, much agitated. 'But I swear I have had no dealings with her. It must be my enemies who have made her say such a thing.'

'What shall we do?' asks Lady Lane, her face dark with terror.

'We can do nothing,' says the Queen shakily, 'unless we want to draw attention to ourselves. We can do nothing but wait for them to accuse us.'

Yet there are no accusations made, and the rumour we heard is soon proved false, for when Anne Askew's confession is printed and circulated, it proves to contain no reference whatsoever to the Queen. We can only surmise that the false tale was put about by those who seem poised to destroy her. From now on, the Queen is more watchful and on her guard. There will be no more banned books smuggled into her apartments, I will swear to that.

Lady Jane Grey

London, July 1546

Katherine and I are enjoying an unexpected respite from lessons. Dr Harding, poor man, is confined to his bed with an evil humour of the stomach, having, it is thought, partaken of too many eels at dinner last night. Much better than that is the absence of our lady mother, who is in attendance on the Queen at Whitehall. The weather is hot and humid, and this morning Mrs Ellen is content for us girls to spend our free time in the brick-walled gardens that surround Dorset House. Katherine weaves daisy chains and draws pictures, while I prefer to curl up under a tree with my lute and a book. It is heavenly here in the sunshine.

After dinner, Mrs Ellen gets ready to visit her sister, who is married to a prosperous butcher and lives with him in a fine timbered house in Smithfield.

'Take us with you!' clamours Katherine.

'Yes, please do!' I entreat. 'We have nothing to do. Take us out!'

'Very well,' agrees Mrs Ellen. 'I'm sure Bessie will be

delighted to welcome you. She loves children, and, having none of her own, will no doubt make much of you.'

As it is such a fine day, we walk to the City, attended by a manservant. We are wearing light silk dresses, but we are sweating in our long sleeves and full skirts. Thankfully we have been excused from wearing our hoods, and enjoy the sensation of our long hair flowing freely down our backs in the breeze. It is good to be out on an excursion on such a day, and we revel in the sense of freedom that it gives us.

Our walk takes us through the Holbein Gate, which straddles the main thoroughfare that runs through the rambling collection of buildings that are Whitehall Palace. North of Whitehall are the gardens and orchards that belong to Westminster Abbey, and at Charing we stop to admire the cross erected by King Edward I in memory of his beloved Queen Eleanor.

'It's such a romantic tale,' says Mrs Ellen. 'The King brought the Queen's body back from the north where she died, and everywhere they stopped on the journey, he raised a cross like this to his dear Queen.'

'The *chère reine*. You see – Charing Cross!' I say, eager to show off my knowledge.

Katherine is quite entranced. A man standing nearby smiles at our reaction.

'They say that, from the top, you could see where her body lay in Westminster Abbey,' he tells us.

As we walk on, I say that's impossible, but Katherine prefers to believe it.

'I doubt that the King took the trouble to climb to the top and cling on to the spire,' I giggle. 'Nor that he could look through the abbey walls to see the body lying there. Use your head, Kat, you silly goose.'

'But it's a lovely story,' she protests.

'Leave it, Jane,' reproves Mrs Ellen. 'You are undoubtedly a clever girl, but a little humility would not go amiss. And I should warn you that your lady mother has complained that you are less biddable of late, and that she intends to deal strictly with any wilfulness.'

I stand chastened, and am instantly full of remorse. I beg Katherine's forgiveness, and she kisses me.

We walk on along the Strand, past the magnificent houses of the nobility, the Hospital of the Savoy and St Clement Danes Church, and so come to Fleet Street. Further along, we enter the City by Ludgate. Here, the prosperity of the citizens is evident in the tall, imposing houses of the merchants, the numerous shops displaying goldsmiths' work and other luxury goods, and the velvets and silks that adorn the backs of the rich burghers and their wives.

The old Gothic cathedral of St Paul lies before me at the crest of the hill, and at its side Paul's Churchyard, where there are many bookstalls. I am keen to linger, and beg Mrs Ellen to buy me a penny chap-book telling the story of Palamon and Arcite, those doomed lovers. Resignedly she obliges, knowing it is her only way of dragging me from the place.

We now pass the great Barbican, the fortified gatehouse set in the City wall.

'Are we nearly there?' asks Katherine. We are quite tired. It seems as if we have been walking for miles.

'Nearly,' says Mrs Ellen. We have left the city centre, yet there are still crowds of people about, and they are all thronging in the same direction. Among them are street-vendors and hawkers.

'Whither are all these people bound?' Mrs Ellen asks a pieman.

'Why, they're all bound for Smithfield, of course, Mistress,' he tells her.

'To a tournament?' inquires Mrs Ellen hopefully. What a fine spectacle that would be!

'Naw!' he scoffs. 'For the burnings.'

'Burnings?'

'Aye. The heretics, Anne Askew and John Lascelles.'

Mrs Ellen looks appalled. I recall her telling me that she had once witnessed a burning in her youth and never wanted to see another.

'If we hurry, girls, we may miss it,' she says, 'but my sister's house overlooks Smithfield, and I know no other way to it than the one we are following. If we hasten, we may get there before the burnings start. I do not want you children witnessing such a sight. Come, come, let's press on.' She grasps us firmly by the hands and pushes through the crowds.

I feel sick. I know that burning at the stake is the punishment for heresy, but, having once singed my finger in a candle flame, I can guess that it must be a horrible way to die, and I do not want to witness it.

Katherine is also trembling and apprehensive. She is only six, and this is no place for one so young. She is begging to go home.

But it is too late for that. The mob surges forward into Smithfield, eager to witness the spectacle. Clinging to each other, we are swept along by this tide of people, unable to resist or turn back, frightened of being suffocated. Jostled and punched, we are thrust nearly to the front, and discover to our horror that the press of people is such that there is now no hope of escape.

'Stay together, girls!' cries Mrs Ellen. 'Don't let go of my hands, do you hear?'

In the middle of the field stand two stout wooden stakes with iron chains hanging from them. Nearby are heaped great piles of faggots. The man who must be the executioner wears a leather mask and apron, and carries an unlit torch. A fire burns in the brazier behind him. I shiver at the sight. Opposite, seated on a bench, well away from the stakes, sits the Lord Mayor of London with his aldermen and sheriffs, and two bishops, all come to witness the executions.

'Girls, I advise you both to close your eyes or turn your backs, if you can, when the burnings begin,' urges Mrs Ellen fearfully. 'This is a sorry state of affairs – goodness knows what your lady mother will say.'

'Excuse me,' says a fat woman pressed close to us. She is poorly dressed in homespun, and has a red face with rolls of chins beneath it. 'They should watch, them young 'uns. Lossa people brung their children, so they can see what 'appens to these wicked 'eretics. That's why they make a public example of 'em.'

'That's as may be. I did not ask for your opinion,' snaps Mrs Ellen. 'A burning's no sight for children, and these are gentle-born. They know what heresy is. And some of us do not rejoice in the sufferings of others. We did not choose to be here, but there is no hope of getting through this crowd.'

The woman shrugs. She's really only interested in what's about to happen in the field.

'Nice weather for it,' observes a man behind us. 'Not much wind.'

'Better for 'em,' says his wife. 'Are they using gunpowder this time?'

'Dunno. Hope so, for the poor buggers' sake. Here, we ought to see if we can buy a copy of her last confession afterwards. There's a man over there selling them.'

'You'll be lucky if he's got any left by then.'

'Yes, specially as it was got from her by torture, or so they say. I 'eard that Lord Chancellor Wriothesley 'imself turned the handle of the rack when she refused to answer their questions.'

The truth of this statement is made manifest as the cart bearing Anne Askew and John Lascelles makes its way slowly through the sea of people, and Anne is lifted out, none too gently, tied to a chair and carried to the stake, her arms and legs hanging uselessly. Thin and pale from long months in prison, her face is drawn with pain, and she seems almost to be cheerful at the prospect of reaching the end of her sufferings. She looks a gentle, kindly, homely person.

'Is she really bound for Hell, as all heretics must be?' I ask Mrs Ellen.

'Well, child,' she replies carefully, 'they say that suffering the flames here on Earth gives a heretic a foretaste of what hellfire is like, and so makes him or her repent before it is too late.'

'And if they do, is the fire put out?'

'Not always. It is often too late. And I have not heard that many do recant.'

I can understand that. The pain must be so great that one would not be able to think of anything else.

The executioner is chaining Anne Askew, still on her chair, to one stake. The man Lascelles is already secured to the other, and some soldiers are piling faggots around him. Soon, the pile reaches his waist. Faggots are heaped around the woman in a similar manner. The man is weeping in fear, but she is calm and her eyes are turned Heavenwards. By all appearances, she believes she is bound for God.

'What has she done wrong?' asks Katherine.

Mrs Ellen stoops down. 'she is a wicked Protestant. She has rejected the miracle of the Mass.'

Katherine looks puzzled. She has again forgotten what the chaplain taught her. Mrs Ellen explains: 'This woman has denied that the bread and wine become the actual precious Body and Blood of Our Lord at their elevation by the priest. She believes they are merely symbolic.'

The executioner now ties a grey cloth bag around the condemned woman's neck. 'That's the gunpowder,' says the man behind. 'It'll make a swift end of her.'

A collective sigh rises from the crowd. It fades to a hush as the faggots are lit, and I hear a light crackling and the voice of a priest reciting the prayers for the dying.

I do not want to look, but I am compelled to. My eyes are riveted to the stakes, as if I have no choice in the matter. Beside me, Mrs Ellen has bent her head in prayer, and Katherine has buried her face in the nurse's skirts, clutching on to her tightly. But I watch unflinching as the flames leap up. The man screams as his clothes catch fire, but Anne Askew sits impassive in her chair, seemingly oblivious to the gathering conflagration. Then she too begins writhing in the fire, but her agony does not last long. The gunpowder soon explodes in a ball of blinding light and acrid smoke, and when the smoke clears it is obvious that the hideous mass of charred flesh and bone that it has left in its wake is no longer a living creature. I can hardly bear to look, yet still I force myself to. At the other stake, the man has slumped forward, moaning piteously, as the fire does its dreadful work. Before long, the two bodies can hardly be glimpsed behind high, hot walls of flame. There is a sickening stench of roasted meat.

Some people in the crowd are jeering at the heretics, others shouting encouragement to them in their ordeal, some even cheering them on. A few eyes are closed in prayer, but not many. As I turn my head away, unable to look at the grisly scene any longer, I espy food vendors making their way round the back of the crowd, and men hawking chap-books about the two heretics. Beside me, Katherine is whimpering in fright, as Mrs Ellen cradles her close to her skirts. The flames are still roaring.

Soon, there is nothing left to see, and the executioner begins raking over the piles of bones and ashes. As the crowd disperses, we make our way around the field to Mrs Ellen's sister's house. There, we two girls are made a fuss of, and given watered wine to drink, but I cannot rid my mind of the terrible scene I have just witnessed, nor forget the incredible courage of the woman Askew, who did not even cry out in the agony of her death throes.

Then an unbidden thought occurs to me. She was so strong and steadfast in her faith that she was prepared to die for it. For a seemingly little matter, the matter of the bread and wine, she was willing to embrace a horrible death.

A tiny voice speaks at the back of my mind. To believe that the bread and wine become the actual body and blood of Our Lord during the Mass is not logical. It is an act of faith. It makes more sense to see these elements as symbolic, doesn't it? And who knows for certain what is the truth of the matter? Who can dare say one person is right and another person is wrong?

I pull myself up. I am horrified at the way my thoughts are tending. I am teetering on the brink of heresy. Were I to speak my thoughts aloud, I too might find myself standing chained to a stake in the middle of Smithfield.

Yet the notion is now fixed in my mind that the miracle of the Mass, as it is called, is against all reason, like the fairy tales and legends I was told as a young child. And yet people are forced to believe it. If they make so bold as to say they do not, they will surely suffer as Anne Askew did.

Her faith shames me. I have never until now thought too deeply about the meaning of the Mass, and I have a dreadful feeling that I will never think the same way about it after today. Surely, if a human being is prepared to endure such a terrible death, theirs must be a faith worth dying for, mustn't it?

But I am not the stuff of which martyrs are made. I believe I would never have Anne's courage, nor perhaps her strength of faith, were I ever to be asked to declare and defend my opinions. But today has left me with much to think about, much that is essential to my spiritual well-being, and I am full of uncertainties where – up till today – I have only been accepting. I can only comfort myself in the certainty that God knows the secrets of all hearts, and in the hope that there might one day come a time when men and women can proclaim openly and without fear what they believe.

Whitehall Palace, July 1546

Oh, joy of joys! My mother, having learned that Dr Harding is still sick and not likely to recover for another few days, has obtained the Queen's permission to bring me to Whitehall. So here I am, and her Majesty herself is overseeing my studies.

Each morning, as before, I go to her chamber and she sets me some work. Most of it is translating, or reading, passages from holy books. Then I must practise my music, or help the ladies-in-waiting with their tapestry. My tasks completed, I wait on the Queen as required, before joining the maids-of-honour in the maidens' dorter at night, where we are all strictly supervised by the Mother of the Maids, a formidable matron who will brook no talking or giggling after the candles are doused.

The Queen is working on another book, *The Lamentations of a Sinner*, which takes up much of her time, and when she is not in her private closet, she can be found with the King, whose bad leg is now causing him such discomfort that he can barely walk, and who sometimes has to be carried around the palace on a velvet-padded chair by sweating attendants. The pain does not improve his temper, which has been less congenial in recent months, but the Queen's serene presence and practical kindness always soothe him, and he gives thanks to God repeatedly for having sent him at last a virtuous wife conformable to his heart.

But there are things going on in the Queen's household that disturb me. The ladies seem to be tense and over-watchful, and conversations sometimes cease abruptly when I enter a room. Once, as I was sitting reading silently in the gardens, I overheard two women speaking very indiscreetly behind a hedge. I am almost certain that it was Lady Suffolk and Lady Lane, but I cannot be sure since they were talking in low tones.

'You-know-who wishes she could express some grief at Anne Askew's death, but she dares not, since she knows it is now more perilous than ever to hold such views,' said one.

'I'm frightened,' answered the other. 'If her enemies could furnish proof against her, even her rank will not save her, for the King is hot against heresy, and she and her friends have been careless in their talk.' The voices faded away into the distance and I sat alone once more.

I am sure they must have been talking about the Queen, but I cannot believe that anyone would wish to harm her. Her reputation as a God-fearing woman is widespread, and even though she enjoys nothing better than arguments about religious doctrine with the King and certain bishops and divines, I have never heard her utter any views that are too controversial.

They are having another debate this evening. Along with my mother, I am attending her Majesty as she sits with the King in his chamber. I am bent to my needlework, and they are chatting amiably with Bishop Gardiner, a hawk-nosed, self-opinionated cleric whom I have never liked. This is one of my great-uncle's bad days, but I can tell that he is making an effort for the Queen's sake.

After a time the talk turns on religion, and the mood darkens perceptibly as her Grace ventures to exhort the King to proceed further with his religious reforms.

'Although your Majesty has banished the monstrous idol of Rome,' she tells him, with ill-concealed vehemence, 'you should now seize the opportunity to rid the Church of England of every last vestige of popery.'

I am astonished at her forwardness, and his Highness's expression shows that he plainly resents being instructed in his duty by a mere woman. He leans forward in his chair, wagging a finger at her.

'Madam,' he says severely, 'it is a wife's duty to learn in silence of her husband at home. As you yourself have written in your book.' The Queen goes red in the face; I believe she is more angry than chastened. The Bishop looks on complacently. He is a stern Catholic, and would probably like nothing better than to see her discountenanced or worse, I suspect.

'Look to your sewing, child,' my mother mutters under her breath.

Rashly, the Queen persists with her arguments.

'Sir, you are right in all you say, but I urge you again to consider purging this Church of all Romish harlotry!'

'Enough, Madam!' snaps the King, and there is an uncomfortable silence. I am startled, for never before have I heard him speak so harshly, and it alarms me. Fortunately, within a short time he reverts to his usual genial self, having deftly changed the subject, inquiring of the Queen how the Prince is progressing with his education. Her Majesty answers equally amiably, apparently not one whit disturbed, and harmony appears to have been restored, for the King looks as lovingly as usual upon his wife and speaks gently to her. Soon it is time for us to leave, and as she rises, he kisses her hand.

'Farewell, sweetheart,' he says, smiling benignly.

The Queen asks me to remain to tidy some embroidery silks that I have accidentally knocked to the floor in a tangle. The King ignores me as I kneel by her vacant chair, hurriedly ravelling spool after spool, and continues conversing with Bishop Gardiner. His Highness is by no means as mollified as he made himself appear to be.

'A fine hearing it is when women become such clerks,' he grumbles, 'and a great comfort to me in my old age to be instructed by my wife.'

'But your Majesty excels all the princes of this and every other age in learning, as well as many doctors of divinity,' soothes the Bishop. 'If anyone knows what is best for this realm, it is yourself. Sir, you know how much I esteem her Majesty, but if you will pardon my forwardness, I must confess that I do think it unseemly for any of your subjects to argue with you as impertinently as she has just done. It is grievous to me to hear it. I fear also that those who are bold in words will not scruple to proceed to acts of disobedience.'

The King nods, looking sorrowful. 'You speak truth, my lord Bishop,' he sighs. 'I must take a firmer line with her Grace.'

Bishop Gardiner, obviously emboldened by his Majesty's response, presses home his advantage. 'Sir, I fear there may be more to this than meets the eye. There is some talk . . . I am sure it is nothing, but one would wish to be reassured that all is as it should be.'

'What are you talking about, Bishop?' interrupts the King testily.

'To be plain, Sir, I have heard things that suggest all is not as it should be in the Queen's household. It may well be mere rumour – it probably is. But I believe I might be able to put those rumours to rest, were I not deterred by the Queen's powerful faction. Your Majesty, may I speak plain?'

The King looks up, his face stony. 'You may.'

'Sir, I wish it were otherwise, but I suspect that the Queen entertains some heretical ideas. Things I have heard her say, and things that others have reported of her and her household, lead me to the conclusion that she believes in doctrines that can only bring about the ruin of the righteous government of princes such as yourself. Such doctrines propound that all things ought to be held in common; they reject the divinely appointed order that ought to exist in any civilised society. Such opinions cannot be tolerated in one so near the throne.'

Kneeling there, holding my breath in horror, I notice that the Bishop has deftly changed his tune. Having first insisted that the rumours are probably baseless, he is now speaking as if the Queen's heresy is an established fact. Very clever, because he has covered himself if his accusations prove false. He can say, it was just a rumour . . . I could not let such a matter rest.

The King is frowning – whether at the Queen's perfidy or Gardiner's outspokenness it is hard to say, but it is clear to me, as I crouch in the shadows behind the chair, my presence apparently forgotten by both men, that he is very angry. But Gardiner forges on, regardless.

'Your Majesty may easily perceive how perilous a matter it is to cherish a serpent within his own bosom. Why, the greatest subjects in the land, defending those views which I suspect the Queen holds, would by law deserve death.' He pauses, perhaps thinking he might have overplayed his hand or gone too far. By the look on the King's face, he probably has. He continues, some-what breathlessly, 'But I run ahead of myself. Forgive me, Sir, this may all be an overreaction on my part to something that is entirely innocent. Yet we must be sure. I cannot act without your Majesty's sanction, because if I do, the Queen and her faction will destroy me. But if you will extend to me your protec-tion, I will have discreet inquiries made.'

The King sits silent, playing with his beard.

'I take it you would not have spoken thus had you not had sufficient cause,' he says slowly. 'I must think on this. We will speak further tomorrow. Attend me after Mass in the morning.'

After the King and the Bishop have left the room, his Majesty heavily leaning on Gardiner's arm, I scoop the tidied silks into a box and fly to the Queen's apartments. My mother is the first person I encounter there, and I am dismayed to find that she is in no mood for confidences.

'You're late, Jane. How long does it take to pick up some silks? It's way past your bedtime.'

'But my lady . . .' I begin.

'Go to the maidens' dorter at once, or you will surely get a ticking off from the Mother of the Maids.'

It is now or never.

'But my lady, there is a plot hatched against the Queen!'

My mother stops in her tracks, astonished.

'What could a witless child like you possibly know of a plot against the Queen?' she asks suspiciously.

In a rush, I relate what I have heard. My lady's face betrays her increasing dismay.

'On your oath, are you telling me the truth?' she asks vehemently, gripping me by the upper arms. 'Because if you have made this up, or imagined any part of it, I will whip you as you have never been whipped before.'

I meet her gaze, willing her to believe me.

'I swear it is the truth, my lady.'

'I am satisfied,' she says, relaxing her grip. 'Leave this with me.'

She disappears into the Queen's bedchamber. A few minutes later, her Majesty emerges in her nightgown, her russet tresses loose about her shoulders.

'What have you overheard, Jane?' she asks, gently but urgently. I relate what has passed, and when I have finished, she looks stricken.

'Dear God,' she says, sinking into her great chair by the fire. 'How has Gardiner found out where my sympathies lie? Who could have betrayed me?'

'None of us who love you, Madam, and revere the true faith,' says my lady with sincerity.

'Then who?'

'A shrewd guess on the part of your enemies?' my mother suggests.

'They have no proof. They *can* have no proof!' The Queen's

voice betrays rising panic. 'We got rid of the books when they were questioning Anne Askew.'

'Indeed you did, Madam,' my mother says. 'I'm sure they were not discovered.'

'Gardiner hates me,' mourns the Queen. 'And Wriothesley. I wouldn't put it past them to fabricate evidence against me.'

I am bewildered by all this. Can it be that the Queen and my mother are both heretics? What else am I to think? Oh, but it is a chilling thought. No wonder her Majesty is terrified. I would be frightened out of my wits were I in her shoes. I try to offer some comfort.

'Madam, the King loves you,' I say, remembering the fat jolly man who has often sat in this very room and joked with us. 'He will not hurt you.'

'Oh, Jane, I wish I could believe it,' she whispers. 'You are a dear, kind girl, and you did well to come to your mother this night.'

My lady is regarding me with something like affection.

'Yes, Jane, I am pleased with you,' she says. Then she turns to the Queen.

'Madam, your only defence at this time is to act the innocent and carry on as if nothing has happened.'

'You are right,' her Majesty replies, bravely composing herself. 'And I must take care to conduct myself with greater humility towards the King. It may not be too late,' she adds. 'His Majesty may be of a different humour in the morning.'

Confirmation of my story comes quickly the next day, when two of the King's guard arrive with a summons for the Queen's sister, Lady Herbert, along with two of her friends and three of her ladies-in-waiting, among them Lady Suffolk and Lady Lane, to go before the privy council and be questioned. The women's faces are white with fear, and as we wait in a fever of anxiety for their return, I notice that the Queen is trembling. After a tense hour or two, the door to the chamber opens and there they are, restored to us.

'They let us go,' says a drawn Lady Herbert. 'No charges have been brought against us.'

'Yet,' adds Lady Lane ominously.

'We were asked if we had in our possession any illegal books,' Lady Suffolk tells the Queen, 'or if such books were kept secretly in your Grace's closet. Of course, we stoutly denied it.'

'But they have searched our coffers, all the same,' chimes in Lady Lane, 'just to make sure we were telling the truth. Fortunately, there was nothing there for them to find.'

After this, life appears to continue as normal, with its daily round of lessons, periods spent waiting on her Majesty, walks in the gardens in the fine summer weather, and the occasional court feast or reception.

The King behaves quite normally, even affectionately, towards the Queen. If he really intends to move against her, he must be a brilliant dissembler. In turn, she takes great care to play the dutiful, submissive wife. Yet I notice that he persists in trying to draw her into arguments about religion, as if he would test her. Thankfully, she is not to be drawn, and defers to him in every respect, taking care that her responses are as orthodox as he could wish for. He appears to be satisfied with them, and we all begin to relax a little, thinking that the moment of danger is past.

I especially have been terrified for the Queen, who has been kinder to me than my own mother, and whom I love most dearly. Some of that terror is for myself, for what would my life be like without her? But I dare not voice my worst fears, or ask anyone what might happen to the Queen if the King were to become convinced of her heresy. Only days ago I witnessed in Smithfield what happens to heretics, and I cannot bear to contemplate so vile a punishment being meted out to such a kind and gracious lady. God willing, it may never come to that, but I am so fearful for her that I can hardly sleep at night, but lie awake, weeping silently into my pillow, praying that Our Lord will protect the Queen, and that the danger is now past.

It is a warm day, and the Queen has sent me on an errand to fetch some fruit cordial from the privy kitchen. The palace corridors are crowded and stink of sweat and old leather, and I am hard-pressed to weave my way through the usual throng of people. Suddenly an important-looking gentleman in a dark damask gown emerges from a doorway and collides with me. I know him from somewhere.

'My pardon, young lady,' he says, doffing his bonnet, then goes on his way, obviously in a hurry. I notice that he has dropped a scroll, one of several he was carrying under his arm.

'Sir!' I call after him, but my voice is lost in the noisy gallery. Then he is gone, swallowed up in the crowd, and I realise I have no hope of following him.

The scroll is lying there on the floor, tied with red cord, with a seal attached. I pick it up, recognising the Great Seal of England. It dawns on me that the man who just careered into me was no less a personage than the Lord Chancellor himself, Sir Thomas Wriothesley. I have seen him only once before, but I'm sure it was the same man.

To judge by his lordship's apparent haste, and the seal, what I hold in my hand must be a very important document indeed. I must take it to the Queen. She will know what to do with it.

The Queen unrolls the parchment, reads it and utters a faltering cry.

'Oh, no! No! Help me! Help me! Oh, please God, help me!'

Lady Lane picks up the scroll that her Grace has let fall, and scans it. She too bursts into tears, as the other ladies crowd round, begging to be enlightened. Lady Herbert, the Queen's sister, snatches the document and reads it, her face growing pale.

'I fear it is a warrant for her Majesty's arrest,' she says in a flat, broken voice. 'It is signed by the King himself.'

Nausea rises in my breast, as the ladies break into floods of tears and lamentations.

'Compose yourselves!' cries my mother. 'Look to her Grace!'

The Queen has begun to scream – harsh, piercing screams that echo through her apartments and probably beyond. She cannot stop herself: her self-control has collapsed in the face of an atavistic fear. Lady Lane and Lady Herbert hasten to calm her.

My lady picks up the parchment from the floor, where it has fallen, and ushers us into the adjoining chamber.

'The King has signed it,' she says grimly. 'Her own husband. Only this morning I heard him bid her a loving good day before leaving to attend to state affairs. And now we know what he was attending to. He was signing this warrant that will commit her Majesty to the Tower of London, just as he once signed two other such warrants for two other wives. Who now lie mouldering in unmarked graves in the Tower chapel.'

'And they were not guilty of heresy,' mutters Lady Suffolk. 'They merely lost their heads.' The tears are streaming down her pretty face.

'Will he burn the Queen?' I ask, fearful.

My mother looks at me. There is more emotion in her face than I have ever seen there. She does not answer me, and Lady Suffolk continues to weep.

The Queen is beyond reasoning. She lies on her bed, still screaming relentlessly – as if screaming will help. On and on it goes, until I have to cover my ears with my hands. When she has no voice left for screaming, distraught with terror, she gasps out her fears of the block, the axe, or – worst of all – the stake and the flames. She imagines she feels the cold metal on her neck, the dizzying horror of the slicing blade, the charring of her tender flesh, the unimaginable agony of the fire consuming her. Would he really go so far? Would he send his wife to her death? But we all know that he would; he has done so twice before and might readily, given sufficient grounds, do so again. But she cannot quite believe it.

After a time, a terrible, long time, the poor Queen recovers her strength a little, but realising that she is trapped, and that it is only a matter of time before the loss of the warrant is discovered and a new one is drawn up, she breaks into fresh shrieks, and nothing we say can calm her, although, God knows, we try everything in our power. I am so distressed that I cannot stop crying, so my mother, fraught with trying to quieten her Grace, sends me out of the bedchamber. But I remain crouched on the floor, near the door, knowing that I might never have another chance to be near my beloved patroness.

Evidently the Queen's ceaseless screaming can be heard in other parts of the palace; before long, one of the King's pages arrives, having been sent by his master to find out what is going on. His Majesty must indeed be puzzled by the to-do, for it is far too soon for the warrant to have been put into effect. I tell the page that her Majesty is grievously distressed, although I am not certain of the cause, and he scuttles away. The next thing we know is that King Henry has sent his own physician, Dr Wendy, a wise and experienced man, to attend to the Queen and stop her screaming. This is an encouraging and unlooked-for development, for surely his Majesty would not be so solic-itous towards one whom he means to destroy?

A little heartened, and with my tears dried, I return to the bedchamber.

Dr Wendy sees at once that the Queen is hysterical with fear and quickly discovers the cause, for the offending scroll is still lying there unravelled on a bench and his eye is immediately drawn to it.

Having read the dread words therein, he dismisses most of the ladies, who are still flapping about the Queen like a gaggle of shocked geese, and allows only Lady Herbert to remain. He does not notice me, small, silent and unobtrusive behind the bed curtains.

'Madam, you must listen and pay heed,' he says urgently to the Queen. 'I have spoken with his Majesty, and he has confided to me that he has doubts about your opinions concerning religion. From what he has said, it is clear that your Majesty's enemies are playing on those doubts. They will bring you down if they can.'

'I know it,' she sobs.

'Your Majesty must conform to the King's mind and will,' he insists, 'and then you will surely find him merciful.'

'I will do anything, anything,' she cries, 'but I fear it will do me no good.' And she bursts into fresh paroxysms of weeping and wailing.

'Listen, Madam,' says Dr Wendy firmly, 'I am going to ask the King to come to you now. The rest is up to you.' Katherine barely seems to hear him. She is lost in her own terror.

As Dr Wendy walks to the door, he espies me.

'Cheer up, little maid,' he says kindly. 'We'll soon have her Majesty feeling better.'

'The King approaches!' cries Lady Lane. 'He comes!'

The women, who have returned to the bedchamber, cease

their ministrations, and I rise shakily to my feet, yet still the Queen wails.

'Your Grace, the King is coming to see you!' Lady Herbert shakes her sister. 'Listen! This may be your last chance to appeal to him.'

The Queen subsides into sniffing silence.

'The King?' she croaks, but there is no more time for conversation, for his Majesty has appeared in the doorway, bulky and frowning. We all sink into deep curtseys, but he ignores us, visibly shocked at the sight of his wife's ravaged face. Quiet now, but trembling in the wake of her outbursts, she sits up and makes to leave her bed, but he stays her with his hand.

'Well, now, Kate, what is all this?' he asks, not unkindly.

'I fear you have grown displeased with me,' she falters, breaking down again, 'and that you have utterly forsaken me. Good God, Sir, what have I done to offend you?' Her tears are flowing freely now, and there can be no doubting her sincerity. He is plainly touched by her candidly confessed fear of losing him, and sets himself to comfort her.

'Calm yourself,' he says, settling painfully into the chair by the bed. 'Why should you have anything to fear?'

'In truth, I know not,' the Queen whispers. 'I can only sense that I have somehow offended your Majesty, something I would not have done for the world.'

'Is that so?' he replies.

'Yes, my lord. I am your devoted and obedient wife and subject.'

'Then calm down, Kate, and let us clear the air,' the King says gently. 'I would speak with you on a matter of religion. I must confess I have been desirous of resolving certain doubts about your opinions, Madam.' He is watching her closely. There is no mistaking his meaning, but the Queen is more in command of herself now, and ready with her answer.

'Your Majesty, if I have given cause for such doubts, I am truly sorry. I am just a poor, ignorant woman. But God has appointed you as Supreme Head over us all, and from you, next after God, I am content to learn.'

It is a good beginning, but not good enough to mollify the King, who is evidently still smarting from having been lectured by her Grace on that previous, fateful occasion.

119

'In truth, Kate, it has not appeared so to us,' he says petu-lantly. 'It has sometimes seemed that you are become a doctor, bent on instructing me.'

'Oh, but your Majesty has mistaken my purpose,' protests the Queen. 'I admit I have said things that have been contrary to your Majesty's mind, yet you must be aware that I have always held it preposterous for a woman to presume to instruct her lord. If I have ever seemed to differ on religion, it was some-times because I needed guidance from yourself, but more often because I wished to engage your Majesty in a lively debate to take your mind off the pain and weariness you suffer by reason of your bad leg, and looked to profit myself from your wisdom.'

The King seems happier now, nodding with approval. It's a marvel how well men respond to flattery.

'I am but a woman,' continues her Grace, 'with all the imper-fections natural to the weakness of my sex. If I am in error regarding religion, I pray your Majesty will instruct me in the truth, and in future I promise I will never again presume to dispute with you, but will refer all matters of doubt and diffi-culty to your Majesty's better judgement, as to my lord and head.'

The King is visibly impressed and positively preening.

'Is that so, sweetheart? And tended your arguments to no worse end?' He smiles. 'Then we are perfect friends again.'

I am mightily relieved, as are all the ladies. But a small part of me is indignant on the Queen's behalf, resentful that such an intelligent and learned woman should have had to abase herself so in order to appease the King's pride. Yet I have to concede that it was cleverly done, for she has certainly saved herself from the machinations of her enemies.

Her Majesty turns to me, her eyes gentle.

'If you had not picked up that warrant and brought it to me, Jane,' she says, stroking my cheek, 'I would not have had the chance to help myself. I cannot thank you sufficiently, and if it is ever in my power, I will return the favour.'

I kneel and kiss her hand.

'Just to have you safe is all I ask, Madam. I rejoice in your restoration to favour.' And, I would like to add, I would give anything to attend on you at court for ever. But I know my mother would never permit it, nor would the Queen ever contemplate taking me from my studies for so long, so there is no point in asking. In ten days, to my sorrow, I will return home. My only comfort lies in knowing that my mother will remain here.

It is the following day, and we are in attendance on the Queen as she takes the air with his Majesty in the privy garden. My great-uncle is at his amiable best, as he and Katherine sit talking and laughing in the shade of an oak tree, while we are sunning ourselves at a discreet distance.

But the trouble is not yet over. Her Majesty looks petrified when she sees the Lord Chancellor advancing in her direction, leading a troop of about forty guards and carrying another ominous-looking scroll in his hand. My heart pounds as panic mounts. I fear the Queen has been tricked. But the King sees her horrified expression.

'You have nothing to fear, Madam. Leave this to me,' he says.

The Chancellor looks puzzled to see the King here: doubtless he expected to find the Queen forsaken and alone, not conversing in apparent harmony with her royal husband. When he sees the scowl on the King's face, he starts quaking visibly; this is not turning out as he planned.

'Well, my Lord Chancellor, what is the meaning of this?' asks the King menacingly, struggling to his feet.

'Your Majesty, I am come as arranged —'

'Enough!' roars his Highness. 'You have done enough. And I want a word with you.'

We watch fascinated as the King draws Wriothesley aside and starts berating him furiously.

'Knave! Beast! Fool!' he shouts. The hapless Chancellor falls to his knees, trying to explain his actions, but his Majesty will have none of it and cuffs Wriothesley about the head, sending him sprawling with a well-aimed kick.

'Get out of my sight!' he snarls, and stumps back to the Queen. Then he turns and grins at the sight of the Lord Chancellor, his dignity in tatters, scuttling back with his men to the palace as fast as their feet can carry them.

For a moment, silence reigns. Then the King's mouth

twitches, the Queen giggles, and soon we are all convulsed with laughter, releasing the tension of the past hours.

'I think I should be a suitor for him to plead his case with your Majesty,' says the Queen charitably. Suddenly the King looks serious.

'Nay, Kate, poor soul,' he says, laying his fingers tenderly on hers, 'you little know how well he deserves such grace at your hands. On my word, sweetheart, he has been a very knave to you. Let him go.'

She bows her head. The matter is closed. But she has learned her lesson, as have we all, and in future will devote herself entirely to her husband's needs, and comply with his will in all matters.

Bradgate Hall and Dorset House, January 1547

We have kept Christmas at Bradgate once more, for the court is closed. We are not supposed to say anything about it in public, but the King is dying. We have talked of little else all through the festive season, although behind closed doors of course.

Normally, we celebrate Yuletide with great festivity, but this year there is little cheer. The yule log crackles merrily in the hearth in the great hall, the house is bedecked with evergreens and we exchange the customary gifts at New Year, but our joy in the holiday is muted, overshadowed by anxiety about what is going on at court.

'It cannot be long now,' my father says. The servants have cleared the table in the candle-lit winter parlour, and my parents are sharing the last of a flagon of wine. I sit reading in the window seat; they have probably forgotten I am here.

'I wish we knew more of what is happening,' frets my lady. 'I feel so out of things buried here at Bradgate.'

'I think we should remove to London,' my father replies. 'Open up Dorset House. Then we will be at hand if we are needed.'

'I doubt the King will summon us.'

'I wasn't referring to the King. I was talking about the regency council.'

'You think it will be that soon?'

'Why else would they close the court? Many are named for the regency council, but Hertford is the Prince's uncle. He'll take charge, you'll see, and he'll be glad of those who will support him.'

'We must show ourselves friendly to Hertford,' my mother declares. 'The Prince being only nine, he is likely to be in power for some time to come.'

'Yes, my dear. And with Hertford in control, the whole balance of power will shift. It'll be an end to the Catholic party. Hertford'll have the whole country turning Protestant, mark my words.'

'I pray it will be so,' says my lady fervently.

'Amen to that,' echoes my lord.

After Epiphany we return to London, so that my parents can be at the centre of events when the new King succeeds. My father visits Whitehall Palace almost daily, but is not permitted access to the royal apartments. Even so, when he returns, he has important news, which he says has been imparted to him by his friends on the privy council, and Katherine and I are summoned to the great chamber to hear it. I am intrigued, as my father rarely sees fit to discuss weighty matters with his children, and I wonder, with a slight chill in my blood, if he will tell us that my great-uncle has at last passed away.

My lord stands before the great stone fireplace, his greyhound curled at his feet. My lady sits very upright and stiff in her chair, swathed in dark furs against the cold of the season. After we have made our curtseys, she indicates that we should be seated on the settle.

'His Majesty, I am grieved to say, is failing fast,' my father begins. 'There is no doubt that God will soon summon him to his eternal rest – although we must not speak of it openly, mind, since it is treason to predict the death of the King. But when he goes, the Prince will become King. However, he is only a child, and his father's only son, and any mishap may befall him. Two years ago, his Majesty passed an Act of Parliament settling the succession to the throne firstly upon Prince Edward and his heirs, secondly upon the Lady Mary and her heirs, and thirdly upon the Lady Elizabeth and her heirs.'

I know this, because Lady Herbert told me it was due to the Queen's kind influence that Mary and Elizabeth were restored to their rightful places in the succession, although the King stopped short of declaring them legitimate, maintaining his firm opinion that he had never been lawfully married to their mothers. The King, muttered Lady Herbert, liked to have things all ways.

'We must all pray,' my father says piously, 'that God preserves the life of the Prince and does not see fit to curse this kingdom once more with a female sovereign. You will have been taught, I trust, of the dreadful anarchy that ensued when the Empress Matilda asserted her claim to the throne in the twelfth century.'

I nod, but inwardly I am puzzled. Dr Harding has taught me that Matilda lost her crown through her pride and arrogance, not because she was a woman. Despite her sex, many men had declared for her, and my studies have shown me that women can be as brave, astute and intelligent as men. What about Boadicea, who courageously took on the might of Rome? Or Queen Isabella, who governed Spain very wisely? Would a queen ruling over England really be such an evil thing? To me, there is no logical reason why a woman should not govern a kingdom successfully – after all, does not my lady mother govern my father? But I dare not say as much, so I tighten my lips and try to quell my rebellious thoughts.

My father rambles on about the frailty of women, taking ages, as usual, to get to the point. Even my mother is tapping her foot with impatience.

'The King's Will, my lord!' she interrupts sharply.

'Yes, the Will. Of course. Well, at the end of December, his Majesty made further provision for the succession, and the position has therefore changed slightly. Now, should the lines of his three children fail, the crown would pass to the heirs of his Majesty's younger sister, Mary, your late grandmother. That means that, if Edward, Mary and Elizabeth were all to die without issue, your lady mother here would be Queen.'

I gasp. The prospect is astonishing. In fact, it is terrible. And my father, who has just voiced his disapproval of female rulers, must inwardly be deeply irked at the prospect of my mother becoming Queen. Presumably he thinks he would rule through her, although I cannot imagine her allowing that to happen. Nor can I bear to contemplate what life would be like with my lady on the throne. To me, the perfect queen would be like Queen Katherine, kind and gracious, and it is hard to envisage my mother being like that.

My mother rises, and already seems to have a regal air about her. She addresses us sternly.

'You will both remember in future that you are the daughters of a possible future queen, and you will conduct yourselves accordingly. I will be even less ready now to tolerate any disrespectful or undutiful behaviour. Our royal dignity must be preserved at all times.'

'Yes, my lady,' we say in unison, eyes downcast.

'Never forget it. This is a great honour for our House, for his Majesty has, in our favour, set aside the stronger claim of the Queen of Scots, who is the grandchild of his elder sister, my aunt Margaret. He has declared that he will never allow England to be ruled by Scotland.'

'We pray, of course, that the Prince will grow to maturity, marry and raise many sons,' my father says, casting a meaningful look at my mother. 'Likewise the Ladies Mary and Elizabeth. We must not anticipate therefore that your mother will ever ascend to the throne, since it is not likely to happen. It is honour enough for her to have a place in the succession.'

It is only later that, as I am at my prayers, it dawns on me that, should my mother die, then I, her eldest child, must be next in line for the crown.

Dorset House, February 1547

Katherine is drawing a picture and I am reciting some Latin verbs for Dr Harding when we hear the church bells solemnly tolling in unison outside our window. Soon afterwards, my lady comes unbidden to the schoolroom. As we scramble to our feet, I notice that her face is pale and sad.

'Forgive the interruption, but I have news of the heaviest import for us all,' she announces. 'His Majesty the King has departed this life.'

She sinks onto the settle, clearly moved by the news.

'When was this, my lady?' asks Dr Harding.

'He died at two o'clock in the morning three days past, at Whitehall,' she tells us. 'At the last, he was beyond speech, but he managed to squeeze Archbishop Cranmer's hand to signify that he died in the faith of Jesus Christ. His passing has just been announced today, and the young King's accession proclaimed.'

I am sorry to hear of the old King's death. I know he could be terrifying and cruel, but he was always kind to me. The real-isation that I will never see him again makes me want to cry. But as my mother is clearly striving to control her tears, so must I.

'There will be no more lessons today,' she declares. 'Jane and Katherine, repair to Mrs Ellen, who will see you are decently clad in mourning garments. Then go to the chapel and pray for the safe passage of the King's soul to Heaven.'

Sombre in our black velvet gowns and hoods, we kneel in our pew, hands folded, listening to the chaplain intoning a requiem Mass for our departed sovereign. Our parents have already hastened to the court to pay their last respects to his body, and to ensure that they are kept abreast of all that is happening in the corridors of power.

We now have a new ruler in England, but it is not the new King, Edward VI, for he is too young, at nine years old, to govern the realm himself. Instead, the late Queen Jane's brother, Lord Hertford, is to be Lord Protector until his Majesty comes of age. My father says that Hertford is to be assisted in his duties by a regency council, which will include Archbishop Cranmer and John Dudley, Earl of Warwick, who my lord says is one of our most experienced politicians and military commanders, for all that his father died a traitor at the beginning of the late King's reign. When I was with the Queen, I heard these men being privately referred to as secret Protestants, and I wonder if our late King was aware of this. Did he choose them on purpose, foreseeing that England itself might one day turn Protestant? I doubt it, as he was quick to punish heresy. But I remember Queen Katherine predicting that, once his father was dead, Prince Edward would embrace the new religion, for he has been brought up and governed by men who are zealous reformists; and with

Lord Hertford in power, I should not be surprised if we are all now commanded to become Protestants. And that, I believe, can only be a good thing.

My mother and I go to the Queen, to offer her comfort. She was not present at the King's deathbed, and is now, according to custom, confined to the seclusion of her apartments for a period of mourning.

'I last saw him on the day before he died,' she tells us. 'He summoned me to his side and said that it was God's will that we should part.' Her voice breaks. It is obviously painful to her to relate what passed between them. 'He said he thanked God for allowing him to die in the arms of so faithful a wife, and he ordered his councillors, who were present, to treat me as if he were living still. I couldn't speak for weeping, and he waved me away. I don't think he could bear to witness my distress. He never asked for me again. And he did not, poor soul, die in my arms.'

I am sure she mourns the King most sincerely. From what I've heard, she did not want to marry him, but he proved, in the main, to be a kind and indulgent husband.

'I did not expect to miss him so much, but I do,' she confesses. 'Shut up here all day, I have leisure to think on my loss, and to wonder what I should do now.'

'I am sure that you should stay on at court, Madam,' ventures my mother. 'The young King is surrounded and governed by men, so I am sure he would welcome a little motherly tenderness.'

Motherly tenderness? I think, surprised. I did not realise my lady knew of such a thing.

'Do you think they would let me see him very often? I doubt it,' ponders the Queen. 'Anyway, there can be no question of me remaining at court, since I can't stand that insufferable Lady Hertford with her barbed tongue, who will doubtless become even more insufferable now that her husband is Lord Protector. Beyond that, I am weary of the court, weary of the ceremony, the intrigues, the very falseness of life here. I crave some freedom.'

'But where will you go, Madam?' asks my mother.

'Fortunately, Frances, the King has left me a wealthy woman. He has also bequeathed me that fine, red-brick palace that faces the Thames at Chelsea. I have a fancy I may retire there. Having had three ageing husbands, and been a dutiful wife to each, I think it is time I pleased myself!'

'High time!' agrees my lady.

But I can hardly hide my sadness. No more visits to court for me – without a queen in residence, there will be no call for ladies to go there. And no more pleasant sojourns with dear Queen Katherine. Unless, of course, she invites me to stay at Chelsea . . .

'How did the King and the Lady Elizabeth take the news of their father's death?' my mother asks.

'Alas, poor children, they collapsed in tears when the Lord Protector broke it to them,' the Queen relates. 'My Lord Hertford said he was hard put to it to console them, but finally he was able to persuade the Prince to sit in the chair of estate to receive the homage of the privy councillors. Poor little boy, he's only nine.'

Her Grace adds that there was weeping also in Parliament when his late Majesty's demise was announced there, and on the streets of London, through which the King's body was carried yesterday, amidst great pageantry, on its way to Syon Abbey, where it rested overnight before being conveyed to Windsor for burial beside Queen Jane.

'And you, Frances – what are your plans now?' asks the Queen.

'Well, Madam, I shall serve our new King in any way I can,' my lady replies. 'Otherwise, I shall look to my daughters' up-bringing, perform my charities, help run the estates. Life goes on.'

'It does, indeed,' sighs Queen Katherine.

Mrs Zouche comes hurrying into the nursery apartments to see Mrs Ellen. She can barely contain herself.

'My dear, you will never believe what I have heard. People are saying that, when the King's coffin was placed in the chapel at Syon, it burst open, and blood and other matter seeped out onto the pavement, causing a terrible stink.'

'How frightful!' exclaims Mrs Ellen.

'That's not all. When men came to repair the coffin – imagine, what a terrible job – they had a dog with them, and the dog licked the King's blood off the floor.'

Mrs Ellen shudders, and I feel sick.

'The prophecy,' says Mrs Zouche. 'You remember the prophecy?'

'I don't think . . .' Mrs Ellen says uncertainly. Katherine and I are agog.

'Well, in the days when the King was determined to marry Anne Boleyn, a friar publicly warned him that, if he persisted in his wicked course, he would be as Ahab in the Bible, and the dogs would lick his blood.'

'Then it would appear it has come true,' whispers Mrs Ellen.

'I fear so, yet some in London dismiss it as popish nonsense, and some deny that the coffin burst at all.'

'It was probably just a coincidence,' says Mrs Ellen, with a sharp nod in our direction. 'Those papists will say anything to disparage the late King's reforms.'

'Soon they will have to hold their tongues,' Mrs Zouche tells her. 'Only this morning, my lady was saying that the country is going to turn Protestant, and that the Mass will be banned. She seems very pleased about it.'

'She and his lordship will follow whatever faith is in fashion, I think,' observes Mrs Ellen tartly. 'Power is more important to them than religion. And don't forget, her ladyship is often with the Queen. I think we can guess where she gets her ideas from.'

'From what my lady was telling me, those ideas are held by many now at court, from the Lord Protector down. And the young King's tutors have seen to it that he is hot for the new religion.'

And I too, I think. Anne Askew's burning first made me question my faith, and then Dr Harding's teaching made me see that a lot of what I had been told about religion was lies. I cannot believe any more in the miracle of the Mass, since it is against all reason. And I do not see why we should have to ask the Virgin Mary and the saints to intercede for us when we can pray direct to God. I also believe that the Bible should be available in English for all to read and interpret. These beliefs, I realise, make me a Protestant. And, in the eyes of the law, a heretic.

For some time, and for obvious reasons, I have kept these opinions strictly to myself. But, listening to the conversation between Mrs Zouche and Mrs Ellen, I have hopes that the time will soon come when I can be honest and open about my beliefs.

The Lady Mary

Newhall, Essex, Spring 1547

As I emerge from the chapel, there is a letter waiting on the table. I pick it up and look at the seal, which bears the Seymour arms. Is this a summons to court from the Lord Protector?

It isn't. My poor eyesight has again deceived me. It's from his brother, Sir Thomas Seymour, who was created Baron of Sudeley in the distribution of honours that preceded the coronation. What on earth could Lord Sudeley want with me?

I open the letter and read it with amazement, for it contains a proposal of marriage. This is staggering. I barely know the man, although I have heard much of his reputation, and I hardly think he is fitted to aspire to marriage with one of the royal House, such as myself. The bare-faced daring of the man! And he says nothing of having obtained the council's permission to approach me. He must surely know that he cannot marry me without its sanction.

I don't like this. I could be compromised by it. My honour, my reputation stained. Yet in some strange way I am excited at the notion of such a man paying his addresses to me. I have carried my virginity like a burden for many a long year, yearned for marriage and the love of a good man, and above all for children. Has Thomas Seymour looked at me and found me desirable, or is he is merely ambitious to be wed to the heiress presumptive to the throne? I cannot deceive myself: it is far more likely to be the latter.

What do I know of this man? He's the younger brother of the Lord Protector and Queen Jane, of blessed memory, and uncle to the King. I suppose he thinks that qualifies him to approach me. At one time, he was said to be bent on marriage to Queen Katherine, before the King my father came along and put paid to it. The court grapevine had it that it would have been a love-match, yet she was a rich widow and would have been a great marriage for him, so I'm not so certain. Then he spent much time abroad, on diplomatic missions and under-taking various duties as Lord High Admiral. He's never held any high political office, though. My late father, God rest his soul, didn't trust him. He called him a rash adventurer.

The very notion of marrying such a man makes my poor flesh tingle. Sir Thomas is a handsome fellow, with dashing dark eyes and boundless charm. Most women, I imagine, would be easy prey. And I too; yes, I think I would, if I were not my father's daughter and the heiress to England.

I must write at once and refuse his proposal. And yet, and yet . . . my pen stays poised in my hand. I am thirty-one, and I am desperate to be married. I cannot imagine what it must be like to bed with such a man. I dare not imagine it, although I suspect I might enjoy the experience, once I had overcome my extreme shyness and modesty. Yet, once again, policy compels me to reject a suitor, even though in my innermost heart I might wish to accept him. And he has been most imper-tinent and presumptuous to propose marriage in so underhand a fashion to a princess of the blood.

Resolutely I write my rebuff: a brief, formal note to say that it would be unseemly for me to consider marriage so soon after the death of my beloved father, and that when I do so, I am determined to be governed by the decision of my brother the King and his council.

There, it is done, I have done the right thing, the only thing. But I fear that, when I am alone in my bed at night, I might feel rather differently about the matter.

I am on my knees in the chapel, praying to Our Lord to turn the hearts of those who have banned the Mass in this kingdom. The prospect of having to live without the consolation of my religion is utterly intolerable to me; how could God allow such a wicked thing to happen?

But God has allowed many wicked things to happen. He does it to test us. As my sainted mother used to tell me, we never come to the Kingdom of Heaven but by troubles. And God knows how many troubles I have had to face in my life. The years spent forcibly parted from my mother, that witch Nan Bullen's vindictiveness and cruelty, the unkindness of my father, and my own craven submission to him. Yet for all that, I loved him, and I miss him now that he is gone.

And now my little brother is King. He has been brought up by heretics, and I fear that his soul is irrevocably lost. I grieve for him, as I grieve for this realm of England, which is being inexorably steered towards perdition and ruin.

'Grant me strength to bear it, O Lord!' I pray, gazing up in rapture at the painted stone statue of Our Lady with the Child in her arms, which stands in its niche above the altar, flanked by two stained-glass windows depicting the Annunciation and the Assumption. 'Give me the strength to bear all my trials!'

The serene features of the Virgin smile tenderly down at me. As I gaze in adoration, ecstasy floods me. With the help of the blessed Mother of Christ, I know I can bear all my trials, because right is on my side, and I follow the path of the true faith.

Five weeks have passed since I turned down Lord Sudeley's proposal, and not a word from him. Today, however, there is another letter. It's from my sister Elizabeth, who is now living with my good stepmother at Chelsea. Astonishingly, she writes to tell me that she has received a proposal of marriage from the Lord Admiral, but has turned it down, telling him that neither her age – she is thirteen – nor her inclinations allow her to think on marriage, and that she wishes to be left to mourn our father a full year or more before contemplating it.

So it was pure ambition, after all. If he couldn't get the second-in-line to the throne, he'd try for the third. Oh, the perfidy of men! What a fool I was to think he could ever have desired me for myself, poor, thin, ailing creature that I am. And how well Elizabeth has dealt with him.

'I made him wait a week or so for a reply, good sister,' she writes. 'I told him he must permit me to decline the honour of becoming his wife. Some honour that would be!'

Something tells me we have both done wisely in rejecting the Admiral. Whatever his schemes are, they are underhand

and coloured purely by self-interest. I think I have just had a lucky escape.

Queen Katherine Parr

Chelsea, Spring 1547

The Lord Admiral stands before me. I have not seen him since long before the King died, so I am unprepared for the impact of his virile good looks. Tall and debonair, with an easy grace, he stoops to kiss my hand, and I suddenly feel as if I am drowning. It was like this when he came a-courting before but that was four years ago, and much has happened in the meantime. I am now a wealthy royal widow, and guardian of the Lady Elizabeth, and I am beginning to enjoy being free of the constraints of court life, not to mention the intrigues and the backbiting.

'It has been too long since I saw your Majesty,' he declares, his eyes roving appreciatively up and down me. 'I am come to offer my condolences on your sad loss.'

'I am growing used to it now,' I say, a trifle tart. 'The King has been dead these eight weeks.'

'Ah, I am sorry I did not come before,' he smiles ruefully. 'I thought your Majesty would need time to grieve. I did not like to intrude.'

'No matter,' I say. 'I appreciate your coming now, my lord.'

'My lord?' He raises an eyebrow. 'You used to call me Tom.'

'I used to be a commoner,' I remind him. 'Now I am a queen. Formality has ruled my life for so long. But you are very welcome . . . Tom.'

He smiles at me. His smile is devastating, revealing perfect white teeth.

'It gladdens my heart to hear it . . . Kate,' he says boldly. I raise an eyebrow but say nothing. I know I should reprove him for his forwardness, but I am enjoying it so.

I was in love with Thomas Seymour before the King claimed me. I would have walked on hot embers for him. He pursued me with flattering ardour, and refused to heed my protests about it being too soon after Lord Latimer's death. He begged me to marry him, and then when I said I would, he laid siege to my virtue.

'We are going to be wed,' he told me. 'What difference does it make?' And the citadel would perhaps have fallen, had not the King made known his interest. Then Tom had no choice but to withdraw and make himself scarce. I mourned his loss desperately, but over the years the pain dulled, as did the hot lust that infused me every time I thought of him, or relived his caresses. I resigned myself to God's will, and in the end the King proved himself a kind husband.

Now Tom has returned, we are both of us free, and the old attraction is still there between us. I cannot take my eyes off him as he seats himself in my privy chamber and jokes with my ladies, a lean and muscular Adonis with a wicked wit that I find irresistible.

The women fetch refreshments and withdraw to the other side of the room, leaving us free to talk in private. Our conversation is not of love or sweet nothings – rather we speak of what is happening at court, although there are naturally other, more personal things that I would rather discuss. But Tom is eager to touch on politics, and soon it becomes clear that he is a disappointed man. Even though the Seymours are riding high in this realm, Tom is bitter because it is his brother, of whom he is jealous, who wields power, and not he.

'I'm forty years old, Kate, and still waiting for preferment. Yet I've been continually thwarted. My esteemed brother' – this is said with a sneer – 'is apparently determined to prevent me, the Lord Admiral – and there's a sop to my pride if ever there was one – from ever participating, however humbly, in the government of the realm. No matter that I have successfully served the Crown on embassies and on the high seas, rather than skulking in corners at court, shit-deep in intrigue like my beloved brother – pardon my language,' he adds with an engaging smile.

I love Tom, but not enough to blind me to his faults. I remember what King Henry said about him, that he was untrustworthy and slippery, and how he refused to give Tom a seat on the privy council. It is true that Henry was suspicious of everybody, especially in his last years, but I suspect there is more to Lord Hertford's attitude than mere cautiousness.

'Your brother is ruled by his wife,' I say.

'That termagant!' Tom sneers. 'Now that you've moved out here, Kate, she's queening it round the court, revelling in the role of wife to the Lord Protector.'

'I can believe it,' I say drily. 'She's appropriated my jewels, the jewels that rightly belong to the Queen Consort.'

'I know, she's flaunting them in public. The woman has no shame. Edward Seymour might rule England, but we all know that Anne Stanhope rules Edward. That's one thing I don't envy my brother.'

'I think she's jealous of her husband's position,' I say, 'and that she sees you as a threat. That's why you are being denied high office.'

'Yes, all I've had are empty honours,' Tom snorts. 'They look good on the surface, but they are meaningless. If he thought to mollify me by creating me Baron of Sudeley and making me a Knight of the Garter, he was deluding himself, especially since he made himself Duke of Somerset, so that my lady can give herself airs as a duchess. Oh, I was grudging and ungracious in my acceptance – and he knew it. He knows that what I really want is a place on the privy council or a great office of state, and he knows that I am able enough.'

I regard him keenly.

'Is that all you want, Tom?' I ask.

Our eyes meet.

'Dammit, I can't fool you, Kate,' he says, smiling deprecatingly. 'Of course I'd like to oust my puffed-up brother from his high place, and supplant him in it. God, what wouldn't I give to do that? But as matters stand at present, I must be realistic and accept that it's not likely to happen. Not yet, at any rate. At the very least they could give me a seat on the council. But the late King forbade it, so they won't. He didn't like me, your husband, not after he found out I'd been chasing you.'

'He never spoke unkindly of you,' I say carefully, though Tom is right.

'Christ, Kate, you know as well as I do that when someone

nominated me to the council, he cried out from his sickbed, "No! No!" And it's not likely, in this present time of mourning, that anyone will venture to go against old St Harry's wishes.'

'Tom!' I exclaim.

'I'm sorry, Kate,' he says wearily. 'I feel I have been unjustly treated. And I feel so frustrated. I have so much to offer.'

He gives me another long look, and I know he is not just talking about serving his country. I glance away. It's too soon after the King's death to be thinking such thoughts. But I am thinking them; I cannot stop myself. All the while he is talking, I am feasting my eyes on him . . .

'I think the best course for me is to get the King on my side,' Tom is saying. 'Of course, the poor lad wields no real power, but he is the King, and his wishes must count for something. And I've always enjoyed a good relationship with him on the odd occasions I've seen him.'

'I know he likes you,' I tell him. 'He admires your gallantry and your adventurous spirit. He told me he wished he could be like you.'

'There's no question but that I am his favourite uncle,' Tom boasts. 'It's no secret that the Lord Protector – God, it grieves me to have to call him that – is severe with the boy and keeps him cloistered up with his tutors and short of money, damn him. And he keeps me from seeing him, although he can't stop it entirely, and when I do, it's obvious to me that the King is angry and resentful at the way he is treated. So do you know what I've done, Kate? I've bribed one of his Majesty's servants, John Fowler, to smuggle generous purses of money to him. I've also instructed Fowler to take every possible occasion to extol my virtues and talents in the King's hearing.'

I have to smile at Tom's audacity.

'And have these strategies as yet borne any fruit?' I inquire.

'Yes, Kate, they have. The King has shown himself very willing to help me. I saw him two days ago at Whitehall, and I, speaking man-to-man to flatter his youth, asked him for his opinion as to which lady I should marry in order to advance my fortunes.'

My heart misses a beat. I had thought him unattached.

'And whom did he suggest?' I ask lightly.

'Anne of Cleves!' he splutters, in great mirth. 'And he wasn't joking. But, seeing my face, in which dismay must have been writ clear, he thought about it a bit more. He's a solemn lad who rarely smiles, but I could see he was pleased with himself. He told me I should marry the Lady Mary, to change her stiff Catholic opinions.'

'He has a great distaste for the Roman faith,' I say, having myself a great distaste for all this talk of Tom's marriage.

'It's those reformers who teach him who have made him a stiff Protestant,' Tom declares. 'His sister's persistence in the old religion is therefore a matter of great concern to him. He seemed quite eager for me to marry her.'

'And are you eager, my lord?' I ask, as nonchalantly as I can.

'Such a marriage could bring me advantages,' he replies, 'but I confess I do not relish the prospect. The Lady Mary might be her father's daughter, but she's a prim, dried-up virgin, and scrawny women like her were never to my taste.' He looks at me intently again, up and down, as if to say that I, with my womanly curves, am very much to his taste.

'You would have to obtain the council's permission to marry the Lady Mary.'

'I tried. They refused.' He puts his head on one side apologetically. 'Well, I felt I should comply with my sovereign's wishes. Mercifully, I was unable to do so.'

The afternoon shadows are lengthening in the chill March sunlight.

'I usually take a walk in the fresh air at this time,' I say. 'Will you join me today, Tom?'

'Nothing would please me better,' he smiles.

As we wander along the path between the flowerbeds, Tom lightly places his arm about my shoulders.

'I still think of you with the greatest affection, Kate,' he murmurs.

Joy threads through me. I did not imagine it. He does still care.

'As well as the Lady Mary?' I banter. 'And Anne of Cleves?'

He roars with laughter, then turns serious once more.

'I know it is early days,' he says, 'but may I hope that you will one day return my affection, just as you did four years ago?'

His hand is still resting on my shoulder. I can feel that touch all over my body.

'It *is* far too soon,' I tell him. 'But I should be glad to see you again.'

'I am content,' he says, smiling. 'For the present.'

Three days later he is back, bearing flowers. He has remembered how much I love flowers. Again, we walk in the gardens, my ladies following at a discreet distance, we two talking of politics, of the court, of mutual acquaintances, of anything, in fact, but the feelings that lie palpably between us. Then we return to the house for wine and sweetmeats before Tom bids me a smouldering farewell.

The days lengthen. I follow my daily round, supervising the Lady Elizabeth's lessons, sewing in my chamber, chatting with my ladies, passing the time slowly. Hoping that Tom will visit again soon.

He has called three more times this week, bringing light and colour once more into my life. And a sense of danger.

'Tom,' I protest, 'people will talk. There will be a scandal, and I have my reputation to consider. With the King so recently dead, many would think it shocking that his supposedly God-fearing widow should be disporting herself with another man.'

'Would to God you *were* disporting yourself with me!' Tom grins, his meaning plain.

'For shame!' I retort, blushing. In answer, he takes me in his arms and kisses me full and lingeringly on the lips. I have never known such bliss, but we are likely to be discovered at any second, for my ladies are not far off, so against my desire I break free and stand my ground.

'I must insist that we keep our friendship a secret!' I declare.

'Friendship?' Tom repeats, raising one eyebrow. 'I'd have called it something different.' He kisses me again, and again I ward him off.

'You must come here only under cover of darkness, for the time being,' I command. 'Send word when you are coming, and I will leave the wicket gate in the wall unlocked. I myself will let you into the house.'

His eyes are dancing in anticipation.

'There is nothing more I wish for than to visit you at night,' he says, his words loaded with meaning. Oh, how I wish I could tell him how deeply I echo his sentiments, but I dare not. Instead, I say, 'My lord! I am outraged by your boldness!'

'Ah, but you like it, my Kate! You love it, in fact!' is his cheeky answer.

'What's happening to us, Kate?' murmurs Tom, as he cradles me in his arms on the settle by the fire. I have cast propriety to the winds, for the sake of secrecy, and we are in my bedchamber. I have warned him that the settle is as far as he is going to get.

I turn to look at him.

'I'm not sure,' I reply, 'but I like the way I'm feeling.'

Tom tenses.

'It's love, isn't it,' he says, gazing at me.

'Yes,' I whisper, and suddenly we are clutching each other in the tightest of embraces, his tongue probing mine in a passionate kiss. It's as if we cannot get enough of each other.

'I can't believe that God has sent you to me,' I tell him.

'We must marry!' Tom declares, as we relax, breathless.

'We must,' I agree, 'but not yet.'

'Why not, my love? We can keep it secret, and I can continue visiting you at night. Except, of course, I will be sleeping with you there in that bed. Or not sleeping, as the case may be.' He looks archly at me, and I feel a sudden sense of alarm.

'And what if I were to conceive a child, so soon after the King's death?' I ask. 'There might be some suspicion that it was his. There would be a terrible uproar. And think of the scandal! We should at least wait until court mourning has ended.'

'Kate,' soothes Tom, kissing me so slowly and sensuously that I feel as if I am melting, 'you are thirty-five. You have had three old men as husbands, and you've been little more than a glorified nurse to them. Think of yourself for a change, of your own happiness. Think how it will feel to have a real man in your bed . . .'

His lips and his fingers are more than persuasive. Why deny myself the thing I desire most, I ask myself, lost to all good sense and reasoning and moral considerations. Before the night is out, I have indeed discovered what it feels like to have a real man in my bed, and I have also agreed to marry him within the week.

Tom has sent a message by Fowler to the King, asking him to give his blessing to our marriage. A large purse of gold coins accompanies this request. Back comes Fowler, with the happy news that his Majesty approves our union and has gladly agreed to keep it a secret.

We are joined in holy wedlock at Chelsea, as the buds begin to open in the April sunshine. No one knows of it except my chaplain and two trusted ladies. For the time being, our joy in each other will remain secret, for we have agreed to postpone the announcement of our marriage until the time seems appropriate. Tom remains at his London house, visiting me by night – oh, what bliss it is to lie in his arms – and sending affectionate letters every day. When he comes to me, there is little time for talk. We have better things to do, for he was ever a man in a hurry, and the stolen hours seem all too short.

Tonight, Tom is in an angry mood when he arrives, and too agitated to make love.

'They are considering the Princess Elisabeth of France as a bride for the King,' he tells me. 'It's outrageous, marrying him to a Catholic. But when I took my lord brother to task for it, he just said it was expedient because we are in no position to court the hostility of France. We need King Henri's friendship. Like a dose of the pox, I said. Who could ever trust a Frenchman? And, I asked my precious brother, does he think the King will accept a Catholic bride, now that the Mass has been banned in this kingdom?'

I draw Tom down beside me on the settle.

'And what did he say?' I ask gently.

'Oh, he muttered some rubbish about hoping that his Majesty would make her see the error of her ways,' Tom replies. 'I told him the King wouldn't like it, and that he would prefer to marry a Protestant bride, but does he listen? Does he listen? No. Once he's set his mind on a plan, however stupid, there's no moving him.'

'Come to bed, my love,' I say, putting my arms round him.

'There's nothing you can do about it tonight. Just put it out of your mind till morning. We have all too short a time together.'

'You're right, Kate,' he says wearily. 'Let's go to bed, darling. Take off that nightgown.'

Dawn is just breaking as Tom wakes me.

'Sweetheart, I've just thought of the most advantageous plan,' he announces.

'Mmmm?' I respond, sensuous with sleep and the sight of his face on the pillow beside me.

'It's a brilliant plan,' he says, 'and it will earn me the King's undying gratitude.'

'What is it?' I ask, yawning.

'Well, Kate,' he answers, curling his arms around me and kissing me, 'there may not be many Protestant princesses in Europe, as my dear brother so irritatingly pointed out, but there is a suitable match for the King to be had for the taking here in England, one who could in truth be considered a princess by virtue of her birth. I speak of the Marquess of Dorset's girl, Lady Jane Grey. She is the King's own cousin.'

I am suddenly awake. Of course, little Jane. She would make a wonderful wife for his Majesty.

'It *is* a brilliant plan,' I echo. 'They are of an age, and what's more, she is formidably intelligent and accomplished, for all her tender years.'

'She's a pretty little thing too,' adds Tom. 'I've seen her about the court. Furthermore, I'd be prepared to wager on her ambitious parents jumping at the chance of such a magnificent marriage for her.'

'Oh, they will,' I agree, thinking of the assertive Lady Dorset, whom I could never like, not just because of her strident bossiness, but also because of her unwarranted unkindness to that sweet child of hers. How Frances and that boring husband of hers managed to produce the Lady Jane I'll never know. 'Edward has not met Jane very often, yet I've heard him speak warmly of her.'

'I'm sure he would infinitely prefer her to Elisabeth of Valois,' Tom says enthusiastically. 'And Jane herself could have little to complain about in such a marriage. What young girl would not give her all to be Queen of England?'

'But how will you go about this, Tom?'

'I will approach Lord Dorset, put the matter to him – he'll be ripe for it, I've no doubt – and then I'll suggest that Lady Jane be placed in my household whilst I negotiate the matter with the King, who will doubtless be overjoyed at the prospect of such an agreeable consort, and so very grateful to the uncle who procured her for him. This is our way forward, Kate. This marriage will bring me the political influence that should be mine already, and will guarantee that I remain the power behind the throne in the years to come.'

Tom departed before first light this morning, and when I arise, I find he has left an early rose lying on the table by the bed. I take it with me to chapel, and then to breakfast, studying its red velvet petals lovingly as I eat my bread and cold meat. When I have finished, I raise it to my lips, but the moment is interrupted by a soft sound behind me, and I turn to see the Lady Elizabeth standing in the doorway, smiling impishly.

'A gift from the Admiral, Madam?' she asks pertly, her eyes mischievous.

'Shouldn't you be at your prayers or your lessons?' I ask, feeling my cheeks flame.

'I hear him leave,' she says, ignoring my question. 'He comes here every night, doesn't he?'

'I don't know what you're talking about,' I reply.

She smiles again.

'Don't worry. I won't tell anyone.'

'There is nothing to tell,' I insist. 'Now go to your tutor.'

'As you please, Madam. But, you know, I pray for your happiness.'

'Thank you, Elizabeth.'

After she has gone, I wish – not for the first time – that our marriage could be made public, as I have already begun to tire of this subterfuge. If the Lady Elizabeth has guessed what is going on, others might have too, and servants talk. And if word of what we have done got out, I dread to think of the consequences for us. I must persuade Tom to tell his brother the truth. We cannot go on living a lie for much longer.

*

But when Tom returns at night, there is no chance of raising the matter because, once again, he is in a bad temper.

'God's blood!' he fumes. 'The stupid, stubborn, ungrateful . . .'

'What has happened?' I ask.

'This afternoon, my man Harington returned from seeing Lord Dorset,' he recounts. 'Harington had laid before him my proposal, but his lordship looked at him as if he were mad. Then he said that nothing would please him more than to marry his daughter to the King, but he was wondering how I intended to accomplish my design when I do not even have a place on the regency council, and when it is clear that the councillors seem to be united in their determination to keep me out of the political arena at all costs.'

'The brazen cheek of the man!' I exclaim.

'God, I was furious at that!' Tom growls. 'And then, when it was suggested that Jane was placed in my household as my ward, his bloody lordship pointed out that I am still a bachelor – if only he knew! – and yet I desire him to send his daughter to live in a household where there is no suitable lady of rank present to oversee her education and welfare. He said it would not be seemly.'

He paces up and down in rage.

'But I'd already thought of that, and I'd told Harington to say that my mother will be coming up from Wiltshire to live with me. But this is not enough for his pernickety lordship, who said he has no confidence at present that I have the ability to bring this match about, and that that was an end to the matter. But it's not. Oh, no, it's not.'

He stops, facing me, and takes my hands in his.

'When the world knows of our marriage, my love, I'll warrant there will be a stampede of noble lords all eager to place their daughters in our household.'

I smile sadly at him. 'I should so have liked to have Jane here. I grew very fond of her when she visited me at court. Her parents treat her harshly, I can't understand why. I think of her as if she were my own daughter. After all, I have none of my own.'

'Dear Kate!' cries Tom, flinging his arms around me. He has sensed the shadow that fleetingly darkened my mood. 'Do not be sad. Soon, we may have children of our own, and the Lady Jane to boot, I'll warrant you.'

'God grant it may be so,' I say tenderly.

Lady Jane Grey

Dorset House, June 1547

Today, I am playing with my sister Mary in the long gallery. She toddles towards me in her ungainly fashion, her disfiguring hump and squat body disguised as far as possible under voluminous lawn aprons and a wide stiff collar. For a while, the poor little thing was shut away, but she is now allowed the freedom of the house. I believe this may be due to the intercessions made by my new tutor, Dr John Aylmer, who is also my mother's chaplain and able to speak to her on such matters. I am already very fond of him.

In recent months, my life has changed dramatically. After Dr Harding announced that he was returning to Cambridge to resume his studies, my parents promoted Dr Aylmer, to replace him as my tutor.

I've known Dr Aylmer all my life. He used to carry me about in his arms, teaching me good diction. It was he who first taught me about the mysteries of faith, in simple terms initially, then later on in profound detail. Like many of his colleagues from Cambridge, he was an early advocate of religious reform, and, like Dr Harding but to a greater degree, he daringly planted in my mind the seeds of several ideas that have blossomed freely in the enlightened climate we now enjoy in England, and borne fruit.

Dr Aylmer's lessons are laced with wit and humour, and he is of the firm opinion that children should be encouraged to love learning, not be forced to it by beatings, as happens so often. I love him because he treats me as an equal. He has even gone so far as to say that I am almost on the same intellectual level as he. I blushed in the face of such flattery. Yet he says I easily grasp the most difficult theological concepts, and insists that my arguments are always well reasoned.

Dr Aylmer is also a great patriot. 'God is an Englishman,' he is fond of saying, and he has instilled in me a strong sense of the history of this kingdom, a history in which I am beginning to realise I might be called to play a part, however small; after all, my parents have never ceased to stress our blood-links with royalty.

Dr Aylmer is a friend of the King's tutor, Dr Cheke. They compare notes over their respective pupils when my father takes Dr Aylmer to court. When he returns, my good tutor cannot resist saying smugly that, from what he has heard, I am well in advance of his Majesty, even though we were born in the same month. I'm not sure that isn't *lèse-majesté*.

I believe it has not escaped Dr Aylmer's notice that my mother is unkind to me. He once gently pointed out, after one particularly severe reprimand, that she is a bitterly disappointed woman, and guilt-ridden too, at not having presented my father with a male heir. Thanks to him, I am beginning to see my mother as a human being with strengths and weaknesses like everyone else, not just as an authoritarian parent, and strangely this gives me the courage to stand up to her on occasion, and not be intimidated by her.

'Catch!' I call, tossing the cloth ball at Mary. As usual, she misses and crawls after it. She's a placid, stolid child who, like Katherine, will take life in her stride, as it happens.

My mother appears at the end of the gallery.

'Time for bed,' she announces. 'Take her to bed, now! Look sharp!'

Why the impatience? Why make it so clear she wants Mary removed from her sight? I cannot help but feel indignant on my innocent sister's behalf.

'Let her have a few minutes more of play, Madam,' I plead.

'Why must you always defy me?' my lady hisses. 'Even over a trifling matter like this?'

I meet her cold stare. For the first time, I do not drop my eyes.

'I said, bedtime,' she repeats menacingly. Then, as I hesitate, wondering if I dare risk a retort, she slaps me about the ear.

'I'll make you obedient, Jane, if it's the last thing I do.'

'Am I a naughty child?' I burst out. 'Am I really? Or is it just that I am not the son you wanted?'

That was unforgivable, but I could not stop myself.

'How dare you!' my mother cries, and pinches me hard on the soft flesh of my arm. Tomorrow there will be a bruise in that place, as there have been bruises on many occasions before. But I do not care. I am too busy releasing my pent-up hurt and anger.

'You punish me for the slightest misdemeanour, even for things I did not do!' I cry. 'I would not mind if I were a bad child, but I know I am not. I try very hard to behave well and not give offence, but it is impossible to please you. If I were a boy, I have no doubt I would receive better treatment. But alas, I am not. I am just an unwanted girl.'

I am shocked at my outburst, and so is my mother, as she is speechless for once. Quickly she recovers herself.

'You must be ill or crazed to speak to me like that,' she rasps. 'Go to your chamber. You will live on bread and water until you repent and beg my forgiveness.'

I endure two days of isolation, and no one speaks to me in my disgrace. Mrs Ellen brings my sparse rations of food and looks tragic, but she is plainly too fearful of my mother's wrath to say anything. At least, I console myself, I have done something to deserve this punishment. Yet why should I be punished for speaking the truth?

I cannot bear it any longer. I go to my lady's chamber, kneel and humbly beg her forgiveness. She nods curtly, her lips pursed, and dismisses me, and it is some days before she will condescend to speak to me again.

I am forgiven, it seems.

'The most astonishing news has come from court!' cries my mother. 'Henry! Jane! Katherine! Listen to this!'

We hasten after her to the great chamber, where she turns towards us, her face flushed with excitement.

'The Lord Admiral has married the Queen!' she announces. 'Lady Hertford writes that the news was disclosed by the Admiral to the Lord Protector, who was very angry with his brother. However, having informed the council of the marriage, he could do little save censure the naughty couple, since they have broken no law.'

'Has the news been cried abroad?' my father asks.

'Yes, it has. The people are not pleased. In fact, public opinion is hot against the marriage.'

'I'm not surprised,' he replies. 'It's scandalous, coming so soon after the death of the late King.'

'I always said she was no better than she should be,' sniffs my mother. I frown: not so long ago, she was honoured to be accounted amongst the Queen's friends.

'At least she has no high belly to speak of. That would have put the cat amongst the pigeons.'

'I take it the marriage was solemnised in the proper manner before witnesses?' says my father. 'And that there is no evidence of any misconduct?'

'It was. But who can say what went on before the wedding? It's the timing that's shocking, I tell you. Couldn't they have waited a decent interval? My poor uncle is scarce cold in his grave.'

My father smiles. 'Doubtless the Duchess of Somerset is much put out by the marriage. She will now have to give place to the wife of her husband's despised younger brother. It must be mortifying for her!'

'It was the King's reaction that surprised me,' says my lady. 'He actually wrote to the Queen and congratulated her on her marriage.'

'But it was against the council's advice. And the Lady Mary is most offended. She sent a scathing letter to the Admiral.

'I doubt she will wish to remain friends with the Queen after this,' my father remarks.

'She is a frustrated spinster,' observes my lady. 'She knows nothing of men or of love.

My father smiles. 'Do you remember how King Henry delighted in testing her innocence, and when he got Sir Francis Bryan to use a very rude word to her? She had no idea what he was talking about.'

'Well, she knows enough about such matters to feel concern about her sister Elizabeth's moral welfare,' my mother replies. 'She has written to her, urging her to leave the Queen's household. Much joy she'll get from that one. Sharp as nails is young

Elizabeth, and she knows which side her bread's buttered. She'll do as she pleases, and I'll wager she'll stay put.'

'She's in no moral danger!' my father scoffs. 'The Queen and the Admiral are married, not living in sin. It's indecently hasty, and I dare say she could have done better for herself, but there we are.'

'She loves him,' says my mother, in a tone that conveys contempt for such weakness. 'She had an eye for him before my uncle wed her. Now she's allowed emotion to override good sense. I would have credited her with more wisdom.'

'Well, they have the King's blessing, so there's no point in criticising them. It seems that Seymour is more in favour with his Majesty than I thought. And, if you think about it, their union may be to our advantage. Remember the Admiral's proposal.' He glances briefly in my direction. 'Let this all die down, and I'll reconsider the matter. After all, the Queen would make an excellent chaperone.'

In some way, I realise, this conversation concerns me. Could it be that the Admiral has proposed that I go to stay with the Queen at Chelsea? If that were so, and my parents were agreeable, which God grant, then I would be the happiest girl alive.

Queen Katherine Parr

Chelsea, August 1547

My Lord and Lady Dorset were our guests at dinner today. Tom was right. As soon as our marriage was made public, Lord Dorset almost fell over himself in his haste to place his daughter Jane in our care. He is a suitor to us now! And so here we are, seated in the privy chamber drinking spiced wine and discussing the proposed arrangements.

Tom is in an ebullient mood.

'Only yesterday,' he is saying to his lordship, 'Bishop Bale, who has the King's ear, told me in confidence that he is convinced it is your daughter, the Lady Jane, whom his Majesty really wishes to marry.'

'Have you spoken with the King himself on this matter?' Dorset asks. I see greed and ambition plain in his eyes, and for a moment I wonder where this will all lead us, and whether we should have entangled ourselves in this coil.

'No, but as I said, I am in the confidence of those who have,' Tom answers urbanely. 'Fear not, my lord, his Majesty will take my advice. He is not happy with the Catholic marriage that the council are forcing on him. I promise you, you shall see Jane placed in an alliance that is much to your comfort, if you will send her to us and appoint me her legal guardian. Then I will be free to dispose of her on my own initiative. In the meantime, her Grace here will be as a mother to your daughter.'

'It will be my pleasure,' I smile. 'Jane is a delightful child.' And if I can make her happy, even for a short time, then I will feel more at ease with myself for participating in this underhand scheming.

'You wish to make her your ward?' Dorset asks cautiously, although he can scarcely conceal how eager he is to conclude this arrangement, which would make Tom Jane's legal guardian, with full control of any lands and income she would inherit in the event of her father's death. I suspect he is doing rapid calculations in his head.

'I do,' says Tom. 'Name your price.'

'Two thousand pounds,' Dorset says bluntly, without hesitation. 'On condition that you arrange Jane's marriage to the King and to no other.'

Tom affects to be taken aback, although we have already surmised that a sum of this nature would be asked. 'A vast amount, my lord.'

'But worth the investment, I trust, and the benefits to all, and to this realm.'

'Indeed,' Tom agrees. 'Shall we say five hundred pounds as a down-payment, five hundred on Jane's betrothal, and the rest on her marriage?'

'Done,' says Dorset, as if he were closing on a land deal rather than what effectively amounts to the sale of his daughter.

'May I suggest that Jane joins our household after Christmas?' I ask.

'That will give us time to prepare a suitable wardrobe for her,' says Lady Dorset, clearly pleased with the transaction.

'I am sure you do not relish the prospect of being parted from her when she is so young,' I feel compelled to say, knowing how unfeeling Lady Dorset can be towards her daughter, 'so please feel welcome to visit her here at any time.'

'Your Majesty is most gracious,' replies the Marchioness, but I have the feeling that it is I, rather than Jane's mother, who feel concern at the prospect of their coming separation.

There is no escaping the fact that my lord's good brother, Protector Somerset, is still in a huff with him. And, of course, he may well have more reason to be so, though he doesn't know it yet. Nevertheless, an appearance of family unity must be maintained, for it would not do for the Seymours' political standing to be undermined by an open rift. The Protector has therefore invited us to join him for a little jaunt along the Strand, to inspect the old Inns of Chancery buildings, which his lordship – prompted no doubt by his socially ambitious wife – plans to develop into a veritable palace for himself, to be called Somerset House.

We alight from our chariot at three o'clock, and find ourselves at the point where the Strand joins Fleet Street. This is the part of town where many lords and bishops have their mansions, with gardens sweeping down to the River Thames; but looming between them, only yards away, is the Hospital of the Savoy, dilapidated and neglected, a haunt of beggars and cutpurses. The Strand is always busy with people making their way between the City and Westminster, and our grooms clear a path for us, waving back the passers-by.

The exterior of Somerset House is swarming with masons, carpenters and labourers, but inside it is near-derelict, and we have to pick our way through the debris that litters the dusty chambers, I holding up my skirts to avoid soiling the rich cloth. Ned – as Tom calls his brother – is lamenting the King's lack of enthusiasm for the French bride selected for him.

'His Majesty was plainly bored stiff during the council meeting this morning, even though he well knows that it is his duty to pay attention and learn how this kingdom is governed. He only woke up when the subject of his marriage was raised, and when we began extolling the virtues of the Princess Elisabeth, he interrupted to ask if she was rich, because he wants a well-stuffed and bejewelled wife, as he put it.'

We laugh. Edward is not his father's son for nothing.

'Well, isn't that what most marriages are all about?' says Tom.

Ned frowns. 'Naturally, but it's still good form to maintain some pretence that there's more to the business than that. It was the bluntness of the boy that was so startling, for all his seriousness, and most of the lords were having trouble stifling their amusement. Of course, I was able to tell him that the Princess will bring a great dowry – we are negotiating on that point at present. And I stressed that the most important advantage she will bring to himself and his realm will be the lasting friendship of France.'

'Which he swallowed whole, I take it?' snorts Tom. 'And pigs might fly.'

Ned shoots him a withering look. 'We need France just now. But the King went wittering on about misliking the Princess's religion, and insisting it be understood by the French that he expects her to convert to the true faith. As Supreme Head of the Church of England, he pointed out, he cannot marry a heretic.'

Tom's face registers smug satisfaction.

Oh, well done, your Majesty, I think. We have just the bride for you up our sleeves.

Ned is still grumbling as we cross the cracked flagstones of the courtyard.

'Then that crafty Warwick said he had no doubt that his Majesty would be able to persuade her she was in error, but his Majesty picked up the irony in his voice, and shot him a sharp look. But I know what the boy really wants, because he told me before this new marriage was ever suggested.'

Both Tom and I look at the Protector with interest. I can guess what my husband is thinking.

'What does he want?' he asks carefully.

'He wants to follow his father's wishes and marry Mary, Queen of Scots. And when I pointed out that she is betrothed to the Dauphin, he retorted that betrothals can be broken, and that anything could happen between now and the time he reaches fourteen, which is when he intends to marry. He's been brought up on dreams of gaining Scotland, which he rightly said would be his if he married Queen Mary.'

'The French will never break the betrothal,' I say. 'They have Scotland within their grasp.'

'Exactly,' replies Ned. 'We have to be realistic.'

We concur. And it is not realistic to expect our increasingly fanatical little King to accept a Catholic bride, especially when there's an excellent Protestant one in the offing.

All things considered, Tom's daring scheme is falling beautifully into place.

Lady Jane Grey

Bradgate Hall and Chelsea, January 1548

Christmas has come and gone, and at Bradgate my chests lie almost packed, ready for my departure for Chelsea. My heart is singing. Since I was informed that I am to join the Queen's household, I have not quite been able to believe my good fortune, nor that I am really about to get away from the intolerable durance of my life under my parents' roof, from the taunts, the criticism, the slaps, the cruelty. I am to escape at last.

I thank God fervently every day for the great mercy He has shown in placing me with the Queen, whose kind heart and gentle manner make her the easiest person in the world to love. Also, I pray to my utmost power that nothing will occur to prevent me going to Chelsea, which sounds to me like a very paradise, and that God will not account me too over-burdened with blessings, for I am taking with me those I love best in the world, faithful Mrs Ellen and dear Dr Aylmer.

I cannot help but wonder why I am to go to the Queen at this time. My mother says it is usual for girls of my rank to be sent to live in a noble household in order to learn the social graces and complete their education, yet I have a strange feeling that there is some other reason, some advantage to be gained from it by my parents. Well, time will tell. I am the beneficiary now, whatever the future holds.

Fortunately, the scandal surrounding the Queen's marriage to the Admiral has been all but forgotten, at least in this household, but just in case my parents were still entertaining any doubts on that score, the Admiral wrote to say that his mother, old Lady Seymour, will be joining his household to assist the Queen in overseeing my welfare, and will treat me as if I were her own daughter. And for company, he added, I will be fortunate in having the society of the Lady Elizabeth, my royal cousin. I am so happy I can hardly sleep for excitement.

When the day of departure arrives, my mother swoops regally into my chamber and quizzes Mrs Ellen and the maids to make sure that everything that should have been packed has been, and that nothing has been forgotten. Then she turns and looks me up and down. This morning I asked Mrs Ellen to dress me in a simple gown of black velvet with sleeves lined with white samite. Few jewels adorn my attire, and my headdress is a plain black French hood and veil. I have recently read that it becomes a virtuous Protestant maiden to dress modestly and discreetly.

'And where do you think you are going dressed like that?' demands my mother, bearing down upon me. I stand my ground. Soon I will no longer have to put up with her bullying.

'I see nothing wrong with my attire, my lady. I thought it looked seemly enough.'

'Everything's wrong with it. You look as if you are in mourning. For Heaven's sake, you are going to stay with the Queen! Out of respect for her, have the decency to dress the part! It's not as if you can rely on your own beauty to blind others to the fact that you cannot be bothered with your appearance. Really, you should know better!'

'On the contrary, my lady, I have taken care with my appearance,' I say quietly. 'I am sure the Queen will appreciate that I desire to dress as becomes a godly Protestant maiden. I have read that fripperies and gewgaws are but papist vanities.' There, I have said it, the thing I have been itching to say ever since I read it. I know I have been rude: the implied insult is clear, because my mother herself is wearing a gown of crimson satin embroidered with gold and edged with pearls and other gems. She is also dripping with jewels.

I wince as my mother's palm lashes my cheek, but I make no murmur. She is breathing heavily, red in the face.

'You will apologise for that, girl, on your knees.'

I say nothing.

'You insulted me, you impertinent minx! Now you *will* kneel and beg forgiveness, and then you will change into some fitting clothes, and leave worrying about such things to your betters. You will not gainsay me. I'll hear no more of such nonsense.'

'My lady, I cannot apologise when I have done nothing wrong.'

Another slap. 'Kneel! Or I write to the Queen and tell her we have changed our minds and you cannot come.'

She has me there. I am in a corner and she knows it. Unwillingly, I kneel.

'I crave your forgiveness, my lady,' I whisper.

'That will suffice,' she says. 'Now, Mrs Ellen, the green damask gown, I think, with the tawny kirtle. And the emerald pendant.'

Mrs Ellen and I exchange surreptitious glances, but there is nothing more to be said. And so, sumptuously gowned and swathed in furs against the January cold, I descend to the great hall and kneel again, this time to receive my parents' blessing. Then I climb into the carriage and set off with my escort for the south, and freedom.

Queen Katherine opens her arms wide as I curtsey.

'No ceremony, Jane. Welcome to Chelsea. I hope you will be very happy here.' I am swept into a warm embrace, and then released so that a smiling Lord Admiral can extend his greeting too.

'Why, you're a handsome little lady,' he says merrily, standing back to look at me. 'And you've grown.'

'Not a lot, my lord,' I reply, knowing he had but meant to be kind. I am aware that I am still small for a ten-year-old.

'The healthy fresh air here will do you good,' says the Queen, leading me from the jetty where my barge has moored, along a path that winds through well-tended formal gardens towards the mellow, red-brick palace, whose many-paned windows glint in the winter sunshine. In the great hall, with its impressive hammerbeam roof and armorial glass, I am presented to my cousin, the Lady Elizabeth, who kisses me on both cheeks and casts appraising eyes over me.

At fourteen, Elizabeth is considerably taller than I, yet there are familial similarities in our looks. We both have the Tudor red hair, and we both wear it parted in the centre beneath a French hood. We are both very slender, with pale, freckled skin, pointed chins and dark, watchful eyes, and we both have beautiful hands with long tapering fingers. I notice from the first that Elizabeth takes every opportunity to display her slender fingers to advantage. My cousin, I fear, is very vain.

'Many princes have asked for my hand,' she boasts later, as we sit talking together in a window embrasure waiting to be summoned to our supper. 'I am expected to make a great marriage some day.'

'Your Grace must be much sought-after,' I say, even though I'm sure she is exaggerating, since her bastard status surely prevents her being in high demand as a princely bride.

'It is a real nuisance to me!' she declares. 'I do not want to marry and live my life at some man's beck and call. I would be my own mistress. And I do not relish the thought of having babies year in, year out. It scares me.'

Her candour is refreshing, if astonishing.

'But it is our duty to marry and bear heirs for our lords,' I say.

'Duty! Katherine of Aragon did her duty, and bore all those dead babies, and was put away for her pains. Jane Seymour died doing her duty. And Katherine Howard . . .' She stops and bites her lip. Doubtless she is thinking of her mother too. 'Never mind. When the time comes, I will be making it quite clear that I am minded to live and die a virgin.'

She turns to me and gives me a piercing look.

'You think it can't be done, little cousin, don't you? Well, let me tell you something. In this world, there are ways of appearing to go along with other people's plans, whilst all the time keeping your own counsel and putting things off. And then, before any confrontation can take place, you often find that events have moved on, and that you can do exactly as you please in the matter.'

I don't really know what she means, so I just nod vaguely.

'That's why you're here, you know,' Elizabeth says.

'Why? What do you mean?' I ask.

'It's so the Admiral can arrange a marriage for you.'

Of course. I had suspected I was not to come to Chelsea just for my health and happiness.

'Did they tell you that?'

'It was something the Queen said,' continues Elizabeth vaguely. 'Of course, I don't know the details. But the Admiral says you are a great prize for any man. Like a heifer!' she giggles.

'I feel like one,' I mutter. 'Is it not unfair that I have not been consulted in this matter?'

'It was ever the case,' Elizabeth tells me. 'We're women. Men think our views don't count. But we are not as weak and feeble as they think. Remember that, Jane. We also have strength and determination and cleverness, and those are qualities to be admired. If you don't like the husband they choose for you, be cunning. There are ways of avoiding an unwanted marriage.'

I can't imagine how I could do any such thing.

'And why should we be obliged to marry anyway?' Elizabeth is saying. 'Surely there is much pleasure to be had in the single life. Pleasure in books, or music, the company of friends, or even a little naughty dalliance with gentlemen!'

I am shocked to hear her speak thus. She looks at my face and laughs.

'Yes, Jane, you can have it all, if you're clever. You can go so far and no further, at your will. You need not forgo all of life's pleasures just because you're not married.'

'My lady, where did you learn such ideas?' I ask incredulously.

'I reasoned them for myself,' she says blithely. 'Come, it's time for us to eat.'

I follow her into the dining hall. My stay at Chelsea is going to be very interesting indeed.

I am in awe of the Lady Elizabeth. She shares her unorthodox and astonishing confidences with me, and swears like a man when no adult is within earshot. There is no mistaking whose daughter she is, and already she carries herself with a regal bearing. She is acutely intelligent, and very witty, and I soon realise that we are going to be competitive rather than close. Yet I never fail to accord Elizabeth the respect due to her rank, and truth to tell, I find her company stimulating and enlightening. We spend many happy hours arguing on points of religion or philosophy, or trying to trip each other up on translations, vying to be the better. We also commiserate with each other over the needlework that the Queen insists we do. We both hate sewing.

I cherish more, however, the company of Queen Katherine, who sometimes sits in on my lessons and stays to discuss them with me. She is a kindly mistress, and is adamant that learning should be tempered with other, less demanding pursuits. Twice during the spring she comes to the schoolroom and insists that Dr Aylmer puts away his books as the weather is just right for a picnic in the garden, and he cannot object, for he is invited too. Then tables are set up under the trees, overlooking the river, and we ladies and our attendants fall to laughing and jesting over our food. It is all very novel for me, and quite exhilarating.

Not that I ever mind doing my lessons. To me, learning is an adventure that stimulates the mind and imagination, and I can never resist its lure.

'You are a delight to teach, Jane,' Dr Aylmer tells me. He is forever, to my embarrassment, singing my praises to Dr Ascham, the Lady Elizabeth's schoolmaster, whose approach to education is similar. There is a healthy, yet friendly rivalry between the two tutors, for each is determined that his own pupil should exceed her rival.

'You are truly gifted, Jane,' Aylmer says. I blush to hear it.

'I shall be guilty of the sin of pride, Sir!' Oh, I am so happy here. I never want to go home.

Queen Katherine Parr

Chelsea, March 1548

Mrs Ellen taps on my door and enters with a tray of cordial.

'Cook asked me to bring this for you, Madam,' she says in her gentle voice.

'Thank you, Mrs Ellen. I'm glad you came. I've been meaning to ask if you are happy here with us.'

'Oh, Madam,' the nurse says, beaming, 'I've never felt so at home in a great household. And I've been watching Jane these past weeks since our arrival at Chelsea and, Madam, I marvel at the change in her. She is no longer resentful, mutinous or reserved, as she was at home, and has become quite joyous.'

'I am gratified to hear it,' I tell her.

'It is because you run a happy household, your Grace. Jane has blossomed under your care.'

'I was concerned about Jane when she arrived,' I say. 'She was a little mouse, stiff and mute, more than she ever was as a young child; but now I hear her laughing out loud or holding her own in an argument. And she no longer shrinks from my lord's hearty teasing, as she did at first. I notice she has become adept at the art of repartee – I'd even swear she enjoys flirting a little with him, which greatly amuses him. Yesterday he told her she looks prettier than ever now, which made her cheeks flush, but I think she really begins to believe it.'

Mrs Ellen smiles. 'For me, too, the change has been beneficial,' she says. 'I love it here. And if Jane is happy, then I am happy.'

In truth, I have never known a nurse who so loves her charge.

'I'm pleased to see that you have made a new friend in Kat Ashley,' I say. Mrs Ashley is the Lady Elizabeth's governess. Like Mrs Ellen, she is a well-meaning soul whose devotion to her charge is manifest, so the two women have a lot in common. When their young ladies are at their lessons, Mrs Ellen and Mrs Ashley may be seen sitting together in the parlour or the garden, gossiping to their hearts' content over a glass of cordial and a plate of march-pane comfits. Sometimes I join them. It is all very relaxed here. I long ago wearied of court ceremonial, and in my own house I insist on only the minimal observance of royal etiquette.

Yet I, as a queen, cannot abandon protocol so far as to unburden my private fears to these two ladies. Some appearances must be maintained, and it would be thought shocking for one of my rank to confide such things to her inferiors.

However, if I go on as I am, I shall go mad.

'Good day, Kate!' cries my lord, stepping into my closet in

high good humour. He stops abruptly. 'Are you ill, sweetheart?'

I wipe my mouth. I feel very fragile.

'I might appear ill, Tom, yet all is well with me. Very well, in fact. Do you take my meaning?'

'You mean you are happy, my love?' he murmurs, kissing me gently on the forehead. 'I made you happy last night, eh? There's no need to be coy about it.'

Despite the rising nausea, I smile at his single-mindedness. He has completely misunderstood my meaning.

'What I'm trying to tell you, Tom, is that I believe I am with child.'

'Why, Kate, this is joyous news indeed!' he cries, kissing me again, boisterously on the lips this time, lifting me up, twirling me round and round.

'I beg you, my lord, desist, for the sake of the little one!' I laugh, glad to see him so thrilled. Every man, be he great or humble, wants a son to succeed him, and Tom is no exception. Five minutes later he is happily planning the future, our son's future, which he envisages being filled with honours and riches.

'We must have a magnificent party for the christening,' he declares. 'I shall invite the King himself!' Indeed, he is so over-joyed at the prospect of his approaching fatherhood that I can say nothing to him of my innermost fears.

As soon as he has gone, whistling, off to the stables, I throw on a nightgown above my chemise and make my way to the chamber of my mother-in-law, the venerable Lady Seymour. She's a wise old soul, not long for this world, I guess, but she has borne ten children and must have some understanding of how I feel.

'Madam, this is a pleasant honour,' she says, rising ramrod-stiff from her chair. Even at this early hour she is fully dressed, and not a hair out of place.

'My lady,' I say, 'I bring wonderful news. I am with child.'

And I burst into tears.

'Your Grace, please be seated!' cries Lady Seymour. 'What ails you? Is something wrong?'

'No, as far as I can tell all is well,' I weep. 'But I am so scared. I am living in dread. I am thirty-six, and this is my first baby.'

'Now calm down, Madam,' says my mother-in-law firmly. 'It will harm the child if you allow yourself to become agitated.'

'You must think me a coward,' I sniff. 'This is not how the Queen of England should behave. And I am no green girl. But I know that childbirth is hazardous to all women, and that the older one is when one is confined for the first time, the greater the danger. I fear for myself, God knows, but I fear even more for my baby. I want to live to see my child grow up, and be there to guide it. I can't bear to think of it being left motherless in this uncertain world.'

'It may surprise you to learn that most women feel that way,' says Lady Seymour. 'It's natural, but you must be firm with yourself. If I know my son, you will have the best care that money can buy. You must pray for a happy outcome, for you are in God's hands, and so is the babe. And remember that frights in the mother are bad for the unborn child. So it is your duty to set aside your fears and be positive. Madam, forgive my boldness, but I speak to you as my daughter, not as my Queen.'

'You are so kind, my lady,' I say, quieter now, and a little reassured. 'I will take your advice, and put my trust in God.'

In the days and weeks that follow, although I make a great effort to banish my fears, I am preoccupied with dark thoughts. Pregnancy, I find, is not easy. I am bone-tired all the time, unable to bear the constant nausea, and in no mood for Tom's embraces. And there's another reason for my misgivings, although to admit it makes me sound like a vain, shallow jade. But, like any wife approaching middle age and beginning to lose her looks, I am worried about the damage that pregnancy will wreak on my face and my figure.

There's something else I must now face too, which is one reason for these seemingly frivolous fears. I haven't imagined it, I'm certain. It breaks my heart to admit it to myself, but Tom's ardour is cooling. Yes, he is still affectionate and respectful towards me, but some of the passion has gone from his loving. I remind myself that many women have husbands who never loved them at all, or who are cruel to them, or flaunt their mistresses, and that in most ways that count, I have been very fortunate. Yet when you have enjoyed such fleshly delight as we two shared in the early months of our marriage, and which I cannot share just now, affection and respect are poor substitutes.

It is sheer anguish to me to dwell on what I have lost.

But that is not all that troubles and torments me. For I and my lord have been entrusted with a great responsibility, and if what I fear is true, then the trust that has been placed in us has been irrevocably violated. Because I am almost certain that my husband is amorously involved with the Lady Elizabeth.

Mrs Ellen

Chelsea, March 1548

It's still too cold to sit outside and enjoy the spring sunshine, so Mrs Ashley and I are taking our leisure in a linenfold-panelled closet, warming our hands on a brazier and discussing our respective charges. Kat Ashley is a garrulous, indiscreet woman who loves to gossip, but today her concerns are serious.

'What I am about to confide must remain a secret,' she warns.

I nod sympathetically. I can tell that she is desperate to unburden herself.

'You can trust me,' I assure her. 'I shan't tell a soul.'

'It started last summer,' she begins. 'The Lord Admiral would often come to my Lady Elizabeth's bedchamber in the mornings, before she was up, and he would tease her and tickle her as she lay in her bed. Of course, I was always present, but he took no notice of me when I asked him, for shame, to leave her be. And, to be truthful, she seemed to be encouraging him. There she would lie, giggling under the covers, and he would yank them off her and slap her on the buttocks, she wearing just a thin chemise.'

'I don't like what I'm hearing,' I say, shocked. 'It's disgraceful. And she not much more than a child.'

'A child in years, you might say,' observes Mrs Ashley darkly, 'but in no other respect. Anyway, when we stayed at Seymour Place in London, my lord continued to visit her bedchamber each morning, and sometimes he came wearing only his nightrobe, and had his legs bare; I tell you, on one occasion his robe was gaping so far open you could see – well, I leave it to your imagination. But it was becoming clear that this was no innocent game between stepfather and child.'

'And how did the Lady Elizabeth react to this?'

'She became embarrassed in the end. She's a forward girl, but her modesty was increasingly offended. She took to getting up and dressing very early, so as to be at her books when he arrived, but he still persisted in coming indecently garbed in the mornings, and at length I took him to task for it. I said I would tell the Queen if it went on, and he just laughed, but he stopped his visits all the same. However,' she sighs, 'when we returned to Chelsea, he was soon up to his old tricks again, arriving earlier and earlier each day. My lady would lock her door, but he had his own key, so when she heard it in the lock, she would jump out of bed and hide behind the bed curtains. But he would come at her, drag her out and tickle her until she cried for mercy. His hands were everywhere, I tell you. One day, he surprised her still in the bed, and made to kiss her, but she pushed him away. I told him that people were beginning to talk, and that he should cease his romps with my lady, but he swore he meant no evil and said she was like a daughter to him. He even threatened to complain of me to the Lord Protector if I spoke of the matter again.'

'But the Queen,' I ask, 'did she know what was going on?'

'That's the odd thing. She joined in these morning romps once or twice. Then, when we were at Hanworth, she and the Admiral chased the Lady Elizabeth through the gardens, and when they caught her, the Queen held her fast whilst the Admiral took a pair of shears and cut her gown to ribbons, they three laughing all the time. I was not best pleased when I saw it, for it had been a good black damask gown for mourning the King her father, and was beyond repair. I tried to remonstrate with the Queen, but she just said I was not to worry, it had been a silly prank. But I did worry, I did.' She looks distressed.

'I had not known any of this,' I say.

'There's more.' She bites her lip. 'Recently something happened to arouse the Queen's suspicions. I don't know what it was, and my little lady will not talk about it – she's a one for keeping her own counsel. The first I heard of it was when the Queen summoned me and told me the Admiral had seen the Lady Elizabeth in the gallery with her arms around a man's neck. Now, the only other man living in the house at the time – apart from Dr Aylmer – was her schoolmaster; not Dr Ascham, for he was away, but Dr Grindal, and he is old and sick, the last person you would suspect.'

'It sounds as if the Admiral was trying to divert suspicion from himself. If so, he went about it very clumsily.'

'Possibly,' says Kat doubtfully. 'But the servants were already gossiping about him, and it was only a matter of time before the Queen heard it. If, indeed, she hadn't heard it already. But she's no fool, Queen Katherine. It's my belief she made up the story herself, not wanting to accuse her own husband to my face. She said I was to be more vigilant with the Lady Elizabeth in future. Which I have been, I assure you.'

'And does the Admiral still come to my Lady Elizabeth's chamber in the mornings?' I want to know.

'No, not since the Queen spoke with me. I think he must have realised she suspects something.'

'Then let us hope that the matter has now blown over,' I say.

'Let us hope so,' she echoes grimly.

I sit silent. I have been more than happy here in the Queen's household, and so has Jane, but I am beginning to wonder if, with all this frightful hurly-burly going on, this is the best place for my little lady to be.

Lady Jane Grey

Chelsea, March 1548

There are disquieting undercurrents here in the Queen's house: chance words overheard, voices hushed as I approach, and a feeling that the Queen is not as happy as she pretends to be. Something is wrong, just as it was that dreadful time at court nearly two years ago, but no one cares to enlighten me. I'm sure Mrs Ellen knows what is going on, but of course she will do her best, as usual, to shield me from anything unpleasant. And it's no use asking the Lady Elizabeth, because I think she is somehow involved, and I know her cunning mind well enough – she'll never willingly reveal her secrets.

Then one day I go to the Queen's chamber to fetch a book. Lady Tyrwhitt is there, the Queen's lady-in-waiting I like least. She engages me deferentially, even fawningly, in conversation, and in the course of it mentions, as if it were public knowledge, my becoming Queen of England one day.

'I?' I ask in astonishment.

'Why, of course, my lady,' replies Lady Tyrwhitt, looking dismayed. 'I thought you knew.'

'No.' I am thunderstruck.

'I spoke but the truth, my lady. The Queen has said as much.'

Frantic, I speed off in search of her Majesty, whom I find in the privy garden, deep in discussion with the head gardener. One look at my face and she puts a finger to her lips, dismisses the man and leads me to a shady arbour where we can be private. I can contain myself no longer.

'Madam,' I burst out, 'Lady Tyrwhitt says I am to be Queen of England. How can that be? The King is in health and has two sisters to succeed him.'

The Queen's face is calm. She takes my hand.

'Jane, when your parents placed you with me, it was in the hope that my Lord Admiral would be able to arrange your marriage to the King's Majesty. These things take time, but we are all confident that my lord will one day bring this to pass. You were not told, in case the matter came to nothing and your hopes were raised in vain; indeed, Lady Tyrwhitt should not have said anything about it, as she was sworn to secrecy, but perhaps she thought you were in our confidence.'

'I, marry the King?' I whisper.

'Yes, Jane. My dear child, you have all the qualities that go to make an excellent queen: you would be a fit wife for any prince. What is more, you and the King share the same views on religion, and I have no doubt that his Majesty is as eager for this match as we are.'

I am quite speechless. So this is why the Queen's ladies are all so deferential towards me. I had thought it was for my birth alone, and perhaps for my learning.

Queen Katherine sees my confusion, and folds her arm around me.

'Jane, you must have known from your early girlhood that a great marriage would one day be arranged for you, a marriage beneficial to your House.'

'I have known, Madam, but I never thought to look so high for a bridegroom,' I tell her. 'My lady mother was more at pains to tell me that love would not be a consideration in the choosing of a husband, but that it would be my duty to love him after our marriage. But that I should be considered worthy to marry the King himself – why, he is the greatest prince in Christendom!'

'And he is not altogether unpleasing to you, I can see,' the Queen smiles.

'I have barely seen him, Madam,' I blush, 'and we are both very young. I do not seek earthly pomp and advancement, as your Grace knows, but I should be grateful to have a husband of my own age who is well favoured in looks and shares my faith and my interests.'

'Indeed,' she replies. 'A husband of the same age can also be a boon. I know several girls who have been pushed into marriage, much against their will, with men old enough to be their grandfathers. But the King is young and shows promise of becoming a handsome man. He's godlier than his father, more serious altogether, and one cannot imagine him pursuing the same matrimonial career!'

'I do believe I could love him,' I say shyly. I have never before thought of what marriage might mean in human terms. 'And I would do my best to follow your Grace's own example in being a good wife and queen.'

Katherine smiles and pats my hand.

Suddenly, I feel a sense of exaltation. 'It must be that God Himself has destined me for this high position,' I breathe. 'His plan is clear. He is to use me, His humble instrument, to help accomplish His will in England. This is to be the purpose of my life, to assist and support our first Protestant king in his divinely appointed work.'

'I pray it may be so,' says the Queen, squeezing my hand tightly.

'It all makes sense now,' I tell her. 'My tribulations thus far were trials sent by God to assay my faith, and to prepare and hone me for the great task that lies ahead. It has been my testing time.'

Her Grace regards me with visible emotion. 'You are sober and wise for one so young. I can't tell you how delighted I am that you have embraced the news in this way. I so want you to be happy, but I also want you to feel that your life has some good purpose. Marriage is more than a political bargain, and you have perceived in this hard-headed arrangement, which is being negotiated by the Admiral and your father, something of the divine, and for that I praise God.'

I smile at her. 'For once, I shall be happy to do my parents' bidding.'

Whitehall, March 1548

At the Queen's behest, I have been brought to court to have audience of the King. She asked the Admiral to tell the Protector that I was such a prodigy in learning that his Majesty should meet and converse with me, as he might enjoy the company of a cousin of his exact age.

The court is much more formal now than in King Henry's day, so the Queen primes me beforehand in the required forms of etiquette. On the appointed afternoon, when I am announced at the door of the royal privy chamber, I curtsey three times as I enter the King's presence, not daring to look up in case I stumble. Then I rise, take three paces and sink to the floor in three further obeisances. Another three paces bring me to the steps of the dais itself, and again I make my curtsey thrice. Then I kneel, as a slender, childish hand, laden with rings, is extended for me to kiss.

'Rise, cousin, you are welcome,' the King says in a high, imperious voice.

Reminding myself that I must kneel again whenever I address him, I rise to my feet, lift my eyes to his and see a slight, copper-haired boy with pointed ears and a pointed chin. He looks a bit like an elf, although a very majestic one. But his eyes are cold and shuttered. I imagine that he will not be an easy person to get close to.

'I have heard that you are something of a paragon,' his Majesty is pleased to say.

I kneel once more, and reply meekly, 'I do my poor best at my lessons, Sir.'

'You're taught by Dr Aylmer,' he says, becoming more animated. 'Dr Cheke has a high opinion of him. You are very fortunate to have such a tutor, cousin.'

This boy is a little younger than me, but his manner gives the impression that he is far older.

'I have the greatest affection for him, Sir.'

'What do you think of this?' the King asks, producing a parchment from his pocket. He hands it to me. It's a translation into Greek, quite ably done.

'Is this your own work, Sir?' I venture.

'Yes. I did it this morning. Well, cousin, what do you think of it? Have you yourself progressed so far?'

A sight further, I think, but of course I cannot say that, and I should not allow myself to fall into the sin of pride. These things come easily to me, and that is not my doing, but God's.

'I am astonished by your Majesty's scholarship,' I say.

'Could you translate it back into the Latin?' he asks, looking at me speculatively.

'I will try, Sir,' I say. I gaze at the Greek, and somehow it resolves itself at once in my mind into Latin. I pretend to hesitate, and stumble purposefully on a word or two, but nevertheless the King looks a little nonplussed.

'Dr Aylmer is to be congratulated on his pupil,' he says when I have finished. Do I detect a trace of irony in his voice?

He has now lost interest in schoolwork, and suggests we play cards. He sits down on a cushioned chair and waves me to a stool. The courtiers, fine lords and ladies in their jewel-encrusted, peacock-coloured clothes, gather round in the tapestry-hung chamber to watch us. We enjoy a spirited game, and I begin to relax in his company. For all the formality surrounding us, he seems to like me. He smiles rarely, and is over-solemn for his years, but he is friendly enough in his reserved way.

When the game is finished, he walks me along his private

gallery, pointing out the portraits of our mutual forebears.

'That's King Henry the Seventh, my grandfather, and your great-grandfather, my Lady Jane. And this is your grandmother, Mary Tudor, Duchess of Suffolk.'

'They say she was very beautiful, Sir.'

'Probably when she was young, but not in that portrait,' he replies candidly.

'I like this one,' I say. It's a likeness of a very fair young woman in a golden dress and hood. The King gazes at it for a moment.

'That was my mother,' he says. 'She died when I was born.' There is no emotion in his voice, and how could there be? He never knew her. But his cool terseness is disconcerting. I cannot imagine anything moving him.

Soon it is time for his archery practice. When he dismisses me, I kneel to kiss his hand.

'Farewell, cousin,' he says. There has been no indication that he has any special affection for me, still less any acknowledgement of the possibility that I might one day be his queen. As I walk backwards out of the presence, curtseying again as two pages throw open the doors, I wonder if I will ever grow to love this cold, dispassionate boy as a wife should.

Queen Katherine Parr

Chelsea, March 1548

It is Sunday morning, and we are preparing for worship in the chapel. This should be a reflective, tranquil time, yet I am uneasy. The Lady Elizabeth has pleaded one of her headaches as an excuse to stay in bed, and my lord is missing.

At the entrance to the royal pew, I pause. I bid Jane be seated, then send Anne Vaux, one of my ladies, back to my private chambers.

'There's still time before the service begins, Anne,' I tell her.

'See if you can find the Admiral, and ask him to hurry up.'

Anne hastens away. She returns five minutes later. She has not seen Tom. He is not in our apartments.

I decide to go and look for him myself, and instruct the chaplain to wait.

As I hasten through the gallery that leads from the chapel, I encounter Mrs Ashley on her way to worship. I inquire after the Lady Elizabeth.

'I've just left her, Madam. She is sleeping.'

I wish I could believe her, but her eyes slide away from mine.

I wait until Mrs Ashley has gone into the chapel, then make my way, not to the royal apartments, but to my Lady Elizabeth's. All is quiet as I approach. But then, from behind a closed door, I hear a girl's muffled giggle.

Taking a deep breath, I push the door open. They are there together, tumbled on the bed, my husband and my stepdaughter, both in a shocking state of disarray. Instantly Tom leaps up, throws the coverlet over the girl's exposed breasts and tugs at his hose. Our eyes meet, and he looks away. There is nothing he can say in his defence, so he just shrugs and spreads his hands helplessly, as I gaze at him in horror. Words will not come, and mutely I turn and flee from the room, as he hurries after me, shouting my name.

We face each other in the privacy of our chamber. I am trembling with the shock of his betrayal, he is aggressive with guilt.

'Do you realise the enormity of what you have done?' I cry, my voice trembling. 'Setting aside the hurt to me, your wife, you have compromised the King's own sister.'

'I have not harmed her,' he retorts.

'By that I suppose you mean you have not deflowered her.'

'Yes. I mean, no, I have not. It was just a flirtation, Kate, that got out of hand. You must believe me.'

'Yes, so out of hand that you felt the need to unlace your breeches. God knows what would have happened had I not interrupted you. Christ, Tom, how can you be so stupid?'

'She bewitched me, the little temptress,' he mutters. 'She's a sorceress, just like her mother.'

169

'That's a feeble excuse. I suppose you had no mind of your own in the matter.'

Tom says nothing. There is nothing he can say.

A terrible thought occurs to me.

'This reflects so badly on me,' I whisper, sounding flat and bitter. 'It is I too who have been remiss. The Lady Elizabeth has been entrusted to my care, and I have been lax in my vigilance. It had never occurred to me that there was any need for it. I believed that you were mine alone . . .' I break down and he moves to embrace me, but I push him away.

'Don't touch me!' I cry. I walk, sobbing softly into my handkerchief, to the window. 'I can only thank Heaven that you have not got her pregnant,' I say. 'I hope to God you are telling me the truth.'

'I am, Kate, I am,' he says brokenly.

'Then I must, for my own sanity, believe you,' I whisper. 'But if the council were to discover what has been going on under my roof, I should not escape the sternest censure.'

'I am so sorry, Kate,' Tom cries. 'Believe me, I am sorry. I was mad, I acted like a fool. It's you I love, you, Kate.'

'Really?' I ask. 'The evidence of my own eyes tells me otherwise.'

Tom falls to his knees, and looks up at me. There are tears in his eyes.

'I'm begging you, Kate, to forgive me. I know I don't deserve it, or you, but I'm only human, with a man's frailties. I love you, sweetheart – doesn't that count for something?'

Something hardens in me. 'It certainly didn't this morning,' I snap.

'You have to believe me!' he cries frantically. 'I love you!'

'Love?' I echo disdainfully. 'You don't know the meaning of the word.'

I walked out on him then, and I have not seen him all day. Nor has Elizabeth shown herself.

Now, Tom and I face each other over the supper table, both of us calmer and more rational. But the fact of his betrayal lies between us like a dark shadow.

I break the silence.

'I am resolved,' I tell him, 'to draw a line under this morning's disgraceful episode.' He looks up hopefully, but I refuse to meet his eyes. He's not going to get off so lightly.

'The Lady Elizabeth, by virtue of her youth, is the innocent party in this sordid affair,' I say. 'It is my duty to send her to a place where she can come to no further harm. I shall say I can no longer take responsibility for her care because of my pregnancy, which obliges me to lead a quieter life.'

Tom hangs his head, cradling it in his palm. 'What more can I say?' he asks pathetically.

'You must pray to God for forgiveness,' I answer, 'because I can give you none.'

Elizabeth is leaving for the house of Sir Anthony and Lady Denny at Cheshunt. No one has been fooled by the official explanation for her departure, and I can tell that the household is buzzing with speculation. Clearly, too many people have seen and heard too many things, and I am fearful in case loose tongues undermine the plans I have made to protect Elizabeth's reputation, not to mention my attempt to conceal the fact that my marriage is in ruins. It doesn't help that, when Elizabeth takes her leave of me, she bursts into weeping, which gives further cause for gossip.

I kiss her kindly, wishing her well.

'Allow me to write to you, Madam,' she sobs.

'By all means,' I soothe. 'Now, farewell.'

And she is gone, leaving me my faithless husband and the perils of childbirth to come.

Lady Jane Grey

Chelsea and Hanworth, March 1548

Ever since I saw the Lady Elizabeth emerge in tears from the Queen's closet at Chelsea, I have wondered if she upset her Majesty in some way, and whether that was the reason for her abrupt departure for Cheshunt. If I'm right, then surely her Majesty has forgiven her, for when Elizabeth left that morning, and the whole household gathered to bid her farewell, I saw Katherine kiss her and smile kindly at her, and stand waving until the little procession vanished from sight. Since then, she has corresponded with the Lady Elizabeth, and sometimes reads her letters aloud so that I and the other ladies can hear news of her.

I fear that Elizabeth's offence had something to do with the Admiral; relations between him and the Queen are visibly strained, and there is a coldness between them that permeates the entire household. I am lonelier than I expected without Elizabeth's stimulating company, so I feel that chill more than most, I suspect, and I therefore pray daily that God will reconcile my kind guardians.

My prayers are answered for, as the spring draws on and the Queen's pregnancy advances without mishap, she and the Admiral are drawn together again by their shared expectations for the future. Her manner towards him thaws, and he is as attentive as ever, boisterously kissing her and chucking her under the chin.

There is no mention of the Lady Elizabeth returning to Chelsea.

It is very warm, even in the shade, in the garden at Hanworth. The Queen sits dozing on a bench, stomacher unlaced to accommodate her swelling belly, and sleeves rolled up indecorously. A woman may display much cleavage in a low-cut gown, yet seemliness demands that arms be covered to the wrist, whatever the season, but the Queen is too hot to care, and we are unobserved in this leafy bower.

I look up to see Katherine dreamily watching me as I sit stitching a tiny bonnet.

'There is no news yet of your marriage,' she says. 'My lord remains at court, trying to win supporters for our plans, but he still awaits an audience with the King. However, he remains optimistic, and has assured me that we will soon see you more well bestowed in marriage than you could ever have hoped for. It's just a matter of being patient.'

I am about to reply when suddenly a look of wonder appears

on the Queen's comely face, and she places both hands on her belly.

'Jane,' she whispers in awe, 'feel this.' And she guides my fingers to the place.

'Can you feel it too?' she breathes. 'He kicks.'

I can. It's like a fluttering beneath my hand. I smile at her and joke, 'He must be a little knave, Madam. Doubtless we shall see him beaten for causing his lady mother so much trouble!'

Katherine laughs. At last, it seems, she has put her sadness behind her.

Queen Katherine Parr

Hanworth, June 1548

The Marquess of Dorset has come to supper. He is alone, for his lady has a head cold and is indisposed. Despite my enjoyment of the good food – I always seem to be hungry these days, with the child due only a few weeks ahead – it is an uncomfortable meal, for his lordship plainly has something disagreeable on his mind and wastes little time on pleasantries.

'Well, my Lord Admiral,' he weighs in, as soon as the turbot has been served, 'you have had my daughter for six months, and so far we have heard nothing about your plan to marry her to the King. May I ask what progress you have made?'

Tom reclines complacently in his chair and answers in honeyed tones, 'My lord, I beg of you to be patient. These things take time.'

'You've had six months.' Dorset sets down his goblet. He is obdurate.

'I await an audience with his Majesty,' Tom tells him, unruffled.

His lordship is not impressed. 'By God, man, if you're in a position to arrange this marriage, how come the King keeps you waiting so long? You told me he was eager for this.'

'And so he is, so he is,' Tom assures him, signalling for a servant to bring more wine. 'But it would not do to be too open about this matter, not just at present. His Majesty does not wish to offend the French by rejecting their princess, so matters have to proceed delicately. England needs the friendship of France, and so it is politic, just for the present, to let King Henri think that negotiations are proceeding satisfactorily. But I promise you I have been working assiduously to build up support for the marriage with my Lady Jane, and that there are many who favour it.'

Dorset looks unconvinced. He's a hard man to please. I smile at him and offer some gooseberry sauce. He ignores me, and pulls on his beard.

'And how long is this little charade for the benefit of the French to go on?' he demands.

Tom's momentary hesitation betrays his uncertainty.

'Only until a secret treaty with the Emperor is negotiated,' he says. 'Then England will no longer be so much in need of the friendship of France.' He is bluffing, I know, lying his way out of a corner. There is no secret treaty with the Emperor in view.

Dorset seems to know it too.

'I'm surprised his Majesty is contemplating an alliance with the Empire,' he says suspiciously. 'The Emperor Charles is a far greater champion of Catholicism than the King of France. All Charles does is incite the Lady Mary to stir up trouble by insisting on her right to celebrate Mass, which, as he well knows, is now illegal in this country. With the Emperor behind her, she knows she can snap her fingers at the law. My lord, do you really believe that his Majesty seeks this alliance? Or perhaps you have been duped?'

Tom's temper flares.

'I assure you, Sir, that an imperial alliance is even now being discussed by my brother, the Lord Protector, and the council,' he retorts fiercely. 'They are negotiating on the very point of the Lady Mary's Mass.'

'Did the Protector himself tell you that?' Dorset is becoming similarly heated. 'I have heard it said at court that you do not enjoy your brother's confidence. And that you have no real influence with the King.'

Tom is hot with anger now, but as he opens his mouth in indignation, the Marquess interrupts him.

'I think, my lord, that the time has come for me to withdraw my daughter from your household and wardship,' he says nastily.

I know I must intervene. If I leave it to Tom, all will be ruined. A display of rage will do us no good.

'Think, my lord,' I urge. 'Be not too hasty in this matter. We have only your daughter's welfare at heart, and our mutual advancement. My lord here is still confident of success – he was only saying as much before you arrived. May I crave your indulgence for a few more weeks, to give him more time to bring this matter to fruition.' I lower my tone and lean forward confidentially. 'We too get to hear the court gossip, and my lord has been credibly informed that you yourself have incurred debts that would prove an embarrassment to the father of the future Queen. Debts, they say, that you have, at present, no means of paying off.'

My bolt shoots straight to the target. Dorset is taken completely unawares, and I guess that the rumours I have heard are indeed true.

'As a token of our goodwill,' I press on, sensing victory, 'my lord here has said he would be happy to make your lordship a loan to cover those debts.'

Tom takes up my drift with enthusiasm.

'Interest-free, of course, as between friends,' he chimes in. 'The only security I ask is that the Lady Jane remains my ward.'

Dorset's confidence in us seems to have been miraculously restored by our offer. As my lord often says, it always helps to smooth the path with a little money. I can guess that the Marquess is thinking it unlikely that we would be willing to commit ourselves to handing over such a substantial sum if we were not optimistic about securing Jane's marriage to the King.

'I will not deny that a loan would come in useful just now,' he says, graciousness itself. 'I thank your Majesty and you, Sir, for your kind offer, and I accept it.'

Lady Jane Grey

Sudeley Castle, Gloucestershire, June 1548

The great cavalcade winds its way slowly through the Cotswolds, passing through villages of mellow stone, trundling along dusty tracks that are free of mud, thanks to the warm, dry weather. I ride with the Queen and Lady Tyrwhitt in a horse litter that jolts over every bump in the road, grateful that we will not have to suffer this discomfort for much longer, since our destination will soon be in sight.

We are bound for Sudeley Castle, near Winchcombe, a house that was granted to the Admiral when he was created Baron Sudeley. It was built over a hundred years ago, the Queen says, and was once owned by the evil, crookbacked King, Richard III, who murdered the two poor Princes in the Tower of London. King Richard extended and improved the castle, and it is still a luxurious residence. The Queen and the Admiral are to set up their court there.

'We plan to live in the grand manner!' her Grace told me gaily. 'We will entertain the local nobility and gentry, and there will be a warm welcome under our roof for scholars, musicians and artists. I want our house to gain a reputation as a haven for hospitality and learning.'

Dreamily she lies on the cushions in the litter, embracing her great belly and her dreams. This is to be a new beginning for all of us.

The Admiral is riding alongside.

'Look!' he cries. 'Sudeley!'

We poke our heads through the damask curtains. In the leafy-green distance, we can see a fine house of honey-coloured stone. As we draw nearer, the details of the castle come into view: the magnificent perpendicular wing with its soaring windows, the chapel standing separate, the stately gardens. The procession enters the gates, and the servants hasten to welcome their master and mistress and to unload the baggage carts.

'What a beautiful, beautiful place!' exclaims the Queen as we walk through the arched entrance. 'A fitting place for our son to be born.'

The Admiral flings his arm around her.

'It is indeed, my love,' he agrees, and kisses her on the cheek. I watch her look up at him. Her love for him is obvious, despite their past troubles. This *will* be a new beginning for them, a fresh start – I feel it in my bones. I pray God they will be happy here.

Sudeley Castle, 30th August 1548

'For God's sake, can't somebody do something?' shouts the Admiral in anguish. 'It's been two days now, and still it goes on.'

'Babies come in their own good time, my lord,' says Mary Odell, the midwife, placidly. Yet beneath her professional air of confidence – she is the best to be found, and knows her worth – Mrs Odell seems a little worried. The Queen, at thirty-six, is old for a first confinement; she has said it herself; and matters progress very slowly.

Her pains started the evening before last, mild at first, then slowly increasing in intensity all through the night. In the morning, inexplicably, they had all but ceased, but by supper time had returned with renewed vigour. By eight o'clock her Grace was in misery, and there was nothing we could do to ease her. Lying down, sitting, even standing with support while she waited for each onslaught to pass – nothing gave her any relief. We all stayed with her, trying to help in our different ways, the older ladies rubbing her back or telling encouraging tales of their own successful confinements, while I, like a good daughter – which is what I am treated as here – flitted to and fro, fetching cooling drinks, scented cloths to mop the Queen's brow, or herbal infusions that were meant to dull the pain, but failed woefully.

At ten o'clock the midwife insisted that her Majesty go to bed, shooing away the Admiral, who had, to her and the ladies' horror, tried to insist that he remain with his wife. Men, Mrs Odell told him firmly, had no business to be in the birthing chamber, for shame! This was women's work, and the women would deal with it. So the Admiral waited impatiently outside in the antechamber, whilst I was deputed to report to him from time to time on the Queen's progress.

It was one of the longest nights I have ever spent. I had been told it was God's will that women should bring forth children in sorrow, as punishment for the sin of Eve, but I had never realised until now what they have to go through to have a child. It is horrible, messy, embarrassing and fraught with perils, and I shrink at the thought that I myself might have to endure this one day. Once one is married, there is really no escape from it. I know now why people speak in hushed whispers of young brides dead within a year of their wedding, or of mothers of large families cruelly taken from them. And I can see why the Lady Elizabeth says she is scared of childbirth and does not wish to marry.

'Please God,' I prayed, 'send the Queen a happy hour. Keep her safe!'

By the middle of the night, Queen Katherine was showing signs of great distress, so the midwife gave her a strong dose of some physic that sent her into a deep sleep, through which her contractions continued sluggishly. As dawn broke, however, the drug wore off, and she woke to worse pains than before, so sharp that she screamed loudly each time the agony began, calling on Our Lord and begging Him to take the pain away.

'Jesus!' she cried, again and again. 'Help me, help me!'

The screaming went on for hours. I, weak from lack of sleep and sobbing in fear, was sent from the room and sat huddled in the Admiral's arms outside. He was trembling too, and to my astonishment I looked up to see tears falling down his cheeks. At one time, when the torment behind the closed door became unbearable, he bade me go down on my knees with him and pray to God to aid the poor Queen, so dear to us both. Never have I prayed so hard.

But the Admiral was in a worse case.

'I have been a bad husband,' he sobbed. 'I never realised till now how much she means to me. Please, dear God, spare her life. Let me make it up to her. Give me another chance.'

I felt I should not be hearing such things, which were private between a husband and wife, and that he should not be saying them in front of me. But plainly he was too unhappy to care who witnessed his outpourings. I'm sure he'd forgotten I was there.

'Dear Lord,' I prayed fervently, 'take this cup from her. Send her a safe delivery. I beseech Thee, do not take her from us.'

The screaming continued, unabated.

Mrs Odell is at her wits' end and no longer bothering to hide it.

'My lord,' she cries, 'with the Queen writhing and shrieking on the bed, it's impossible to talk sense to her or even attempt an examination. Her pains are almost continuous now, so it cannot be long, and it is time for her to push out the babe, but her Majesty is too far gone to heed my bidding, and her strength is failing. I fear she has wasted much of it on screaming. This is a bad sign.'

The Admiral leaps up.

'Let me talk to her.' He disappears into the bedchamber, the midwife at his heels. Five minutes later he emerges, shaking his head, and sits with his face in his hands.

An hour passes, and there is no change. The Queen's distress is terrible to hear.

'My lord,' says Mrs Odell, 'this case calls for firm intervention. So far, I have held back out of respect for the Queen's rank. I've begged her to let me examine her in order to check the babe's progress, but she will not allow me. She doesn't even hear me.'

'Mistress,' says the Admiral, 'you must assert the authority of your profession. I command it.'

'I will need all the assistance I can get,' she replies.

So I am called back into the birthing chamber, which is foetid with the stench of sweat and blood. The Queen lies on her disarranged bed, her hair damp and tangled, her face drawn with suffering. She sees nothing; she is withdrawn to a place where we cannot reach her. Her cries are mere moans now, for her strength is failing.

I am called upon to bathe her hot brow, and watch in shocked fascination as Mrs Odell instructs Lady Tyrwhitt to take one of Katherine's legs, and Lady Lane the other. They try to cooperate, but the Queen, despite her failing strength, manages to kick them away.

'Hold her fast!' commands the midwife, perspiring visibly, for this is one patient she dare not lose. The ladies, struggling, raise their mistress's legs so that Mrs Odell can examine her.

'Your Majesty,' she shouts, 'I can feel the baby's head, almost ready to be born. Madam, you must push hard, now!'

By some miracle, the Queen hears her and, summoning her remaining reserves of energy, does as she is bidden.

'Again!'

Straining, Katherine complies. The violence of the actual birthing horrifies me – has every woman to endure such agony? But then the child thrusts its tiny wet head into the world, and the rest is easy. I am conscious that a wondrous miracle has taken place.

There is a blessed silence. Outside, the Admiral must be wondering what is happening, but I cannot tear myself away to tell him.

The infant lies, blood-smeared and apparently lifeless, at the foot of the bed. The Queen has slumped back exhausted on her pillows, apparently neither knowing nor caring if it lives. For her, the dreadful pain has ceased, and that is probably enough for now.

Mrs Odell takes one look at the crumpled little face, already turning blue, and moves quickly. She deftly snips the umbilical cord, cleans the mouth and nostrils of mucus, lifts the child by its feet and slaps it hard on the back. No response. She lays it down and kneads its tiny chest with both hands. And then – oh, joy – it gives a tiny mew and begins to breathe, the healthy pink colour returning to its cheeks.

Wrapping the infant in a fine cloth, Mrs Odell lays it beside its mother.

'Your Majesty, you have a beautiful baby daughter,' she announces.

Sudeley Castle, September 1548

Both parents are so relieved that mother and child have come through their ordeal safely that the sex of their infant is of little moment to them. Of course, the Admiral had wanted a son, but when he sees his little girl lying in her mother's arms in that joyful moment of reunion, his face is suffused with love and pride, and I feel a pang, knowing it was not thus with my own parents when I was born, and that their disappointment in my sex is still a cross they bear. But the Admiral is sanguine, confident that sons will follow, and that this little maid will make a grand marriage to increase her father's fortunes.

The Queen is delighted with her daughter, and thrilled with her lord's reaction to the child.

'I am so at peace with the world, Jane,' she declares on the day after the birth, 'that I want nothing to mar our happiness.' Contentedly she lies there in her flower-filled bedchamber, recovering her strength and giving thanks to God for His manifold blessings.

As for me, I think the baby is the most wonderful thing I have ever seen. I sit gazing for ages at her as she lies snuffling, blinking milky-blue eyes at me. Indeed, she can't do much else, since, according to custom, the midwife has ordered that she be swaddled to ensure that her limbs grow straight. Tightly bound and wrapped in a rich crimson damask shawl, she lies in her vast oak cradle. A young girl has been employed to rock it, but she often finds that I have usurped her place, for I love nothing better than to sit by the babe, crooning to her, and I hasten there as soon as my lessons are over. A wet-nurse has also been taken on, a wholesome village girl whose own baby died at birth, for naturally a queen should not suckle her own child. A wife's duty is to provide her husband with sons, and breastfeeding, so Mrs Ellen says, will prevent her conceiving again. I cannot imagine her Grace welcoming another pregnancy so soon, not after the ordeal she has just suffered in childbed, but the midwife has assured us that things will be easier next time.

I cannot help but fear that the Queen's child, like so many other new-borns, might not survive infancy. No one has said as much, but within hours of her birth the Admiral summoned the household chaplain, who quickly baptised the sweet angel and named her Mary, in honour of the Lady Mary. Her Grace has just received a letter from the Lady Mary, who hastened to write and heal the rift between them as soon as she learned of Katherine's pregnancy, and agreed to be godmother. Now, if the poor babe should die, at least her soul will be safe.

The Queen did not attend the baptism; custom does not require it, but she would have been too weak anyway. Then the days passed, and still she did not recover her strength. Today she is very sick, and to my utter heaviness, Mrs Odell has just come to the Admiral to warn him that there is grievous cause for concern. Her Grace is suffering from childbed fever.

'What is that?' I ask fearfully.

'My lady, it is a condition that affects many new mothers during their lying-in period,' she says. 'Sadly, there is nothing anyone can do but wait for the fever to reach its climax, and pray.'

The Queen has been in a delirium for several days now, God save her. She barely knows her child, nor any of those around her. Whenever the Admiral comes near, she shrinks from him, and after hearing her tormented ravings, we are all distressed to realise that she is brooding over some real or imagined infidelity of his. This puzzles some of the ladies.

'I have ever thought him a devoted husband,' whispers Lady Tyrwhitt.

'And I,' says Lady Lane, shaking her head. But Lady Herbert, the Queen's sister, says nothing, and I think I can guess why. I fear that the suspicions I had at Chelsea – that the Admiral and the Lady Elizabeth had somehow offended the Queen – are confirmed when Katherine keeps muttering the name Elizabeth. The ladies think she asks for her stepdaughter, and debate whether they should send for her.

'Best not,' says the Admiral, when asked for his opinion. 'I heard only recently that the Lady Elizabeth has been unwell herself.'

'So did I, my lord,' says Lady Herbert, fixing him with a glacial look. Their eyes lock in a brief, tense moment. The other ladies are staring at them.

'It is unlikely that the Lady Elizabeth is fit to travel,' the Admiral continues, his voice dropping like a stone into the silence. He turns his back and returns to his wife's bedside.

*

'Is the Queen going to die?' I ask him later, after he has made yet another fruitless attempt to offer comfort to his wife.

He looks at me with pity; his eyes are heavy with unshed tears, defeated. Mine must be red from weeping.

'We should put our trust in God,' he says, covering my small hand with his large one. There is little hope in his voice.

On the fifth day of her fever the Queen briefly becomes lucid, although she is still hot and shivering.

'I feel so ill, I believe I cannot live,' she tells Lady Tyrwhitt in a weak voice.

'Nonsense, Madam!' replies that lady, a shade too briskly. 'I see no signs of death in you. The fever will soon pass.'

But Katherine is not listening. She has retreated to some twilight world in which she hovers between dreams and reality.

'I saw them together,' she murmurs fretfully, 'there, on the bed. Oh, my lord . . .'

I think Lady Tyrwhitt has heard only the last three words. 'I'll get the Admiral,' she says, rising.

Seeing how it is with his wife, my lord tenderly takes her hand, smiling sadly down upon her, then looks startled as she grips his fingers with surprising force and exclaims, 'Lady Tyrwhitt, I am not well handled by this man. He cares not for me, but stands laughing at my grief.'

'My lord, she is delirious,' cries Lady Tyrwhitt, seeing his stricken face and looking intensely embarrassed. 'Pay little mind to what she says! She knows not what she is talking about.'

'Sweetheart, I wish you no hurt,' the Admiral says gently, turning to the Queen and stroking the damp hair back from her brow.

'No, my lord, I think so,' she answers with some bitterness, 'but you have given me many shrewd taunts.' And she turns her head away from him.

'I cannot bear much more of this,' he says despairingly. 'What can I do? Shall I lie beside her and comfort her?'

'I think that would be a great solace to you both,' says Lady Tyrwhitt gently, whereupon we ladies tactfully withdraw to the far corner of the chamber, bend our heads to our needlework and converse quietly amongst ourselves.

Behind us, the Admiral lies down on the bed and takes his

wife in his arms, murmuring private words of love without regard for the presence of others nearby. We cannot hear what is being said, but we are aware that, for an hour or more, the Queen continues to pour out her grief and bitterness.

Later in the day the crisis passes, but although the fever subsides, it leaves Katherine drained and all but lifeless. While she sleeps, we pray for a happy outcome. In her cradle, little Lady Mary Seymour slumbers soundly.

Two days pass, without improvement. The Queen, drifting in and out of sleep, knows that there is little hope of recovery. At the suggestion of the chaplain, she makes her Will, and when it is drawn up and witnessed, asks the Admiral to bring their daughter to her. As he sits on the bed with the baby cradled in his arms, the Queen stretches out a feeble hand to touch the downy little head and whisper a last blessing. Tears are running down her cheeks, and I can only imagine how she must feel to be saying her final farewell to her child, this child she longed for so much.

'God keep you, my husband,' she whispers. 'It is His will that we must part. But I hope we shall be reunited in Heaven.'

'Don't leave me, Kate,' sobs the Admiral, his shoulders heaving.

'Jane, come here.' I can barely hear the fading, beloved voice. I lean over the bed to receive the whisper of a kiss on my forehead, then fall on my knees weeping, as this dear lady, who has been as a mother to me, bestows a fond last look on her lord, squeezes his hand and passes to her eternal rest. I have lost my beloved protector.

The chapel looks dark and sinister, hung with black cloth that has been hastily embroidered with the royal arms of England quartered with those of the Parr family. Mourning cloths are also draped over the altar rails, and stools and cushions have been provided for the more important members of the congregation.

First in the funeral procession are the officers of the Queen's household, carrying their staves of office; they are followed by Somerset Herald in his richly coloured tabard. Then comes the leaden coffin, borne on the shoulders of six black-clad stalwarts, and behind it, the chief mourner, myself.

I must look a diminutive figure in the midst of all this sombre pageantry. I wear a gown and hood of black banded with purple, the colours of royal mourning, and my long train is borne by a maid-of-honour. I carry a prayer book and keep my eyes downcast. The Queen's six ladies-in-waiting come after me, leading a procession of ladies, gentlemen, yeomen, tenants and members of the late Queen's household.

One person is, of course, absent, for etiquette precludes his attendance. Racked with grief and, perhaps, remorse, the Admiral has kept to his chamber today. He is not expected to parade his sorrow in public at the funeral, which is why I, as the senior lady of rank here at Sudeley, am chief mourner.

I stand stony-faced and dry-eyed as the coffin is set down on trestles before the altar rails, and remain so while the psalms are sung and the service performed. It would be undignified to cry, but indeed, even were I able to let myself go, I would have no tears left to flow. They have all been spent in private.

I try to concentrate on Dr Coverdale's sermon, but tragic thoughts of the dear Queen we have lost, and her motherless babe, keep intruding. When he has finished speaking, and the coffin is lowered into the open vault beneath the altar pavement, I think that I could never feel more miserable than I do now. The household officers break their staves of office and cast them in after the coffin to signify the ending of their service to the Queen; then it is all over, and my heart is as dead as a stone.

'Oh, Mrs Ellen!'

I am cradled on my nurse's lap, crying on her shoulder as if my heart will break. It is late evening, and the mourners have either ridden home or gone to bed; as soon as I could, I escaped to Mrs Ellen's chamber.

'I cannot bear it! I miss her so dreadfully.'

'It's always hard, my pet, to lose someone you love,' says Mrs Ellen, stroking my hair. 'It takes time to come to terms with it.'

To be truthful, my tears are as much for myself as for her whom I have lost.

'I dare not think what my life will be like without her,' I weep. 'I have been so happy here. I like the Admiral, but I do not think my parents will allow me to remain here now that the Queen has died.'

'No, child, it would not be fitting,' says Mrs Ellen sadly, 'not without a lady of rank present to act as your chaperone. And more's the pity, because I have been happy here too.'

'Lady Seymour could chaperone me,' I venture.

'I doubt your parents would agree to that, Jane. Lady Seymour is getting on in years, and keeps mostly to her rooms – you know that. What's more, she doesn't have the social standing of the late Queen, which I'm sure was one of the chief reasons why your parents placed you with the Admiral.' Mrs Ellen sighs. 'I see nothing for us but to go home.'

'I don't want to go home,' I sob. 'This is my home now.'

'You have to go home, child, if your parents command it. You are all but eleven years old.'

I wonder inwardly what will become of the Admiral's plans to marry me to the King, but of course I cannot discuss them with Mrs Ellen because I have had to keep them a secret. If only my marriage could be brought forward – then I might not have to go home, or not for very long, anyway. Yet in truth, I have little hope of the Admiral's chances of success in arranging my marriage to the King, and even if he did, I should have to wait three years before the Church would permit us to live as man and wife.

Thinking this through, I am calmer, though still emitting the occasional sob as I lie in Mrs Ellen's arms. But my passion is spent, and with it my desperation. If they insist, I will go home without complaint, however miserable it makes me. After all, I couldn't feel much more miserable than I do now.

'I have written to all my friends and acquaintances to inform them of this dire loss,' says the Admiral a week after the funeral, as we sit at dinner with the late Queen's ladies and a few remaining guests. 'I have also sent a letter to the Lady Elizabeth.'

He does not reveal what he said in it, nor do I ever find out if he receives a reply.

'I am concerned about what is to happen to you, Jane,' he tells me for the fifth time. I am not so green that I don't realise how valuable an asset I am to him. 'I have written to your father to ask if you might remain with me. I have told him I believe you to be sufficiently mature to order your own affairs.'

If only that could be so, I think.

'I also informed him,' the Admiral continues, helping himself liberally to some pigeon pie, 'that I have retained the services of my dear wife's maids-of-honour, so that you would be suitably chaperoned and attended.'

'I do hope my lord father will agree, Sir,' I say. Sad as this household is now, it is infinitely preferable to my home, which I can only envisage as a perennial field of conflict.

'He has already replied.' Looking grim, the Admiral produces a letter and passes it to me. To my despair, it is a demand for me to be returned home. With mounting indignation and embarrassment, I read that I am too young to rule myself without a proper guide, and for want of a bridle might take too much head and be forgetful of the manners and good behaviour taught me by the Queen. My father knows nothing of me! In sum, I am to be restored to my mother's care, to be framed towards virtue, sobriety, humility and obedience.

Remembering with a shudder what that will entail, I sit crestfallen, utterly wretched. I *cannot* – no, I *will* not – go back! I had thought to have put the misery of home behind me for ever, and that I would in due time go from the Queen's household to the King's. But I know I have no choice: I am bound to obey my parents. It is my duty, and God will be justly displeased with me if I rebel against it.

The Admiral is watching me speculatively, but I fear there is nothing he can do or say to make things better. He knows as well as I do – as, indeed, the world knows – that without the Queen his wife, he counts for little in the corridors of power. The King might be fond of him, but for the present the King is his brother Somerset's creature, nothing more. I suspect there is now little likelihood of the Admiral being able to bring about the royal marriage he and the Queen planned. My parents, too, must be of this opinion, if they are ordering my return.

The Admiral bends close to me. 'Cheer up, little one. I shall refuse to let you go. I intend to write this very night to your father, and assure him that his Majesty has said he will marry none other than you.'

'*Has* he said that?' I ask, astonished.

'Of course he has,' he replies, smiling broadly. 'And if that is not enough, we will sweeten your father with a nice fat payment towards the price of your wardship. You wait and see – all will be well!'

Hanworth, October 1548

My parents are here! We have removed to Hanworth, which is more convenient for them than Sudeley, and the Admiral is receiving them downstairs now. I wait, trembling, in my chamber, with Mrs Ellen – who is almost equally agitated – for the summons. Today my future will be decided.

The quarter-hours pass. I cannot settle to anything. It seems as if they have been talking for hours.

'Someone's coming!' says Mrs Ellen. It is the summons, at last. It is all I can do to restrain myself from racing down the stairs, so anxious am I to find out what has been decided for me. But I take care to hold myself decorously as I enter the great chamber and make my curtsey, hardly daring to lift my eyes to my parents', in case I read my future in them.

My lord and lady are alone, the Admiral having tactfully withdrawn.

'Greetings, Jane,' says my father. He is wearing hunting leathers and a jaunty plumed cap. He seems cheerful enough.

'God's blessings on you, child.' My mother, seated in a high-backed chair and wearing a magnificent pink damask gown, is looking me up and down, no doubt to see if I have grown or been cured of my freckles. I cannot deduce very much from her expression.

'I am pleased to see you, Sir, Madam,' I reply dutifully.

'Sit down,' says my lady, pointing to a stool at her feet. I sit, arranging my skirts neatly around me.

'As I am sure you are aware, we have been discussing your future with my Lord Admiral,' my father says, 'and we want you to know that we have accepted his offer to have you remain with him.' I bow my head in relief. I had not expected this.

'I still have my doubts as to the wisdom of it,' my mother comments. 'I should tell you, Jane, that we have been considering seriously an offer for you from the Lord Protector himself, for his son.'

I am astonished, not only at this revelation, but also at my parents' willingness to use me as barter in this way. If you can't have the King, snare the Lord Protector's son. Either will bring our family influence and greatness, although in different measures. It's the way of the world, of course, but so cold, so calculating, and so dismissive of my feelings in the matter.

'Sometimes one has to be realistic,' my mother continues. 'We heard nothing from the Admiral on the matter of your marriage for a long time. We had doubts that he could keep his promises. I have to say that I am not yet convinced –'

'We *should* accept Lord Sudeley's offer, Frances,' interrupts my father. 'As yet, the Lord Protector has given no firm indication that he is interested in an alliance with us. He hints shamelessly, but will commit to nothing.'

I try hard to remember what the Lord Protector's son looks like, but no image comes to mind. Perhaps I've never met him.

'At least,' my father says, 'the Admiral has given us a substantial sum as tangible proof of his good intentions. He also proposes that Jane remain in his household until she is of childbearing age. That will give him more time to arrange the marriage. Moreover, by then the King will have reached his majority, and will be able to choose his own bride, and our matter will go forward more smoothly, God willing.'

'Well, you must do as you think fit,' says my lady, tart. 'But I agree, there is not much chance of us finding another suitable husband for Jane at this present time. I've had enough of the Protector's delaying matters. I hope you are aware, nevertheless, that the Admiral has his own ambitions.'

'Which ride with ours,' replies my lord. 'He speaks sense, and I for one am prepared to give him another chance.'

'You were ever easily bought, husband,' my mother observes.

'Sweetheart,' he replies, with heavy irony, 'the Admiral is hardly likely to have outlaid all this money to no purpose.'

'So be it, then. I just hope that old Lady Seymour is a fit guardian for Jane. From what I've seen and heard here, she's an ailing recluse.'

'She is a virtuous lady, Frances, and must be used to governing a large household,' my father says firmly. 'Jane will come to no harm under her rule, I am sure.'

'Madam, she is a most pleasant and kind lady,' I venture.

'Soft, I make no doubt,' my mother replies. 'I hope she won't spoil you.'

They have gone. What a blessed relief. And they have left me behind, for which I thank God. It has been an anxious fortnight. The Admiral summons me and Lady Seymour to celebrate our victory with a cup of wine. I am strangely happy, despite the grief for the Queen that never leaves me and has me weeping into my pillow every night. I never realised it was possible to be both happy and sad at the same time.

Troubles, however, never come singly. Within days, there is a disturbing rumour in the household. Mrs Ellen, having got wind of it, sits me down and says she must tell me what is being said. I am bewildered at her urgency.

'This is serious, child,' she tells me. 'I am shocked to hear it being whispered around that the Lord Admiral's true intention is to marry you himself.'

'What?' He is far too old to think of such a thing, surely. He is forty-two! And the Queen his wife so recently dead!

'Has he said anything at all to you that might indicate he means to wed you?' Mrs Ellen demands.

'Nothing,' I answer, astounded, thinking back hastily to his dealings with me over the past weeks, and finding nothing. But doubt begins to nag me. 'Although, when I think about it, such a plan could explain why my marriage to the King goes forward so slowly. My lord has told me that it must now wait upon his Majesty coming of age, but . . .'

'That could just be an excuse,' Mrs Ellen finishes. She looks stern and worried. 'Jane, if your parents knew of this, they would summon you home at once.'

'Please don't say anything!' I beg. 'It is, after all, just a rumour. That doesn't mean to say there's any truth in it.'

'Yes, but you often find, child, that there's no smoke without fire,' Mrs Ellen observes. 'I have a responsibility towards your parents, mind you, and I warn you, the first hint I get that rumour speaks truth, I shall write to them. I should have no choice, for your honour would be compromised by remaining under this roof.'

'Then I pray the rumour is false,' I say fervently.

It is evening. The Admiral and Lady Seymour are entertaining a guest, a courtier friend of my lord's, and I am to join them for supper. It is early yet, but I am impatient to be downstairs. Mrs Ellen, who is to attend me, is not yet ready, but says I may go ahead.

In soft slippers, I descend the great oak staircase. The door to the dining hall is ajar and I can hear voices. A mention of my name stops me short. They are talking about me.

I know that eavesdroppers never hear anything good about themselves, or so Mrs Ellen tells me, but I cannot resist stopping to listen, since there is no one to observe or reprimand me.

By the sound of it, the Admiral is already a little drunk. He is slurring his words slightly.

'Yes, there has been a silly tale of late that I shall wed her,' he is saying. 'I tell you this but merrily!' He laughs. 'Aye, merrily! But I have my eyes on a bigger fish.'

A bigger fish? Who can he mean?

A footfall from above interrupts my listening. Clasping my hands decorously on my stomacher, I advance into the room to greet our guest.

I lie sleepless in bed, thinking on what I have learned. Thanks be to God I am not, after all, the object of the Admiral's matrimonial ambitions! But it is evident that he is pursuing an even more foolhardy scheme. Who can he mean by a bigger fish but the Lady Elizabeth? Is he mad? She would not stoop to have him; nor, I am sure, would the Protector and the council allow it, which proves that it must be a stupid and wicked plan. I am beginning to realise that not all adults are as wise as they would have us children believe.

Hanworth, November 1548

One of my greatest pleasures is playing with the Admiral's baby daughter. Little Lady Mary is now two months old, and her rosy face breaks out in gummy smiles when I approach her cradle and say hello. I like nothing more than to take over from the rocker, gently lulling the baby to sleep, or making her wave her chubby arms in excitement as I play peek-a-boo or shake her gold rattle at her.

Lady Seymour has come to the nursery today to make her inspection and question the lady governess and wet-nurse as to her granddaughter's progress. Satisfied that all is well, she sits by the fire sewing, rocking the cradle with her foot, while I kneel on the hearth-rug, gazing at the sleeping infant.

'These are dreadful times we live in,' she says tetchily. 'All change, for change's sake. I dread to think what the world will be like when this little one grows up. I thank God I won't be there to see it.'

I let her ramble on in this vein for a while. There is little I can say by way of an answer.

'I know what my son is plotting,' she says suddenly. 'I wish he'd desist. It's dangerous meddling in these affairs. But he's too headstrong by far. Won't listen to me.'

'I must do what my parents command,' I say defensively, feeling that in some way she thinks I am at fault too.

'What are you talking about, child?' asks the old lady. 'I wasn't referring to that madcap scheme to marry you to the King. No, I'm talking about my son's foolish ambitions concerning the Lady Elizabeth.'

Her indiscretion alarms me, and I quickly look up to see who is within earshot. But fortunately we are quite alone, the nursery staff having taken advantage of our minding the baby and gone off to do tasks elsewhere.

'The Lady Elizabeth?' I ask.

'Aye. He wants to marry her, don't you know?'

Of course, I had guessed. But I am nevertheless shocked.

Two weeks have passed, and the gossip is rampant. The Admiral's schemes are now the subject of common specula-tion – I've even heard people talking about it in the street when I go with Mrs Ellen to the shops in nearby Feltham. They say that the Admiral has launched himself on a head-long course towards disaster. Surely it is just a matter of time now before my parents take fright and recall me, which fills me with dread.

This talk of marriage to the Lady Elizabeth is exceedingly dangerous. Even I know that it is high treason to marry a princess of the blood without the sanction of the council, so surely the Admiral must know it. But I fear he has made his intentions all too plain.

People in this household are saying that the Lady Elizabeth can hardly be averse to the idea in view of what went on between them before.

'What did go on between them?' I ask Mrs Ellen.

She hesitates. 'Jane, this must go no further, because if it did, several people would get into trouble. There was some illicit dalliance between the Admiral and the Lady Elizabeth, when we were living at Chelsea. The Queen stepped in before it went too far, and sent the Lady Elizabeth away. Now, it seems, the Admiral would like to revive his connection with her.'

Of course. I had suspected as much.

'Read this letter, Jane,' says Mrs Ellen. 'It's from Kat Ashley.'

Mrs Ashley writes that her young lady has said she will not refuse the Admiral, if the Lord Protector and the council give their blessing.

'If you ask me,' Mrs Ellen says tersely, 'the Admiral has no intention of asking for it. I've even heard it bruited that he hopes to be in his brother's place before very long. I fear it is only a matter of time before someone points a finger at the Admiral and accuses him of treason.'

That is a terrible prospect.

'Shouldn't someone warn him of the danger?'

'That one? He enjoys it, dicing with danger! Do you think he would listen? His mother's already tried remonstrating with him. He told her to get back to her embroidery.'

'But someone should do something . . .' I think of that dear little baby, sleeping innocently in her nursery. 'For the Lady Mary's sake.'

'He won't listen to the likes of us,' sighs Mrs Ellen. 'We can but pray that matters have not advanced so far, and that he wakes up to reality before it's too late.'

Seymour Place, London, January 1549

All is in uproar; the Admiral has been arrested and is held for questioning by the council. It was true, I fear: he was plotting to overthrow the Protector, his brother. Yet the manner of his arrest was shocking.

Lady Seymour, near broken in grief, sits in the great chamber as her maid dabs her temples with lavender water, and tells the tragic tale, as she had it direct from her son, the Lord Protector. Nearly everyone in the household, from the chamberlain to the kitchen boys, has crowded into the room to hear it. I am on my knees at Lady Seymour's feet, holding her gnarled hands tightly, in a vain attempt to comfort her.

'It began when Fowler went missing,' she says. 'You know, Fowler, by whom my lord sent money to the King from time to time. The Admiral told me he was worried because Fowler had not come back. In fact, the man had been discovered on his secret errand and taken before the council for questioning.'

She shudders. 'The next thing was that the Admiral himself was summoned by the Lord Protector. My own sons, both of them, and the one summoning the other! Tom was ever a hothead – he refused to go. He wrote back to say it was not convenient. Then he told me, only a few nights ago in this very room, that he felt a net was being tightened inexorably about him. He decided to take drastic action.' She pauses, breathless. 'He took the reckless decision to seize the King.'

'But how would he manage such a thing?' I gasp.

'He had forged keys to his Majesty's apartments, Madam,' sniffs Lady Seymour, reaching for her handkerchief. 'Fowler got them for him, in return for a substantial bribe. So he was able to enter the King's lodgings by stealth at the dead of night, with the intent to kidnap his Majesty. With such a valuable bargaining counter in his hands, none would have dared gainsay him.'

There are tears in the old lady's eyes, but she bravely presses on with her story. Some of the ladies are crying, others shaking their heads incredulously. I find myself weeping too; I was fond of the Admiral, for all his faults.

'As ill luck would have it,' Lady Seymour is saying, 'although the guards were asleep outside the door of the King's bedchamber, his Majesty's spaniel began barking furiously as the Admiral let himself quietly into the room, and made to attack him. Stupidly, he shot it dead with his pistol, and after that there was no hope for him. The guards came running, and the King, who was horrified at the killing of his pet, ordered Tom's arrest.'

'But the King is a friend to the Admiral!' I cry. 'He loves his uncle.'

'He lifted no finger to save him,' whispers Lady Seymour. She bends her head to hide the brimming tears.

How can this be? I ask myself helplessly. Surely the Admiral will be saved – his own brother and nephew would not condemn him? He has often said how close he is to the King. That must count for something.

'But there is more,' says poor Lady Seymour. 'At every opportunity Tom has voiced loud criticisms of his brother's rule. He has even gone so far as to build up a following of his own, with a view to overthrowing the Protector. He offered bribes to many in an attempt to buy their support. He even kept a chart on his closet wall. I saw it there myself, and wondered what it was for. It made no sense to me. But it was a list of the names of the men he had cozened and those whom he had yet to approach. To keep such a thing so openly – it beggars belief!'

How foolish the Admiral has been. And how unthinking of the consequences of his rash and ill-considered actions.

'Then there is the marriage he planned with the Lady Elizabeth,' continues Lady Seymour, shaking her head. 'He boasted too openly about it. Now she herself, and her servants, are to be questioned.'

Mrs Ellen looks at me in alarm. I know her thoughts are with Mrs Ashley. And what of Elizabeth herself? Will her wit and her courage avail her now?

By all reports, the pile of incriminating depositions against the Admiral mounts daily, and I fear there can be little doubt of his malevolent intentions towards his brother, or that he is a danger to the realm. There is much talk of his impertinent plot to marry the Lady Elizabeth, and it is even known that he was scheming to marry me to the King; they say he meant to rule through us, as the power behind the throne, and I can well believe it, although I find the very idea shocking. I feel so used, as if I myself had never mattered to him, and I wish my name were not being bruited about so shamefully by the gossip-mongers, for I have done nothing to deserve it.

Lady Seymour plans to take me to Wulfhall, the family seat in Wiltshire, in order to escape the gossip and the scandal, but we are still at Seymour Place in London when my father's messenger arrives and seeks me out.

'My lady, the Marquess commands you to make ready with all haste and return with me to Bradgate. My lord has told me that, this very day, the Admiral was taken to the Tower of London. He says this is no place for you to be.'

He turns to Lady Seymour, who has dissolved into heart-rending sobs. Poor old soul, she had not known that her son had been sent to the Tower.

'I am truly sorry to bring you this news, Madam,' says the messenger. 'I wish I could give you further tidings, but I only know what my lord has told me. He is at court just now, but he wishes the Lady Jane to return to her mother in Leicestershire. I should be grateful if you could give orders for her gear to be packed ready for her departure.'

With a great effort, Lady Seymour recovers herself and summons Mrs Ellen, who hears the news with an obviously heavy heart. She must guess how sorowful I feel at the prospect of being returned to my mother's care, but there is no gain-saying my father – nothing that anybody can do. I cannot compromise my birth, my blood or my marriage prospects by remaining in the household of a suspected traitor, nor can I risk my family's honour being tainted by association with him.

My face set, I stumble blindly upstairs to my chamber, where the maids are already dragging out chests, garments, books and other possessions, the detritus of the two happiest years of my life. My belongings lie on the bed, looking pathetic and out of place. Dr Aylmer comes in to see what all the commotion is about, and when I lift my face to tell him, he sees my tragic expression, and spontaneously takes me into his arms and hugs me.

'Fear not, Jane,' he says. 'I will be with you, and we will have our theology, philosophy and literature as consolations.'

'I don't think I can bear it,' I whisper against the woollen hardness of his chest, feeling uncomfortable at this unaccustomed contact with a man, yet still appreciating his strength and warmth.

'God never sends us tests He thinks we cannot bear,' soothes Aylmer, 'and remember, we never come to the Kingdom of Heaven but by troubles. You must go home now, but another place is waiting for you. Think on this. In the meantime, you are a princess of the blood, and you must frame your mind towards marriage, accepting the path that God means you to follow. I doubt not that many others before you have railed against their fate, but that they made the best of what destiny brought them. And you must do likewise. Now, hadn't we better pack your books?'

Bradgate Hall, January 1549

'So you're back,' says my mother, eyeing me appraisingly. 'You haven't grown much in the time you've been away, although you've got a better colour, and you're beginning to fill out.' Her eyes fall on my budding breasts, just apparent beneath the smooth black velvet of my bodice. 'I see you're still wearing those sombre clothes,' she sniffs.

'It is out of respect for the late Queen,' I tell her.

'Christ, child, court mourning ended two months ago! You must change, put on something more becoming. Doubtless your insistence on going about garbed like a papist nun had some bearing on the Admiral's failure to arrange your marriage. The King took one look at you, I'll wager, and changed his mind.'

'Nay, my lady,' I answer defiantly, 'I fear the Admiral exerted less influence over his Majesty than he liked to think.'

'He was a fool,' says my mother with feeling.

'But I think he will pay dearly for it,' I reply. 'What will they do to him?'

'What they do to all traitors, I expect,' she answers grimly. 'He will lose his head.'

'Then I am sorry,' I falter, for truly I had grown rather fond of the Admiral, who was always kindly and funny and never uttered a harsh word to me. The prospect of him kneeling at the block, waiting for the blow to fall, is too horrible to contemplate, and I wince.

Suddenly my lady's hand is gripping my shoulder, shaking me.

'Don't waste your sympathy on the likes of him,' she hisses. 'He is best forgotten. Your father regrets ever having become involved with him, and has laid evidence against him before the council. Now you must put all this behind you, and frame yourself to obedience and virtue.'

I lower my eyes.

'Off to your room, child,' she says. 'I have things to do, and you will need to help Mrs Ellen unpack.'

She turns away to her writing table. She has not seen me for weeks, but she has already forgotten that I am here.

At night, I cry myself to sleep. It is not often that I give way to tears of self-pity, but it seems that my life stretches out before me as one long, unending tunnel of misery. Nothing has changed. I doubt my lady even missed me those two years I was away. I know it is my duty to love my mother, but at this moment I can feel only hatred for her, and it is a terrible feeling, for I know I must be displeasing God by my undutiful thoughts. So I lie awake, praying for help and understanding, and wishing beyond reason that I could be back at Chelsea in the tender care of the Queen. But, alas, those days are gone for ever, and I do not think I shall ever be as happy again.

Bradgate Hall, March 1549

News from London takes several days to reach us, but my father writes regularly from court, so we are kept abreast of events. He tells us that there is enough evidence to send the Admiral to the block, but that the council are staying their hand because they are deeply disturbed by reports of his relations with the Lady Elizabeth. I am shocked to learn that, although Elizabeth is being held in the comfort of her house at Hatfield, her servants, including Mrs Ashley, have been sent to the Tower for interrogation. Poor Mrs Ashley, she is not a strong character, I fear, and I tremble to think how she will fare.

My lord writes that Mrs Ashley has confessed to scandalous goings-on at Chelsea, such as might lead God-fearing persons to suspect that the Lady Elizabeth is no longer as pure as she should be. My mother asks me if I knew anything of this, but I say truthfully that I saw nothing, and keep my own counsel about my suspicions.

Now, even the Lady Elizabeth herself has been subjected to rigorous questioning, and she only fifteen years old. My father says she has given away nothing, nor said anything to incriminate herself and the Admiral. He writes that the council gave up in the end, realising that the little minx, as he puts it, is too clever for them. Yet she remains under a cloud of displeasure, and is to stay away from court and live in retirement. Before long I hear, to my great satisfaction, that she is ostentatiously attiring and conducting herself as a virtuous and sober Protestant maiden in an attempt to redeem her tarnished reputation.

But the Admiral does not get off so lightly.

My lady comes to my room one morning with a letter.

'You must prepare yourself for ill news, Jane,' she says. 'Parliament has passed an Act of Attainder against the Admiral, condemning him to lose his life and possessions, and three days ago his head was struck off on Tower Hill.'

I feel sick. Involuntarily my hands go to my throat, as I shudder to contemplate what it must be like to meet such a dreadful death. I remember the Admiral as I knew him, a big, vital man, full of life and vigour. Now he has been cut down, literally, in his prime. At night, I find my sleep is haunted by nightmares similar to those I suffered in my early childhood after learning of the fate of Katherine Howard.

By day, my prayers are all for poor little Lady Mary Seymour, the baby daughter of the Queen and the Admiral, who is now orphaned and penniless, as a result of her father's attainder. I hear she has been consigned to the care of my step-grandmother, the Duchess of Suffolk. I shall miss her sorely, the sweet child.

And now there is covert talk of another baby, a baby that the Lady Elizabeth is rumoured to have borne the Admiral in secret, and who was destroyed by agents of the council. I cannot believe that the Lady Elizabeth, who is so very clever in many ways, could have stooped to such immoral and stupid behaviour. Surely, in this case, the rumours are unfounded. I cannot credit them, and am consumed with pity for my cousin, whose life, like my own, has been so cruelly turned around. Even if she had been seduced by the Admiral, the fault was his alone, for she was little more than a child at the time, and he not a man to be gainsaid. It doesn't seem fair that she should suffer for another's wrongdoing, but then life is not fair. That is a hard lesson I have learned already.

John Dudley, Earl of Warwick

Ely Place, London, Autumn 1549

Looking in my mirror, I see a bull of a man with cold black eyes. Not a handsome face, but then vanity has never been one of my vices. I'm a soldier first and foremost, with a talent for strategy that has served me well both in the field and in the council chamber. There are those who call me ruthless and, looking at me, you might well believe it, but I prefer to see myself as a pragmatist, for whom the end justifies the means.

I am ready now, ready to meet my guests, and soon I am seated at the head of the table in the richly appointed dining hall in Ely Place, my palatial London residence, regarding the soberly dressed noblemen and bishops around me with a shrewd eye. I believe I can trust them all.

'So, gentlemen, we are of one accord,' I say. This is not the first of our discussions; we have met before, and I have spoken with each man privately, so I am sure I can be candid.

Every eye is upon me.

'We are agreed, then,' I declare. 'We want the Lord Protector replaced. His insufferable arrogance has alienated not only the King, but also many of his councillors.' Several are present, among them Archbishop Cranmer and the Earls of Arundel and Southampton, and I nod in their direction.

'Furthermore, he has pursued disastrous wars with Scotland and France. Far from covering England's name with glory, these wars have impoverished and humiliated her. And his callousness in sending his brother to the scaffold is viewed by many – and by you yourselves, as you have told me – as nothing less than foul fratricide.' I pause for effect. 'And as if this is not enough,' I thunder into the hush, 'Somerset has angered numerous lords who might have been his friends by opposing the sensible policy of enclosing agricultural land, and by allowing his offensively liberal views to prevail in all aspects of government. It is enough. Somerset must go!'

'Somerset must go!' echo several voices. 'Aye! Aye!'

I hold up my hand for silence.

'What England needs now,' I tell them, 'is a firm hand, wielded by someone who will stand up to the Lady Mary, who has continued obstinately to uphold the Catholic religion. She still insists on celebrating Mass in the face of repeated censures and threats by the government, which she ignores, knowing that, if things get too hot for her in England, she can always appeal to her cousin the Emperor for aid. This is not to be tolerated!'

'Nay! Nay!' The response is unanimous.

I stand up and lean forward, resting my hands on the table.

'We need a ruler who will steadfastly maintain and promote the Protestant religion. One who is sufficiently experienced in a military capacity to ensure that England's security, and her reputation in Europe, are protected from any Catholic threat.'

'Aye! Aye!'

They look questioningly at me.

'But who should that ruler be?' The speaker is my good colleague, the Marquess of Dorset. No great politician, but loyal and well versed in intrigue, and a useful ally to have, given that his wife has a claim to the throne, and that they have three marriageable daughters with rich and valuable Tudor blood in their veins.

'We must give that due consideration,' I reply, but in my view there is only one man in England who can do all these things, and that is myself.

'It should be yourself, my Lord Warwick,' Dorset declares,

and is enthusiastically and flatteringly echoed by a dozen voices.

'I see you are all of the same mind, gentlemen,' I say. 'I am gratified that I can count on your support.'

'We pledge it,' they assure me.

'I am grateful,' I tell them, sitting down. 'Now, our first task is to plan when and how the Lord Protector should be removed.'

Later, when the rest have gone, Dorset and I share a flask of hippocras before the dying fire.

'I know what people say about me,' I muse. 'That I am the son of a traitor. But I've never let the injustice of my father's execution prevent me from being loyal to the Crown. Fortunately, I've fared rather better than my father. And I got where I am today on the strength of my own abilities.'

'You've done very well,' acknowledges Dorset. 'Master of the Horse, Lord High Admiral, privy councillor. There's none more influential on the council.'

'I thank you, my lord. And I have been blessed in my wife and children. Of the thirteen she's borne me, seven yet live.'

'And five are handsome, strapping sons,' says Dorset, wistfully. It's well known that he has been disappointed in his expectations of a male heir. 'You are lucky, Sir, that God has so blessed you, and that your children have found favour with the King and his sisters. We all noticed how, when she was at court, the Lady Elizabeth and young Robert were inseparable.'

'Yes, God has been bountiful,' I agree. 'But this is no time to be complacent, Henry. I have my enemies too, and they are only too happy to go about smearing my reputation.'

'What man has not risen to power without making enemies?' he asks.

'I know my reputation for toughness is not entirely undeserved,' I tell him. 'I am aware that many of the men who are pleased to call themselves my friends are simply scared of crossing me.' I smile. 'Of course, at times it has been necessary to use a degree of, shall we say, intimidation when building up alliances, but I have taken care to temper this with bonhomie and open-handedness.'

'Any man who would rule must display a certain ruthlessness,' observes Dorset. 'Bonhomie on its own never won battles.'

'Never underestimate the power of calculated bullying and veiled threats!' I tell him. 'It's my conviction that, when it comes to politics, a tender conscience can be an inconvenience. Somerset has a conscience, an unfashionably liberal one, and look where it's got him. He's arrogant too, although that's no bad thing in a ruler, almost a necessity. I too can be arrogant, and to far deadlier effect, but when it comes to laying my quarry, I can pile on the charm at will. Unlike Somerset, I am not burdened with scruples. What has to be done has to be done. Let them call me greedy and ruthless, and accuse me of looking only to my own interests. Every man worth the name does the same, especially those of us who inhabit the court.'

'If something stands in your path, you must eliminate it, by fair means or foul,' says Dorset, looking me straight in the eye.

'Indeed,' I say, and smile grimly. We both know that I intend to be the supreme power in England. By God, no one is going to stop me, and Dorset means to back the winner. He knows I have the young King in my hand, thanks to a policy of calculated friendliness and deference, and that with his confidence in my pocket, I am unassailable. Let none dare offend me, for they will find me a dangerous adversary.

We are prepared to use force, but, when it comes to it, Somerset puts up only a weak show of resistance. He knows he is no match for me.

Now he is a prisoner in the Tower, and I am Lord President of the Council and the effective ruler of England.

Lady Jane Grey

Bradgate Hall, January 1550

Outside the window the landscape is white, hidden under a blanket of snow. There is a horseman, swathed in furs, riding through Bradgate's main gate into the courtyard. I watch as the steward hurries out, clicking fingers at stable boys and greeting the unexpected guest.

It is Master Roger Ascham.

I knew he was expected. Dr Aylmer, in a state of joyful anticipation, told me a week ago that he would be coming.

'Sadly, Jane, it is not in the happiest of circumstances,' he confided. 'Master Ascham wrote to me that he was weary of the Lady Elizabeth's service, the backbiting and intrigues in her household, and the resentment of her treasurer, Parry, who went behind his back to poison the Lady Elizabeth's mind against him. It is as well, he says, that her formal studies had come to an end on her sixteenth birthday, since, if he had not been quick to resign, he would certainly have been ignominiously dismissed. For the Lady Elizabeth believed all Parry's lies.'

'That is a shame,' I said. 'I thought her to be intelligent and astute. Yet once her opinions are set, there is no moving her. '

'Poor Master Ascham returned to Cambridge,' Aylmer continued. 'His intention was to resume his studies. But almost immediately – such is his fame – he received a letter offering him a post as secretary to England's ambassador in Brussels. He was delighted to be afforded such an opportunity and accepted at once, thinking it would alleviate the sadness caused by the Lady Elizabeth's betrayal. But listen to this! When I told your parents of his imminent departure abroad, they invited him to visit us here beforehand, to enliven us all with his wit and learning.'

'And was that at your prompting, Sir?' I asked mischievously.

'Oh, yes; they'd never have thought of it themselves,' he replied, his eyes twinkling with merriment.

And so Master Ascham has arrived at Bradgate, and there is no one to receive him, for they are all out hunting. All except me. I stayed behind, reading by the fire.

'Master Ascham,' I smile, stretching out my hands in welcome. 'It is a pleasure to see you again. Do come into the parlour – it's warm in here.' I lead the way, calling for refreshments as I pass the bowing steward, and while we are waiting to be served we exchange courteous pleasantries. All the time, however, I can sense that Master Ascham is regarding me speculatively.

'Did you not wish to go hunting with your mother and father?' he asks, once we are alone. I pour some wine, thinking how gentle his tone is, how inviting of confidences. It would be easy to unburden myself to him.

I pull a face. 'I loathe hunting. No, I was happily absorbed in a book and wanted to finish it. Have you read it?' I pass him the leather-bound volume of Plato's *Phaedo*. He looks at it in astonishment.

'You prefer this to a jaunt in the park?' he asks.

'Infinitely,' I reply with feeling. 'Their sport is but a shadow to the pleasure I find in Plato. Poor souls, it seems to me that they do not know what pleasure means.'

Ascham is grinning at me.

'And how, Madam, did you come to this true knowledge of pleasure at such a tender age?'

'You are mocking me, Sir,' I blush.

'My apologies, my lady,' he says, bowing. 'I am not joking. Tell me, what chiefly drew you to it, this knowledge of what pleasure is, seeing that few women and not many more men have arrived at it?'

'I will tell you a truth, which perhaps you will marvel at,' I say. 'One of the greatest benefits God ever gave me is that He sent me – who has such sharp, severe parents – so gentle a schoolmaster as Dr Aylmer. If it were not for him, I think I should go mad.'

I break off, biting my lip. What am I saying, to this man who is merely an acquaintance? What will he think of me for speaking so disloyally of my father and mother, or being so forgetful of the consideration due to a guest?

'I do apologise, Sir,' I say humbly. 'I fear I have said too much. This is no kind of talk for a social occasion, as my lady mother would no doubt remind me.'

Dr Ascham leans forward and lifts my chin. His eyes are so kind.

'You can talk to me, my Lady Jane,' he says gently. 'I will respect your confidence. Sometimes, if our minds are disturbed or troubled, it helps to unburden ourselves.'

I hope my gratitude is evident in my face. I have needed to unburden myself for so long. I take a deep breath.

'You will think me undutiful, I am sure, but I cannot help myself.' My words are tumbling out now, in an impassioned torrent. 'You see, Master Ascham, when I am in the presence of either my father or my mother, whatever I do – whether I speak, keep silence, sit, stand or go, eat, drink, be merry or sad, be sewing, playing, dancing or doing anything else – I must do it, as it were, as perfectly as God made the world; or else I am so sharply taunted, so cruelly threatened, yes, sometimes with nips, pinches, slaps and other ways, which' – I can feel myself blushing – 'I will not name for the honour I bear them.' I shiver. He is watching me closely. He must guess how deeply I have been humiliated.

'I am so unhappy,' I continue, with increasing vehemence, 'that I think myself in Hell; that is, until the time comes when I may go to Dr Aylmer, who teaches me so gently and so pleasantly, and makes learning so enjoyable, that I think of nothing else whilst I am with him. But when I am called from him, I start weeping, because whatever else I do seems to land me in great trouble. That, Sir, is why my book gives me so much pleasure. Compared to it, all other pleasures are but trifles and troubles to me.'

I bend my head so that he shall not see the tears in my eyes, but they have not escaped his notice, for he covers my hand with his.

'I am so sorry,' he says. 'I would I could do something to help you. Yet under the law, parents are entitled to discipline their children as they think fit, and there are those who would not account yours unduly harsh.'

There is an uncomfortable silence. Sympathy is not enough, but there is nothing he can do, and we both know it. So he clears his throat and changes the subject.

'You are indeed fortunate in your tutor, my lady. It has always been my opinion that learning should be made easy and agreeable, and that unkind punishments should form no part of it. I believe it is the tutor's role to encourage, not to force, although I know there are many who disagree with me. Go to any grammar school, and you will see the boys beaten until they know their lessons. '

'Well, Sir, you have the right of it,' I tell him. 'Learning should be an adventure.' I have now recovered my composure.

'Would you do me the honour of showing me some of your work?' Dr Ascham asks. Delighted at his interest, I fetch a pile of papers and books, and lay before him some of my translations from the Greek.

'These are your own work?' he asks admiringly. 'They are excellent.' Then he asks me several questions in Greek, to which I make answer. 'Madam, you are faultless!' he exclaims.

An hour passes in such stimulating exchanges, until the sounds of the returning hunting party can be clearly heard beyond the latticed windows.

'My Lady Jane, would you do me the honour of corresponding with me?' Master Ascham asks, rising. 'I should gain infinite pleasure from exchanging letters with so brilliant a princess.'

'The honour will be mine,' I reply, deeply touched and flattered. To have this great scholar speak to me in such a way, with gentleness and understanding, warms my heart. 'How shall I write to you? In English, Latin or Greek?'

'All three!' he grins. 'But I shall discuss that with Dr Aylmer. How I am looking forward to your letters. I have scholarly and learned friends abroad who will be amazed to learn of your achievements. You are an example to your sex. Now, I believe your parents have returned. I shall impress upon them how well you have entertained me. Perhaps that will win you a small reprieve from their unkindness.'

I smile, happier than I have been for a long time.

Bradgate Hall, Spring and Summer 1550

Master Ascham has been as good as his word. With the approval of my parents, and the aid of Dr Aylmer and Dr Harding, who has been promoted to household chaplain, he has instituted a correspondence through which I have had the great honour of becoming acquainted with some of the finest minds of our age. Letters now pass between Bradgate, Brussels and Switzerland, where religious reformers such as the celebrated Henry Bullinger profess themselves honoured to write to a mere girl. They flatter me with descriptions that make me blush, calling me a shining luminary and an ornament of the Protestant religion! I tell myself that this is mere literary conceit, but secretly I am basking in it. Yet on another level, the praise they give me only makes me resolve to try harder and be a better Christian, and a truer Protestant. I cannot possibly be worthy of all this praise, but I can try my best to merit it.

They send me treatises to read, which we discuss afterwards in our letters, and I have asked for help with learning Hebrew, because I want to read the Old Testament in its original texts. In all my dealings with these worthy men, I strive to remain modest and self-effacing, always thanking God for my erudition; and as I acknowledge faith to be God's gift, so I acknowledge my little learning.

As the months pass, I grow in confidence and understanding. Aylmer says he has noticed the change in me. He says I have benefited greatly from my discourse with these learned men. At his prompting – and no doubt with an eye to my future – he asks Henry Bullinger to send me a copy of his famous treatise on matrimony, so that I can translate it from Latin to Greek. Dr Aylmer peers over my shoulder as I am writing.

'Jane, I do not think that among all the English nobility for years past there has been a single person as devoted to learning as yourself. Not only are your translations excellent, but your music and needlework are in every respect as good as your scholarship. If you were to marry the King, as your friends hope, you would make a truly noble, Christian queen.'

'I am not such a paragon as you think, Dr Aylmer,' I protest. 'No one can be as perfect as that.'

'Ah, Jane,' he smiles, 'if you have a fault, it is that you are too dogmatic in your opinions. Perhaps you should make allowance sometimes for the frailties of others, or accept that people might not always agree with you.'

'I cannot do other than my faith tells me to do,' I say, startled by his criticism.

'Then you must keep it in mind that not every tenet of faith is set in stone,' he replies. 'You are young, child, and the young are often dogmatic. Wisdom and moderation are said to come with age, but looking at the world today, I have my doubts about that. Just remember what I have said, and learn to temper zeal with charity.'

'I am sorry for my faults. I will try to improve,' I say. 'I do not wish to displease you or anyone, but my life is not easy. In fact, I feel I am leading two lives. In one, I am the learned correspondent of great men, who praise me beyond my merits. In the other, I am the ill-tempered, despised daughter of parents with unrealistic expectations, whose cruelty is at times unbearable.' I cannot help my tears. 'I am in an earthly prison, and in this earthly prison I pass my days as if I were dead, whereas you, Dr Aylmer – you are alive, not in captivity.'

Aylmer's face is taut with compassion.

'I have been unfair,' he says, shaking his head. 'You have enough burdens without my adding to them. Let us hope that you will soon make a glorious marriage. Then, I make no doubt, your life will be much happier.'

'God, let it be so,' I pray.

Oxford, Autumn 1550

I rise from my curtsey to the King, who nods solemnly at me. He has grown taller, more angular and, if anything, more majestic in his manner. Behind him stands the Earl of Warwick, beaming jovially.

'Welcome to Oxford, cousin,' says the King in his high-pitched voice, which shows no signs of breaking yet, although he, like me, is now thirteen. I step backwards to join my parents and sister. This is Katherine's first visit to court, and my mother's hawk-like gaze is upon her as she in turn makes her obeisance. My youngest sister Mary who is only five years old, has been left at home with her nurse. I doubt my parents will ever permit her to attend the court.

The King addresses my father. 'I trust you had a good journey, my lord.'

'We made good time, your Majesty, I thank you. I trust your Majesty is enjoying his progress.'

'Well enough, my lord,' replies the King. 'We have been most loyally received everywhere, and it is gratifying to find that our subjects are in general obedient to our laws governing religion.'

'His Majesty is looking forward to the jousts tomorrow,' puts in Warwick.

'I would prefer to be taking part rather than just watching

them,' complains Edward, suddenly an adolescent boy rather than a king.

'Now, your Majesty knows that that would be unwise. Were any accident to befall you, which God forbid, there would be nothing to prevent the Lady Mary from succeeding to the throne and restoring the popish faith.'

Edward frowns, once more the King.

'I dare say you speak truth,' he sighs. 'I would I could reform my sister's opinions. She is the most obstinate lady.'

He turns again to my parents.

'We hope very much that you will join us for the sport tomorrow.'

'With pleasure, your Majesty,' replies my father, recognising dismissal and retreating backwards, bowing low, towards the door, with us following in his wake.

The next morning, my mother comes to my chamber in a flurry of excitement.

'Jane! The King wishes you to sit beside him in the gallery overlooking the tiltyard while he watches the sport. This is wonderful news! Now, you must look your best; none of this dowdy black and white! Mrs Ellen, the gold damask, if you please, and she can wear it with the ruby pendant that Queen Katherine gave her.'

I stand patiently as Mrs Ellen fetches the gown and begins to dress me, but eventually I dare to protest. 'Madam, the King prefers ladies to be soberly attired. Would it not please him more if I were to dress modestly?'

'Pshaw! You cannot appear at court garbed as a nun. We've been through all this before, and I don't want to hear it again. I've had a good deal more experience of the court than you, and I know how a lady is expected to appear. Now stand still and let Mrs Ellen lace up that bodice.'

I dare not gainsay her further.

The knights in their polished armour and plumed helms thunder at full speed towards each other, lances couched. As they clash across the wooden palisade, the watching crowd cheers itself hoarse. My fingers tensely grip the window-ledge of the gallery, where I am sitting with his Majesty and a small group of favoured courtiers.

'He's down! Sir Robert's down!' cries the King, as one rider crashes to the ground.

I lean further forward. 'I hope he is not hurt, Sir,' I breathe.

'I don't think so,' he replies. Fortunately, the unhorsed knight is getting to his feet. He waves to the spectators and earns himself a round of applause. Meanwhile, the victor of the joust, Sir James Knollys, is approaching the gallery on his steed and doffing his helm with a flourish.

'Yours be the honour, my Lady Jane,' says the King, handing me a golden arrow to present to the knight.

I rise, blushing.

'For your valour, Sir,' I say, handing the trophy to Sir James, who takes my outstretched hand, kisses it and bows in courtly fashion.

'My thanks, fair lady,' he cries. 'I am honoured indeed!'

I sit down, abashed by such public attention, as he rides away.

The Marshal of the Joust is already consulting the names and shields on the Tree of Chivalry at the far end of the lists to see who will next enter the contest. Beside me, King Edward is fidgeting in his chair.

'I would it was me out there,' he says. 'My father was a great champion of the lists – they would not have gainsaid him. But I – I am forever condemned, it seems, to be a spectator.'

'That is a shame, Sir,' I venture. 'Could you not insist on taking part? You are the King, and must be obeyed.'

'Ah, Jane, how little you know.' He sighs. 'They won't let me joust in case I get killed. Then the Lady Mary would be Queen, and imagine what that would mean.'

He looks glum. It's proving to be an uncomfortable afternoon, in more ways than one. My leather corset is tight and restrictive; it has not yet moulded itself to my developing figure, and I sit rigid and stiff-backed on my stool beside the King's cushioned chair, wishing I could breathe properly. Next to me, his Majesty sits morosely watching the joust and no longer seems to notice that I am here, or the presence of Lady Mary Dudley on his other side. If he does speak at all, it is only to comment on technical points to the young gentleman who stands behind us. Once or twice I catch the twinkling, admiring glance of this fair-haired Irishman, Barnaby FitzPatrick, whose blue eyes keep appraising me appreciatively behind his master's back. I smile at him uncertainly, unsure whether it is proper to return a young man's look. To be on the safe side, I try to keep my eyes on the tournament. I am all too aware of my mother, seated not very far off, watching me with an eagle eye.

When the interval comes and refreshments are brought in on gold platters, the King turns to me.

'I recognise that pendant,' he says. 'It was my stepmother's. Master John painted her wearing it. She was a good woman. I miss her.'

'I, too, your Majesty,' I say wistfully.

'Her husband, however, was a foolish and dangerous man,' Edward goes on, his voice colder now. 'He was a traitorous schemer. He killed my dog.' (I cannot be sure which he regards as the worse crime.) 'Do you know he was plotting to have us betrothed?'

'I – I had heard something of the sort, Sir,' I say warily.

The King looks at me uncertainly.

'Several people consider it a good idea,' he declares, in a lower voice. 'I mean, that you and I should marry. My tutors have spoken well of it, and tell me it is the dearest hope of many of our reformed faith. They offer numerous good reasons for such a match, and perhaps they are right. What do you think, my Lady Jane?'

Astonished that he should broach such a subject, I am struck dumb until I realise that the hopes of many people depend upon my answer.

'I – your Majesty,' I say earnestly, 'I will do whatever you and my parents wish. I have been told that I will one day make a very good marriage, but I never thought to look so high. Sir, I am your good servant, and I know my duty.'

'We all know our duty, cousin,' Edward says severely, 'but what of our personal inclinations?'

'Your Majesty does me too much honour. I scarce know what to say –' I break off, unsure of what he wants me to reply.

'What I mean,' says the King, coming to my rescue, 'is, would it please you to marry me and become Queen of England?'

'Your Majesty need not ask,' I answer, feeling my cheeks grow hot. 'It is the greatest honour any lady could wish for, and more than my desire.'

There is an uncomfortable pause. Have I said too much? My mother is watching us intently from her place nearby. I can tell she is desperate to know what we are saying.

Edward sighs. 'Unfortunately, I cannot ask it of you. For state reasons, I am betrothed to the Princess Elisabeth of France, and my councillors are of the opinion that those state reasons override all other considerations. But I wish you to know that, were I just Edward and you just Jane, I would prefer to marry you. We accord well together, and have similar views. The Princess is a Catholic, and I will have to change her opinions. God send she does not prove stubborn. Kings,' he adds sadly, 'cannot make their own choices. I wished you to know that.'

'I understand, Sir,' I say. I am startled – is this an end to all my parents' grand schemes? – and strangely relieved. I have a feeling that marriage to this cold, haughty, insensitive youth would be no easy life. And I have no wish to be Queen of England, although I would have embraced it if God had shown me that my duty lay that way.

'Oh, one thing more,' says the King, wiping cake crumbs from his mouth and reaching for his goblet. 'This conversation is to remain privy to ourselves only.'

'Of course, Sir.' The last thing I would do is tell my parents. I am quite happy to let them go on thinking that my marriage to the King is a possibility. At least that will deter them from looking about elsewhere for a husband, which in turn will buy me precious time before I submit to the bonds of wedlock.

Tilty, Essex, Autumn 1550

The masque goes on interminably. Although the Earl of Oxford's players are among the best to be found and provide a lavish spectacle with wonderful costumes and scenery, I cannot enjoy it. A throbbing headache torments me and although I often suffer thus with my monthly courses, they are not the cause of it this time. A weariness and lassitude portend that I am, as Mrs Ellen would say, 'coming down with something'.

Trying not to betray my discomfort, and fighting my urgent need to sleep, I look surreptitiously along the high table to see if any other guests are showing signs of boredom. Our hosts, Lord and Lady Willoughby, great landowners in this part of Essex, are sitting there with bright smiles on their faces, nodding appreciatively in time with the music. After leaving Oxford, my parents took us to stay at the houses of several noble acquaintances, before settling in for two months as guests of their friends, the Willoughbys. In a couple of days we will be returning home, much, I suspect, to our hosts' secret relief, and this splendid banquet and entertainment have been arranged to mark the end of our stay.

Between Lord and Lady Willoughby sits the Lady Mary, who has ridden over from her house at Newhall to grace the proceedings as guest of honour. She too seems to be enjoying herself, but it is hard to tell if she is happy. The Lady Mary is thirty-four, and looks much older. There are lines of disappointment and sorrow on her face, a few grey streaks in her red hair, and she is as thin as ever. Everyone knows that life has not been easy for her, especially during the last few years; she has fought a bitter, ongoing battle for her Mass, and although she is misguided in her beliefs, she must have suffered greatly through it. I have heard it whispered that, earlier this year, she was on the point of escaping from England to seek shelter with her cousin the Emperor, but was deterred at the last minute by friends who warned her that, should the King die without heirs, her chances of succeeding to the throne would be severely jeopardised if she were not in England. So here she is, still defying her brother and the council.

Although she knows that my family is of the reformed faith, the Lady Mary greeted us warmly enough today. She might deplore our conversion as much as we do her obstinacy and error, but her sense of kinship is plainly strong, and when she raised my mother, her cousin, from her curtsey, she kissed her affectionately. 'How do you, my Lady Dorset? Well enough, I hope. And this is your daughter, Lady Katherine, is it not? She is a fair maid, I declare, favoured with beauty. May the blessed saints guide her, for earthly comeliness can lead to earthly temptations. And this of course is Lady Jane.'

Although she kissed me on both cheeks, and has shown great courtesy to me since, I sense a certain chill from her. Perhaps she is aware of how much I deplore her for adhering to the Roman faith and insisting on clinging to the old, discredited ways, when we have all been shown a new and truer way to God. I watch her as she sits there, absorbed in the masque, a spare, stiff-backed little woman who is dressed gaudily and extravagantly, as I would expect a Catholic to be. She is too openly emotional, too quick to burst into laughter at the antics of the players. And too ready to burst into tears, or so my mother says. I have seen for myself how she dwells far too much upon the past, forever making embarrassing references to her 'sainted mother', or brooding on remembered hurts. She peppers her conversation with allusions to her faith – to 'Our Lady' or 'the blessed saints' – as though she is unaware of the King's wishes or the demands of the law. It seems to me she goes out of her way to provoke those of us who have embraced the true religion.

At last the interminable evening ends, and we make our way back to our lodgings.

'The Lady Mary has invited us to visit her at Newhall when we leave here the day after tomorrow,' my mother announces, as we cross the courtyard. I stifle a groan.

The next morning, I awake with a high fever and know little of what is happening until three days later, when I am myself again, although much weakened. Mrs Ellen has been tending me, and is obviously pleased to see me making a recovery.

On the fourth day, I am better still, although as yet unfit for travel.

My lady mother looms beside the bed.

'I am glad to see you improved, Jane,' she says. 'I think you should get up for a bit. We have delayed our departure for Newhall because of your illness, and cannot keep the Lady Mary waiting any longer. I'd like to see you ready to travel in the morning.'

'But Madam,' protests Mrs Ellen, 'the Lady Jane is still quite weak. It will be two days at least before she can travel.'

My lady looks at me with narrowed eyes.

'She looks healthy enough to me,' she says. 'I don't believe in mollycoddling children. Now, Jane, get up, have something to eat and prepare yourself for the journey tomorrow. We really must move on.'

After she has gone I slide slowly out of bed and stand up. My head is spinning and Mrs Ellen has to hold me steady to stop me from falling. I sink into a chair by the fire, and she hastens to put a shawl round my shoulders, then brings me some warming pottage. As I spoon it up, she sits watching me.

'You don't want to go to Newhall, do you, Jane?' she asks perceptively.

'No,' I say. 'It is a Catholic house. And I don't think the Lady Mary likes me very much.'

'I understand that,' she answers. 'But Jane – you wouldn't pretend to be ill just to avoid going there, would you?'

'No, I would not,' I say truthfully. 'I am indeed feeling poorly. But I also know my duty to my parents.'

'I never doubted it,' she says, smiling. 'Yet I could tell your lady mother had her suspicions. Now, eat that up – it'll do you good.'

I am still weak and light-headed when we climb into our coach in the morning, having taken our leave of Lord and Lady Willoughby. And as the unsprung vehicle trundles off on the dirt-track that passes for a road, bound for Newhall, I sit there fighting the rising nausea and longing for my bed.

Newhall, Essex, Autumn 1550

Newhall is impressive! It's a vast perpendicular palace with a five-hundred-foot-long façade, beautiful oriel windows and spacious courtyards. My great-uncle Henry VIII owned it, and improved it, so my father says, at enormous cost. It was he who set up the colourful royal arms above the entrance door and, thanks to his bounty, the palace boasts luxurious royal apartments, a fine long gallery and a tennis court.

I cannot but marvel at the splendour in which the Lady Mary lives, although I know that she is the heiress presumptive to the throne and a great magnate in her own right. Yet I am shocked at the all-too-obvious reminders of her popish beliefs that taint the beauty of the house. There are even statues of saints in the chapel, which must offend any good Protestant, never mind flout the law. I am relieved therefore when my parents decline, politely but firmly, to attend Mass, because it means that I must follow their example. Nevertheless, I take care not to offend my good hostess, and plead illness as an excuse.

'She breaks the law with impunity,' my mother observes to my father. Almost the entire household is in the chapel for Compline, and we are at leisure in the privy chamber. Katherine and Mary have gone to bed, but I have been allowed to stay up for a little.

'I don't know why the council let her get away with it,' my lord replies, draining his goblet.

'The King has to be careful,' my lady points out. 'He knows he risks the wrath of the Emperor if he takes any proceedings against his sister.'

'He has put a great deal of pressure on her,' my father observes.

'It is not enough. She is his subject, like the rest of us. That she should have her Mass is intolerable.'

'I fear for the Lady Mary,' I say.

'You do right to fear for her,' says my father with feeling. 'She is courting the gravest danger.'

'I didn't mean that,' I tell him. 'I fear for her soul. She is in peril, and she doesn't seem to realise it. And she is imperilling the souls of all the folk in her household. I wish she could come to an understanding of the truth.'

'She was ever obstinate, like her mother,' my lady retorts.

'Someone should point out the error of her ways,' I persist.

'Many have tried,' my father says drily. 'Even threats haven't moved her. Let her go to perdition, I say. It'll be her own fault.'

I am shocked at his flippancy.

'In charity, someone must show her the way,' I insist.

'Are you suggesting that you yourself could succeed where others have failed?' my mother asks, grimly amused.

'If it were to save her soul, yes, I could try.'

'You? A girl of thirteen, to preach doctrines to a princess of thirty-four, no less? The very idea. As if she would listen to you. She would see it as gross presumption.'

'You just keep out of it, Jane,' my father instructs. 'You mean well, but there may come a day when we need the Lady Mary's favour, so it would not do to prejudice her against us now.'

'Very well, Sir,' I say, but inwardly my heart burns with zeal to bring the Lady Mary to the light.

The next day, I am following Lady Anne Wharton, one of Mary's ladies, through the empty chapel on my way to the royal lodgings, which lie beyond it. I am startled as Lady Anne stops and curtseys to the altar, on which is set what Catholics call the Blessed Host: the bread and the wine used in the Mass.

'Why do you curtsey?' I ask her. 'Is the Lady Mary in the chapel?' I look about me, fearing that I have neglected to show the proper courtesy to the Princess.

Lady Anne frowns.

'No, Madam,' she replies. 'She is not here. I make my curtsey to Him that made us all.'

I cannot help feeling shocked at such blatant papistry, and at the dangerous ignorance of this poor woman.

'Why?' I ask. 'How can He be there that made us all, when it was only the baker who made Him?'

It is Lady Anne's turn to be shocked.

'My Lady Jane! That is blasphemy, to so denigrate the Sacred Host. Have you no respect?'

'I meant no offence, my lady,' I protest. 'But I am of the belief that no miracle occurs in the Mass. The bread and wine remain just that, and only when the priest blesses them do they become symbolic of Our Lord's sacrifice.'

'May God have mercy on you for your heresy!' she cries, and hurries me out of the chapel, as if I should contaminate it simply by being there.

The Lady Mary is not in her apartments. Later, I meet her in the gardens, walking her dogs; she is wrapped in a fur-lined velvet cloak against the cold wind. Her ladies trail behind her.

'My Lady Jane,' she says, extending her hand. Her manner is decidedly cooler than when we last met. As I make my obeisance, I realise that Lady Anne has probably told her what I said in the chapel. 'I trust you are quite recovered now,' the Lady Mary continues. Her voice is frosty.

'I am quite well, your Grace. I hope to resume my lessons soon.'

'You are well taught, child,' she observes. 'But too well taught for your own good, and those who have had the rearing of you have much to answer for. Remember, a little knowledge is an unwise thing. And a little humility never goes amiss.'

I would like to speak out, but I dare not. My father's injunction has stayed with me. So I bow my head meekly.

'I am your Grace's most humble cousin,' I say.

But the damage is done, and the rest of our visit passes in a rather strained atmosphere. Yes, I was unpardonably rude: even though I had the right of the matter, I should have held my tongue. I don't know what demon gets into me these days. I was never so hot with my passions and my opinions when I was younger, but now I feel so strongly about things, and surprise even myself! Mrs Ellen says it is something to do with my age, and that I must learn to temper my strong views and curb my tongue.

'Remember, there are two sides to every argument,' she tells me.

'But when it comes to faith, there can only be one,' I insist. 'There is only one way to God, of that I am convinced.'

Bradgate Hall, August 1551

The plague known as the sweating sickness has returned, as it does most summers. People are dying in the stinking streets of London, and the wealthier subjects of the King have fled to their country houses to escape the contagion. We are therefore at Bradgate, where my parents occupy themselves through the long summer days with hunting and entertaining. One of their guests is my lady's young stepmother, Katherine Willoughby, Duchess of Suffolk. She arrives swathed in mourning, bringing news of great import.

Some years before I was born, on the day Anne Boleyn gave birth to the Lady Elizabeth, my grandfather, Charles Brandon, Duke of Suffolk, married this Katherine Willoughby. She was then a great beauty, half-Spanish — her mother had been one of Katherine of Aragon's ladies-in-waiting — and only fourteen years old. My grandfather was then forty-eight, but he was besotted with her. The new Duchess later became one of Katherine Parr's ladies, which was how I got to know her well, and also a staunch Protestant. Before my grandfather died, she bore him two sons, Henry and Charles, my step-uncles.

Now the Duchess is at Bradgate, in great grief. Her two little boys, successive but fleeting Dukes of Suffolk, have both died of the sweating sickness. She weeps in my mother's arms in the parlour. She cannot find the words to tell of her tragedy.

'They succumbed within days of each other,' she sobs at length.

My parents' eyes meet over her shaking shoulders. This news, terrible though it is, is of great significance to them, for my mother is now her father's only remaining heir and, as such, inherits his title and wealth. As her husband, my father may hold that title in her right – which means that they are now Duke and Duchess of Suffolk, raised to the highest echelon of the peerage.

As soon as poor Lady Suffolk has retired for the night, my lord calls for wine to toast his advancement.

'Who would have believed it?' says my lady delightedly. 'Not that I do not mourn my little brothers. But God moves in mysterious ways, and always for a purpose.'

My father pours the wine and hands round the goblets. Even Katherine gets one.

'To their Graces the Duke and Duchess of Suffolk!' he cries.

We drink the toast.

'You know what this will mean for us all?' my lady says to Katherine and me.

'Will you have to wear coronets?' Katherine asks.

'Yes, but only on state occasions,' my father smiles.

'Dukes and duchesses take precedence over all other ranks of the nobility at court,' my lady explains. 'We will enjoy many privileges there. We will be entitled to lodge in one of the most comfortable apartments, to have more servants attend on us, and to keep more horses in the King's stables.'

'And I believe we'll also get a bigger daily ration of bread, ale, firewood and coal,' chimes in my lord, grinning broadly.

'Most important of all,' continues my lady, ignoring him, 'is the likelihood of our enjoying greater influence with the King and with his Grace of Northumberland. And for that reason, husband, I think we should take ourselves to court without delay. I hear his Majesty has removed to Richmond.'

'We should leave at once,' he agrees. 'First thing in the morning. Have our chests packed now.'

'What of Lady Suffolk?' I ask.

'Oh, dear, I had forgotten . . .' says my mother. 'Not to worry. She can stay here as long as she likes. You can look after her, Jane.'

They have been back at court a week, and I am wilting under the strain of having to console poor Lady Suffolk, when the messenger arrives.

'Our lady mother is ill,' I tell Katherine, after reading my father's letter. 'They thought it was the sweating sickness at first, and it was feared that she would succumb within hours.'

'Poor Mother!' cries Katherine, concerned.

'Fortunately not. It's just a low fever. But I am summoned to Richmond to help tend her and cheer her convalescence.'

'You might see the King,' Katherine says, her eyes shining with excitement.

'I might,' I agree.

'Can't I come?' she asks wistfully.

'No, sweeting, I'm sorry. My lord writes that you must play the hostess in my absence.'

She looks crestfallen.

'And you must look after Mary too. We can't leave her all on her own.'

I embrace my sister.

'If I could stay here, I would. I have no taste for court life. But I am commanded and must go. I have no choice.'

'I would I could change places with you,' Katherine says.

'So do I!' I say fervently.

Frances Brandon, Duchess of Suffolk

Richmond Palace, Surrey, October 1551

It is October, and I am perfectly recovered, ready to enjoy my new status as Duchess of Suffolk. With the arrival of colder weather, the sweating sickness has abated and the councillors and other nobles have returned to court. At last Henry and I begin to enjoy the privileges of our ducal rank and can revel in the deference shown us, and in our new prominence at court feasts and state occasions. We are closer to the King than ever.

Others, also, are enjoying the benefits of advancement within the peerage; the Earl of Warwick, plainly determined to consolidate his power by rewarding his supporters, has had the King make several new creations. William Herbert, that was Queen Katherine's brother-in-law, is Earl of Pembroke; William Paulet is Marquess of Winchester; and Warwick himself is made Duke of Northumberland to ensure his seniority above his colleagues. Others have received knighthoods.

Henry says that the Duke of Somerset, the former Lord Protector, who was released from the Tower some time ago to serve his King once more (albeit in a humbler capacity, and provided he cooperates with the new regime), sees in this distribution of honours a move by Northumberland against himself, since his has been of late a lone voice of protest against John Dudley's rule.

Northumberland is too quick and deadly for Somerset. He accuses him in council of treason, and consigns him again to the Tower. Few emerge from that place once, after being tainted by treason, let alone twice.

The mood at court is subdued, as the council busies itself in assembling a case against the fallen Duke. It is lightened somewhat in November by the news that Marie of Guise, the Queen Regent of Scotland, is to grace the English court with her presence on her way back from France, where she has been visiting her daughter, the young Queen of Scots. Great preparations are being made for the Queen Regent's reception, and entertainments are being planned. Accordingly, we order ourselves sumptuous new clothes.

John Dudley, Duke of Northumberland

Richmond Palace, Autumn 1551

'Your Majesty,' I urge the King, 'we should invite the Lady Mary.'

'Whatever for?' asks Edward, coldly. 'We are most displeased with her.'

'Ah, but your Majesty could take advantage of her presence at court to have her questioned once more as to her obstinacy over the Mass and her dealings with the Emperor.'

He thinks about this.

'True,' he nods. 'It might be politic. In fact, my lord, I shall speak to her myself.'

'Excellent,' I beam. The Lady Mary is a threat to my own position, and I want her eliminated as soon as possible. I know she hates me, for I have hounded her over this matter of the Mass. And if Edward were to die childless, the Lady Mary will be Queen and her revenge swift. The sooner the boy is married and the father of a son, the better.

The smile still on my lips, I bend confidentially towards the King.

'I have this day sent to France for a portrait of the Princess Elisabeth.' I have, in truth, done no such thing, but will soon remedy that. 'I hear it reported that her beauty increases each day. Let us see if rumour speaks truth.'

'I am looking forward to seeing her likeness,' says the King. Then, lowering his voice, 'Tell me, is she . . . er, does she have a comely bosom?' He reddens. I laugh, and just stop myself in time from clapping my sovereign on the back.

'Indeed!' I roar. 'I see your Majesty is more than ready for the marriage bed. We shall have to hurry these negotiations along.'

'Nay, my lord, not so fast,' protests Edward. 'There is the matter of her religion still to be resolved.'

'All in hand, Sir,' I assure him. 'I believe she is willing to convert.'

'I shall want it in writing,' declares my young master. 'Then we shall think on carnal matters.'

The Lady Mary

Hunsdon House, Hertfordshire, October–November 1551

I look at the King's summons with dismay.

'I can guess what lies behind this.' My voice sounds gruff, as it does whenever I am moved to emotion. 'It is a trap in which to ensnare me. They mean to interrogate me again. Well, I will not go, much as I would like to meet the Queen Regent of Scotland.'

Susan Clarencieux, the dearest and closest of my ladies-in-waiting, frowns.

'But, Madam, this is from the King himself. It is a command.'

'The King is a child, in the hands of the Duke of Northumberland.'

I sit down at my desk and write a note excusing myself on the grounds of ill-health, which I lead my brother to believe is worse than usual. Everyone knows I am not a well woman. Next, I write another, more private missive, addressed to the Emperor's ambassador, one of my most loyal friends. In it, I explain the real reason for my not attending the court.

'There is another letter here, Madam,' says Clarencieux, passing me a sealed scroll. I unravel it and peer closely at it. My eyesight was never good.

'It's from my cousin, Frances Suffolk. She informs me that she and her family are to be present at the reception for the Scottish Queen, and expresses the hope that I will be there too.' I sigh. 'You know, Susan, despite our differences over religion, I am fond of Frances, and I wonder if I have been over-harsh in my judgement of her eldest girl, Jane, who is, after all, but fourteen, and of an age to be pedantic in her opinions and generally difficult.'

'She was very rude to your Grace,' Clarencieux points out.

'Yes, but as I have often told my brother the King, much to his obvious annoyance, young people of her age lack the wisdom to decide important matters like religion for themselves, and are easily led astray by those who make it their business to corrupt them. Jane is doubtless in thrall to her heretical tutors and the pernicious influence of the court. Yet I do not doubt that, given the opportunity, and kindly guidance, she could be made as staunch a Catholic as she is now a Protestant.'

'I doubt it,' sniffs my companion.

'Kindness, that is the key. God knows, it's often been lacking in my life. You know – none better – that I long for the kindness, yes, and the love, that so many enjoy within the security of a happy family, so I understand something of what Jane feels. Hers is not a happy family. If only I had been given the chance to marry and have children – and God knows how I have longed for that – I know I would make a far more loving mother than my cousin Frances. She has not been kind to Jane.'

'Madam, I know it. It is talked of. No one knows what the child has done to deserve such treatment.'

'Perhaps I am naïve, Susan, being but an ageing spinster . . .'

'Oh, Madam!'

'Yes, Susan, I do not deceive myself. I know what I am. But I firmly believe that, if it is the harshness of her parents that has turned Jane Protestant, then kindness might win her back to the true faith. So I must resolve to be especially kind to her in whatever ways I can devise.'

'Your intentions are noble, Madam,' says Clarencieux, lips pursed, 'but I doubt you will enjoy much success.'

'We shall see,' I say, rising.

Remembering myself at Jane's age, I decide that what pleases young girls most is finery. It is deplorable that Frances, ever garbed like a peacock herself, keeps the poor child dressed dowdily in black and white. At my desk, I write an order to my tailor for a beautiful – and costly – court gown of gold tinsel and scarlet velvet, embroidered with gold and seed pearls. I shall have it sent to Lady Jane – it is just the kind of gown I myself loved to wear when I was fourteen, and I am only sorry I will not be there to witness the girl's gasp of wonder when she opens the package.

When the gown is delivered, and wrapped ready to send, I enclose a note, asking to be remembered in her prayers.

Lady Jane Grey

Dorset House and Westminster Palace, November 1551

I stare horrified at the heap of rich fabric lying on my bed.

'What shall I do with it?' I ask Mrs Ellen.

'Marry, wear it, to be sure,' she answers. 'It is very fashionable, and quite appropriate for a state reception.'

'No . . . no . . . I cannot!' I stutter. 'It would be shameful to go against God's word and follow the Lady Mary by wearing such apparel! I know it is beautiful, but I should be emulating the example of the Lady Elizabeth, and dressing as a devout Protestant maiden should.'

Mrs Ellen looks disapproving. 'It's a shame you reject pretty clothes, Jane. With your striking red hair and your sweet face, you could be one of the beauties of the court. Instead, you persist in wearing these severely cut black gowns and plain hoods.' Seeing my pained expression, she pauses. 'I'm sorry, child. What am I thinking of, when you are so virtuous and so far unlike some of the little jades at court? Yet I have to say, it is gratifying on occasion to see you finely dressed in bright colours. I know I'm old-fashioned, but I can't help regretting that some of the old customs have fallen out of favour. They assuredly did little harm.'

'But surely I must stay true to what I think is right?' I protest. However, it does me no good, for Mrs Ellen's arguments are supported, rather more forcefully, by my mother. She is overwhelmed by the Lady Mary's thoughtfulness and generosity – especially considering how impertinent I was to her – and insists, brooking no arguments, that I wear the gown to the Queen Regent's reception. And so I suffer it being put on me, with rebellious thoughts and a set mouth and, thus attired, I go to greet the Queen Regent of Scotland, another Catholic.

The King has sent my father and the Earl of Huntingdon to escort Queen Marie to Westminster. They lead her in procession to Westminster Hall, accompanied by many lords and ladies. I walk beside my mother, behind the Queen Regent.

Marie of Guise is thirty-six, but looks far older. Her face is careworn and melancholy, although when she smiles she has a certain charm. When I was presented to her before we set out on our stately progress to meet the King, she received me warmly, patting my cheek as she raised me from my curtsey. She must hate being parted from her little daughter, the Queen of Scots, whom she has just visited in France; it was surely agony to say goodbye to her, not knowing when – or if – they would meet again. And far from wearing the gaudy clothes I would have expected a Catholic queen to sport at a state occasion, she is clad in decorous black velvet, bordered with pearls. Later, I learn that she is in mourning for her son by her first husband, who died while she was in France. Poor lady, I feel so sorry for her.

The procession wends its way through the great doors of the hall, and the Queen advances to greet King Edward, who descends the steps from the dais and comes forward to kiss her on both cheeks. He then takes her by the hand and escorts her to the apartments that have been prepared for her in nearby Whitehall Palace.

In the evening, Queen Marie is seated at the King's right hand at the banquet given in her honour in Westminster Hall. Afterwards the musicians play for her, and then she retires to bed. She will leave for Scotland early in the morning, and doubtless I will not see her again.

I am glad to return home to Dorset House and retire to my room. I can't wait to take off this hateful gown, in which I have felt so unpleasantly conspicuous. As Mrs Ellen unlaces me and pulls the thing over my head, I tug at the sleeve, and it rips at the seam.

'Oh, dear, I have torn it!' I exclaim.

Mrs Ellen gives me a knowing look.

Tilty, Essex, December 1551

When, at the beginning of this month, the Duke of Somerset was tried at Westminster Hall and condemned to death, the people made such great and alarming demonstrations of loyalty for their 'good duke', whom they believe to be the champion of their rights, that the Duke of Northumberland was obliged to defer having the sentence carried out. Instead, he sent Somerset back to the Tower to await his fate. My father says he assured the condemned man that he would do all in his power to save him, but no one believes it.

Now it is Christmas once more, and we and our over-large entourage are spending the festival at Lord Willoughby's house at Tilty in Essex. Since the Lady Mary is guest of honour for the twelve days of Yuletide feasting and revelry, the old customs and traditions are to be observed, although I prefer not to join in — I do not feel it would be fitting for a well-brought-up Protestant girl to do so. Instead, I sit stiff and unsmiling through the celebrations, and only participate when viciously prodded by my irate mother.

'I am embarrassed and mortified by your gross discourtesy,' she growls.

'What about my discourtesy to God, Madam?' I whisper back. She thinks me difficult, but in truth I wish to be obedient. It is God whom I must obey, though.

'Bad manners are a discourtesy to God, especially at this season,' she retorts. 'Get up and look interested!'

The Lady Mary, on the other hand, seems resolved to win my friendship by relentless kindness. But no matter how many smiles and kindly words she bestows on me, I can never relax in her company; indeed, I find her almost irritating. I wish it were otherwise, and deplore my own reactions to her affectionate overtures, but I cannot reciprocate as I should. It is a great sadness to me that our different faiths come between us.

On Christmas Day I contrive to disappear for several hours, spending my time at prayer in my bedchamber, so that I can avoid

228

entering the chapel, which I feel certain has been contaminated by covert Catholic worship and where I cannot commune with God as I would wish.

Mary's ladies plainly disapprove of me. In the evening, when I have had no choice but to join the gathering in the great hall, the chief of them, a veritable dragon by the name of Susan Clarencieux, bends over my shoulder and mutters in my ear.

'There's nothing wrong with singing the old carols, my Lady Jane. Everyone else is joining in. But you, I have noticed, seem to take pleasure in spoiling what should be a merry occasion. There's no need for such a long face – it's Christmas!'

'I am sorry,' I answer, shamed into an awareness of my impolite conduct. 'I intended no harm.'

'Then cheer up! The Lady Mary says, in truth, she finds it hard to be charitable towards you, although she reminds us constantly that you are young and that your circumstances are not easy. Yet I know many other children with equally strict parents, and I make no doubt that they would at least know their duty to their hosts.'

My cheeks are burning now. I am mortified. I do not want others to think ill of me, despite my earnest desire to please God. Again, I say I am sorry. I remind myself that Christ did command us to love our enemies, but I am burning with indignation at the unjustness of it all.

On Twelfth Night, the former Feast of the Epiphany, there is a final evening of jollity, during which a masque is performed. At the end of the evening, according to time-honoured tradition, gifts are exchanged. For weeks, Katherine and I – and even little Mary with her clumsy stitching – have been embroidering purses, bookbindings, and partlets for hoods, which we distribute amongst the guests, receiving in return a variety of trifles as well as some presents of great value. Mine include a clock, from my parents, a garnet brooch and three pairs of gloves of the softest kid.

But my gift from the Lady Mary is the most splendid of all.

'Her Grace wishes to see you, my lady,' says Clarencieux, eyeing me warily. I cross the room to where the Lady Mary is seated on the dais beside our hosts. A pile of unopened gifts lies to one side of her chair, while those she has received and unwrapped lie strewn on a table the other side, a jumble of rich fabrics, jewels and plate.

'Ah, Jane.' She smiles as I make my curtsey, then reaches down and picks up a rectangular package wrapped in silver tissue from the pile on the floor. 'With my good wishes and my blessing,' she says, presenting it to me.

'I thank you, Madam,' I say, and pull off the wrappings, revealing a silver coffer. Inside is a magnificent necklace of great rubies interspersed with hanging pearls. I gasp with delight – I have never owned anything so beautiful or valuable.

'Your Grace, I thank you most humbly,' I say, warmly. Her generous gift has touched me. 'I am overwhelmed by your kindness and bounty.'

'I thought you would like it, Jane,' smiles Mary. 'It will suit your colouring.'

My mother joins us, eager to see what I have been given, and her eyes stretch wide when she see the jewels.

'Madam, you are too generous!' she exclaims. 'Jane, I hope you are sensible of the value of such a gift, and that you have thanked the Lady Mary's Grace sufficiently!'

'She has indeed, Frances,' says my benefactress. 'And I am sure Jane knows that the value of a gift lies not in its cost, but in the goodwill and affection of the giver.'

'Indeed, I know it well, Madam,' I reply. And I will try, I vow, to be worthy of that goodwill and affection.

We finally retire in the small hours of the morning, and before I go to bed I cannot resist trying on my new necklace. Mrs Ellen helps me with the clasp, and then stands back to see the effect. But as I gaze at my reflection in the candle-lit mirror, I am startled by the stark image that confronts me, for in the flickering light the red stones look disconcertingly like gouts of blood around my neck.

'What's the matter, Jane?' asks Mrs Ellen. 'It looks wonderful.'

'Do you see it?' I ask, shuddering.

'See what? My dear child, what are you talking about?'

'The rubies . . . They look like blood.' My voice is husky, trembling.

'Nonsense!' Mrs Ellen is brisk. 'Pull yourself together. It's just a trick of the light – and your vivid imagination!'

'Take it off!' I say urgently.

'Jane, don't be silly,' she replies impatiently.

'Take it off!' I repeat, fumbling ineffectually with the clasp. 'Help me!'

'I don't know what's got into you,' Mrs Ellen mutters, unhooking it. 'It's a beautiful necklace. You've got yourself into a state over nothing.'

'Let's put it away,' I say. I am surprised at myself. I usually scorn superstition as nonsense, but I am filled with a terrible sense of dread, as if what I saw in that mirror portended something awful.

Tower Hill, January 1552

I didn't want to come, but my father insisted. Not only is this to be a salutary lesson in what happens to traitors, but it is supposed to be riveting entertainment. I know I shall not find it so. How can watching another person's suffering be entertaining? I don't care that lots of people from court are come to see the spectacle – I do not want to be here.

But I am here. I had no choice. At least my lord insisted that we, like nearly everyone else of noble birth who is present, go in disguise. We are done up against the cold in voluminous hooded cloaks lined with fur, such as prosperous city merchants wear, and I am warm despite the bitter chill.

Behind me, I am conscious of the grim bulk of the Tower of London, a place that has witnessed much tragedy and misery and has become notorious since two queens, Anne Boleyn and Katherine Howard, met their bloody ends there. Few who enter the Tower's portals as prisoners ever go free: there is no escape but via the block or the noose – or worse. I've heard terrible tales. Torture is not lawful in England, but it is said that several wretches have endured the horrors of the rack and the thumbscrews in that place. Then there is rumoured to be a cell called the Little Ease, in which a man may not stand or sit or lie down, since it is too small to permit it. If I were confined in such a cell, I would go mad, I know it. I shudder.

The procession is late. The crowd grows restive.

'You know, the King agonised for weeks before signing the warrant,' my father tells us.

'Doubtless my lord of Northumberland put much pressure on him,' my mother says.

'Somerset *is* his uncle,' my lord reminds us. 'He has already been constrained to send one uncle to his death. But the Duke warned him again and again that to show mercy would be unwise, and that he cannot permit such seditious traitors to flourish.'

Suddenly the cry goes up: 'He's coming! The good Duke is coming!'

It takes some considerable time to march the condemned man through the vast crowds assembled around the scaffold. The mood of the mob is angry.

'If I were the Lieutenant of the Tower, I'd be worried in case my prisoner is snatched from his guards and spirited away,' says my father. 'I wouldn't put it past them.'

Yet the little procession successfully pushes its way through the press of humanity, and Somerset mounts the steps to the scaffold. It is strange to reflect that a man who once wielded such power, and who even sent his own brother to his death in this same place, could be brought so low. A tall fellow in front shifts position, and I can see the wooden block, standing in the straw. I shudder again. What must the poor Duke be thinking as he looks upon it? How must it feel to know that, within minutes, you will be dead, your life severed at the neck? It is too horrible to contemplate.

'Now, Jane,' my father is saying, 'according to custom, a prisoner always makes a speech from the scaffold, preferably confessing his guilt and praising the King's justice, and asking the people to pray for him.'

Sure enough, the Duke has stepped to the rail of the scaffold and is holding up his hand to hush the crowd, but before he can open his mouth, the people begin yelling, 'Reprieve! Reprieve!' as a small troop of soldiers can be seen approaching at a gallop across the Tower's drawbridge.

The Duke of Somerset stares at them disbelievingly. He must, poor soul, have prepared himself for death, have steeled himself for the final blow of the axe. His face registers shock and longing: he must desperately desire to live.

We can see the headsman, sinister in his black hood, speaking to his assistant. The soldiers are nearly at the scaffold.

'Reprieve! Reprieve!' the crowd is chanting, parting ranks to let the troop through.

'My Lord Lieutenant, there is no reprieve,' announces their captain in a loud voice. 'The Governor of the Tower thought it prudent to send reinforcements in case of any trouble. You men, surround the scaffold!'

There is a furious roar from the crowd. The Duke looks as if he might faint; how terrible for him, having to face the renewed reality of death after having his hopes so cruelly raised. Yet in a firm voice he calls for the people to be quiet and delivers his prepared speech. Then he raises his hand once more.

'I am the King's loyal subject!' he declares.

In all too short a time the grim formalities are dispensed with, and he kneels in the straw before the block. I have to close my eyes: I cannot watch, but beside me I can sense that my parents are tense with expectation. There is a pregnant silence, a sickening thud, then roars and screams of disapproval. When I dare to look again, heaving, shoving bodies are scrambling beneath the scaffold, and hands are frenziedly dipping handkerchiefs and cloths into the blood that drips through the boards, seeking a relic of their hero.

'For sure, he is a martyr!' a man cries.

'A true martyr for the Protestant faith!' another yells.

I stand, nausea rising, unable to bring myself to look upon the mangled thing that lies on the scaffold. Around me, men and women are shouting and weeping in a frenzy. I swear that, at this moment, there is no more hated man in London than he who has supplanted the Good Duke – His Grace of Northumberland.

Westminster Abbey, April 1552

It is cool in Westminster Abbey. We have sat here in our privileged places near the altar waiting a long time for the arrival of the King. Today is St George's Day, and although, by law, saints' days may no longer be observed in England, St George is regarded as a national hero. He was certainly no papist priest or martyr, but a knight errant who embodied the ideals of chivalry still held dear by the King and the nobility, and therefore it is thought right, and indeed patriotic, to celebrate his feast day.

Spring is blossoming outside, but I am wearing my customary black, much to my mother's evident disgust. Fortunately, by the time she saw me, it was too late to change. I am gratified to see that the Abbey has been stripped of all its idolatrous Roman ornaments. Even so, it is still lavishly appointed by Protestant standards, but it is the greatest royal mausoleum in the land and houses the tombs of many kings and queens.

My mother frowns at Katherine, who is simpering at a handsome youth sitting near us in the nave. This impudent young man is making sheep's eyes at us both, and my mother nudges my father sharply, alerting him to what is going on.

'I wouldn't worry, my dear,' he murmurs. 'That's the Earl of Pembroke's heir, Lord William Herbert. No bad catch for any young lady of good birth.'

'He's too cheeky by far,' snorts my lady, unbending.

'It's just his age. They're all either moonstruck or randy as tomcats. I recall that I was the same. But there's no harm in him eyeing up our girls. A young lord of his rank will know that it can go no further. Unless, of course, his father and I come to some agreement. How would that please you?'

'For Jane?' asks my lady. I look at them, startled. My father bends his head close to my mother's ear.

'No, for Katherine. There's a bigger fish to fry for Jane.'

My mother silences him with a look.

This brings to mind a conversation that took place between my parents a month or so ago, when we were all three taking our ease after supper in the winter parlour at Bradgate.

My lady was harping on, as she does from time to time, about the likelihood of my marrying the King.

'But you are forgetting, my dear, that he is still betrothed,' my father pointed out.

'Betrothals can be broken, and often are,' she retorted. 'Wait until he is declared of age, and then we'll see. I haven't given up hope. But to be plain with you, I can't see Northumberland relinquishing power when the King comes of age. Not without a struggle.'

'Oh, I don't doubt he intends to remain chief minister, and who could blame him? We'd all do the same, given the chance. But even he must realise that the King has to grow up and come into his own. And if I know his Majesty, he'll assert his authority sooner rather than later. He's already growing restive at being subject to his councillors. Mark my words, he'll be another such as his father, given his head.'

'I'll wager he'll be even more of a fanatic than King Henry,' my mother declared. 'My late revered uncle burned heretics, but mainly because they espoused beliefs that conflicted with his policies. With the son, policy takes second place to religious principles.'

'Our daughter is of like mind, in case you hadn't noticed,' said my father wryly, looking at me.

'Oh, she's just difficult for the sake of it,' retorted my lady testily, missing the humour. 'I don't know what gets into her.'

Sitting here now, in the cool of the Abbey, I reflect that it would be wonderful to be Queen, if only to be able, just once, to put my mother firmly in her place!

The trumpets sound the arrival of the royal procession, and the entire congregation rises to its feet. The King passes along the nave, preceded by the Knights of the Garter, whose feast day this is. Edward's slender figure seems engulfed by his blue velvet Garter mantle. He was unwell recently, and it was first given out that he was suffering from an attack of the measles; then they announced that he had smallpox. I conclude that, as his pale skin shows no sign of pockmarks, it must have been measles after all. His resumption of royal duties hopefully betokens a good recovery, but he still appears tired and seems to have lost some weight, although it is hard to tell in those robes. I'm sure his face looks thinner.

Fortunately, the court is soon to leave Whitehall for Greenwich, where the fresh air will hopefully bring back some colour into his Majesty's cheeks. I know that many lavish entertainments are planned, and rumour has it that the King is to be permitted to tilt at the quintain – the nearest they will ever allow him to jousting in the lists. Then, from Greenwich, the court is to depart on a long summer progress, so that his Majesty can see – and be seen by – his subjects throughout the south and west of England. I fervently hope he will have recovered his strength by then.

On my knees in the Abbey, I pray that King Edward makes a full and speedy recovery. I do this not so much because I am fond of him – it is hard to be fond of one who is so detached and cold – but because it is unthinkable that the Lady Mary should ever come to the throne.

John Dudley, Duke of Northumberland

Salisbury and Windsor, September 1552

The progress is to be curtailed. The lords of the council inform me that, after carrying out what they describe as a punishing schedule of public engagements and lavish entertainments, the King's health has broken under the strain. Fearing that his Majesty will not be able to go on, they have summoned me from London, where I have been attending to the business of government during the King's absence.

Arriving at Salisbury, I am shocked at Edward's appearance. When he left on his progress at the end of July he seemed restored to health, as robust as ever, and of good colour. Now, just over a month later, he looks ghastly, thin and white, and even his lowlier subjects are beginning to comment on it.

I bow deeply, trying to conceal my dismay. The implications of what I see are manifold, and I need time to think about them. For now, however, I put on my most avuncular manner, saying kindly, 'I am most distressed to see your Majesty so unwell.'

'It is of little moment, my lord,' replies the King. He sounds weary.

'Perhaps your Majesty should return to London,' I suggest.

'I cannot disappoint these good people. Some of them have gone to great trouble and expense on my behalf. Kings should not give way to weakness.' He coughs.

'They should when the welfare of their kingdom is at stake,'

I tell him firmly. 'If your Majesty, by persisting on his progress, makes himself ill, then what of his duty to his people and to the true religion? Sir, your councillors are alarmed, and I too am concerned about your health. I must remind you that your heir is the Lady Mary. Now, for the sake of England and its Church, I beg you, go home and rest.'

The other lords present add their pleas to mine, and the King, knowing himself defeated, gives in with good grace.

'But please have our secretaries write to those we have disappointed and extend our heartfelt apologies for our absence,' he insists.

'It shall be done,' I assure him. 'And now you must set all cares aside, and lie down.'

He looks relieved as he rises from his chair of estate and walks slowly towards his privy chamber. At the door, he pauses.

'Thank you, my lords. I do confess I have never felt so ill in all my life.'

We are at Windsor. Despite having rested and submitted to the attentions of a whole team of royal physicians, who all declare themselves puzzled by his Majesty's illness, Edward shows no signs of recovering. In fact, his condition grows worse.

Desperate for a remedy, I send to Italy to summon the eminent and renowned doctor and astrologer, Girolamo Cardano, to England to examine the King. Cardano duly arrives, consults the royal physicians and disappears into the royal bedchamber, where he remains for the next hour.

The doctors stand in a little group, keeping an eye on the door and conversing in low voices, so that I cannot hear what they are saying. Do they know more than they are telling? Are they too frightened to disclose their fears? Or are they reluctant to have their ignorance exposed?

Dr Cardano and I sit facing each other in my private closet, where the most secret business of the realm is conducted.

'You may speak plainly,' I say in Latin, grateful that the Italian is fluent in that language. There is an ominous pause.

'I am very impressed with the excellent virtues and singular graces of his Majesty, which can only be a gift from God,' Dr Cardano begins. 'I cannot say enough to commend him: he is such a worthy prince, despite being so tender in years. For his mature wisdom, his wit and his princely bearing, I have met few his equal.'

'Yes, yes,' I interrupt, desperate for him to come to the matter in hand, 'but what of his Majesty's health?'

Cardano's smile disappears.

'Such a paragon is too good for this world, I fear, my lord. I regret to inform you – and I cannot stress how deeply – that the King shows all the symptoms of a consumption of the lungs.'

I feel as if cold fingers are streaking down my spine.

'I must confess to you,' he continues, 'that before I visited his Majesty, I took the liberty of casting his horoscope, even though I was aware that such things are not permitted in your country. I assure you, it was purely for the purpose of making a diagnosis. I saw therein the omens of a great calamity, and when I was admitted to the King's presence, I observed unmistakable signs in his face denoting an early death. There is no cure for this disease. His vital powers will weaken, and he will die.'

'How long?' I bark.

'It is impossible to say with any certainty. Months, a year at most, no more.' He bows his head.

I sit silent, digesting this terrible news. I feel I have aged ten years in a single moment. But this is no time for self-pity. I must safeguard my interests and play for time. I tell the doctor, 'The council will wish to be told the results of your examination. May I remind you that in England it is treason to predict the death of the King?' I smile meaningfully. 'Say whatever you like, fob them off with platitudes, tell them that his Majesty needs a period of rest in order to recover, but I warn you, do not even hint at the seriousness of his condition. If you manage to allay their fears, you will be well rewarded, and may congratulate yourself on having done me a signal service. Because what I need now – what this kingdom needs, and what the Church of England needs – is time.'

Lady Jane Grey

Hampton Court, October 1552

After resting for several weeks at Windsor, the King has risen from his sickbed and travelled to Hampton Court for his fifteenth birthday celebrations. My family and I are among the many lords and ladies attending a state banquet held in King Henry's great hall with its magnificent hammerbeam roof.

Because of our near-kinship, my parents (and consequently myself) are among the very few people who have been made aware, to our sorrow, of the gravity of the King's condition, and we have been sworn to secrecy. Until today, however, the reality of the situation was not brought home to me, but now, seated with my father and mother towards the end of the high table, I have a good view of his Majesty, and am appalled to see him looking so ill, with sunken, flushed cheeks and swollen limbs. What is more, to judge from the furtive glances and alarmed expressions along the tables, others are shocked too. I watch my poor cousin as he toys with his food, leaving most of it, and from time to time I see him hold his chest with one hand and cough into a fine lawn handkerchief held in the other; once, I swear, I see that handkerchief come away spotted with blood. The King's cough is harsh, racking his body, and it interrupts him every time he tries to speak.

I turn to my lady and whisper, 'Madam, I fear his Majesty is far more ill than I had expected.'

'Hush!' she hisses fiercely. 'You must not speak of such things here. Remember, we have been told by my lord of Northumberland, for the King's sake, to act as if all is well. Very few people know how ill he actually is, and for very good reasons.'

'But surely people notice? And surely the King himself realises how sick he is?'

'The Duke wants everyone to believe that he is slowly

improving. I hear that the King himself has been told he will recover in due course,' she murmurs. Poor, deluded soul, I think sadly. 'Now, enough,' my mother adds briskly. 'This is a festive occasion, and should not be spoiled by mournful talk.'

I cannot help but feel mournful, though. That poor boy. He cannot recover: it should be obvious to everyone, himself included. Death sits upon him as clear as day. He should be warned of it and, in charity, given time to prepare his soul.

I am disgusted to see Northumberland carrying on as normal, sitting on his Majesty's right hand, laughing and jesting. Already he is planning, for the King's delight, a number of elaborate and costly entertainments for Christmas, which is probably the last Christmas Edward will ever see. My father says the Duke is also trying to hurry along negotiations for his Majesty's marriage to Elisabeth of France, hoping no doubt that my poor cousin will father an heir before he dies, although my lord says that, looking at him, he doubts he would be capable of it. Yet Northumberland continues with his charade, intent on deceiving the world. It is even said that the Duke has made belated friendly approaches to the Lady Mary, with an all-too-transparent motive, and it is certain that he has banned the Lady Elizabeth – who is far too astute for his comfort – from visiting her brother. Without a doubt, he is playing for time and arming himself against several contingencies. But can the insensitive man not see that, by maintaining the fiction that the King's illness is just a temporary indisposition, he is imposing an intolerable strain on Edward, who is plainly far too ill to be co-operating in all this deception?

The Lady Mary

Newhall and Whitehall, February 1553

'I don't like this at all,' I confide to Sir Robert Rochester, the comptroller of my household. 'Everywhere I go, and even in my own house, I hear rumours that the King is seriously ill; and yet from the court, and in particular from that villain Northumberland, nothing apart from this.' I wave the document that has just arrived. 'I have sent letter after letter, begging to know the truth, and I am just fobbed off with extravagant pleasantries. Does it not occur to you, Sir Robert, that a year ago they were sending me threats? Now they seem to be falling over themselves to win favour with me.'

'It does seem suspicious, Madam,' my comptroller agrees.

'The Emperor's ambassador tells me that Northumberland has taken over the Treasury and begun hoarding huge sums of money.' I twist the rings on my fingers in agitation. 'Now I receive this invitation from the Duke to attend a masque to be performed at court at Candlemas. All he tells me is that the performers are a group of very talented children, and that I might be amused by their antics. It beggars belief: the King might be dying, yet all he can write to me is of mummeries!'

'I beg of you, Madam, do not accept,' urges Sir Robert.

'Oh, but I must, my friend, I must,' I insist firmly. 'For all my reservations, I must see for myself how my brother is. He may have fallen grievously into error, but I was ever fond of him. And I am next in line to the throne, never forget that. I should see for myself how matters stand.'

'It may be a trap,' he warns.

'Fear not, I will take with me a goodly entourage – shall we say one hundred stout knights and their ladies? And we shall go very publicly in procession through London. I know I may say without vanity that the people love me, if only because I am my father's daughter. I am sure they would suffer no harm to come to me.'

'I admire your courage, Madam,' says Sir Robert sincerely, 'but my mind will not be eased until you return safely home again.'

I smile at him affectionately. He has served me faithfully and well for years.

'I appreciate your concern, Sir Robert, and will take good care of myself, trusting in God and Our Lady to protect me. Now, I must have my gear packed. The Duke writes that he has arranged for me to stay in the former priory of St John at Clerkenwell' –

I sigh – 'another great religious house turned over to secular use. Well, I am sure I will at least be lodged comfortably.'

I make my ceremonial entry into London, and the people turn out in large numbers to greet me and pour blessings on me. Northumberland himself receives me most cordially at Mile End and escorts me to Clerkenwell.

'A fine day, Madam,' he observes, riding by my side.

'Unusually fine for the season,' I agree.

He bends towards me.

'I regret that his Majesty is too unwell to receive your Grace today,' he murmurs. 'May I suggest that you come to Whitehall tomorrow? He will be better then, I hope.'

I have no choice but to concur.

The next day, at the palace, I am astonished to find Northumberland and the whole privy council waiting to receive me, bowing low as I approach. This, more than anything, convinces me that my poor brother is indeed dying. Of course, they are anxious to court favour with their future sovereign, no doubt hoping that such excessive courtesy and demonstrable goodwill will erase any bitter memories of the cruel way in which they relentlessly persecuted me in the past.

Nevertheless, I wait three days to see the King. By this time I have heard the latest worrying rumours that are circulating at court, and am more than ever persuaded that he cannot last long. I am also deeply troubled by allegations – admittedly made by those who have no love for Northumberland – that the Duke is poisoning his Majesty. But why, I ask myself, would he do such a thing? It would be madness. He has far more to gain from keeping Edward alive, for he must be aware that he has nothing, or worse, to hope for from me. Indeed, I have already made up my mind that John Dudley will receive short shrift when I ascend the throne: the man is a heretic and a traitor, and it galls me to have to show courtesy towards him. But the time will surely come when a reckoning must be made.

On the fourth day, I am relieved to hear that his Majesty is well enough to receive me. Nothing, however, not even the wildest rumour, has prepared me for the sight of my brother lying weak and wasted in the vast state bed. Northumberland has just informed me that he is on the mend, but how could I ever believe it now?

'Good sister, it is kind of you to come,' says Edward in a tired, cracked voice, extending his hand to be kissed. I kneel by the bed and put my lips to his fingers, trying not to wrinkle my nose at the putrid smell coming from him. The poor boy looks mortally ill, and I am grieved to see it, remembering his youth and the fact that, for all his wrong-headed opinions, he is my brother. For a short while we converse, touching only on safe matters, and avoiding contentious ones such as his health or our religious differences, but before long Edward closes his eyes.

'I cannot talk further,' he mutters. 'I . . . must . . . sleep.'

'Sleep well, Sir,' I whisper, and quietly leave the room, tears blinding my eyes.

'His Majesty looks dreadfully ill,' I say accusingly to Northumberland.

'Your Grace speaks truth,' he answers smoothly. 'He has good days and bad days. He seemed better this morning, but I fear that any excitement overtaxes and exhausts him. I regret that I have had to cancel the children's masque. I hope your Grace is not too disappointed.'

'Not at all. My concern is for the King my brother. What do his doctors say?'

'They say he will recover, given time.' The Duke's face is impassive, impenetrable.

'And do you believe them?' I persist.

'I am in their hands, Madam. They are the experts.'

'Doctors have been known to be wrong before.'

'Madam, we have had several opinions, and all concur. I can do no more. We must be patient.'

I do not believe him – I am no doctor, yet I can see my brother is dying. But there is nothing more to be said.

'Very well, Sir, I will return to Newhall tomorrow.' I wait for him to find some excuse for detaining me at court, but he merely bows.

'I hope you will keep me informed of the King's progress,' I say.

'Of course,' he assures me. I know he will not keep his word.

I had thought, when I came to London, that I was walking into a trap, and perhaps I was. If so, I foiled my enemies by coming so publicly and so staunchly attended. I leave with the distinct impression that the wily Duke had invited me as part of another plot entirely, and that he has not finished with me yet.

John Dudley, Duke of Northumberland

Greenwich Palace, Kent, March 1553

In my closet at Greenwich, I sit alone, deep in thought. There is no escaping the fact that God will soon call the King to Himself, and it is obvious that a radical solution to the problem of the succession is called for, if I am to survive. And, of course, the Church of England.

So far, I have been cautious. In February the King enjoyed a period of remission from the consumption that is eating away at his lungs, and felt fit enough to open Parliament in person. There was, however, much furtive comment about how ill he looked. Somehow I managed to allay the fears of both Lords and Commons, and convinced them – and, for that matter, the King himself – that his Majesty is in truth convalescent after recovering from a serious illness. Wiser souls at Westminster might have read something sinister into the announcement that the King, at fifteen, had now attained his majority and would from henceforth assume personal control of the government of his realm. But I, who know the real state of the boy's health, have merely placed sovereign power in his hands in order to lend legality to the plans forming in my mind. I know very well that he is no fit state to govern, and that he is happy to delegate everything to his faithful servant – myself. It should be no matter, therefore, to persuade him to agree to my scheme for preserving the Protestant religion – and of course, my own power.

But the time is not ripe for that yet. To all appearances, Edward is getting better. With Parliament dissolved, the court has moved to Greenwich, where the healthful air is known to be beneficial to invalids. His Majesty believes that, given a few weeks here in the springtime, he might soon be his old self again.

I, however, am preparing for the worst. I have before me a copy of the late King's Will, and the scroll on which is enshrined the Act of Succession of 1544, brought to me by the Master of the Rolls. I scrutinise both, looking for loopholes that will justify my plans, but find none. If it were merely a matter of altering King Henry's Will, it would be simple enough: the wishes of a deceased sovereign hold no force in law, and the Will could be overridden by another written by Henry's successor. But an Act of Parliament can only be altered by another Act of Parliament.

Of course, Parliament could be summoned again to debate the matter, but the King, worn out by his state duties last month, has returned exhausted to his bed to recover his strength, and is certainly too weak to open a new session. Either his absence or his appearance would give rise to the panicky rumours I have worked so hard to avoid by issuing reassuring bulletins on his Majesty's health. I need time now to plan carefully for the future – my future – and more time for those plans to be put into effect. Yet I only have to look at the King to see that time is running out.

It is essential that the public, and even the council for the present, be kept in ignorance of his Majesty's true state of health for as long as possible. The last thing I want now is Mary's supporters rallying to her cause. Fortunately, I believe I have been successful in lulling her into a sense of false security.

As it is, I fear that when I lay my plan before Parliament, it will meet with such opposition as to ensure that it never becomes law.

The only course open to me, therefore, is to act independently of Parliament. The King's consent to my proposals should be sufficient to quell any protests. Such a course might not be entirely lawful, but too much is at stake to pay heed to legal niceties.

I read over the Will and the Act for the third time. The old King's intentions are clear: after Edward come Mary and her heirs, then Elizabeth and hers, and after them the heirs of Henry's sister, Mary Tudor. That means her surviving child, Frances Brandon, Duchess of Suffolk, and Frances's daughters in turn.

It is plain enough, but I dare not contemplate the consequences to myself, or to England, if the Lady Mary succeeds. The Catholic faith would certainly be restored as the official religion of the kingdom, and the Church of England would once more come under the dominion of the Pope in Rome. Protestants in England would be regarded as heretics, and I should not be surprised if Mary brought back burning as the punishment for heresy. She is obsessed with her faith, and no doubt desirous of being revenged on those who have persecuted her for it. My own destruction is assured.

Mary, therefore, must never succeed, and I am confident that I can make my fellow councillors see the sense of that. I know I have enemies amongst them, but even they must realise what Mary's accession will mean for them — they have all supported me in my battle against her Mass. And while the King has great reverence for his father's memory, and might have scruples against changing his Will, he is a zealous champion of the reformed faith, and will desire to safeguard all his good work.

What of Elizabeth then? She is a dark horse, and I do not trust her. She rarely comes to court, and when she does visit the King, she appears meek and pious, but I am not fooled. Beneath that dutiful mask, I have no doubt, lies a devious and dangerous character. I would not like to tangle with Elizabeth — she has no worth for my purposes. No, what I require for the success of my plans is a candidate who is young and malleable; someone who will submit without complaint to my guidance and rule, and comply with what is required of them. Elizabeth is not that person.

There is justification for passing over Mary and Elizabeth, since both were declared bastards when their mothers' marriages were dissolved, and no bastard can sit on the throne. But they are popular with the people on account of being King Harry's daughters, and I must tread carefully.

If I manage to exclude Mary and Elizabeth from the succession, that leaves Frances Suffolk, a Protestant to be sure, but even less likely than the princesses to be meek and biddable. She would certainly never submit patiently to my tutelage. Nor would there be any need for her to do so, for she is thirty-six and quite capable of ruling autonomously.

But if my Lady Suffolk could be persuaded to waive her right to the succession in favour of her eldest daughter, the Lady Jane Grey, then all would fall into place.

Greenwich Palace, April 1553

Lying in his sickbed at Greenwich, the King is restless and fretful. Whilst striving to accept God's will, he plaintively wonders aloud why He has chosen to inflict such suffering upon His faithful servant, and why, when his Majesty has done so much to promote the true religion, and there is still so much left to be done, He has decided to cut down His most devoted son in the first flower of his youth.

For it is as plain as day that, whatever the rest of us may say to reassure him, the King has guessed the truth.

'I know there will be no reprieve for me, my lord,' he tells me, fixing me with those cold, impenetrable eyes. 'You can stop pretending. Comfort yourself in the knowledge that I am strong in my faith and can face death with courage and patience.'

In truth, death stalks him through every waking hour. It is apparent in his wasted limbs, his laboured breathing, his racking cough and in the vile, stinking sputum he hawks up, which was until recently greenish-yellow, but is now increasingly streaked with bright blood. Yet, for all his brave words, the fear of death haunts his dreams, so that he lies wakeful yet weary, fighting off sleep, while complaining that he is too tired to make the necessary preparations for the salvation of his soul.

'What is hardest to bear, my lord,' he whispers, 'is the knowledge that, once death has done its terrible work on me, all that I have striven for will be undone by my misguided and wrong-headed sister. It sickens me to think of an England returned to the Roman yoke, bedevilled once more by popish superstition and corruption; an England whose people will have scant hope of Heaven, but may face everlasting damnation. It is unbearable to contemplate.' But contemplate it he does as he lies there, hour after hour, his book lying unread on the counterpane, and the warm sun streaming in through the mullioned window.

I leave him to his terrible preoccupations so that I can mould him to my purpose when he is sufficiently demoralised. Sitting by his bedside, I speak mainly of state affairs and the grievous condition of his health, taking care to hint at the horrors that will engulf us under Mary's rule; this has the gratifying effect of heightening the King's fevered anxiety. Like a dog with a slipper, he worries around the problem constantly.

'What remedy is there?' he cries. 'Should not Parliament be summoned to approve a new Act of Succession, passing over the Lady Mary and giving the throne to the Lady Elizabeth, my sweet sister Temperance, who is a loyal Protestant?'

I take my time answering, as though considering the matter. 'Parliament might not agree to set aside the Lady Mary,' I warn, frowning. 'If they pass over the Lady Mary, they may, on the same grounds, pass over the Lady Elizabeth, for both have been declared base-born.' I pause to let this sink in. 'Permit me time to think on this, Sir. There may be a better way forward.'

Thus I play on his fears. Perhaps he suspects I have some scheme in mind. No matter. By the time I have finished with him, he will be very grateful for it. I just pray that God grants me time to bring my plans to fruition, for I fear that the King is not long for this world.

Lady Jane Grey

Dorset House, April 1553

Katherine and I stand before our parents in the great chamber at Dorset House.

'We have sent for you,' my lady begins portentously, 'to tell you that we have invited his Grace the Duke of Northumberland to dinner here tomorrow, and that he has asked for you both to be present.'

My lord adds, 'It is essential that you conduct yourselves in a manner befitting your rank, and make a good impression on his Grace.'

'Yes, Sir, yes, Madam,' we reply, almost in unison. There follows a silence, as if some question needed to be asked and answered.

'That is all,' says my mother. 'Oh, and Jane – dress appropriately.'

'Something is going on,' I observe, as we climb the stairs to our rooms.

'What do you mean?' asks Katherine. She is a pretty, docile twelve-year-old, but not very perceptive.

'The Duke is coming to dinner. Why? He wants us there. Why? To inspect us for some reason. I tell you, I smell a rat.' I know it could not be anything to do with my mooted marriage to the King, for the King is very ill, probably far too ill to wed. Anyway, how could that involve Katherine?

'But why should he be interested in us?'

'That's what I should like to know.'

Northumberland is his most urbane and charming self at table. He compliments my mother on her cook's efforts, discusses sporting pursuits at length with my father, and even condescends to speak to us girls, enquiring about our academic progress and our accomplishments. Katherine speaks up for herself in a pleasing manner, but I am more guarded. I dislike the way his smile never seems to reach his eyes. He is all falsity. I am sure he senses that I do not like him.

I am afraid, but I do not know why.

Frances Brandon, Duchess of Suffolk

Dorset House, April 1553

If it's a marriage he's after, Jane might be a great prize by virtue of her birth, but she has little else to offer any suitor. At fifteen, she's small for her age and slightly built. There's not much bosom beneath that stiff corset, I'll wager, and her hands are positively childish, while her complexion is still marred by those wretched freckles. Her only good points are her lips, which are full and cherry-red, her dark eyes and perhaps her hair, which tonight she is wearing loose about her shoulders. It is the mark of our royal heritage, that hair: all the Tudors have it. It's Jane's greatest asset.

Thank goodness the girl appears modest and keeps her eyes downcast unless she is spoken to. It annoys me that, when someone addresses her, she answers boldly, with a steady, disconcerting gaze. Fortunately, the Duke has not conversed much with her, otherwise he might be concluding, and with good reason, that she is not as biddable as she looks! But she will bend, she will bend to my will and it will do her good in the long run, for she must soon, God willing, submit to the rule and instruction of a husband. Is this what the Duke has come about?

The table has been cleared, the cloth removed and the girls dismissed to bed, along with the servants. We and our guest retire to the parlour with a flagon of the best Burgundy.

'Madam,' says the Duke, 'there is a matter of great weight that I must discuss with you.'

I glance at Henry and read in his face that he already knows what this is about. My irritation rises, for I feel myself at a disadvantage. These men have already made an important decision without me, I am sure. Well, I will not give it my blessing until I have scrutinised it from all angles.

'I am going to tell you something of vital importance, which you must not divulge to anyone,' Northumberland continues. 'The King, I am saddened to say, will not live out the summer. What we have to ask ourselves is, do we want the Lady Mary to succeed him?'

I think of the frail boy at Greenwich, once his father's pride and joy and the surety for the future of the Tudor dynasty. We knew he was seriously ill, but not that the end would come so soon.

'I am grieved for his Majesty,' I say slowly, 'and for England.'

'Yes, for England,' echoes the Duke. 'It is for England that I fear. I cannot sleep at night for worrying what will befall this fair land when Edward is gone – and what will happen to us.'

'Us?' I ask, surprised.

'Yes, us. For we have all been accomplices in establishing the Protestant faith in this realm, particularly your husband here, Madam. Do you really think the Lady Mary will show favour to us when she is Queen?'

'She has always been most friendly towards me and my family, despite our differences in religion,' I point out. 'I am, after all, her cousin.' While you, my lord, are not. I smile sweetly.

'Ah, but she will require you, like everyone else, to change your religion when she comes to the throne,' Northumberland pursues relentlessly. 'She will not tolerate any Protestants in her court. And if you refuse, what price kinship and friendship then? Madam, you have not dealt with her as I have; you do not know how stubborn she can be, how fixed in her opinions. She is a fanatical Catholic, and regards the rest of us as heretics. Your husband here, my lady, has been one of the chief promoters of the reformed faith. How will she deal with him? With me? If we do not recant our beliefs, she will put pressure on us. First, we will fall from favour, then we will go in fear of our lives. And,' he adds meaningfully, 'our property.' A shrewd thrust, that. Well he knows that my lord and I, like many others of the nobility and gentry, have grown rich on the pickings from dissolved abbeys, priories and chantries. 'Mary will give it all back to the Church of Rome.'

I shudder. With sudden clarity, I perceive what a calamity the death of the King will be. Yet, as I struggle to control the rising panic, I am also aware that, of the three people in this room, Northumberland has the most at stake. Clearly, he is scare-mongering in the hope of gaining support. Being of the same royal blood as Mary, I cannot quite believe that she would treat unkindly with me and my family. Yet it is indeed true that my lord has vigorously supported Northumberland – and Somerset before him – in the sweeping religious reforms of this present reign, and there might well be cause for concern there.

When it comes to religion, I must admit in my heart that my faith is not deep-rooted. I was brought up a Catholic until, influenced by Katherine Parr's circle, I secretly flirted with the reformed faith, but with no great conviction. Then after King Henry's death, I was happy to proclaim myself a Protestant: I needed no persuading. And if it comes to it, I will have few qualms about converting back to the religion of my childhood, if the law requires it of me; after all, we all pray to the same God. But I fear my husband is of another mind entirely.

'Mary will never make a Catholic of me or my daughters,' he is saying. 'I am as committed as yourself, my lord, to the Protestant cause. And I suggest you now tell my lady wife what you have in mind.'

Northumberland clears his throat and turns to me.

'I have been studying the late King Henry's Will and the Act of Succession, as well as other records, and it is clear that the Ladies Mary and Elizabeth are legally bastards. In the normal way of things, bastards are incapable of inheriting titles and property as a lawful heir would inherit. The Crown is regarded as property in that sense by many judges; I have taken legal advice on this. Thus,' he goes on smoothly, 'it might be possible to pass over their claims to the succession, and in that case, Madam, the rightful sovereign of England would be yourself.'

Well, I had worked that out already. I shiver with anticipation, and something else less pleasant. Myself, Queen of England! The glory and riches of England to be mine . . . But would I want to bear the burdensome weight of government? I like my life the way it is: I enjoy many comforts, much leisure for sport, and the privileges of high rank without too much responsibility. True, I am ambitious and, yes, greedy (I freely admit it), but my freedom and a degree of privacy are just as precious to me, and my acceptance of the crown would deprive me of both. Moreover, could I, a woman in a man's world, control my councillors and advisors? And, of course, Northumberland, who would be revelling in the role of queen-maker, and competing for ascendancy, no doubt? I shake myself inwardly. Of course I could rule – I am a match for any man. But would I want to? Would I not be happier remaining as I am, a private person?

The Duke is watching me intently, studying my face.

'Does the idea appeal to you, Madam?' he asks.

'No, it does not.' I have barely needed to think about it.

'I thought as much,' he answers, with a significant look at my husband.

'You have both discussed this,' I accuse them. Henry looks uncomfortable, but Northumberland smiles.

'Some sounding out was necessary, Madam. The success of

my plan is vital for the future of England and our faith, and it is essential that we are all of one mind.'

'It's vital for your own surety too,' I point out, with a touch of malice.

'Naturally,' he agrees, unruffled. 'But to be plain with you, Madam, I had not laid any plans to put your Grace on the throne. You are not well known by the people, and it is doubtful they would support your claim against that of the Lady Mary, whom they obstinately revere, if only because she is the late King's daughter.'

'So what *is* your plan?' I demand.

'I believe, Madam, that the future security and welfare of this realm and the Church of England lie in the hands of the next heir, your daughter, the Lady Jane. No, no, hear me,' he urges, as I make to interrupt him. 'Should you renounce your claim, the Lady Jane could become Queen. She is young and pretty, which is ideal for my purpose, and she is biddable. Above all, she is famed, not only in England, but throughout Europe, for her learning and her love of the true religion. I have no doubt that, given the right kind of persuasion, the people would accept her as their sovereign.'

'Think on it, Frances,' chimes in Henry. 'Our daughter as Queen of England; a new dynasty on the throne; us three as the power behind it. It is a wise choice.'

'It is the only choice,' declares Northumberland with feeling. 'There is no other. Not if we are to survive.'

'I agree with you, my lord,' I tell him, 'and I cannot deny that I am ambitious for my daughter. This is indeed beyond my wildest expectations for her, and I will offer her my wholehearted support and loyalty if it comes to pass. But I must ask you two things.'

'My lady?'

'First, this is a course fraught with dangers. We have our daughter's safety to think of. I take it you have thought it through and planned for every contingency?'

'We have discussed everything,' says Henry.

'No, my lord, let me explain to your good lady,' puts in the Duke reassuringly. 'Madam, I have planned this down to the last detail. When the King dies, his death will be kept secret for as long as possible. Soldiers will be dispatched to take the Lady Mary into honourable custody, and, if necessary, the Lady Elizabeth. I assure you, neither will be harmed, simply placed under house-arrest at some secret location, where they will be well looked after. Only then will the King's passing be made public and your daughter proclaimed Queen. Many lords will support us because they too fear a Catholic resurgence. I have no doubt that the people of England will quickly come to see the wisdom of my plan, and even if they do not, there are strict laws for dealing with those who spread sedition or incite riots. Does that set your mind at rest?'

'It seems infallible,' I say, with grudging admiration. 'But I must also ask you what advantage there is in this plan for you, my lord Duke.'

'Great advantage, Madam, but not only for me. The House of Suffolk will benefit more. But remember, Madam, this plan cannot go ahead or succeed without me. I control the court, the government, the militia and, above all, the King. What I am proposing – to seal our success and mutual advantage – is an alliance between our two families, to be cemented by a marriage between our children.'

Well, he couldn't be more candid than that. As for a marriage between our children – the advantage will all be his. He might be a duke, but his father was a traitor, while our daughter is of royal blood. It's as plain as day: Jane will be Queen, but Northumberland plans to rule England through his son, her husband.

'I have five sons,' he tells me. 'John, Ambrose, Harry and Robert are all married. Only Guilford is unwed, and it is he whom I am proposing as a bridegroom for the Lady Jane. He's a virtuous boy, and only a year older than she. He's his mother's favourite, and a dutiful son. He will make an excellent consort.'

'I dare say,' I respond wryly. I know for a fact that the Duchess has spoilt that boy, but no matter. He'll meet his match in Jane – *if* we agree to the marriage. Just now, there are more pressing issues to discuss.

'I must be certain,' I say, 'that Jane's title to the throne is sound. It will be, won't it? It will be a legal title?'

'Of course,' the Duke answers, but he does not meet my gaze.

'And you would wish Lord Guilford to become King Consort?'

'Naturally. Who could contemplate a female sovereign ruling without recourse to the guidance of her husband?'

'Who will be subject to the guidance of his father,' I add, smiling.

Northumberland is immediately on the defensive.

'Madam, with respect, I know how to govern this realm. These young people as yet lack the wisdom of age, and have little experience of life. My aim is to guide them until they are capable of ruling unaided – with your help, of course, and that of my lord here. Once Jane and Guilford are steering a safe course, they will have no further need of us, but I am sure they will not forget those who launched them upon it, and thereby I see for us all a glorious future crowned by a peaceful and prosperous old age.'

'God willing,' I say.

'God,' he retorts, 'helps those who help themselves, Madam. Now, what say you? Will you give Jane this chance to fulfil her destiny?'

Why should I hesitate? The glory of a crown without the burden of one. There is no question in my mind now as to what I should do.

'I am with you,' I declare. 'I give my consent. I will waive my right in favour of Jane.' Both dukes beam at me triumphantly, but the smile soon disappears from Northumberland's face as he hears what I have to say next. 'I have but one condition. I do not want the marriage consummated until all is assured. Your plan, my lord, might fail; nothing is certain in this life. And an unconsummated marriage can be annulled with little difficulty. It's merely a wise precaution, in case anything goes wrong. I'm sure you can understand that we have to protect our own interests, and our daughter's.'

Henry is staring at me in admiration, but Northumberland is clearly riled.

'I fail to see what can go wrong, Madam,' he says stiffly.

'I have every confidence that all will go as planned,' I reply. 'You seem prepared for every contingency. But I feel that caution should be our watchword. We should not be too precipitate. I too want to be prepared for every eventuality.'

Ah! I have him there.

'Very well,' he agrees, his reluctance plain to see. 'The consummation will wait until the crown is on Jane's head.'

'There is one small matter,' Henry says, a little later.

'Yes?' asks Northumberland.

'We have for some weeks had an understanding with the Duchess of Somerset that Jane is to be betrothed to her son, Edward Seymour, Earl of Hertford.'

'But they are not formally betrothed?'

'Not yet.'

'Good. Then break off your understanding. Say you have reconsidered. Young Hertford is a traitor's son. The Lady Jane is far too good a prize for him.'

'I agree,' I say. 'One question, my lord. Why did you ask to see our younger daughter, Katherine, tonight?' I suspect that Henry already knows what Northumberland will answer.

'Madam, I am seeking to retain the support of the chief men of the kingdom,' the Duke explains. 'I believe the Earl of Pembroke to be stout in our cause. His son, you may be aware, has expressed an interest in the Lady Katherine. Should you agree to their marriage, we could bind Pembroke more tightly to us by ties of kinship.'

I recall the bold young man in Westminster Abbey. A handsome youth, and a good match for Katherine. I look at Henry.

'I have already given my consent in principle,' he says, somewhat abashed. 'If you approve, my dear, we will go ahead.'

'Well, it's good of you to consult me,' I say tartly. 'But as it happens, I heartily approve.'

'Excellent!' cries Northumberland. 'And now, if I may, a toast to the future?' He raises his goblet.

'To the future,' we echo.

John Dudley, Duke of Northumberland

Ely Place, London, April 1553

I smile as Guilford enters the room.

'Be seated, my boy,' I say, appraising him as he sits opposite me at the table. Fair hair flopping over his eyes, full lips, elegant blue-velvet doublet and breeches. He's sixteen now, already over six feet tall, and long and lean with it. My wife says he's very graceful for a man, and very good-looking.

She is partial – he is too immature for his years in my opinion. His older brothers were men at his age. Of course, his mother has spoiled him, right from his infancy. She's soft, and I suspect she has made sure that I don't always get to hear of Guilford's transgressions, of which I'm sure there are many. Oh, she reproves him, but she has as sharp a bite as a kitten. He runs rings round her, smiles charmingly, says he loves her when she's angry, and gets away with murder. She doesn't know the half of it. If she heard one whisper of what my spies have told me of Guilford's activities, she'd collapse in horror.

I know for a fact, because I had him followed, that last night my son frequented The Cardinal's Hat, a notorious brothel in Southwark. I know that his friends paid for him to have a whore there, as he had spent all his money on drink. I suspect that this morning he is suffering from a sore head, at the very least. God grant he has not got the clap or the pox.

'I have something very important to tell you,' I say, watching him closely. 'Last night, I dined with the Duke and Duchess of Suffolk. We discussed many matters of great consequence – among them, your marriage. It's high time you wed, don't you think?'

'My marriage?' He is unprepared for this, of course. He looks shocked. I don't know why this should be, because his brothers were all married off while they were young; but then, of course, Guilford lives only for the moment.

'Yes, your marriage,' I say, with some emphasis. 'It's high time. More than timely, if what I hear is true.' He has the grace to look both bewildered and embarrassed. 'It has been arranged that you will marry the Suffolks' eldest daughter, Lady Jane Grey. I saw her last night, and I am happy to report that she is a prize for any suitor, with her royal blood, her learning and her comely appearance. You are a lucky young man, Guilford, luckier than any of your brothers. I hope you appreciate that.'

'Er, yes, Sir,' he stammers. 'I'm sure I've seen the Lady Jane at court, but I . . . I can't remember her.'

'Is that all you have to say?' I ask, exasperated.

'No, I mean, yes, no. I am most honoured, Sir,' he stutters, plainly reeling at the thought of what marriage will mean to him. The loss of his freedom, the responsibility of a wife, the likelihood that children will follow hard on the heels of the wedding night. No more jaunts to the stews of Southwark! It will do the boy a power of good. Of course, he's not ready for it, and no doubt his mother will have something to say, but it will do him no good, as my mind is made up.

'You'll get used to the idea, Guilford,' I tell him. 'I did, when I was your age. We all have to. And remember, this marriage will bring you more status, wealth and power than you can ever have dreamed of. The Lady Jane is a princess of the blood, a member of the royal House. What other youngest son, such as yourself, could hope for such a bride? I tell you, I have done well by you. It is the most brilliant match. And I have no doubt that, when Jane meets you, she will like what she sees. Remember, my boy, marriage has its advantages. I take it I need not spell them out.'

I grin at him, watching the flush redden his cheeks. I decide to bait him by pretending in his innocence.

'It's alright, Guilford, you need not worry yet about that aspect of wedlock. For political reasons, which I will explain in due course, we have decided that you will not immediately consummate your marriage, but will wait until we deem the time to be right.'

'But why, Father?' He looks surprised.

'For reasons of state. You may rest assured that there is no other cause. May I take it that you are content with your good fortune?' I ask, with some irony.

'Yes, Sir,' he answers. 'I am content.'

His scowl belies his dutiful reply.

Lady Jane Grey

Suffolk House, London, April 1553

Once they became Duke and Duchess, my parents took possession of Suffolk House in London. It lies in Southwark, hard by
the residence of the Bishop of Winchester and the former priory
of St Mary Overy. The house is virtually a palace, having been
given to my grandmother, Mary Tudor, Duchess of Suffolk, by
her brother, King Henry VIII. Its magnificence underlines our
family's royal connections.

We have now abandoned Dorset House for our new abode,
and are more than comfortably installed here. My sisters and
I occupy sumptuous apartments in the turreted west wing,
which are furnished with exquisitely carved furniture, family
portraits and bright tapestries. I'm sitting here by the open
window, on a fresh morning in the middle of April, engrossed
in a treatise denying the Real Presence of Christ in the
Eucharist, when Mrs Ellen brings a summons for me to attend
my parents immediately in the great chamber on the first floor.
Reluctantly laying down my book, I smooth my skirts,
straighten my hood and hasten on my way, Mrs Ellen following.
What have I done, I wonder, to merit such a peremptory
summons?

When I arrive, I find to my astonishment that my lord and
lady, seated either side of the fire, are beaming at me as I make
my curtsey. This is more alarming than if their faces bore
menacing frowns.

'Come and sit with us, Jane,' invites my mother. I take the
proffered stool.

'Will you tell her, Henry?' she asks, archly.

'No. You're her mother. You know best how to put these
things.' My father rises, plants his feet firmly in front of the

fireplace and begins caressing the head of his mastiff, which has loped over to his side, tail wagging.

'Well, Jane, we have some excellent news for you,' my mother says. 'You will remember the night my lord of Northumberland came to dinner. After you had gone to bed, he suggested an alliance between our two families, to be cemented by a marriage between yourself and his youngest son, Lord Guilford Dudley. He is the only son who is as yet unwed. Lord Guilford is a virtuous and . . .'

'I beg your pardon, Madam, but did you say that I am to be wed to a Dudley?' I interrupt, shocked into rudeness. 'But why? You have told me yourself that they are upstarts, traitors and hypocrites. How can you contemplate such a marriage?' The idea of it repels me: I am breathing fast and am flushed. 'Lord Guilford cannot be my husband – everyone knows he is but a spoilt little mother's boy.'

'That is enough!' shouts my father, since my mother looks astounded at my outburst and is, for once, lost for words. 'I tell you, my fine lady, you will marry Lord Guilford, mother's boy or no. He comes of good Protestant stock, and the marriage will bring us all splendid advantages.'

'Good Protestant stock?' I echo, my temper rising. For years I have bent the knee, and often my back, to my parents' will, but this is the proverbial last straw, and all the pent-up anger at years of abuse and humiliation now bubbles to the surface. I will not let them do this thing to me – I will fight them until I have no breath left in my body. 'Good Protestant stock?' I repeat, registering their appalled expressions. 'Traitor's stock, you mean. Northumberland's father was sent to the block by Henry VIII, or have you forgotten that? And I dare say that, if all were known, he himself would deserve the same. Look how he treated the Duke of Somerset! I marvel that you can contemplate giving your daughter to the son of such a self-seeking, opportunistic tyrant.'

'Listen, Jane.' My mother has found her voice. 'Listen – before my patience runs out. You are young, and although you are learned, you are innocent in the ways of the world. You cannot be expected to understand matters of state, and make no mistake, my girl, this marriage is a matter of state, as you will find out in due course. There are many sound reasons for it, and they are all to your, and our, benefit.'

'To my lord of Northumberland's benefit, you mean!' I fling back.

'It does not become you to speak ill of the Duke,' says my father sternly. 'He is a great and powerful man, and if such talk as you have uttered today went beyond this room, you would be in a dire pass indeed. And so would we. Now, on your duty to me and your mother, you will not say one more word against my lord of Northumberland. You will obey.'

I stand vibrant with anger, forcing myself to silence. I am being sold to that horrible, unscrupulous man for my parents' gain, I know it. It is intolerable! My only chance is to stand against it with every objection I can think of.

'His Grace apart,' I say, laying as much contemptuous stress on the title as I dare, 'I have no inclination to marry, and even less to marry Lord Guilford Dudley. I refuse his offer.'

My father makes a visible effort to master his impatience.

'I understand your reluctance,' he says gruffly. 'It is but natural for a young maiden to fear the marriage bed. But look at your mother and me! We have been contented in our union, and we accord well together, even though we were strangers at the beginning. And when you have children, you will discover that they are a great blessing. There is no reason to think that Lord Guilford will not prove an excellent husband. Forget the court gossip: I have it on his father's word that he's a virtuous, upstanding lad who is eager to make you a happy bride. Now, set aside your fears, and compose yourself for your betrothal.'

My mother chimes in, 'Remember, Jane, if you have any particular concerns, you can always have a quiet word with me or Mrs Ellen.'

'I have no fears about marriage!' I cry. 'But I know that it must be the union of two souls, made in the sight of God, with the consent of each. How can God be pleased with such a union if one of the partners has been forced into it against their will?'

'You will grow to love your husband in time,' insists my lady. 'It is your duty.'

'Never!' I am passionate now. 'I will never marry him. Nor can you make me. I have obeyed you in every other thing. I wear these awful, extravagant clothes because you say I must, even though I know they are offensive to God. I have accompanied you week after week on your brutal hunting expeditions, even though the agonies of the kill turn my stomach. I have endured blow after blow for misdemeanours I never committed. I have borne your criticisms and your cruelty because I know the right duty of a child to its parents, and I bear the bitter knowledge that I am not the son you wanted. But now you want to marry me to an upstart fool I can never love, because it is to your advantage. Well, I will not. When I get to the altar, I will refuse to pledge myself, even if you beat me in the face of the congregation to make me.'

'You'd not dare humiliate us thus in public!' bawls my mother, rising in fury. She slaps me hard across the face, once, twice, thrice. 'You've said enough, you ungrateful girl!'

'And by God's blood, you will apologise at once!' thunders my father.

'I will not,' I sob, my cheek stinging and tears spilling from my eyes. 'It is you who should be apologising to me for all the hurts and the unkindnesses – and now this!'

'How dare you!' spits my lady, raining blows on my head and shoulders. 'I tell you, I curse the day I bore you. You have been nothing but trouble ever since you came into this world. But I promise you, for all that, I will not neglect the duty laid upon me, as your parent, to expunge this evil streak of rebellion from your malicious heart.'

I am beyond heeding her. I crumple into the chair, cradling my head against the blows and wailing as if my heart will break. Mrs Ellen hastens to me, but my mother waves her away.

'My whip, Mrs Ellen, if you please,' she commands. 'I see I shall have to beat this wickedness out of her.'

John Dudley, Duke of Northumberland

Greenwich Palace, April 1553

I am gratified to see the Duke of Suffolk at Greenwich so soon after our discussion, especially since his Grace and his lady seemed to have had some reservations about co-operating with my plans.

'I had not expected to see your lordship for several days yet,' I tell him affably.

'Ah, but my lord, we do not look a gift horse in the mouth, if you will pardon the expression,' Suffolk smiles. 'No, I am here to tell you that our daughter is delighted at the prospect of marrying your son, and that she is happy to proceed to the betrothal without delay.'

'Excellent, excellent,' I say, beaming at him. 'I will set the lawyers to work at once to draw up the contract. Perhaps you and her Grace could bring the Lady Jane to court two days hence to conclude the formalities.'

'Of course,' he agrees. Do I detect a certain hesitation?

'Now there is another matter I wanted to speak of,' I continue. 'Again, this is in confidence. I have found out that the Earl of Pembroke is wholeheartedly with us in our matter, for he has said he is eager to join our alliance, and has agreed that his son should marry your younger daughter, the Lady Katherine.'

The Duke looks suitably gratified. I know he likes and respects Pembroke, and that he must therefore welcome this proposed marriage.

'Will you have a word with the Earl and sort out the preliminaries?' I ask.

'I shall be pleased to do so,' he answers. 'I must say I am more than satisfied with the way things are turning out.'

'Yes,' I agree, 'I confess that I too find matters to be proceeding more smoothly than I had anticipated. This augurs well for the future, my lord, for with every day that passes it seems more likely that our plans will prove successful.'

Lady Jane Grey

Suffolk House and Greenwich Palace, April 1553

I have given in. I lie face down on my bed, my back and shoulders sore from the most vicious beating that my mother has ever administered. I could bear the pain better were it not for the fact that I suffered it in vain. But in the end I had to capitulate to their demands, and they forced me to grovel abjectly. I did it because I was unable to endure further punishment. How I hate myself and deplore my spineless weakness! Christ Himself never gave in, even though they nailed Him to the Cross, but I, who pride myself on being His dutiful follower, I gave in because my agony was too great. I cannot help but despise myself!

And now, according to a message from my father brought to me by Mrs Ellen, I am to prepare myself to go to court, on the day after tomorrow, to make my betrothal pledges and sign the precontract. Above all, I am to look pleased about it, or else! Frankly, I doubt I will be able to raise myself from the bed by then, let alone endeavour to look pleased. Anyway, what is there to look pleased about? And what would they say at court if they could see the stripes on my back?

He's such a peacock, strutting about in his gaudy clothes and giving himself airs. He'd be good-looking if it were not for that pouting underlip and the permanent scowl. None of his posturing impresses me; in fact it repels me. This is my husband-to-be. How can I ever love such a person? There appears to be no finesse, no humanity in his manner – just indifference and petulance. Doubtless rumour spoke truth, and he *is* spoilt. God help me, how will I endure living with him? How can I bear it?

We are standing either side of a table in the Duke's luxurious lodgings, encircled by parents, lawyers and clerics. My wounds still smart beneath the heavy fabric of my dress, and I am constrained to hold myself stiffly. I feel utterly wretched, but when it's appropriate, I attempt a smile; otherwise I keep my eyes modestly downcast to the floor. Even my mother could not argue with that!

Thus I go through the whole charade – the betrothal promises, the giving of the ring and the placing of it on my finger, and the congratulations of the witnesses. I can hardly believe this is truly happening. Tomorrow there is to be made a public announcement of the forthcoming wedding, but for now, the formalities completed, we move into a private chamber where wine and sweetmeats have been set out.

Goblets in hand, Guilford and I come face to face again.

'My Lady Jane,' he says, bowing low.

'Lord Guilford.' I curtsey.

We have nothing to say to each other. We fill the void with the small talk that is expected on such an occasion, and for a few minutes we discuss the weather and the quality of the wine, all the while sizing each other up. The absurdity of it all strikes me forcibly, while my betrothed looks bored and vexed. It is I, however, who venture into deep waters first.

I lean towards him.

'I just want to say that, if I were allowed to follow my own inclinations, I would not marry you,' I declare in a low voice. 'It's nothing to do with you, my lord – I do not wish to marry anyone at all.'

He snorts with amusement.

'What makes you think I want to marry you?'

'Then we are of one mind.'

'Yes – but what of it? We have no choice in the matter. That's been made very plain to me.'

'And to me,' I tell him. 'At least we have something in common.' I venture a tight smile.

'I hear you are very bookish,' Guilford says.

'Yes. I find much comfort in my books. I would have preferred a life dedicated to study.'

'Well, I have no objection to your continuing your studies,

provided you don't expect me to share them,' he declares. 'Your leisure time will be all your own, as long as you keep me company in public – and in bed.' He leers at me knowingly. Involuntarily I shudder, and he notices.

'Ah, so that's the cause of your reluctance!' he laughs. 'Well, my little bookworm, let me assure you, it's not as bad as all that. Really, it's quite pleasurable, as I shall teach you. We'll have some good sport, when they let us.'

I flush with indignation, mortified that he should refer to such intimacies, and then I remember that soon he will have every right . . . The thought is hateful to me.

But there is no time for a reproof because both sets of parents are now bearing down on us, obviously gratified to see us at least talking to one another. I bite my lip, trying to control my indignation, while Guilford takes refuge in an excessive outpouring of gushing pleasantries. Simmering, I force myself to respond politely and ignore his smirking face. What a sham, I think. What a pretence! And that is what my life will be henceforth.

Durham House, London, Whitsunday, 25th May 1553

The weight of my gown and train, made of gold and silver brocade and embroidered with hundreds of tiny diamonds and seed pearls, obliges me to walk in slow and stately fashion through the panelled rooms and galleries of Durham House, a royal property on the Strand, once the London residence of the bishops of Durham. My wedding is to be celebrated in the chapel here. Behind me in the procession walks my sister Katherine, also a bride this day: for her, I swear, that means little more than the chance to dress up in a gorgeous gown and be the centre of attention.

Northumberland has prepared for this double wedding with especial care, for its trappings are to reflect what he insists is its political importance – as if there were something unusual about such alliances between great families. The ancient walls of Durham House have been hung with magnificent new tapestries, its flagstones covered with Turkish carpets, and its mullioned windows and arched doorways swathed in swags of gold and silver tissue.

The King himself – who, I am told, has heartily given his assent to these marriages – has personally commanded his Master of the Wardrobe to provide the brides and bridegrooms, and all the important guests, with rich stuffs for our wedding attire. For once, my lady does not have to exhort me to dress as beseems my rank, for I would never dream of disobeying the express wishes of the King, good Protestant that he is, especially after he has sent, from his sickbed, generous wedding gifts of fine jewellery for us all, four young people whose marriages he is too ill to witness.

As I am borne on my father's arm into the chapel, the whole privy council of England rises to its feet. Northumberland is there, garbed in his customary black, and Guilford awaits me at the altar rails, a tall, resplendent figure in white satin, his fair hair flopping over his blue eyes.

This should have been a joyful occasion, the fulfilment of my hopes and dreams, but it is not. Not for me, anyway. I make my vows unthinkingly, not daring to reflect on their deeper meaning, and avoid looking at Guilford when he tries to catch my eye. I did not miss the glance of lustful appreciation he threw me when he caught sight of me in my wedding finery, and it fills me with trepidation. I can only be thankful – indeed, it is the sole thing I have to be thankful for – for my parents' decree that he and I shall live apart for the present, on account of my tender years, or so I have been told. This is a little strange, for many girls are married at fourteen and sleep with their husbands from the first, but I'm not going to ask questions. It's a welcome respite, and long may it last!

The nuptial ceremony is over – I am Lady Jane Dudley. The hated name is mine. We take our places for the feast in the great hall and are served course after course of rich and exotic food. I can eat little of it, but beside me Guilford is wolfing mouthful after mouthful with relish, and washing it all down with copious amounts of the best Rhenish. Presently, a troupe of players enters the hall and begins performing a masque portraying the god Hymen with his bridal torch, who dances suggestively with a bevy of adoring nymphs. It has barely started when Guilford announces that he feels sick, and crashes out of his chair. A moment later he has spewed up his dinner, and a lot else, on the costly Turkey carpet, and has to leave the room in an ignominious hurry, lest he further disgrace himself in front of the company.

I remain at table, mortified and embarrassed, pretending to watch the masque and wishing that this interminable evening would come to an end, so that I can return with my parents to Suffolk Place, and retire to my virginal bed and the tender ministrations of Mrs Ellen. I long to cast off my heavy gown, in which I am sweating profusely, and slither between cool linen sheets. But first I have to do my duty by my guests.

Further along the high table, Katherine is radiant as she gazes into the adoring eyes of her groom. Clearly she and Lord William Herbert have struck up a warm rapport. He seems entranced by her, and justifiably so, for she is surely the beauty of the family, with her fair hair and her eyes the colour of cornflowers. It's a pity, then, that the consummation of their marriage is also to be postponed, since – to judge by the way they are behaving – they are ripe for it now. Perhaps they will find a means to outwit our parents.

At last the festivities come to an end, and I can take my leave of a very drunk Guilford and walk with my parents across the sloping lawns leading down to the river and our waiting barge. It's a warm, starry night, and most of the company are tipsy and in high good humour. I have no inclination to join in their jesting. Despite the heat, I feel an inward chill: I am cold to my soul, and doubt that the sun will ever shine for me again. The deed is done, I have been sold into bondage, and there is no remedy. I long to get back to my bedchamber and my books, the only comforts I have left.

Lady Jane Dudley, formerly Grey

Suffolk House, 27th May 1553

Servants do gossip, and gossip travels swiftly, for London is a small world.

'I do not like what I hear,' says Mrs Ellen, coming into my

chamber one evening with some dried herbs to scatter in the clothing chests.

'What have you heard?' I ask, abandoning my book.

'You will remember, my lady, that on the night of the wedding, the Earl of Pembroke took his son and your sister to his London residence, Baynard's Castle.'

'I do remember,' I reply. 'I hear that Katherine is being housed there in palatial style and that my lord Earl cannot do enough for her.'

'And very proper too, I say,' observes Mrs Ellen. 'But already she has displeased him. I have it on good authority, from one of her maidservants, whose brother is a groom in this house, that on the wedding night Lord William was caught by his father in the act of stealing into her chamber, and she all undressed ready to welcome him. Well, the Earl ordered them both back to their separate beds, telling them they must be patient a little longer. He was not best pleased, I can tell you.'

'Poor Katherine.' I recall the radiant, ardent bride.

'I don't like it a bit,' Mrs Ellen repeats. 'It's not natural. The Lady Katherine is nigh thirteen, of full age to be a wife, and why she should not be one I cannot understand. It's the same with you, and you're even older. Is it that my lord of Pembroke does not trust your lord father, or your lord father does not trust my lord of Northumberland? In truth, that does not augur well for the future. Why make such marriages in the first place, if you're not willing to let husband and wife bed in the natural way?'

'Why indeed?' I ask. None of it makes sense. But, in very truth, I am quite content to leave things as they are, and not ask questions.

Syon Abbey, Middlesex, June 1553

I wake up in a strange bed. For a long time now, it seems, I have been inhabiting a shadow world, suffering – I vaguely recall – from constant vomiting, fever and a humiliating looseness of the bowels. But today I am myself again, although very weak and shivery.

'Thank God you're looking better at last, child,' says Mrs

269

Ellen fervently, reverting from the formal title by which she must now address me to the old, familiar endearances, and stroking the hair from my forehead. 'I do declare that there was a time when everyone feared you might die, so virulent was your fever.' There are tears of relief in her eyes. Was it that serious, then? I have blurred memories of leeches being applied to my body, to bleed me of evil humours.

Mrs Ellen plumps the pillows and raises me gently in the bed. Then she pulls off my sweaty shift and replaces it with a freshly laundered one. My exposed body looks thin and wasted; of course I have not been eating. When I am decent again, Mrs Ellen rebraids my hair. I ask for my mirror, and she hands it to me. One glance reveals skin stretched taut over delicate cheekbones, and eyes over-bright with the aftermath of fever. Surprisingly, I am not ill pleased with what I see, for illness has lent a strange, ethereal beauty to my face.

I remember that I fell ill at Suffolk House three days after my wedding.

'I do think, Jane,' says Mrs Ellen, as we discuss it later, 'that your collapse was caused by nervous strain and unhappiness. I don't believe there was anything more to it. Do you remember what you were saying at the time?'

'No, I do not,' I murmur. 'What did I say?'

Mrs Ellen's voice drops to a whisper. 'You thought that it was due to something more sinister. In your more lucid moments, you expressed the fear that his Grace of Northumberland did not like you and was trying to poison you.'

'I said that?' I am shocked.

'You did indeed. Naturally we all dismissed it as an absurd fancy, the ramblings of a mind crazed by sickness. In fact, the Duke and Duchess, and your husband, all expressed their deep concern, and sent regularly to inquire after your health. And then, when your condition deteriorated alarmingly, the Duke placed his mansion here at Syon at your parents' disposal, because the air is more healthful in these parts than in Southwark.'

I realise I am in the former abbey of the Bridgettine nuns, by the Thames at Isleworth. The nuns were turned out by my great-uncle during the dissolution of the monasteries. The Duke of Somerset, and Northumberland in his turn, took possession of their house, and a glance around my bedchamber with its fine furniture, rich carpet and rare tapestries suggests that they both turned it into a very comfortable residence indeed.

Mrs Ellen places a clutch of papers on my bed.

'The Duke and his family wrote to you,' she says. I pick up the papers and peruse them. They are heartening letters, expressing concern, a sincere desire for my return to health, and the hope that I will soon be back in London. I am tempted to feel touched by such overt kindness, but remind myself that it doubtless springs purely from self-interest.

There comes a morning when I am strong enough to join my parents and sister Mary for a slow stroll along the gallery, as it is too wet outside to venture into the gardens. We inspect the many portraits that hang there; among the sitters are several we know personally, or recognise, and my mother is particularly taken with a group portrait showing her grandmother, Queen Elizabeth of York, with her four young daughters kneeling behind her. She points to the third daughter in line.

'That's my mother, Mary Tudor. How fair she was,' my lady remarks, gazing at the pretty child with long blonde curls.

'Think you it is a true likeness?' asks my father sceptically. 'Her sister Katherine is shown as a full-grown child, yet you told me she died an infant.'

'I can see a likeness,' says my mother, considering. 'Perhaps the artist was told to make Katherine look like her sisters.'

Suddenly, shockingly, an axe wielded by a bloody hand comes crashing through the wooden panelling next to the portrait. My mother has the rapid presence of mind to push my father aside to avoid his head being cloven in two, before he is even aware of the danger. Mary and I scream in horror – later, Mary tells me she thought it was a spectral apparition, although it looked horribly real to me. But as my father reaches for his sword, the axe crashes to the floor and the gory hand is withdrawn through the splintered gash in the wood.

Tentatively my lord examines the rough slit; there is nothing to be seen behind it but a dark, empty cavity. He shouts for strong men to attend him with cudgels and axes, and when they come hurrying, he directs them to chop down that section of

271

the panelling. Within minutes, holding aloft a lantern, he is able to enter the space behind. As we peer through, a hidden passage with bare stone walls can be seen. My father disappears down it, his retainers at his heels, still brandishing their weapons.

'Careful!' cries my mother in alarm. We girls are huddled together in terror, fearful of what might ensue.

After a time my lord returns, grim-faced.

'God, it's dark and dank in there,' he exclaims. 'There's only room for one man at a time to get through. The passage leads to a spiral stair, which we descended until we came to a cellar. And there we found our axe-man. These good fellows here laid hold of him, and by the tried and trusted method of pointing my dagger at his throat, I extracted a confession from him. It seems he was once a lay brother here at Syon, and that he has nourished his bitterness at its dispossession these past thirteen years. He said he'd survived by doing odd jobs as a labourer, and on the occasional charity of the local people. He longed, he said, for the chance to have his revenge on the House of Tudor, and was gratified to hear that the King's own cousins had taken up residence at Syon. This morning, he slipped into the house unchallenged, made his way to the south gallery and was gratified to find that the secret passage and stair were still there behind the panelling, untouched by the renovations. And there he hid, his axe grasped in his hand. It was meant for you, my dear.'

My father puts an arm around my mother's shoulders. I have never seen her look so discomposed: she is fighting to retain her customary dignified manner.

'Is he still down there?' she asks, her face pale. 'I hope you've tied him up!'

'As it happens, my dear, he's quite dead,' my lord tells her. 'He managed to wriggle free, grabbed my dagger and stabbed himself with it.'

The men exchange glances. My father fixes them with a steady gaze. I cannot take this all in.

'Take him away tonight and bury him at a crossroads,' he commands them. 'He has offended God by taking his own life, so he may not rest in hallowed ground. He tried to murder my good lady here, and he almost murdered me.' The men seem about to say something, but he stills them with another look.

'Say no more about this to anyone. I do not wish to cause my wife and daughters any further distress. If anyone asks what you are about, say you found his body in the woods.'

They leave, and my father hurries us back to our private chambers, permitting no further questions. And that is an end to the matter, although I am left to wonder just what did happen in that cellar, and whether murder was committed this day after all.

Northumberland, my father says, is rarely far from the King's side these days. Something ominous is in the air, and today a messenger in the royal livery came cantering to Syon, although I don't know what his errand was.

I am still a little frail after my illness, and spend my days reading in the great parlour, or strolling with Mrs Ellen through the beautiful gardens that Somerset planted. The roses are in bloom just now, and I enjoy savouring their heady scent, and the sensual whisper of the warm breeze on my face.

It is late afternoon, and the sun is a golden ball slowly moving westwards. As we are about to return to the house for supper, we espy two horsemen trotting through the main gates.

'It's Lord Guilford,' I say, startled. I have not seen him since our wedding day, and I have not missed him, either. What could he possibly be doing here? The other rider is obviously a manservant, for he wears the Dudley livery.

Guilford sees us and waves, reining in his horse.

'Good day, my lady!' he calls. 'I hope I find you better.'

I dip a brief curtsey. 'Much improved, Sir, I thank you,' I reply politely. 'What brings you here?'

He dismounts and walks towards me, a lean, graceful figure in tawny velvet.

'You may go,' he says curtly, addressing Mrs Ellen. Startled by his rudeness, I shoot her a pleading look that begs her to remain within earshot, and she quietly withdraws into the next garden, behind a high box hedge.

Guilford looks down at me. He is so tall, and his eyes are very blue. Reluctantly I find myself admiring his perfect features, even while reminding myself that I have no cause to admire his character.

'I came, my lady, at my parents' behest. Were you not informed?'

'I know nothing,' I answer in some bewilderment.

'Oh. I thought you were waiting for me.' He seems at a loss for words.

'Of what should I have been informed?' I ask, in mounting trepidation, for I begin to think I can guess the answer.

Guilford draws a deep breath.

'That we are to consummate our marriage,' he says, with an odious leer. 'I am to make a true wife of you. My father says the King wishes it, and your parents have agreed.'

There is a silence while I try to compose my thoughts, which are now plunged into fearful turmoil.

'I did not know,' I stammer at length. 'I am unprepared. They should have told me. And I've not been well. This is impossible!'

He looks at me in dismay. 'But my father sent a messenger.'

'I am unprepared,' I repeat. 'They said nothing.' He must be able to detect the panic in my voice: I sound to myself like a trapped animal.

'There is nothing to fear,' he says. 'I would not hurt you. Trust me.' He tilts my chin upwards with his fingers and our eyes meet. I feel myself flushing. Again I think, how handsome he is! And how I wish I liked him better. Then I reprove myself for going over to the enemy. But he *is* very good-looking, and for the first time he seems disposed to be kind.

Young as I am, I have learned, over the years, to accept the hand that Fate has dealt me, even if I occasionally rail against it. My situation could be a lot worse. I have heard of girls wedded to greybeards who can do little in bed save indecently paw their young wives, while yet expecting those same wives to bear them sons. At least I will not have to suffer an old man's caresses. Instead, my duty bids me submit to this fine-looking youth, whom Fate has set in absolute authority over me as my husband. Many girls would envy me, I make no doubt, but they are not the kind of girls who look beyond a beautiful face and a muscular body. What irks me most is that I have been sold for gain, and I cannot help my resentment running high.

Guilford is watching my face and has the wit to read my conflicting emotions. Tenderly, to my surprise, he bends and kisses me on the mouth.

*

Supper in the evening is a horribly embarrassing occasion. My parents have welcomed Guilford warmly, obviously aware of the purpose of his visit. For my part, I cannot forgive them for keeping me in the dark. During the meal, which we take in the private parlour, they make excruciating bawdy innuendoes and jokes. I squirm when my father, seeing me blush, observes that I am lucky to have been spared a public bedding ceremony.

'Unlike your mother and me,' he winks, expansive with good wine. 'They stripped us naked in front of all the company.'

'Don't remind me,' says my lady. 'I thought I should die for shame. And then they returned an hour later with the loving cup and demanded to know if we had performed the act. They even inspected the sheets.'

Guilford is sitting there smirking. I wish I was anywhere else.

It is an utter relief when the cloth is lifted and spiced wine and wafers are set out in honour of the occasion. We all raise our goblets in a toast, then my lord claps Guilford on the back.

'To your labours, my boy! Do your duty and provide me with a brace of grandsons!'

My mother leads me to the state bedchamber, which has been made ready for the occasion, and helps Mrs Ellen disrobe me and dress me in a beautiful chemise of white silk embroidered in gold. My long hair is brushed until it shines, then spread becomingly over my shoulders as I lie in the vast bed, which is hung with painted oriental curtains and spread with herb-scented lawn sheets and a counterpane embellished with the Dudley arms. I rest on the pillow stony-faced as my mother kisses me – a rare occurrence – and departs with Mrs Ellen.

All the lurid female gossip I have ever heard about virgins being deflowered has surfaced in my head, and I am doing my very best not to panic or burst into tears. Once, one of my mother's ladies said the pain was so great that she had screamed out loud, and even then her husband had not been able to penetrate her, though he went repeatedly to the assault like a battering ram to the siege-tower, she shrieking in agony every time.

Please God, I pray, let it not be like that for me.

Guilford, clad in a red velvet nightgown, places the candle on the table and smiles uncertainly at me.

'Blow it out,' I whisper.

'No. I want to see you,' he says with that leer, pacing towards the bed and throwing off his nightgown to the floor. I have never seen a naked man before and lower my eyes, not daring to look at the virile nudity so blatantly displayed before me. He climbs in beside me, taking me in his arms and kissing me hard on the mouth. The feel of his bare flesh is a shock to me.

'Take off your shift,' he orders, his voice hoarse. Mutely I obey. Snuggling down under the covers, I unlace the ribbons threaded through the bodice and wriggle out of the garment, thrusting it under my pillow, ready for when I can put it on again. I am desperate with embarrassment, but Guilford allows me no vestige of modesty. He wrenches back the bedclothes and exposes not only my nakedness, but also his own. I close my eyes for shame.

'Look at me,' he insists. 'Look at me, Jane.'

'I cannot,' I whisper.

For answer, he grabs my hand and guides it to his erect penis. Startled, I open my eyes, and am again shocked at what I see and feel. It seems to have a life of its own, for it throbs and swells at my touch. It is horribly big.

Guilford starts touching me, fingering me hastily from breast to thigh.

'Squeeze me,' he demands, breathing heavily. 'Go on! Hard!'

Timidly, I venture a squeeze.

'Harder!' he rasps. 'Harder!'

My hand tightens. His manhood is taut beneath it. I cannot believe how large it has become, and draw my fingers away involuntarily.

'Will it not hurt me?' I whisper fearfully. He makes no reply. He has gone red in the face, and it is as if he is no longer truly aware of me. It is only my body that he wants, as he writhes against me, rubbing me vigorously and panting with increasing fervour. His strength is fearsome: I cry out as he jabs me with an elbow, but he takes no notice. Suddenly he leans up on one forearm and pushes my legs apart with his free hand. His fingers boldly explore the secret place between them, briefly caressing every crevice, then suddenly, brutally, thrust inside me. A hot splinter of agony pierces my core, and with unwilling tears spilling down my cheeks, I use all my strength to pull his hands away, but he is too strong, too insistent, forcing his fingers further inside, invading, probing and wounding.

'Hold me!' he grunts, mercifully withdrawing his hand and clamping mine to his pulsating member, which seems even bigger than before. He is in a passion of excitement, an animal with only its primeval urge to satisfy. 'Let go, you bitch,' he snarls, pulling my hand away. 'Not now.' Then he mounts me, heaving himself on top of me and violently forcing his penis into me. Deeper and deeper he thrusts, and the pain is terrible, sharp and stabbing. I would be screaming, but he has rammed his lips close on mine, and I can only whimper and squeal, squirming beneath him, almost suffocating, and praying for him to stop. But he is jerking against me, slamming into me faster and faster, hurting me savagely, yet intent only on his own pleasure. Then suddenly, mercifully, he ceases his awful thrusting, tenses and holds still, clutching me painfully tightly and gasping in what seems like agony. I feel him pumping his seed into me before he slumps on me, his erection slowly subsiding.

The torment ended, I lie entangled with him, ravished, violated, unbearably sore, not daring to move. Is it of this that the poets write such heavenly verse? How could any woman ever achieve pleasure from such brutal couplings? And oh, dear God, will I have to endure it again?

To my astonishment, Guilford is smiling sleepily at me, his face close to mine on the pillow. He is still lying across me, heavy, hairy and sweaty, and I can hardly breathe.

'That was good,' he mutters hoarsely. 'Very good. You were so tight. I could feel every sensation.'

I cannot speak, I am so distressed. The pain inside my female parts is an agony.

Guilford frowns. 'What's wrong with you?'

'It was horrible!' I burst out, tears welling up. 'Horrible. Worse than they told me. You hurt me.' I am weeping uncontrollably. 'You hurt me. Oh, oh.'

'For Christ's sake, it couldn't have been that bad,' he says, as if I am making a fuss about nothing. This makes me cry all the more pitifully.

Guilford rolls off me and lies staring up at the tester. The sheets are in a tangle and he is obscenely exposed, flaccid now, damp. There is blood on his penis. My blood.

I pull the covers around me and curl up into a ball, facing away from him. I am sobbing my heart out, but he makes no move to comfort me.

'What on earth is wrong with you?' he asks impatiently. 'God, what a little misery you are. I should have guessed you'd be like this. Or perhaps you don't fancy me, and would prefer to be fucking that sex-starved tutor of yours.'

That is beyond enduring.

'How dare you insult me so!' I cry.

'You are my wife, God help me,' he answers. 'I'll use you as I think fit. Now pull yourself together and stop snivelling.'

I respond to this by breaking into a further torrent of weeping.

'Oh, go fuck yourself!' he swears and flings himself across the bed, dragging all the covers with him. I lie naked, exposed and vulnerable, and scrabble under my pillow for my chemise. But Guilford is too quick for me. His face blazing with anger and something else, he rears up to his knees, seizes my hands in a grip of iron and forces them back on the pillow. This renders me helpless, which immediately, and strangely, has the most unfortunate effect on him. His expression changes to a lustful contortion and, kneeling over me, he begins roughly sucking my breasts, kneading them with one hand and gripping his member with the other.

'NO!' I scream, pushing him backwards with all my might.

He slaps me on the cheek. 'Yes!' he roars. 'You will serve my pleasure. Whenever I like, and as often as I like.' He is above me now, forcing my legs apart with his knees, then driving into me again with a violent urgency. The pain is white-hot, knife-sharp, but my husband is relentless in his lust and ignores my pitiful cries.

'You will obey me, you bitch!' he gasps, shuddering to a climax.

I have died, I think, and gone to Hell.

For hours I lie awake at the edge of the bed, as far from Guilford as possible, steeped in misery. Eventually, sheer exhaustion sends me off to sleep. When I awaken, he has gone and it is morning. Gingerly I sit up, inspecting my bruised body. There is dried blood on the sheets.

By the time Mrs Ellen comes in to dress me, I have made myself decent, but she must see from my face how distressed I am, for she makes the rare gesture of putting her arms around me to comfort me, something she has not done since I left childhood behind. Somehow she knows I cannot talk about what has happened to me, not even to her.

'Alright now, my lamb?' she says, handing me my shift.

If anyone in the household heard me cry out in anguish in the night, they do not betray it by word or look. I am unable to sit, stand or walk without discomfort, and eat my breakfast by sheer effort of will, hiding my inner despair. What has been done to me is too shameful, too awful, for words, and my pride forbids me to disclose it to anyone. I feel dirty and sullied.

Guilford, Mrs Ellen tells me, departed at first light, apparently eager to get back to Greenwich. He dares not face me, I think. Even my mother and father are looking at me with concern. My lady takes me aside.

'I take it your marriage has been consummated?' she asks.

I can only nod. I cannot speak of it.

'I hope, then, that you will soon find yourself pregnant,' she says. 'Then you might settle down to a more normal life, and dwell a little less upon intellectual matters. I'm beginning to wonder if we made a mistake in educating you so well. It has given you unnatural ideas and made you discontented with your lot. Well, no matter – you will soon learn where your true duty lies.'

I am bereft, remembering a world I have lost, and to which I can never return. The very idea of pregnancy fills me with fear. Pregnancy and childbirth are hazardous matters, to which I have now laid myself open, albeit unwillingly. Like the rest of womankind, I must risk my life to provide my husband with heirs. Within a year, I realise with horror, I could be dead.

A week passes, and still Guilford has not returned, I thank God. After my illness and my ordeal in the marriage bed, I am fragile. Inside, I am numb, closed-up and leaden-hearted, carrying my sorrow and shame locked away in my heart. I'm sure Mrs Ellen is worrying about me, for she complains I am too thin and not eating properly, and that if I continue this way I will never recover my strength.

I do not think I could care less.

Chelsea, June 1553

I am back at Chelsea now in the house filled with bitter-sweet memories of Katherine Parr. How happy I was then, and how sad it is that we do not always realise we are happy until happiness is gone. Now, instead of the late Queen's kindly nurturing, I have to endure the harsh rule of my mother, who seems indifferent to my suffering and still takes every opportunity to criticise me. Now it is because Guilford still has not returned to see me; his absence must, of a certainty, be due to some fault in me.

At Chelsea I live quietly. With the King so ill, it would be wrong to do otherwise. I spend my days trying to absorb myself in my studies, and praying that I will not be disturbed by any visits from my husband. My wounds heal slowly, and to my utter relief my monthly course arrives as usual. I dare to hope that Guilford will not think it worth repeating the dreadful marriage act, since I was such a disappointment to him. After all, it's not as if he is his father's eldest son, with an obligation to carry on the family name; nor do I lack sisters who can provide my parents with grandchildren. If only they would all just leave me alone with my books and my letters, I would be content to let life, and the world, pass me by.

John Dudley, Duke of Northumberland

Greenwich Palace, June 1553

Lady Suffolk sends me regular bulletins on the Lady Jane's health. I am concerned about this new daughter-in-law of mine.

I was told she was a modest girl, but at first, to be honest, I thought she looked more sulky than shy, and I have wondered ever since if she will prove as amenable as I had hoped. Then there is her health, which is not good. She's too thin for a start, and over-prone to illness, which is more cause for misgivings. Truly, I fear, I have invested all my hopes in a weak and unpredictable vessel.

Fortunately the marriage has been consummated. Guilford has openly said so, although I was not pleased to hear today that, when he visited her at Chelsea, she refused him her bed. That is a very serious breach of duty on a wife's part, and one calling for me to act. But I must go carefully: the Duchess of Suffolk tells me that her daughter has some malady of the spirit that prevents her from making a full recovery from her recent illness.

I discuss the matter with my wife. Guilford has complained to her also of the wretched girl's intransigence.

'I think she is very wilful,' my good lady says. Of course, she will take Guilford's part: in her eyes, he can do no wrong.

'Yes, that may be so,' I reply. 'But could he be in any way to blame?'

'Of course not! He has merely claimed his lawful rights. Really, John, this foolish wench is making a lot of fuss about nothing, and I mean to visit her and tell her so.'

'No, wait,' I counsel. 'She's been unwell, and it will not do Guilford any good if you interfere. He must sort this out himself – woo her back to compliance if need be. But first, I suggest we allow the Lady Jane time to fully recover her health. That's why I had her moved to Chelsea – her father mentioned how happy she was there with the late Queen. Moreover, it's close to London. I would like the Lady Jane near at hand in case she is needed.'

I look down on the wretched example of human suffering that was once the pride of King Henry. Edward VI is on the brink of the next world; I don't need the royal physicians to tell me that. But it is a hard, drawn-out death. The boy has no rest because of his harsh, tearing cough. The putrid matter he brings up is black, viscous and stinking. His feet and ankles have swollen to twice their normal size, and he can hardly eat anything. Sleep eludes him unless he takes the noxious cocktail of medicines and draughts prescribed by his doctors. He is beyond human help now.

'Your Grace, we can do nothing more,' Dr Owen tells me.

'How long will he last?'

'A week or two at the most, I would say.'

And that, I know for certain, is not enough for all that must needs be done to secure the succession to the Lady Jane.

'Can you do nothing more to keep him alive?' I urge the doctors.

'My lord, we have done all we can. He is in God's hands now. It is only a matter of time.'

With a brusqueness born of anxiety, I dismiss the physicians. Later, after a confidential interview with one of my agents, I am glad I have done so, because with what I have in mind, I do not want them poking and prying around, for I know that they will surely guess what is afoot. My priority is to keep the King alive long enough for my plans to mature, so that I can obtain the support of the great nobles of this realm and commit Edward's sisters into custody. Above all, I must cozen his Majesty into lending some veneer of legality to what would otherwise, I am aware, be a blatant attempt to subvert the law of the land.

All this requires secrecy and time. Time, time, time. I am becoming obsessed with it, and sick of worrying about it and the ever-present need for urgency. But my time will surely run out when the King dies, or soon afterwards, since even I cannot keep the death of a sovereign a secret for long.

So I am profoundly relieved when my trusted agent – a man who is troubled by as few scruples as myself – comes to me with the name of a woman who may be able to prolong the King's life.

'She's a Welshwoman, Tegwyn Rhys by name,' says Yaxley. 'She was left widowed and childless at a young age, so she came to London to seek work, and inevitably turned to prostitution. I've had some dealings with her' – he reddens – 'and found her to be bright and, shall we say, versatile. It got so that she was very much in demand, and managed to stash away quite a bit of money, enough for her to abandon that profession and set herself up in a modest shop in Cornhill.'

'Where she sold?' I inquire.

'Potions. Cures.' Again his cheeks flush.

I lean forward.

'For what?'

'All kinds of complaints,' says Yaxley, clearly uncomfortable.

'And your interest was?'

'To be frank, my lord, I'd been one of her regular clients in the past, and I used to drop in on her from time to time at her shop. Later, after I got married, I experienced some small difficulty –'

'Impotence?' I inquire.

He squirms. 'Something like that, yes. Tegwyn gave me a potion for it, which did the trick.'

Or rather, you believed in it so much that it did, I reflect.

'So what has all this to do with his Majesty?' I ask.

'Well, my lord, after that, whenever I or my wife needed any physic, I went back to Tegwyn's shop. Her prices have always been reasonable, and her cures often work better than those expensive ones prescribed by the court physicians. I became a good customer, you could say. Well, more than that.'

'You frequented her bed as well as her shop?'

He nods.

'We're good friends. I could talk to her about anything, she's that kind of woman. Yesterday, I was sitting in the shop as she was locking up, and we were talking about how dangerous some drugs can be. I was surprised to hear her say that arsenic, while it can be deadly, can also prolong life, if used in the right way.'

Understanding dawns. This is what I have prayed for.

'Summon her to Greenwich at once,' I command. 'I want to talk to her.'

The woman sits before me in my panelled closet. She looks awestruck by her surroundings; of course, she's never been in a palace before. She's comely in her way, if you like the overblown rose type, but her eyes are sharp. I read in them intelligence and cunning. It takes a fox to know a fox.

'I have been told that you can help me,' I say.

'I can try, Sir,' she says. 'Is it a confidential matter?'

'Very confidential. Not one word of what we say must be repeated beyond these walls.'

'You can trust me,' she says, low. 'Is it a – you know – personal matter?'

I laugh briefly.

'Oh, no, nothing like that. Much more serious. Tell me, Mistress Rhys, how come you are so gifted in curing people? My man, William Yaxley, has been singing your praises to the skies.'

'I got it from my mother, Sir. Seventh child of a seventh child, she was, and regarded by many as a wise woman with a gift for healing. She taught me all kinds of lore.'

'I take it all this is quite legal?' I inquire, fixing my stare upon her. 'No magic, no witchcraft?'

'Oh no, Sir. Just herbs and simples.' The flush on her cheeks tells me she is lying, and that there's a great deal more to it than that. 'I rely only on time-honoured remedies.'

'And poisons? Master Yaxley mentioned arsenic.'

Ah. I've got her there. She looks like a hare cornered by dogs.

'I've never harmed anyone,' she protests.

'I'm sure you haven't, but others might wonder. That's why I think you will help me.'

'Help you?' she echoes.

'Yes. I understand you can prolong the life of someone who is ill.'

'Prolong life?' she asks, plainly baffled.

'Yes, by the use of arsenic. Is that correct?'

'Well, yes, I – ' She is more on her guard now. 'I've heard it can be done.'

'But you have never used it yourself for such a purpose?'

'Never, Sir. Never.' The emphasis suggests she is lying.

'Then how come you told Master Yaxley that it could be done?'

'I just repeated something I'd heard about years ago. From an old monk.'

Clever touch, that. Most people nowadays would believe any monk capable of such infamy.

'Well, wherever you learned it, what I want to establish is: would you yourself know how to use arsenic to prolong life?'

'I dare say I could,' she says slowly, considering. 'Is it for yourself, Sir?'

'No.' I take a deep breath. 'It is the King's Majesty whose life we are discussing.'

'The King?' she gasps, her eyes terrified.

'Indeed, sadly so. He is dying, and there are urgent matters of state for him to attend to. I fear, however, that God will call him to Himself before these can be brought to a satisfactory conclusion, and that the kingdom will then be plunged into chaos. If you can help his Majesty, Mistress Rhys, you will be doing England a great favour.'

'I can't,' she says, plainly horrified.

'Why?' I ask, trying to conceal my impatience.

'I can't. It would be cruel.'

'Madam, I am asking you to prolong the King's life, not end it.'

'The old monk told me,' she says, picking her words with care, 'that to administer arsenic in this way can cause the greatest suffering and pain to the patient. Sir, you must realise what it will mean for that poor boy, King or not. It would be callous and inhuman – akin to torture, you might say.'

'But will it prolong his life? And for how long?'

'It would assuredly prolong his life, and probably for a week or more, maybe even a month, but – oh, Sir – at a terrible cost. I beg of you, do not do it.' Her vehemence tells me she has seen the suffering she describes at first hand. But I cannot afford to heed her remonstrances.

'Would you be prepared to take over his treatment? From today? You will be handsomely rewarded, of course.'

The woman slumps in her chair.

'And if I refuse?' she asks.

'Well, Master Yaxley has been rather free with his confidences. Inquiries might need to be made . . .' I allow her a moment to think about this. She must know that the penalty for witchcraft is death.

'I will do it, then,' she says.

I can feel my shoulders sagging with relief.

'Good. But remember,' I say sternly, 'speak of this to no one. There must be utter and absolute secrecy.'

The King looks grey. His young face is disfigured by a grimace of pain, and his frail body is unnaturally bloated. The stench in the royal bedchamber is worse than ever, as if he is rotting already, and it is all I can do not to clamp my handkerchief to my nose as I approach the bed.

'Your Majesty, there is an urgent matter I need to discuss with you,' I begin.

'Pray proceed,' croaks Edward.

'Sir, I am very concerned about the succession. In the interests of preserving the true faith, would you not agree that it is the duty of a good and devout prince to set aside all considerations of blood and kinship where there is any risk of endangering the spiritual welfare of his subjects? Sir, I fear that, if a king were to do otherwise, after this life, which is short, he might be punished for it at God's dreadful tribunal.'

'I know that well, my lord Duke,' says the boy, with feeling. 'I worry about it constantly. The prospect of my sister Mary succeeding is even more terrible to me than my present sufferings and approaching death. It haunts my thoughts, and robs me of the peace of mind that would allow me to prepare my soul in quietness for eternal judgement. God has given me this sacred trust, to lead my people to the true faith, and in abandoning them to a Catholic ruler, I feel I am betraying both Him and them. I am relieved to hear that you share my concerns.'

'Your Majesty, the Lady Mary must never come to the throne.' I speak urgently and sincerely, my fears plain in my voice. There is no time for mind games now.

'I know,' answers the King, no less urgently. 'But my father and Parliament have so ordered matters that her accession cannot be avoided. She is my legal heir.'

'She is a bastard, Sir, and in law a bastard cannot inherit the crown. I have taken advice on this. Your Majesty has the power to disinherit her, and I pray you will do it. So much is at stake.'

'You do not need to remind me, my lord. If there is any lawful way out, I assure you, I will take it.'

'It only requires your Majesty's signature on a legal document.'

'Then we shall have it drawn up.' Edward pauses, breathless. 'Tell me, my lord, if the Lady Mary is removed from the succession, shall the crown go to my sister Elizabeth?'

I answer smoothly. I am prepared for this. 'Sir, she too is a bastard; if the Lady Mary is disinherited, the Lady Elizabeth must be also. Mark my words, as unmarried female sovereigns, one or the other of them would certainly marry a foreign prince and thereby surrender not only England's independence, but also all her ancient rights and privileges. Your Majesty should consider again and again. Kings owe protection to their subjects and must defend them from such calamities.'

'Then who should succeed us? The Duchess of Suffolk? She is next in line after our sisters.'

'It is a possibility, I agree. At least she's a good Protestant, and she's married to an Englishman.' I hesitate. 'Shall I summon her?'

'Yes, do. We would speak with her and see what mettle she has to carry on our great work.' He coughs painfully, hawking up phlegm, and waves me away.

The Duchess rises from her curtsey and listens gravely to what the King is saying. I have warned her of what she is about to be asked, and together we have rehearsed her reply.

'Your Majesty,' she says at length, 'I must confess I have no wish to be Queen. I am a weak woman, unfitted for the task. With your consent, I hereby relinquish my claim.'

'That leaves your Majesty's cousin, Lady Jane Dudley,' I say, after Lady Suffolk has withdrawn.

Edward nods slowly. The afternoon's discussions have exhausted him.

'Since she married my son Guilford, I have come to know her better,' I continue, 'and I can say with surety that she has matchless qualities that befit her, more than any other, for this high dignity. Your Majesty will doubtless recall the agreeableness of her conversation, and her zeal for religion. She has imbibed the reformed faith with her mother's milk, and she is married to a loyal Englishman of wealth and probity. Your Grace, I know, has always held this excellent lady in affectionate regard.'

'Indeed I have,' agrees Edward. 'But while she certainly embodies all the requisite virtues, she is not of my father's line.'

'Sir,' I say severely, 'you are bound by your duty to God to lay aside all natural inclinations towards your father's House. Yet remember, the Lady Jane has Tudor blood by virtue of her descent from your grandfather, King Henry VII, and she was born in lawful wedlock, unlike your sisters. And there is a precedent for her succeeding in her mother's lifetime, for did not that same King Henry VII, of blessed memory, succeed whilst his mother, who had the prior claim, was still alive?'

'You speak the truth,' Edward says. 'My lord, I must confess I am beginning to like this proposal you have laid before me, for it seems to offer real hope for England's salvation. But I am tired now, and cannot discuss it further. I will think on it when I have rested. Attend me tomorrow morning to hear my answer.'

I withdraw. In the ante-room to the bedchamber I encounter Edward's closest friend, and gentleman of the privy chamber, Sir Henry Sidney.

'How is my master, my lord?' he inquires anxiously. 'He had a very bad night. He was in terrible pain.'

'A little amended.' I smile. 'Sir Henry, if you wish to do his Majesty a service, you can entertain him, when he wakes, by singing the praises of the Lady Jane Dudley, making much of the high esteem in which she is held by all for her character and her piety.'

'Yes, my lord, of course.' He seems nonplussed at this request. Hopefully he will conclude that I am seeking some patronage for my daughter-in-law. Poor fool, he would never guess the truth.

But the King needs little convincing. When I return in the morning he has had himself propped up on the pillows and is once again, briefly, his father's son.

'Your Grace,' he announces, 'we have decided to agree to your proposal that the Lady Jane should succeed us. Have our clerks draw up our Will, or whatever document is required, and then bring it here for us to sign.'

Inwardly jubilant, I hasten away to do my sovereign's bidding. Later, I present him with a draft of his Will, in which is enshrined the new order of succession: the crown is to be left to the Lady Jane and her heirs male. The King reads it over, sends for writing materials and laboriously and shakily copies out the text in his own hand, signing it with a travesty of his usual flourish.

'Praise be to God, we may now sleep peacefully in our beds at night,' I say fervently. 'Sir, one thing: I want you to rest assured that, even though the Lady Jane is married to my son, in this matter my chief interest is in the welfare of your Majesty's realm.'

'I know that well, my lord,' he replies. 'We have both worked hard to establish true religion in this kingdom, and I know every-thing will be safe in your hands after I am gone. Now I can die content, in the knowledge that our labours have not been in vain.'

But there are still the formalities to be dealt with. The Lord Chief Justice, the Solicitor General, the Attorney General and all the lords of the council have been summoned to the King's bedside to ratify his new Will. There are protests from the judges that this document cannot overturn an Act of Parliament, and that it is high treason even to attempt to alter the Act's provisions, but I firmly override them.

'Obedience to the King's will can never be treason,' I declare.

'But this Device, as his Majesty is calling it, has no validity in law,' objects the Lord Chief Justice.

Edward's bloated face flushes with fury.

'Raise me! Sit me up!' he commands, his voice rasping. His attendants hasten to obey.

'I will hear of no objections,' he tells the assembled lords sternly. 'Make quick dispatch!'

It is several days, however, before the final version of the Will is signed by the King, and the councillors and judges give their unwilling consent to it. Even those who wish to see the Lady Mary dispossessed are doubtful this is the right way to proceed. But I suspect another concern lies behind the general antipathy: several lords are jealous of my power, but are too fearful for their own skins to oppose me openly. So I decide it is prudent to provide some indemnity for the future. I insist on the lords signing a second document, drawn up by me, in which they promise to support the future Queen Jane to the uttermost of their power, and undertake never at any time to swerve from this resolution.

And there I have them.

I am still concerned that the Emperor, on learning of the Lady Mary's exclusion from the succession, will attempt to intervene on her behalf, and therefore, as a precaution, I swear all the lords to secrecy. Then, thinking that there is no harm in discreetly preparing the ground in England, I order that prayers for the King's sisters are henceforth to be omitted from church services. Too late, I realise that this is a mistake, for it signals my intentions to the Emperor's ambassador. Why else would the Emperor promptly send three special envoys to England merely to enquire after the King's health? No, they have instructions to protect the Lady Mary's interests, I am sure, and if it comes to it, they will probably make representations on her behalf and try to persuade me from my chosen course.

I fear they are destined to failure and disappointment.

I look down dispassionately at the living corpse on the bed. The King is in mortal agony, that is obvious, and his constant prayer is that God will think fit to deliver him from this torment and grant his speedy release to Heaven. His body, skeletally thin, has swollen up like a pig's bladder: his stomach is distended, his legs bloated. His skin is turning a livid purple and black in places, and gangrene has attacked his extremities. His nails and hair have fallen out, and he can hardly breathe. Speech is now especially difficult for him.

Mistress Rhys is looking pleadingly at me from the other side of the bed. She has just told me, in the privacy of my closet, that she can take no more of this.

'I have done as you asked,' she cried, 'and shut my ears to his pitiful cries. Why can you not leave him to die in peace? He'll not last much longer anyway, so what is the point of prolonging his agony?'

I nod at her. I have no further use for Edward now, or for this woman. I lead her from the bedchamber and back into the closet, where I hand her a heavy bag of coins.

'For your services. Remember, not a word of this to anyone, or there will be consequences.'

'Yes, Sir,' she replies, suitably frightened, but obviously relieved to be free of her duties, and unable to conceal her eagerness to see how much is in the purse.

'It is late. You may stay in the palace tonight,' I tell her, 'but you must leave at first light.'

I summon one of my retainers.

'Take this lady to her lodging. First door on the left in the outer court, third floor up.'

I watch them leave. My man has his orders. Mistress Rhys

has been assigned an attic room above an empty courtier apartment that is scheduled for renovation. The attic is clean but sparsely furnished, quite sufficient for her needs. But of course she won't be using it for long. In the small hours of tomorrow morning, my very precise orders will be carried out. Her body can then be disposed of under cover of darkness.

The retainer has been told he can keep the purse. That should keep him quiet.

Greenwich Palace, 2nd July 1553

Despite my precautions, rumours that the King is dying have proliferated throughout the land. To avoid panic or alerting the Lady Mary, I issue regular soothing bulletins announcing that his Majesty is out of danger and recovering his health; I even say that he is taking the air in the gardens at Greenwich, or exercising in the galleries of the palace. These fool no one, I'm certain – a king must be visible to his people, and Edward has not been seen in public for months.

Today I am furious to be informed that in London posters bearing prayers for the King's recovery, which are normally requested only when a monarch is at death's door, have been mysteriously nailed to a number of church doors in the City. Who put them there is anyone's guess, but they have their effect. Before long, huge crowds are converging on Greenwich Palace, on foot or by barge, demanding to see their sovereign.

I order the park gates to be closed, and send a gentleman of the privy chamber to calm the crowd.

'Go back to your homes!' he cries above the clamour. 'His Majesty is resting. The air is too chilly to permit him to come out of doors and greet you today.'

But the crowd will not disperse.

'We want the King! We want the King!' the people chant, their mood growing uglier by the minute.

'What shall we do?' The lords of the council are clearly frightened.

'We will give them what they want,' I mutter grimly. I march into the King's room and order his appalled servants to get him up and dress him in his rich robes. He protests feebly at such treatment, but I'm in no mood to be opposed. The mob outside could prove a danger to us all. So the wasted body is dragged from the bed, wrapped in a velvet gown and feathered bonnet and propped up at the window, its head lolling forward, its eyes unable to focus.

I can see in the people's response their realisation that he is doomed. They are struck silent, dismayed and shocked. After a short while they begin drifting quietly back to London. There will be no more hopeful bulletins.

Frances Brandon, Duchess of Suffolk

Chelsea, 3rd July 1553

We were anticipating another quiet day enjoying the summer sunshine in the gardens, but there's been a great hurrying and scurrying here at Chelsea this morning because the Duchess of Northumberland has arrived unexpectedly. Now we have kitchen staff flying in all directions to prepare fitting refreshments for her, whilst I, my green silk gown hastily smoothed, perform the part of hostess in the great chamber.

Jane Guilford is a pale, insipid-looking woman whose mousy exterior belies her inner toughness and determination. I've known her for years, and I recall that, from childhood, she always aspired to greatness. Back in those days she was convinced, on the basis of a silly, unfounded rumour, that her grandfather, Sir Edward Guilford, was in fact the elder of the two Princes in the Tower, and therefore the rightful King of England. To utter such a claim during the reign of my late uncle would have been the direst folly, so Jane was obliged to keep quiet about it; whether she still believes such nonsense or not, I don't know, but she certainly acts as if she were royally born.

Marriage to Sir John Dudley, as he was then, was not the

glorious match she thought was her due. Orphaned by his father's execution, and adopted by Jane's kindly father, he was no great prize, yet their marriage has turned out to be remarkably happy and successful, and his extraordinary rise to power has no doubt been ample compensation for his tainted blood. Their union has also been abundantly fruitful. I suspect that the Duchess's frustrated ambitions are now focused on her son, Guilford, who, by the grace of God, will soon be our King Consort, and, in the fullness of time, the founder of a royal Dudley dynasty.

Very much on her dignity, the Duchess sweeps into the room and delicately kisses me on both cheeks. Inwardly I bridle: I cannot abide her presumption, for although we both enjoy the same rank, she is far beneath me by virtue of her birth. I wonder why she has come.

'You are welcome, my good sister,' I say, beckoning to the steward to serve some wine. 'I trust you will do us the honour of staying to dinner?'

'That is most kind, but time is pressing, and I cannot,' replies the Duchess, bestowing on me a tight smile. I nod at the steward.

We seat ourselves either side of the fireplace, which, on this warm day, is filled with flowers. After enquiring about the health of my family, the Duchess asks if 'our' daughter Jane is at home.

'Yes, she is,' I tell her, 'but she has not yet fully recovered her strength after her illness, and usually takes a nap at this time. But if you wish, I will ask her nurse to fetch her.'

The Duchess does insist, and within ten minutes Jane has joined us. I am not pleased to see that she is wearing one of her drab black gowns, with only a simple pearl pendant, but at least she has not forgotten her manners, for she makes a pretty curtsey to her mother-in-law.

The Duchess is regarding her with disapproval. I'm sure she is thinking, and quite rightly, that the girl could make more of herself. Nevertheless, her ladyship attempts a frosty smile.

'I am come to tell you news of great import, my dear,' she says, 'which will concern your mother also. It is my heavy duty to inform you that the King is dying. When God sees fit to summon him to His mercy, it will be needful for you, and the whole court, to go immediately to the Tower of London. You should know that his Majesty has named you heir to his realm.'

Jane looks blank. Did she not hear aright? She stands there, staring at the Duchess and looking stupid.

'Jane!' I bark. 'Did you hear what her Grace said?'

'Yes, Madam,' she replies, still looking bewildered.

'Has the child taken leave of her senses?' asks the Duchess. 'She appears to be dumbstruck. I said, Jane, that when the King dies, you are to be Queen, and must remove to the Tower when you are summoned. It is customary for a new sovereign to stay in the palace there before being crowned.'

'But that cannot be!' Jane has finally found her voice, and I soon wish she hadn't. 'The Lady Mary is the rightful heir, then the Lady Elizabeth, and then my lady mother.'

'Not any more,' the Duchess informs her. 'His Majesty has set aside the claims of his sisters, and your lady mother has relinquished her own claim, so that you can succeed.'

'The King has done this?' Jane cries, in a rare passion. 'He would never order such a thing. Rather it is my lord of Northumberland who has done it, in defiance of both Parliament and King Henry's Will! This is treason, my lady, and I want no part in it. Nay, I will not listen further!'

And with that she rudely hurries from the room, to my utter mortification.

The Duchess is clearly trying to control her temper. 'Her behaviour is most immoderate,' she hisses. 'I wonder you do not whip her for her impertinence.'

'Oh, I shall whip her, never fear,' I mutter.

'I am beginning to wonder if she is beyond your control,' the Duchess says tartly. 'My son has already come to me with a string of complaints about her undutiful behaviour towards him. Did you know she has dared to refuse him her bed?'

I had suspected something of the sort, judging by Lord Guilford's petulant demeanour when he left Chelsea after his one and only visit. I did ask Jane about it, but met with a blank wall of silence: she said she had no idea why her husband was so out of humour.

I assume an innocent air for the Duchess's benefit. 'You are certain this is the case?'

'The marriage was consummated, there's no doubt about that. Twice, in fact, I believe. But Guilford told me that Jane resisted him, and that she seems unaware that it is a wife's duty to submit to her husband. Madam, it was your responsibility to ensure that she was prepared for marriage, and it appears that it was ill done, or not done at all.'

I grow hot with fury. How dare this woman lecture me on my duty? I am just about to rebut the accusation when I recall something that may be significant. More than once on the bridal night I heard Jane cry out, and I remember thinking that she sounded more distressed than the occasion would warrant. Perhaps Guilford – young, inexperienced and therefore unsure of himself – was over-rough and insensitive with her. Of course, it was her duty to endure it, and I suspect that her sullen and unwilling demeanour that evening may have gone some way towards provoking her husband, but whatever my private opinion of Jane's conduct, no Lady Northumberland is going to berate me for my supposed failings as a mother!

'I will speak with Jane,' I say through clenched teeth, 'but I have good reason to believe that Guilford is to blame for her reluctance.'

'Guilford?' The Duchess is almost screeching. 'Madam, how dare you blame your daughter's shortcomings on my son, who has tried his hardest to win her love! He is in no way to blame – it is she who is at fault. You have only to recall the wilful manner in which she flounced out of this room. Guilford has assured me that he has shown her every consideration. He does not deserve this unwifely treatment.'

'Really?' I am on my mettle now. 'Well, Madam, from what I heard on the wedding night – and my lord and I were lying just along the gallery from their bedchamber – your son was repeatedly hurting our daughter. I heard her cry out, not just once, which might have been expected, but several times.'

'I am sure you exaggerate. Guilford would not hurt her intentionally,' the Duchess insists. 'He is a kindly boy.'

I pull a derisive face.

'This is insufferable,' she fumes. 'You cannot even see what is under your nose – or you will not. Well, I must tell you that I have confided to the Duke my husband my concerns about the Lady Jane, and he has ordered that she is to come and stay with me at Durham House until she is summoned to her great destiny. Both of us think she needs framing to her new duties, and parents are often not the best people to do it, being too tender of their child's feelings.'

Even I, angry as I am, can see the irony in this: that I, who have ever been strict with my daughters – for their own good, mark you – should be accused of being too soft with them. If it were not so insulting, it would be laughable. Yet this is no light matter, and I am in a corner. Northumberland is all-powerful, and his word is law. Besides, a wife's place is with her husband. I realise I have no choice but to let Jane go to Durham House.

'Very well,' I say icily. 'I will have her gear packed.'

Lady Jane Dudley

Chelsea and Durham House, 3rd–5th July 1553

There is a frosty silence as my mother and the Duchess of Northumberland wait for Mrs Ellen to finish packing my travelling chest.

'She will not need much,' the Duchess instructs. 'I do not anticipate that her sojourn with us will be long.'

'We'll await you downstairs, Jane,' my lady says, escorting her Grace of Northumberland from the room.

Alone again with Mrs Ellen, I throw myself on the bed and burst into a distraught passion of weeping.

'If only you knew, dear Mrs Ellen, what is in store for me!'

My nurse hastens to comfort me.

'Hush now, my lamb. Nothing's as bad as all that.' But her voice betrays her anxiety.

'I am forced to live with Guilford,' I sob, the words coming brokenly between shuddering storms of tears. 'You could not imagine . . .'

'Oh, but I can, pet, I can,' she says sadly. 'Some men are like beasts. I'm not blind, Jane. I saw your bruises, and the blood on the sheets. I guessed he'd been rough with you.'

'He's an animal,' I weep. 'No, that's unfair to animals. They but act instinctively. We humans are supposed to be rational beings, but he showed no finer feelings. And there's no way out. I am bound to endure it.'

Mrs Ellen is weeping too. 'Oh, my precious child – that you should be at the mercy of that callous, brutal youth . . .'

'But there's worse,' I cry, 'far, far worse.'

'In the name of God, what?' Sorrow gives way to alarm in her face.

'They are going to make me Queen,' I say, sitting up. 'When King Edward dies.'

Mrs Ellen looks aghast.

'This is Northumberland's doing,' I continue, my tears subsiding as anger takes the place of sorrow. 'Of course, I will resist it. I will not let them do this. I refuse to cooperate.'

'But how can the Duke bring it to pass?' she asks, incredulous.

'I do not know, save by underhand dealings and subversion of the law. And the law says that the Lady Mary should succeed her brother. She has the unassailable right. I know what her accession will mean, but I cannot be a party to depriving her of that right. And anyway, I should hate to be Queen. I am a private person. I do not want to live my life in the public glare, nor do I relish the burdens of sovereignty. Power and glory hold no attraction for me.' The unfairness of it all hits me forcefully. 'Oh, Mrs Ellen, why does God visit me with so many miseries? All I ask is to live my life in peace.'

'It is not for us to question the will of God,' she reminds me.

'I tell you, dear nurse, this cannot be the will of God. He would not permit such an unjust thing to happen.'

I sit twisting my hands. There is much to be done if I am to be ready to depart with the Duchess anon. Mrs Ellen makes a visible effort to pull herself together, and drags out my gowns. I make no move to help her; ordinarily, when I am going away, I pack my own books and personal things.

'I don't want to go,' I say, breaking down again at the sight of Mrs Ellen snatching clothes from pegs and presses. 'I do not want to live with Guilford, or his parents. His mother hates me, and I fear his father. I cannot comprehend the sheer effrontery and awfulness of what they have all been plotting: I want nothing to do with it. I am no traitor.'

There are no words of comfort that can still my raging heart. Mrs Ellen knows that. She does not attempt to gentle me with trite solecisms; instead, she puts her arms round me and holds me tight for a space, neither of us saying anything.

When she finally delivers me to the Duchess, I am still tearful and angry. Yet I dutifully kiss my mother farewell, and kneel for her blessing.

'Remember your duty,' she says briefly. Clearly there is no help to be had from that quarter.

My mind in a turmoil, I meekly follow the Duchess to the splendid barge moored by the jetty; it will take us along the Thames to the Strand.

Sitting in the barge, watching the sun-sparkled water lap by, I cannot speak. It is obvious that my mother-in-law is highly displeased with me, and I suppose I can understand why, for I have been unpardonably discourteous. Yet I am not, under any circumstances, going to be a party to treason. I have resolved to resist becoming involved in their plots with every ounce of my being.

On arrival at Durham House I am shown to my chambers, which overlook the river. They are dark, being panelled in old oak and having small, diamond-paned windows. On the wall is a portrait of Katherine of Aragon, who lived here many years ago, the Duchess says. The picture disturbs me: it is not just my awareness of that Queen's staunch Catholicism that makes me uncomfortable; it is also the knowledge that I have been chosen as the instrument through which unscrupulous persons mean to perpetrate a great wrong against Katherine's daughter, the Lady Mary. Even though I deplore Mary's religious beliefs, I know for a certainty that her right to succeed her brother is just and lawful.

Mercifully, Guilford is with his father at court, so I do not have to endure his company. But there are other trials in store for me. In the evening I am violently sick again, and for the next two days I cannot keep even water down. I am in a very poor case, suffering painful and humiliating attacks of the flux, and ghastly stomach cramps. I even begin to wonder, yet again, if Northumberland and his insufferable wife are trying to poison me.

298

On the third day, plainly alarmed in case I die whilst in her care, the Duchess sends me back to my mother at Chelsea.

Here, in familiar and once-loved surroundings, I begin to mend.

The Lady Mary

Hunsdon, 4th July 1553

Sir Robert Rochester and I are sitting in the room that serves him as both office and study at Hunsdon House. I frown, peering short-sightedly at the two letters I hold in my hand.

'My lord of Northumberland writes that the King my brother is getting better, and suggests that I come to court to cheer him during his convalescence,' I tell Sir Robert. 'Yet the Emperor's ambassador informs me, in his letter, that his Majesty is thought to be at death's door, and that I should under no circumstances come near the court. Now who should I believe?'

'I think your Grace knows the answer to that question,' he replies. 'I would not trust the Duke.'

'I agree. I should like to see my brother, but if I go to Greenwich, I will be putting myself in a very vulnerable position. I am a lone woman, my health is not good, and I have little political influence and few friends there. But if I do not go, the Duke might smell a rat. And if the King *is* getting better, he might take my absence unkindly.'

'I have heard,' says Sir Robert, who has his own friends at court, 'that there are those on the council who are sympathetic to your Grace, and those who might be reluctant to offend you at this time. On consideration, my advice is to go to court as you did before, attended by armed men and a great retinue. Then you will see for yourself how his Majesty really is, and you should also be able to assess how much support you can count upon. Remember, Madam, if the Imperial ambassador is correct, you would be wise to be at hand to claim the throne as the rightful heir.'

'You speak sagely, old friend,' I smile. Dear Sir Robert: he has served me faithfully for years, and I know that his affection for me goes beyond mere duty. My welfare is always his chief priority.

'Then take my advice,' he says firmly, smiling back.

'I will. I shall summon my escort and leave for Greenwich today.'

John Dudley, Duke of Northumberland

Greenwich Palace, 4th July 1553

De Scheyfve, the Imperial ambassador, keeps giving me odd looks. Calculating looks. As if he knows something I don't. Or knows something I don't want him to know.

Could it be that he has found out about the King's Device for the succession? And if so, who could have told him? The lords here are in the main an untrustworthy bunch, but they're all in this with me up to their necks; should any fool betray me, I would hope that the rest would turn and savage him like wild dogs, but all I can do is pray that the ambassador's price is less than the rewards any man hopes to gain when the Lady Jane is on the throne.

But if de Scheyfve has got wind of my plan to seize the Lady Mary as soon as the King is dead, he might warn her. And that will not do.

Time. It cannot pass quickly enough now. God, when will the boy die?

I have written to the Lady Elizabeth, who is staying at Hatfield House in Hertfordshire, informing her, as I informed the Lady Mary, that her brother the King is on the mend and invites her to court to bring him some good cheer.

God forbid that my foxy lady is too clever for me. Elizabeth's as sharp as nails, and is more likely than her sister to suspect a trap. If she doesn't come to court, I'll have to send soldiers to drag her here.

Greenwich Palace, 6th July 1553

Henry Sidney, that faithful friend since boyhood, is keeping vigil by the King's bed. He's been sitting there for a long time, heedless of the foetid air in the chamber, from which most of us cannot help but recoil when we enter. He is visibly grieving for his young master, the tears trickling unashamedly down his cheeks.

There is only one physician in attendance, Dr Owen. I fear it has been too dangerous to allow the rest access to the King. Owen poses the least risk, since he's getting on now and his eyesight isn't what it was. He served the late King Henry for years, and has known his Majesty all his life, so his presence is a comfort to Edward. The good doctor has done what he can to make his patient comfortable, although his skills avail him little. I'm pretty certain he doesn't suspect anything.

I stand at the foot of the bed, looking down on the King. It's as well old Harry can't see his beloved son. Edward's wasted body is covered with sores and ulcers. He can no longer eat, so his stomach is fearsomely distended, and he retches frequently. Most of his hair has fallen out, and his once-fair skin is blotched and discoloured. He is a living corpse. Fortunately, his periods of lucidity are less and less frequent: he either sleeps fitfully, or lies there rambling deliriously. No one can understand much of what he says, but we can make out enough to realise that the King is still fretting about the future of the Church he has established.

'My lord,' whispers Dr Owen. 'In my opinion, His Majesty is *in extremis*. Do I have your permission to summon the other doctors to assist me in helping him die in peace? You will understand that I don't want to shoulder the responsibility alone. Men are always too ready to point the finger in the wake of a tragedy, and I fear they might accuse me of malpractice or worse.'

'You have my permission,' I say reluctantly, telling myself that it must be safe now for the doctors to see the King. Presently they file into the room, looking grave. They know they can do little for him save give him useless draughts and pray for his release. (As I pray for it – God, I do pray for it!)

The physicians go through the motions of examining their patient, then withdraw to a corner to confer, looking like so many black crows in their sombre gowns and bonnets. I watch them covertly, and realise they are doing the same to me. I should dearly love to hear what they are saying, but their voices are too hushed. They are frowning, shaking their heads. Even if they do have their suspicions, they cannot prove anything. And, of course, it would be very unwise for any of them to make wild accusations.

They move again to the bed, and make a great play of checking the King's pulse and mopping his brow. They ask for a specimen of his urine. It's a charade, because they can do nothing to help him. His breath is coming in laboured gasps, and he keeps coughing up bloody sputum. It cannot be long now.

Sidney is still weeping.

'Dear God,' he cries, 'let my master be taken before his sufferings become unbearable!'

Edward stirs. Outside, a church bell strikes three o'clock. It's a hot and sultry afternoon, and the room is stifling. The doctors fear that fresh air might bring with it noxious vapours, but young Sidney has had enough. Ignoring Owen's protest, he goes to the casement and throws it open. Not that it makes much difference, for the air outside is so humid that the sluggish, clammy breeze that barely lifts the curtains offers little respite from the close atmosphere in the room.

As I look out, the sky suddenly darkens. We're in for a thunderstorm, which is about to break any minute.

Perhaps sensing this, his Majesty wakes. Henry Sidney hastens to his side and lifts a wine cup to his lips, but he cannot drink.

'I thank you for your care of me, Henry,' he croaks feebly, and sighs deeply. 'I feel so bad,' he falters. 'I entreat God that He will deliver me.' Then, in a firmer voice, he prays aloud: 'Lord, Thou knowest how happy I shall be to live with Thee for ever; yet I would live and be well for the sake of Thy people.'

He turns his ravaged face towards Sidney.

'I am so pleased to see you near,' he whispers, and falls asleep again.

*

It is nearly six o'clock. The storm has been raging for two hours, and his Majesty has awoken once more. Henry Sidney and Dr Owen are seated either side of the bed, while I maintain my position at its foot. We have been joined by Edward's chaplain, who is quietly reading aloud words of spiritual consolation from the Scriptures. It is clear that Death is at hand, hovering in the shadows.

The King makes an effort to speak, but cannot, for very weakness, yet he manages to whisper a last brief prayer. Weeping unrestrainedly, Henry Sidney takes the frail body into his arms and holds it close as Edward's young life ebbs away.

At length, the rasping breaths cease, and Sidney tenderly lays the inert form back on the pillows, closes the eyes and folds the hands over the still breast. As he does so, there issues from the brooding skies above a mighty clap of thunder. In the weeks to come, ignorant folk, bred to superstition, will assert that the storm was sent by old King Harry, in anger at the setting aside of his Will.

The Lady Mary

Hoddesden, 6th July 1553

Early evening, and we are approaching the outskirts of Hoddesden when we see cantering towards us a messenger, soaked and spattered with mud. He says he has been sent by Sir Nicholas Throckmorton, one of my most loyal friends at court.

'Turn back, my lady!' urges the messenger. 'A trap is laid for you by your enemies. You are in great danger!'

I need no second bidding. Scribbling a quick note to the Emperor's ambassador, I inform him that, as soon as I hear news of the King's death, I intend to have myself proclaimed Queen. Then I wheel my horse around and ride like the wind through the night, making for my well-fortified house at

Kenninghall in Norfolk. Once there, I shall summon my loyal tenantry of East Anglia to my support.

John Dudley, Duke of Northumberland

Greenwich Palace, 7th July 1553

It is imperative to keep up the pretence that the King is still alive, even though rumours to the contrary have been buzzing around the court for several days. Meals are being delivered as usual to the royal apartments, and solicitous ambassadors are being informed that his Majesty is resting, but will receive them as soon as he is better. I don't think de Scheyfve, for one, believes a word of it, but diplomatic etiquette forbids him to contradict me.

The immediate problem is what to do with the King's body. I need to keep his death secret for as long as possible, at least until we have apprehended the Lady Mary. Fortunately, she is even now on her way to court. Once she is in custody, I can have the Lady Jane proclaimed Queen without fear of Mary retaliating or drumming up support in her own favour, or even trying to raise an army.

But the King's corpse is still lying on his bed. It's already begun to decompose in this hot weather, and it cannot be left where it is. A lying-in-state and a ceremonial funeral are out of the question at present; nor can I have the body secretly buried in Westminster Abbey, the sepulchre that his late Majesty requested, for fear of awkward questions being asked when his death is finally announced. And the last thing I want – which I fear my colleagues might demand – is an autopsy. Changing the succession is one thing, poisoning an anointed sovereign quite another; and the penalty for it is hanging, drawing and quartering. Even my power and influence would not survive such a revelation.

With the stink from the locked bedchamber becoming ever more noticeable in the ante-room, I realise I have to act quickly.

It has proved necessary, and useful, over the years, to retain certain unsavoury characters in my pay. I summon four of these ne'er-do-wells to my closet, admitting them pair by pair.

To the first two, I say, 'I will pay you twenty gold crowns each if you can find and bring to me the fresh corpse of a boy, aged about fifteen, with reddish-yellow hair and of slender build. No questions will be asked, but mark you, there must be no sign of violence on the body. Have it nailed down in a coffin and hidden in the woods surrounding the great park beyond the palace. Then come straight to me.'

'When do you want it, my lord?' asks one.

'Tonight. Without fail.'

To the second pair of ruffians, more brutish and slow-witted than the others, I give orders that the body resting in the royal bedchamber is to be sealed in lead and buried hastily, at dead of night, in Greenwich Park.

'Oh,' I add, 'and if you are wise, you will cover your noses with kerchiefs. There are twenty crowns each in it for you, payable upon satisfactory completion of the job, but your lives will be worth nothing if you tell a single soul what you have done. You will be marked men, I warn you.'

And thus it comes to pass that his late Majesty, King Edward VI, is laid to rest in a shallow and unmarked grave in the great park, while the body of a murdered Deptford apprentice, embalmed beyond recognition, will later be interred, with great pomp, in the vaults of the Henry VII Chapel in Westminster Abbey, at the feet of the founder of the Tudor dynasty.

Greenwich Palace, 8th–9th July 1553

All is going awry. The Lady Mary, I am informed, has flown the trap, and I realise I can no longer afford any delay in implementing my plans. I therefore summon the Lord Mayor of London, with his aldermen and sheriffs, and receive them in private.

'My Lord Mayor, Sirs, I have heavy tidings,' I announce. 'The King's Majesty, God rest his soul, has departed this life. On his deathbed, wishing to preserve the true Protestant religion in this realm, he drew up a new Device for the succession, and named his cousin, the Lady Jane Grey, as heiress apparent. Very shortly, gentlemen, she will be proclaimed Queen.'

These are clever, successful men, wise in the ways of law and commerce; they are the bedrock on which the City of London has been built. But they are standing there looking at me blankly and uncomprehending.

'With respect, my lord Duke,' says the Lord Mayor, 'who *is* the Lady Jane Grey?'

'She is the great-granddaughter of King Henry VII and the great-niece of the late King Henry VIII,' I tell them. 'She is virtuous and well educated, and an ornament of the Protestant faith.'

'What of the Lady Mary?' asks an alderman.

'Yes, and the Lady Elizabeth? What of King Harry's daughters? Don't they have a better claim?'

I make myself smile, suppressing my rising irritation and concern.

'Both were declared bastards by King Henry, if you remember. The Lady Mary is a staunch Catholic, and the Lady Elizabeth's persuasion is uncertain. But the Lady Jane is a firm Protestant, and zealous for the faith. This was his late Majesty's overriding priority in changing his royal father's Will. I am sure that, when you see the Lady Jane, who is young, comely and intelligent, and possessed of every feminine accomplishment, you will applaud his Majesty's choice. There is none more fit to rule this land.'

They are nodding now; some even look approving.

'Two things, gentlemen,' I say, raising my hand. 'You are sworn not to disclose any of this to anyone, lest the Lady Mary gets wind of what is afoot and appeals to the Emperor for aid. And secondly . . .' I pause for effect, frowning. 'If it became known that any man had spoken ill of the Lady Jane – or Queen Jane, as we must soon call her – it should be accounted a great and treasonable offence.'

There. I have them now. They will think twice before questioning his late Majesty's provisions for the succession.

The Lord Mayor steps forward.

'Your Grace, I think I can speak for my brethren when I assure you of our unquestioning allegiance to the excellent Lady Jane as our future sovereign lady.'

'Aye, aye!' echo the rest eagerly.

Inwardly I congratulate myself. The first hurdle has been successfully negotiated.

I now secure the Tower, the chief fortress in the kingdom, placing it under the control of a trusted associate, Lord Clinton, and order the execution of a number of Catholics imprisoned there, so as to deprive the Lady Mary of potential supporters. I have already sent my son, Lord Robert Dudley, off in hot pursuit of Mary, with instructions to take her prisoner and bring her without delay to London, where I will ensure she suffers the same fate as that awaiting her friends in the Tower.

Presently, Robert sends encouraging news of his swift progress northwards. His next message, however, is less welcome. The Lady Mary, he informs me, was warned by some traitor of his approach and has managed to elude him. Dressed like a servant girl, she rode at full speed behind a guide provided by a local adherent of hers, and has now, it is believed, reached Kenninghall. I pray God that Robert apprehends her before she has raised her supporters.

It must have been de Scheyfve who sent word to Mary that the King is dead. How he found out, I have no idea, but at any rate she knows the truth now. That much is clear from a letter she has sent to the privy council, which has just been placed in my hands. Expressing herself in the most regal terms, she writes of her astonishment and indignation at our failure to inform her of her brother's death or to have her proclaimed Queen, and asserts her right to the crown. She concludes by commanding us all, on our allegiance to God and to herself, to have her accession announced forthwith.

Instead, we have already ordered the Bishop of London to proclaim both Mary and Elizabeth bastards in his next Sunday sermon at Paul's Cross.

Even now, I still stay my hand when it comes to making public the King's death. We have yet to prepare the ground for the Lady Jane's accession, and for that I need more time.

Lady Jane Dudley

Chelsea and Syon House, 9th July 1553

I am reading in the garden when, late on this warm afternoon, the arrival of Northumberland's daughter, Mary, Lady Sidney, is announced. Summoned by my mother to the great chamber, I am surprised to be greeted warmly, with a curtsey and a kiss on both cheeks, by this dark beauty with the dancing eyes, the wife of the King's closest friend. I had thought I was *persona non grata* with the Dudleys.

'Madam,' Lady Sidney announces grandly, 'I am sent to bid you to come this night to Syon House to receive what has been ordered for you by his Majesty the King.'

It is what I have feared, I am certain. Immediately I am on my guard. I step back.

'I regret, my lady, that I have been unwell of late, and am still too weak to travel,' I protest. But Mary is having none of it.

'Madam, I'm afraid I must insist. It is necessary that you come with me, and your lady mother too.' Her tone has changed; it brooks no opposition. 'Please hasten and make ready.'

I flee to my chamber, trembling.

'I cannot go,' I tell Mrs Ellen distractedly. 'You may guess what is about to happen. You know I want no part in it.' Of course, Mrs Ellen knows of what I am speaking. She tries to soothe me, but fails miserably.

I am so alone. There is no help to be had from any person. It is as if I am stepping off dry land onto a boat that is about to encounter swift rapids, and I will not be able to get off before disaster strikes, yet I am powerless to walk away. Set-faced, I stand silently shaking while Mrs Ellen dresses me in a black velvet gown bordered with silver, then replaits and coils my hair and sets upon it a French hood banded with little diamonds and pearls. In the mirror, my face is white and my eyes look haunted. Ready now, I emerge from the safety of my bedchamber and descend the stairs, then allow myself to be led by Lady Sidney to the waiting barge that boasts the Dudley arms. The Suffolk barge departed minutes ago, I am told, bearing my mother to Syon.

On the short journey upriver, neither of us speaks. It occurs to me that the only way to escape my fate is to leap into the murky water and let it sweep me away, out of the hands of those who would use me so iniquitously. But I do not do it. I am capable, it seems, of nothing. We disembark at Syon stairs and are escorted to the house by a chamberlain wearing the Dudley livery, who leads us to the deserted great hall, where we are asked to wait.

Suddenly, the doors are flung open and the entire privy council, headed by Northumberland, files into the hall. Each man in his turn bows to me and Lady Sidney. I see undisguised interest and speculation in their faces. A hush descends as the Earls of Pembroke and Huntingdon walk towards us. To my unutterable dismay, they both kneel before me and, one after the other, kiss my hand with great reverence.

How dare they so honour me? I am not the one to whom is due such fealty, nor am I worthy of it. I am wise to their purpose, and will stand my ground. This must not be! Nevertheless, as Northumberland approaches and asks me to proceed with him to the presence chamber, a deep fear possesses me. They really mean to do this.

My alarm increases as I am led to an empty throne, set upon a dais beneath a crimson canopy of estate. The chamber is packed with ranks of lords, ladies and courtiers, all standing in order of precedence, all wearing black. As the Duke steers me through the throng, his hand in a vice-like grip on mine, I am dimly aware that people are making obeisances to me. My heart pounding, I see my father and mother, both smiling triumphantly in my direction; the Duchess of Northumberland, her thin lips slightly upturned at the corners; and Guilford, his handsome, dissolute features set in a knowing smirk.

Panic mounts. There is an unpleasant jarring sensation in my head that has me frantically looking for succour in what I know is to be my hour of trial. It passes, but leaves me feeling faint and shaky. With an immense effort of will, I try to steady myself, fearing that I will either pass out or even drop dead from fright in front of all these people. I pray for strength and guidance, and that God may reveal His will in this great matter.

The thought strikes me, that perhaps this *is* the path that the Almighty, in His usual subtle way, has chosen for me. Is it possible that I, a poor weak vessel, am destined to be His instrument? His ways of working out His purpose are so mysterious as sometimes to appear incomprehensible to mere mortals. But how can I know whether this business is the will of God or the work of the Devil? I am desperate to understand! I must hope and pray for a sign.

I stand trembling at the foot of the dais as Northumberland wheels me round to face the company. There is a hush.

The Duke speaks in ringing tones: 'As Lord President of the council, it is my sad duty to proclaim to you all the death of his most blessed and gracious Majesty, King Edward VI.' He pauses to allow this momentous, dread news to sink in. That poor boy! How I pity him . . . But now is not the time to weep. Few of those present look surprised, and I suspect that most have already heard or guessed of the King's passing.

Numb in my misery, I hear the Duke drone on, praising the late King's virtues and giving thanks for his most Christian death. Then it comes: his late Majesty, in his wisdom, says Northumberland, devised a new Will, which is to be enshrined in an Act of Parliament, disinheriting his sisters and decreeing that whosoever takes them for his undoubted heirs is a traitor to both God and the realm.

All eyes are now on me. To my horror, I see Northumberland turn towards me.

'Be it known that his Majesty has named your Grace as the heir to the Crown of England,' he declares. 'He has also appointed that your sister will succeed you in default of your lawful issue.'

All are silent. I stand mute, in agonised turmoil, reeling from the impact of his words and unable to respond in any way.

The Duke seems to take my silence for assent. He smiles. 'Madam, your title has been approved by all the lords of the council, the great nobles of this realm, and all the judges of the land. There is nothing wanting but your Grace's grateful accept-ance of the high estate that God Almighty, the sovereign disposer of all crowns and sceptres – never sufficiently to be thanked by you for so great a mercy – has advanced you to.' He pauses, his smile becoming more strained as I remain appar-ently stupefied by my good fortune.

'Therefore,' he concludes, 'you should cheerfully take upon you the name, title and estate of Queen of England, receiving from us the homage that will shortly be tendered to you by the rest of the kingdom.' Now he falls on his knees, followed by everyone else present in the chamber, until I am the only person left standing, looking down on rank upon rank of bowed heads.

'Each one of us would willingly shed his blood for you, exposing our lives to death!' Northumberland assures me dramatically. But I cannot hear him properly. Waves of dizziness and nausea are engulfing me, and I crumple to the floor in a dead faint.

When I open my eyes, I am still lying there. I realise, aghast, that not one person, not even my mother or my husband, has stirred to help me. Is this what being a queen will mean? I am alone, utterly alone, and will be so for the rest of my life. This realisation is just too much to bear, and my composure breaks. Lying on the floor, I bury my head in my arms and fall to weeping piteously, great racking sobs tearing at my body. This is wrong, I know it! We must surely be damned to Hell for all eternity, I along with them, even though I am forced to be their accomplice in this evil.

Northumberland is staring down at me without emotion. He clearly thinks me a foolish girl who does not appreciate her good fortune, but he makes no move to stem what, to him, and in these circumstances, must be an immoderate display of feeling. Perhaps he, and the rest, believe that I am suffering from shock after hearing of the death of my cousin Edward, and trust I will soon remember that such loss of control is ill-bred, and compose myself.

There is no point in crying if no one takes any notice. I am sobbing softly now and after a few minutes, realising they have no intention of comforting me, I wipe my eyes and sit up. The Duke stretches out a hand to support me, and I rise shakily to my feet. I know now, with surprising clarity and moral certainty, what I must do.

'The crown is not my right,' I declare in what sounds like a high, childish voice. 'This pleases me not at all. The Lady Mary is the rightful heir.'

There is a ripple of shocked excitement in the chamber. Northumberland's eyes flash with anger. He cannot believe I have dared to defy him: a slip of a girl against a mighty duke. No doubt he thought he could deal with me easily and firmly.

'Your Grace wrongs yourself and your House,' he cries stridently. My parents, looking as appalled as he, and embarrassed, weigh in also.

'You are an ungrateful girl!' thunders my father, his face flushed. 'Have you forgotten your duty to us, who have helped to order this for you? Not to mention your obedience to the Will of his late Majesty, nor to the decision of your chief subjects here present?'

'You will do as you are told!' spits my mother.

'I must do as my conscience dictates,' I say firmly, determined to hold my ground in the face of their hostility and my fear and bodily weakness.

'And do you think King Edward, of blessed memory, would have acted in an ungodly fashion in thus willing the crown to you?' asks the Duke in a voice that suggests he is making an effort to show patience with me.

'He was ill, and not in his right mind, of that I am convinced,' I reply steadily. 'And it appears he was overborne by others who look only to further their own ends.'

The mighty Northumberland is visibly taken aback by my candour; I doubt that many people have ever spoken so plainly to him, and certainly not his fellow councillors. Yet here am I, a mere girl, who owes him the respect due to a father, insinuating openly that he is corrupt and self-seeking.

My parents seem poised to swoop to the attack once more, their mouths open in protest, but suddenly, at his father's nod, Guilford steps forward and lays his hand on my arm. I recoil at his touch, and the Duke frowns, but Guilford persists. Of course, he has a vested interest in my compliance, and no doubt the Duke has briefed him beforehand: how touching, the handsome young husband gently persuading his reluctant wife to do her duty.

'Sweet Jane,' he says gently. Now I know he's playing a part. It's even been scripted for him, as his next words prove: he's probably been reciting his speech all day. 'I pray you,' he continues, 'be mindful of your duty and accept this sovereign honour that God has seen fit to bestow on you. There is, I know well, no one more fitted by descent, learning and religion for it, and it is clear that God has designated you to be the saviour of His faithful people.'

I stare at him in astonishment. If a donkey had spoken, I could not be more surprised.

'The crown is not my right,' I repeat.

'Think,' Guilford goes on – his father is watching him closely. 'Think on the good you can do for the true Church, and think also of what would happen to those of our true faith if the Lady Mary were to come to the throne. If you refuse the crown, you will be responsible for their fate. Think on it, Jane!'

God chooses the strangest instruments, for Guilford's words strike home with more impact than I could ever have imagined. The Duke is looking at him with new admiration. Possibly Guilford said more than he was told to say, but it was enough to plant a doubt in my mind. The assembled courtiers appear to be collectively holding their breath, waiting on my response.

I struggle to collect my thoughts. I am wavering at the prospect of true Protestants suffering persecution for their faith, as they will surely do under Mary's rule; the prospect makes my heart quail. My husband is right: I hold their fate in my hands.

What shall I do, Lord? I am praying inwardly. I am unfitted in every way for this high honour, which is not mine by entitlement, but I fear for Thy elect if I refuse it. Direct me, show me, I beg of You, what I must do.

'I must pray for guidance,' I say, and fall to my knees.

Although my eyes are shut, all must witness the struggle taking place within me. But the battle is quickly fought and won: I understand the Divine Will now. The true faith must take priority over a doubtful title. It is my duty to be its defender – there is no other course I can take. It is a bitter cup, but I must drink it; my fateful decision is made. Northumberland looks on approvingly as I open my eyes and call on God to be my witness:

'If what has been given to me is lawfully mine, may Thy Divine Majesty grant me such spirit and grace that I may govern to Thy glory and service, and to the advantage of the realm.'

With a great effort I rise to my feet, mount the dais and sit down on the throne, gripping the velvet armrests.

The Duke bends to kiss my hand, his relief – and his irritation – evident. Looking down on his bowed head, I feel a wave of revulsion and it is all I can do not to snatch my hand away. I resolve that, at the earliest opportunity, I will rid myself of the hated Dudleys.

Coolly I nod my acceptance of the Duke's homage and watch him retire, making way for the next in the long line of lords and officers seeking to offer their allegiance. It gives me a frisson of pleasure to see Guilford on his knees before me. From now on, I decide, he will treat me with courtesy and respect, or I will send him away.

My father glowers as he bends his head, and mutters under his breath, 'A fine dance you have led us all, Madam!' My mother, waspish in victory and determined to have the last word, is standing at my elbow.

'Queen you may be,' she whispers, 'but you'll not forget your duty to your parents. And after today's sorry performance, I look to see some improvement in your conduct. You have shamed us all.' Strangely her sharp tongue has lost its power to move me. I realise I am now in a position where I may choose to ignore it, and it dawns on me that queenship will have one advantage at least – that of keeping my parents, and particularly my mother, at a safe distance. And let them dare gainsay me!

But this is small compensation for the unsettling feeling in my bones that, however good my reasons, I have done wrong in accepting a crown that can never rightfully be mine. I fear I have been imprudent, but it is too late now. I have made the hardest decision of my life. I have charted my course, and must now stick to it, whatever tempests threaten, and however my conscience troubles me. I will endeavour to be a good and merciful queen, and a champion of the true faith.

It feels very strange to be sitting in my high seat and listening to my – yes, *my* – privy councillors acquainting me most deferentially with the arrangements for my state entry into London, which is to take place tomorrow. Although it is customary for a new monarch to go in procession through the City streets to be acclaimed by his or her subjects, my councillors feel that, with the Lady Mary still at large, the proclamation of my accession, followed by my reception at the Tower of London, shall be sufficient for the present. Northumberland says the Tower is the safest place for me, and the council too, just now; and of course it is traditional for a sovereign to lodge there prior to being crowned.

I do not question these arrangements: it seems as if it is all happening to somebody else, and does not concern me. Nor do I dare ask what will happen to the Lady Mary when they catch up with her. If they catch up with her. For if Mary succeeds in reaching the coast, she could take ship to the Emperor's dominions and there raise an army in support of her claim, a Catholic army that might well be used to force this kingdom back to obedience to Rome. The very thought keeps me true to my chosen path.

It is late now, and after such a momentous day I feel drained.

'My lords, I will retire now,' I announce, surprising myself and, clearly, my hearers with the ring of authority in my voice.

Guilford stands up with the rest. His constant presence at my side throughout these past hours has irritated me, yet I realise that, short of being unpardonably rude to him in public, there is nothing I can do about it.

'Allow me to escort you to your chamber, Madam,' he says courteously, making his obeisance with a flourish. The hair flopping forward over his face does not quite conceal the glint of lust in his eyes. Doubtless he finds the prospect of bedding the Queen of England stimulating. Northumberland and his Duchess are watching me closely, as is my mother. Well, I am learning to dissemble. I will give them no cause for criticism.

'I thank you, my lord,' I reply coolly, giving Guilford my hand. Together we walk past the bowing lords of the council, as the doors of the state chamber are flung open for us. Beyond them, Mrs Ellen is waiting.

'Your Majesty,' she says, with a formal curtsey that startles me.

'Attend me, please,' I respond, gratefully. I turn to Guilford. 'I beg you to excuse me, my lord, but I am weary beyond measure after this long day's business. I bid you good night.' The doors behind us are still wide open, and the lords are beginning to spill out of them. Guilford has no choice but to acknowledge defeat: he will not risk the shame of his wife's rejection being made public. He bows again and kisses my hand.

'Good night, Madam,' he says, meekly enough, but his expression is petulant.

Queen Jane

The Thames and the Tower of London, 10th July 1553

Soon after midday the flotilla of barges draws away from Syon steps. Ahead go those bearing the privy councillors and the chief officers of the royal household, whilst the state barge emblazoned with the royal arms of England brings up the rear. I am seated in its cushioned and canopied cabin, the curtains tied back so that my subjects can get a good view of their new Queen. My gown and headdress are in the Tudor colours of green and white, embroidered with gold thread and encrusted with jewels that glitter in the blazing afternoon sun. Beside me sits Guilford, dazzling in a suit of white satin trimmed with gold and silver. He is holding my hand and rather overacting the part of attentive husband. If he bows his head again when I speak to him, I think I will scream. But even his presence cannot make this real.

Behind us sits my mother, clad in crimson velvet and perspiring heavily. She has been designated my train-bearer on this great occasion. I can sense from her pursed lips and rigid bearing that she is still mightily displeased with me, but this is the least of my worries.

I am, I have to admit, very nervous, because the news from the City is not good. This morning, the royal heralds proclaimed me Queen in three places: by the Eleanor Cross in Cheapside, on Tower Hill and outside Westminster Hall. But the people received the news in silence, stony-faced. The Duke has sent bands of armed guards into London to deal with any disturbances, yet this does not prevent some naughty fellows shouting out from the river-bank that it is the Lady Mary who should be queen. For this, they will later be sentenced to have their ears cut off and stand in the pillory. It is not an auspicious start.

As the barges glide downriver, I see more clusters of people along the shore, but there is no cheering. The mood is hostile, and most stare insolently at me or gawp incredulously. I feel intimidated by their silence and antipathy, and dare not wave or even acknowledge them by a nod of the head. The journey seems endless, and it is with relief that I see the great white bulk of the Tower looming in the distance.

'Nearly there,' says Guilford unnecessarily. 'You should put on your chopines now.' I reach for the three-inch-high clogs at my feet; I have been told I must wear them to give me height so that I can be seen by those at the back of the anticipated crowds. I begin to wonder if there will be any crowds at all.

As the barges pull in towards the Court Gate at the Tower, the cannons along the adjacent wharf salute me with a deafening report. Assisted by Guilford, I alight from my barge, my mother holding up my heavy train, then take my place beneath a canopy of estate borne by six waiting peers. Followed by the lords of the council, I walk in procession through the Tower precincts, which, to my utter astonishment, are packed with people, all craning their necks to see me. Even more amazing, some are actually cheering!

'God save Queen Jane!' they cry, throwing their bonnets in the air. 'God save your Majesty!'

Heartened by this, I press on, smiling, although my knees feel weak and my heart is pounding.

At last, the entrance to the palace is in sight. Here, the elderly Marquess of Winchester, Lord High Treasurer, waits with Sir John Bridges, the Lieutenant of the Tower, to receive me. The Marquess falls creakily to his knees to present me with the great keys of the Tower, but before I can take them, Northumberland, standing nearby, snatches them up and himself places them in my hands. His action is blatantly symbolic, as if he himself confers upon me the privileges of sovereignty. I bridle inwardly – his arrogance is breathtaking!

But there is no time for feeling indignant, for I am now being escorted up the stairs into the White Tower, the massive keep built by William the Conqueror to guard the City of London. We proceed to the presence chamber, where a vast throng of noblemen and ladies fall on their knees as I enter. Among them, I glimpse the pretty face of my sister Katherine; she is with her young husband and his father, Pembroke. As I seat myself on the throne, my lord father and Northumberland approach me and, kneeling, officially bid me welcome to my kingdom.

These formalities completed, at the Duke's bidding I lead the court upstairs to the Norman chapel dedicated to St John the Evangelist. Here I am supposed to give thanks to God for my accession. Yet, as I kneel on my cushion before the altar rails, I find I cannot pray, for my thoughts are in too great a turmoil. I try desperately to recapture the sense of conviction I felt when I accepted the crown, when I believed I would be God's instrument in saving His faithful, but it eludes me now, when I most need it. How can I give thanks to God for this crown to which I have no true title? It would be dishonest, and He is never deceived. And while I compound my sin, He might turn His face against me. Indeed, my inability to commune with Him now might be the first indication of His disfavour. I know in my heart that I have wronged the rightful heiress, the Lady Mary. I feel bereft and alone; without God to sustain me, I cannot bear this burden.

Yet I must, I *must*, for the court is rising to its feet and there are further ceremonies over which I must preside. Promising myself that, as soon as I am alone, I will kneel and crave forgiveness and guidance, I resolutely compose myself and lead the way back down to the presence chamber. Here I sit enthroned again, flanked by Guilford and, at my own request, Mrs Ellen, who henceforth is to be my chief lady-in-waiting. Next to her stands a family friend, Mrs Tilney, who will also attend me from now on.

Now the Marquess of Winchester and other lords advance, bearing on velvet cushions the crown jewels, brought up from the Tower vaults for the occasion. I stare at the crown, that same crown that was worn by my late great-uncle, King Henry, who had it made, having decided that the diadem worn by his predecessors was insufficiently magnificent for his greatness. His crown is set with the jewels taken from that earlier crown of the Plantagenets; they wink and glisten in the light of scores of candles.

I panic. This is not mine! I have no right to it, whatever anyone says. To accept it is to court disaster, I am sure of that. So when the Marquess lifts the crown and makes to place it on my head, I recoil.

'My lords,' I say firmly, though I am shrinking inside, 'this crown has never been demanded by me or anyone acting in my name.' I place some stress on the word 'my', looking pointedly at Northumberland. 'It is not your place, my lord of Winchester, to offer it to me or to set it on my head. I tell you, I will not wear it, for it is not mine.'

The Duke frowns and looks exasperated, but Winchester – who is, after all, a practised diplomat – chooses to ignore the substance of my words.

'Your Grace may take the crown without fear,' he says avuncularly. 'I merely wish to see how it becomes you, and if it fits.'

I am aware of Northumberland and my parents glaring at me, and my courage fails me. I nod, and Mrs Ellen steps forward. She removes my headdress and unbinds my coiled and plaited tresses. The Marquess now places the crown on my head, and the courtiers break out into hearty applause. Again I feel faint, and grip the arms of the throne to steady myself. It is done, for better or worse.

Winchester is speaking, but I pay him little heed, so I'm not sure if I actually heard him say that he means to order another crown for Guilford. Later, alone in my apartments with Mrs Ellen, I discover that I did hear aright, and am perturbed and displeased. How I wish I had been in a fit state at the time to make it very plain to all that I have no intention whatsoever of making Guilford Dudley King.

I sit at the centre of the high table, toying with my food. All around me, at this banquet given in honour of my accession, lords and ladies are chattering animatedly, apparently enjoying themselves, while I, the focus of it all, feel detached and unreal. Guilford, on my right, is bored with playing the devoted husband, and pays more attention to his mother, who sits the other side of him, flashing the occasional frosty look in my direction.

To my left sits Northumberland. His outward good humour seems forced; he looks strangely deflated. Perhaps he feels less in control of the situation than he could wish. The Lady Mary is still at large, and if she flees abroad before Lord Robert Dudley catches up with her, it will almost certainly mean war. But my father warns that England's depleted treasury cannot bear the expense of defending the realm from invasion.

'If the Emperor does choose to lend the Lady Mary his support, we will all very likely be doomed,' he predicts gloomily.

I have decided to put myself in God's hands; I will not give way to my fears. But the Duke cannot hide his anxiety. He had expected me – I make no doubt – to be docile and easy to manip-ulate, a willing tool in his hands; it must be disconcerting for him now to discover that I am nothing of the sort. I am deter-mined not to be governed by him, and have resolved to start as I mean to continue. He must not be allowed to go on believing that his rule will continue indefinitely, for I mean to declare myself of age and be rid of him and his whole family at the earliest opportunity. Kings before me have attained their majority at my age, fifteen – King Edward did – so there is no reason why the Duke should rule in my name. He must know that I mean to assert my authority and do what is right and needful.

The noise in the dining chamber has reached a babel when a messenger from the Lady Mary is announced. A hush falls as the Duke beckons the man to come forward and takes from him a letter. After breaking open the seal and perusing it rapidly, my lord rises to his feet, his dark brows beetling.

'Your Majesty, my lords and ladies, you shall hear what the traitor Mary has to say.' He reads the whole defiant letter aloud. After lamenting the death of her dearest brother the King, the Princess writes that no one can be ignorant of the provisions of the Act of Succession. Then, using the royal plural, she continues:

It seems strange that, our brother dying, we had no knowledge from you thereof. We had conceived great trust in your loyalty and service, but nevertheless, we are not ignorant of your consultations and the provisions you have forced through. We understand that political considerations may have moved you to act thus, so doubt not, gracious lord, that we take all your doings in gracious part, and will remit and fully pardon them. Wherefore we require and charge you, for that allegiance which you owe to God and to us, that you cause our right and title to this realm to be proclaimed in our City of London and other places, as our very trust is in you.

The silence that greets these words is broken only when my mother and the Duchess of Northumberland begin lamenting how Mary had obviously been warned in advance of the plan to apprehend her, and wondering who it was that got word to her.

'Of course,' Northumberland declares, 'we will ignore her outrageous demands. How can we proclaim her Queen when Queen Jane here is already acknowledged the rightful ruler?' He turns to me. 'Rest assured, Madam, my son, Lord Robert, will track the Lady Mary down and take her prisoner. I assure you, she is a lone woman who has no friends in this realm, and poses no serious threat to your throne. And now, I pray you, good my lords and ladies, continue with the feasting.'

He sits down, but for all his brave words, his discomfiture is plain to see, and I notice also that few councillors have the appetite to finish what is on their plates.

The messenger is still standing before the high table, looking uncomfortable. Northumberland beckons to one of the Yeomen of the Guard, who stand to attention behind us.

'Have that man put in a dungeon,' he says in a low voice. Then he looks again at me. 'Madam, I will summon the privy councillors to a meeting this night. We will draw up a document repudiating the Lady Mary's claim, and have it published, so that there can be no further dispute over the matter.'

'I hope, my lord,' I say sweetly, 'that that will indeed be the case.'

The state apartments in the Tower, which are situated between the keep and the river, are old and have been little used since the last century. Their decaying splendour is that of a bygone age: the walls are gaily painted with heraldic designs in indigo and vermilion, floors are laid with chequered tiles, the narrow arched windows are filled with stained glass and the furniture is in the Gothic style. Yet I find myself occupying some state apartments that are more modern than the rest; my bedchamber boasts linenfold panelling, a tester bed with embroidered hangings and mullioned lattice windows. There is a beautiful frieze of gambolling *putti* below the gilded and battened ceiling.

As Mrs Ellen turns down the covers, I stand in my nightgown, waiting for her to brush my hair. I notice that the linen pillow-covers are embroidered with the initials H and A.

'Whose initials are those?' I wonder.

'I think they stand for Henry and Anne,' says Mrs Ellen shortly. 'Mrs Tilney was telling me about it. Her cousin waited on Anne Boleyn when she occupied these rooms before her coronation – that would have been twenty years ago. They were refurbished especially for her. Mrs Tilney says that Anne also lodged here before her trial.'

'But she was a prisoner,' I point out. 'Surely she was not housed in the palace?'

'She was at first, but she was moved to the Lieutenant's House after being condemned to death. From her window there, she watched them building the scaffold on Tower Green. She and her ladies didn't get much sleep those last nights, because of the noise made by the workmen.'

I shiver, despite the night being warm.

'Poor lady. I cannot imagine how she must have felt. They say she faced death bravely.'

'Oh yes, she had courage, for all her faults.'

'I don't suppose many people have slept here since.'

'Only King Edward, Madam, on the night before his coronation.'

I sit down so that Mrs Ellen can attend to my hair.

'I don't like this place,' I confide to her. 'It disturbs me. So many bad things have happened here. Anne Boleyn, Katherine Howard, and those little Princes who were murdered by Richard III. Aylmer told me that they never found their bodies, so I suppose their bones must still be here somewhere. I think the Tower is an evil place, Mrs Ellen, and I shall be glad to leave it.'

'I wonder how long it will be before we can do that,' she muses. 'Perhaps, Madam, it is best not to dwell on the past. Think about more pleasant things.'

'What pleasant things?' I ask flatly.

Suddenly the door opens and Guilford appears, carrying a candle.

'You may go, Mrs Ellen,' he orders imperiously. I realise at once that he is drunk.

'No, stay,' I command.

'By God, she will do as I say, or I will throw her out!' he growls.

I nod bleakly – I cannot put off this confrontation any longer. With a pained look of commiseration, Mrs Ellen curtseys and hastens from the room.

I round on my husband, my anger blazing.

'How dare you gainsay my command!' I cry. 'I did not want the crown, but now that I *am* Queen, I expect to be obeyed. Even by you!'

'You forget,' he flings back, 'that you took a vow to obey me when we were wed.'

'Which is greater, the authority of a husband or that of a sovereign? The latter, I make no doubt. You took an oath of allegiance to me, may I remind you?'

'Madam,' says Guilford, gripping my arms and pinching the tender flesh beneath my nightgown, 'in this bedchamber I am lord and master, and you will do as I say. Do I make myself clear? I am claiming no more than my lawful rights as a husband, and no law in the land can prevent me, so I suggest you submit with good grace. Do you hear me?'

'I hear you all too well,' I hiss, 'and under no circumstances will I allow you to abuse me again. I am your Queen. One word from me, and those guards outside the door will send you packing. Then all the world will know the truth about our marriage. *That* won't please your father.'

His fair cheeks are pink with fury.

'The world, Madam, will know you for an undutiful wife. You forget that I am King of England and, as such, am entitled to equal respect and obedience.'

His presumption takes my breath away. So *this* is his game.

'No, Guilford,' I declare firmly, keeping my anger in check, 'you are not King, and never will be, unless I authorise Parliament to make you so, and that I will never do. But if you promise to leave me alone – and only if – I will consider making you a duke, which is far more than you merit or deserve.'

He looks momentarily stunned, but his temper quickly flares again and, like a child deprived of a hoped-for treat, he throws an unedifying tantrum.

'I *will* be made King by you!' he screams. 'And by Act of Parliament! My father will see to it.'

'Oh no, you will not,' I say, more composed now, which further infuriates him. I know – as does he – that this is one argument he cannot win. Even his father, powerful as he is, may not make Guilford King without my consent.

His handsome face is suffused with rage. He stands before me shaking, then, to my disgust, bursts into noisy tears.

'I shall tell my mother of you!' he sobs, and crashes out of the chamber.

Exhausted, I sink down on the bed, too drained to concern myself with what might happen next. All I want to do is sleep. I would banish my cares, my fears and the ghosts into the shadows, and seek blessed oblivion on the pillows.

No sooner have I drifted off into a blissful stupor than I am rudely awakened by the door bursting open and the Duchess of Northumberland sailing into the room like a galleon at battle stations.

'How dare you, Madam!' she spits at me.

'And how dare you intrude into our bedchamber like this!' I retort, surprisingly regal for one who is still gathering her wits.

'You may be the Queen, but you will not forget that it is my husband who has made you what you are, and that to him and his House you owe a debt of gratitude and a filial duty. My lord has deemed it advisable that Guilford shall be King, and you will not oppose it.'

I stand up, bristling with fury.

'Since when has a subject had the power to decree who will, and who will not, be King?' I ask. 'It may not be done without my consent and that of Parliament, and who would be such a fool as to place a crown on the head of that snivelling boy?'

She looks as if she would like to slap me for that, but she dare not. So she tries another tack. 'Queens need heirs, Madam, and if you want sons to inherit your crown, I suggest you start treating your husband with respect. Otherwise you risk him abandoning your bed.'

I almost laugh. Does the Duchess really believe that such deprivation would cause me grief? She must indeed be a fond, deluded mother.

'I am sorry to disappoint you, Madam, but that would come as a relief to me,' I tell her. 'I would rather die barren than bed with him again.'

She glares at me.

'That is a foolish, short-sighted attitude. How can you treat Guilford so cruelly? He has done nothing to deserve such contempt.'

'I beg your pardon,' I retort, 'but you were not there when he raped me on our bridal night, nor did you see him bullying me, then whining and crying like a spoilt child in this room not one hour ago. I think, your Grace, that few woman would find joy in such a husband.'

Seeing her dreams of being the mother of England's King and matriarch of a royal Dudley dynasty shattering before her very eyes, the Duchess is reduced to weeping.

'You are indeed cruel, Madam,' she sniffs. 'I regret the day that my son married you. You must be taught a lesson. You might think you can live without a husband, but time will teach you otherwise, and then it may be too late. You must consider how it will appear to your subjects, who will look askance at Guilford being banished from your bed and board. Rumours have a habit of spreading fast, and rumours, I might remind you, can be easily set on foot. Your reputation could be ruined by such a scandal, and your court divided. There will come a day, mark you, young lady, when you will regret your rejection of a husband who has only demanded what is his by right. This is no way to begin your reign. The people will not love you for it. I hope you will see sense and reconsider the rash decisions you have made tonight.'

'I have no intention of doing so,' I say firmly. 'But I *have* offered to create a dukedom for Guilford.'

To my surprise, Guilford opens the door. He must have been eavesdropping outside.

'I will not be a duke: I will be a king!' he cries. I look at him with contempt.

'You may save your breath, my son,' the Duchess says. 'We are wasting our time here. If you have any sense, you would do well to abstain from the bed of this lady – she is an unnatural and undutiful wife. Instead, I suggest you come with me to Syon House, after we have spoken with your lord father.' And, with the sketchiest of curtseys, she strides purposefully out of the room, leaving Guilford no choice but to follow her. The look he flings over his shoulder at me is venomous.

My first reaction is one of relief that they are gone. Then, by and by, it dawns on me that my mother-in-law may be right, and that so public a separation from my husband so early in my reign would be damaging to my reputation as a champion of religion. Of course, I cannot allow it to happen.

Late though it is, I send for the Earls of Arundel and Pembroke, who come hastily dressed, rubbing sleep from their eyes. Briefly I explain the situation.

'For private reasons, I do not want to keep Lord Guilford company at night,' I tell them, and am warmed by the unexpected sympathy in their eyes. They can surely tell what kind of man my husband is. 'But by day his place should be at my side. Go quickly and tell him that the Queen forbids him to leave the Tower. Her Grace of Northumberland is, of course, free to depart.'

'We are your Majesty's to command,' say the Earls, bowing themselves out.

Within ten minutes, they later report, a furious Guilford and his mother are back in their apartments, forced to obey my command. Alone again, I lie in bed, very vexed, vowing that in no circumstances will I let the Dudleys rule or overrule me. I will be a queen in very truth, or no queen at all.

The Tower of London, 11th–12th July 1553

I have to struggle hard to remember where I am when I wake in the morning. I have slept late, worn out by the momentous events of the previous day and my disturbed night, so I rise hastily, splash cold water on my face and hands and say my morning prayers. Then I summon Mrs Ellen, who is surprised to hear that I wish to be dressed in a rich gown that becomes the dignity of a queen. She brings, for my approval, a crimson dress of figured damask, its wide square neckline edged with pearls, and a bejewelled hood with a latticed snood of silken cords picked out with pearls. I nod.

Thus attired, and followed by my two ladies, I walk along the old stone passages to the council chamber in the keep, ready to attend to affairs of state, for I mean to take my responsibilities seriously.

Pausing in the palace's great hall, I stare at the vast tiers of wooden benches standing against the walls, and am informed by Mrs Tilney that they were built there for the trial of Anne Boleyn, which took place here in this very hall.

'Two thousand people attended, Madam.'

Everywhere I go in this place I am reminded of its grim past. The atmosphere is oppressive, brooding, and it weighs down on me as I make my way to the council chamber and order the guards to open the doors.

'Your Majesty, I crave your pardon, but the council is in session,' says one, clearly embarrassed.

'I am the Queen. If anyone is entitled to enter, it is I. Open the door.' I draw myself up to my full height, and although the guard towers over me, there is no mistaking my authority. Without further protest, the doors are opened and I advance into the room. There is a hasty scraping of chairs as the councillors scramble to rise and bow, but I am not looking at them. Instead, I stare in outrage at the high chair at the head of the table, which should be reserved for me, but is occupied now by a smug-looking Guilford. At his right hand is his father, the Duke. They both stand up reluctantly. There is a tense silence.

Northumberland is the first to find his voice.

'Good morning, your Majesty. As you see, we are already about the business of your realm.'

I hope my displeasure is evident on my face.

'Why was I not summoned, my lord Duke? You have no right to proceed without me.'

Northumberland smiles deprecatingly.

'You forget, Madam, that in law you are still a minor and unable to govern for yourself. We, your Majesty's most loyal servants, are therefore gathered to make decisions in your name, as was the custom in the late King's time. Your husband, who has already attained his majority, has been appointed to represent you. You may, of course, rely on him to protect your interests, for they are his own.'

I understand at once. I am to be a puppet queen, no more. This is their revenge for my refusal to bestow a crown on Guilford. And he, that stupid, grinning weakling, is to be his father's willing tool. I can guess all too well who will be making the decisions, though, and whose interests will take priority.

My anger wells up, but I know better than to make a display of it. I must learn to dissemble and to subvert Northumberland's power in subtle ways. Once I am crowned, I will declare myself of age and be rid of him and his treacherous tribe. And in spectacular fashion, I promise myself. It is merely a matter of biding my time and keeping a smile on my face.

'Very well, my lords,' I say. 'I thank you for your favour shown to me.' And with as much dignity as I can muster, I turn and walk from the room.

I spend my morning closeted in my chamber, engrossed in my studies, which I have thankfully resumed. Later, dinner is served with great ceremony in the presence chamber, where I preside over the high table. The meal lasts for two hours and is an ordeal for me, as I am obliged to make polite conversation with Guilford, my parents and the Duke and Duchess of Northumberland; I am at odds with most of them and can think of little to say.

In the afternoon a charade is acted out: I sit enthroned under my canopy of estate, while my father and the Marquess of Winchester inform me of the decisions that have been made in my name this day, and bring me documents to sign, all of which I read carefully. Then, dipping my quill into the ink-pot they offer me, I inscribe my signature, *Jane the Queen*. This marks the extent of my regal duties.

Afterwards I retire to my apartments to read and, later, eat supper in private. Then it is time for evening prayers and bed. Such is the life of a queen!

On the second night in the Tower, after Mrs Ellen has tucked me into bed and departed, Guilford comes to me.

'I will brook no refusals, Madam,' he says, his purpose plain in his taut demeanour and bulging codpiece. 'You ordered me back to play the husband, and I demand the full privilege. You are my wife and have no right to say me nay.'

'I am your Queen!' I retort.

'A queen without her crown is the same between the sheets as any common whore,' he sneers, seizing hold of me. I struggle in his grip. 'Hold still, or it will go worse with you,' he snarls, forcing me back against the pillows.

I open my mouth to scream for help, but before I can utter a sound, his hand is clamped over my mouth, so heavily that I fear I will suffocate. I realise at this point that all resistance is futile because Guilford is far stronger than I, and cease struggling, bracing myself to endure whatever he might do to me.

'That's better,' he mutters. 'Now, shall we see if we can fill that empty belly of yours with a lusty prince, an heir to England?' He is fumbling with the laces of his codpiece, and when he has them loose, he tears at my nightgown and rams himself into me, again and again, with no thought for whether he is hurting me or not. Yes, he *is* hurting me – not just my body, but my pride also. And they call this the act of love. It is rape, no less, whatever the law may say about a husband's right to use his wife as he thinks fit.

At last Guilford spends himself, and the torment ceases. Several minutes pass while he lies slumped across me, panting, saying nothing. Then he simply gets up and adjusts his clothing. I quickly cover myself and turn my back to him so that he will not see the humiliation and loathing in my face. I just want him to leave without arguments or confrontations. He has won this round, just as he scored his victory in the council chamber, but I will never give him the satisfaction of knowing how much he has wounded and enraged me. In my silence lies my strength. He might possess my body, but my mind and soul are my own. He shall never have those.

At length, after fumbling about in the semi-darkness for a time, Guilford manages to unlock the door.

'I bid you good night, Madam,' he says quietly. 'Let us hope your womb soon quickens with our son, then we can abandon all pretence that we enjoy our coupling. For my part, I would rather roger a poxed tart from the stews of Southwark. At least they fuck with a smile on their faces.'

I steel myself to ignore his taunts and his coarse language. I no longer care what he says or does. It doesn't matter any more. I am detached, contained in my own private world where he cannot reach me. It is my last refuge.

By the evening of my third day in the Tower, the strain of it all is beginning to tell on me. There is still no word of the Lady Mary's whereabouts, and the councillors are growing ever more anxious. The longer Mary remains at liberty, the more likely it is that she will be able either to escape abroad – if she has not already done so – or raise support for her claim. Of course, there is no way of knowing how many would rally to her. Every man here knows his neck is at risk until she is taken. Not to mention my own neck. But Mary will surely understand that I was forced to accept the crown against my will, and that I had no choice in the matter. She must understand that.

At present, I am not primarily concerned about the Lady Mary. I have a far more immediate and pressing worry, for I fear I am being slowly poisoned.

The first symptom I noticed was my hair falling out. Not just the odd strand here or there, but great clumps that leave bald patches. Then I began suffering griping pains in my belly, and lost my appetite. Now my skin is beginning to peel. Anxiously I recall what I have heard of King Edward's terrible sufferings in the weeks before his death: *his* hair fell out, and *his* skin peeled. Of course, this could have been caused by the consumption that killed him, but there are other, more sinister rumours – rumours that accuse Northumberland of hastening the King's death by arsenic poisoning.

Could he be doing the same to me? Does he mean to be rid of me, troublesome thorn that I am, so that he can set Guilford up in my place, a more malleable puppet to dance to his tune? Surely even the Duke could not expect the people of England to allow it! Yet he is a frightened, desperate man, whose crucial schemes are in jeopardy, and I myself am causing him further problems. I am aware he was deeply displeased by my initial rejection of the crown, and that he has certainly resented my outspoken defiance expressed in several ways since. I know that he is angered by my categorical refusal to make Guilford King;

he cannot be happy either about my more personal objections to Guilford as a husband. All in all, the Duke has got himself a bad bargain in exchange for setting me up as Queen, and he surely guesses what fate I have in mind for him once I am crowned. We are locked in a power-struggle, middle-aged opportunist and untried girl, and we both know it. Hence I think it is not illogical to fear that Northumberland is trying to do away with me.

I dare confide in no one. I am glad now that my involvement in state affairs is minimal, for it means that I can stay in my chamber for most of the day and have as little to do with the Duke as possible. At dinner, I take care to eat only from the same dish from which he helps himself, and I have all my food assayed by a food-taster. In the evening, I send Mrs Ellen down to the kitchens to supervise the preparation of my supper.

Yet still my hair continues to fall out, and my skin to peel.

Henry Fitzalan, Earl of Arundel

The Tower of London, 12th July 1553

Long after the Queen has retired, a group of us, all members of the privy council, gather in my lodgings and sit drinking late into the night. Thrown together with these men in the claustrophobic atmosphere of the Tower, I have become aware, during the past day or so, that some are of like mind to myself. A hint here, a muttered remark there, and here we all are, closeted together in secret, confessing our fears for the future.

'I, more than most, have little reason to love Northumberland,' I say resentfully. 'After Somerset fell, he had me imprisoned on the flimsiest of charges. I was utterly humiliated.'

'Your lordship did regain his place on the privy council,' the Marquess of Winchester reminds me.

'Aye, but at the price of my own integrity, I fear,' I tell him. 'I am asking myself – I, whose family can be traced back to the Conquest – how I could ever have allowed myself to become a tool of this upstart Dudley. And what concerns me is that the Duke is becoming infinitely more arrogant as the father-in-law of the Queen than he ever was as mere President of the Council.'

The Earl of Huntingdon, in whose veins runs a thread of royal blood, and whom some secretly considered to be a viable alternative to the Lady Jane, although he is further in blood from the royal line, agrees with me.

'I am even more worried about the influence of that blockhead Suffolk, who knows of little but horses and hounds,' he confides. 'And I am certain I do not want Guilford Dudley as King.'

The Marquess of Winchester heartily concurs. 'It was that, above all, that convinced me that the Duke has gone too far. The whole scheme looks suspicious. This is less about preserving the true religion than about keeping the Dudleys in power.'

'It's just a transparent plot to put the Dudleys on the throne,' I growl. 'We've all been hoodwinked.'

'Who would you rather have on the throne then, Guilford Dudley or the Lady Mary?' asks Huntingdon.

'The Lady Mary has the best and most rightful claim,' answers Winchester. 'I always knew it, but when it came to approving King Edward's device for the succession, I had my own skin to consider.'

'As did we all,' I chime in, as anxious as he to exonerate myself from complicity in Northumberland's plot. 'And now might has prevailed over right.'

'There is still no word of the Lady Mary,' says Huntingdon.

'There will be soon, make no doubt, and it may not be what Northumberland wants to hear,' puts in Pembroke. 'With every day that passes, his position grows more precarious. Until I know which way the wind is blowing, I'll not let my boy consummate his marriage to Lady Katherine Grey. If the Lady Mary prevails, I'll have it annulled.'

Queen Jane

The Tower of London, 13th July 1553

Late in the morning, Northumberland himself brings a sheaf of documents for me to sign. He is obviously under some strain, and makes a visible effort to appear his usual urbane self.

'A slight problem, your Majesty,' he begins, with what proves to be breathtaking understatement. 'I learned last night that the traitor Mary is still at liberty, and it was decided in council this morning that your Grace should dispatch orders to all your lord lieutenants in the shires, commanding them to defend your just title to the crown, and to assist you in the apprehension of the Lady Mary.'

I nod, guessing that the situation is worse than he cares to disclose.

'Very well,' I say, and put pen to parchment. Then I look up, innocent as pie, at the Duke.

'Tell me, my lord, is it not possible for *you* to lead an army against my cousin? You are an experienced soldier, and ably fitted for the task.'

He is astonished at my boldness, and momentarily at a loss.

'Nothing would please me more, Madam,' he stutters, 'yet my duties compel me to remain here in London.' That's a lie, I'm sure. He is frightened to leave the Tower, but of course he can't admit it. He goes on, 'Today, Madam, I have put in hand arrangements for a general muster of troops at Westminster, and my officers are busy even as we speak, recruiting more men. Every man is to have a month's pay now.'

It all sounds providential and grand, but I'm not stupid: I can guess he is only paying the soldiers handsomely in advance in order to ensure that they do not desert, should it come to civil war. And where, I wonder – considering the emptiness of my treasury – is the money coming from?

Later, Northumberland returns with some councillors, beaming.

'Two thousand men stand ready to defend you, Madam, as well as the Yeomen of the Guard, who will remain here. I have placed at the army's disposal thirty great guns from the Tower arsenal.'

'Then we may sleep peacefully in our beds tonight,' I observe.

'Indeed, Madam,' he replies. 'Furthermore, five warships are to patrol the coast of East Anglia to prevent the Lady Mary from escaping by sea.'

'Is there further news of her whereabouts?'

'Yes, Madam. She is at Kenninghall still, where a few lewd and base persons have rallied to her banner. Yet your Majesty has no cause for fear, since your army will shortly be ready to march into Norfolk to put down this rebellion.'

I look directly into his eyes. Here is my chance to be rid of him.

'And who will lead it?' I ask challengingly.

'I suggest your lord father, Madam.'

'My father?' I echo. 'Oh, no, my lord, I could not spare him.' And, taking a handkerchief from my sleeve, I pretend to dab away a tear.

The Duke does his best to reassure me.

'Your father is the finest soldier I know. No other is as experienced. You may be certain he will deal with these rebels in no time, and come safely home to you.'

'No,' I say, putting my handkerchief away and sitting straight-backed. 'You, my lord, are the best man of war in this realm. It is you who should lead my forces.'

Before Northumberland can open his mouth to protest, Pembroke, Arundel, Huntingdon and Winchester all break out in a chorus of approval, which is most heartening to hear. The Duke looks staggered. Now he must know he is beaten. He must also guess, as I do, that they are beginning to turn against him. They too want him gone, and in a position to take the blame if things go wrong. Taken at the head of an army, in open rebellion against his rightful sovereign, what chance would he have? Whereas these lords left in the Tower could lie brazenly to absolve themselves from any willing part in his conspiracy.

I suspect the Duke has deliberately lied to me and his colleagues as to the extent of Mary's support. If he has so speedily mustered an army of two thousand men, her forces must be great: he would not need as many to put down a few yokels.

'I am your Majesty's to command, of course,' Northumberland is saying belatedly, breathing heavily. 'I will do as you ask.'

'I thank you most humbly,' I reply demurely. 'I pray you use your diligence, and wish you Godspeed.' This victory to me, then, and it might well prove the crucial one.

But Northumberland must have his revenge. Without consulting me, he announces almost immediately that I and my husband are to be crowned in Westminster Abbey a fortnight hence.

I am outraged as I sit here, impotent, on my throne. Have I not expressly refused to make Guilford King? But the Duke is determined to ignore that, so anxious is he to secure his own position before his departure. Wait, I counsel myself. Just wait, and have patience. Soon he will be gone, and I will have more freedom to order affairs myself. The lords will almost certainly support me – witness how they did so today, to devastating effect – and I conclude that they must be as resentful of the Duke's tyranny as I am. And there is always the possibility that his lordship may never return.

Northumberland is still speaking. 'Henceforth, any servant approaching either the Queen or her lord husband will do so on bended knee, and both will be addressed as "your Grace".' He turns to the throne and bows.

'Your Grace,' he tells me, 'an envoy has been sent in your name to your good brother the Emperor to announce your undisputed succession and to declare to him how the traitor Mary is bent on disturbing the peace of the realm.'

I incline my head regally, whilst responding with a touch of sarcasm.

'Let us hope that will be sufficient to deter the Emperor from aiding and abetting our enemies.'

The Tower of London, 14th July 1553

The next morning, I am aware of a buzz of activity in and around the Tower. Emerging from my chamber, I am informed that the Duke has ordered his troops to muster outside Durham House, and is preparing to depart.

Arundel approaches me, doffing his cap and bowing.

'Your Grace, I would speak privately with you.'

I lead him into my apartments and dismiss my two ladies.

'You have news, my lord?'

'Bad news, I regret, Madam. We had tidings in the night that the whole of East Anglia has risen in support of the Lady Mary, and that the Earl of Derby has proclaimed her Queen in Cheshire. Even that Protestant troublemaker, Sir Peter Carew, has done the same in Devon. Worst of all, for my lord Duke, is the report that his son Robert, realising he could not hope to apprehend the Lady Mary, himself proclaimed her Queen in King's Lynn.'

I feel faint and nauseous. Northumberland's edifice is crumbling, unable to withstand the tempests, and God's will is prevailing, despite the efforts of foolish, proud men to thwart it. And although I am shaken by the news, I am glad – glad to my soul – of the likely outcome. For, as the Almighty is my witness, I never wanted to be Queen. I have worn my dignity unwillingly and hated every minute of it, these last days in the Tower. Now, it appears, the treacherous charade is nearly over, and when it is, the hated Dudleys will receive just punishment, and I will happily relinquish my borrowed title and go home to Bradgate, there to live in peaceful obscurity with my books. That Mary will allow this, I cannot doubt: she is a merciful, kindly lady, and wise enough to understand that I consented to accept the crown only under unbearable pressure and with extreme reluctance. Heaven knows, there are plenty of witnesses who could tell her so. Thus, for myself, I have no undue concern.

'Several councillors have fled,' Arundel is saying. 'They left the Tower at dead of night.'

'Ought we to leave too?' I ask.

'Your Majesty is probably safer remaining here,' he advises.

'It is hard to judge the mood of the people, and anyway, if you flee, you proclaim yourself guilty in the Lady Mary's eyes. The day is not lost yet, Madam.'

'I thank you for your counsel, my lord. Will you remain?'

'I will dissemble until the time is ripe for declaring my true allegiance – saving your pardon, Madam,' he says candidly. 'The Duke may yet prevail. If he does, you may count on my loyalty. But we must all look to our own necks.'

'And the rest?'

'They too will swim with the tide.'

I smile to myself. Is there a man of principle among them?

Shortly afterwards Northumberland arrives to receive from me his formal commission.

'I bid you farewell, Madam,' he says. 'In a few days I will bring in the Lady Mary, captive or dead, like the rebel she is.' And, with a sweeping bow, he is gone.

Northumberland and his eldest son, the Earl of Warwick, have left London at the head of their army, much to my relief. My advisors assure me that the Duke will be victorious: is he not, after all, the finest soldier in the kingdom?

'I wonder if I might remain Queen after all,' I confide to Mrs Ellen. 'I am certainly resolved at least to behave like one until the outcome of the matter is known. After all, if God has called me to rule England and further establish the reformed religion here, I must not let Him down. I just pray that His will is evident in the events of the next few days, so that I may know my course is the right one.'

'We are all in God's hands,' Mrs Ellen says quietly.

The tension in the Tower is palpable. Several councillors have announced their intention of visiting their homes, there to wait upon events, but my lord father has persuaded them – not without difficulty – to stay. They do so with plain reluctance, for the news is not good for those who have thrown in their lot with the Duke. Mary has been proclaimed Queen in four counties now. Off Yarmouth, the crews of Northumberland's warships have mutinied in her favour, and two thousand sailors have deserted and gone to join her at Framlingham, where a vast army is gathering around her. And how the people are flocking to Mary's standard! Even that stern Protestant, Bishop Hooper, is urging his flock to support her. It is becoming increasingly obvious that the people of England will not bow to the ambition of John Dudley.

Ashen-faced, my father turns to me.

'Madam, the lords are restive. They whisper that yours is a lost cause. That damned Treasurer of the Mint – may God curse him! – has absconded with all the gold in your Grace's privy purse, and you may be sure that others are planning to follow him. I suspect that, even now, some of them are in touch with Mary's supporters in London.'

'Then we must pray that my lord of Northumberland is victorious,' I say drily. My father gives me a look; he has not missed the irony in my voice.

Later in the day he is back, very agitated.

'Madam, this is beyond me. Two lords of the council have just been stopped by the guards whilst attempting to leave the Tower by stealth. None of us has the authority of Northumberland, and the number of waverers is increasing by the hour. Who shall prevent them if they are determined upon going?'

'I will,' I declare, rising to my feet. I will not let them leave me to face the consequences of Northumberland's folly alone. 'Pray summon the privy council to attend me now.'

There are several empty chairs. I rest a stern gaze on the men before me. Some meet my eyes, others look shiftily away. I know that I cannot rely on their loyalty, but I will do my best to make them take responsibility for what they have done. And in order to bring them to obedience, I must dissemble, and dissemble again.

'My lords,' I say, 'I thank you for coming so promptly. I have called you here to inform you that, in the absence of the Lord President, I myself, your sovereign lady and Queen, will assume the government of my realm. I will henceforth preside over all your meetings, and every order will be issued by me in person. I do assure you, I mean to rule as well as reign, with the guidance of Almighty God.'

No one speaks, but some of the peers are regarding me with undisguised admiration. No one ventures to challenge my assumption of power – at least, not openly.

'I propose,' I continue, 'to write to the sheriffs of certain counties to remind them of their allegiance. I intend also to give audience to the Bishop of London, to ask him to use his sermon next Sunday to put our subjects in mind of their loyalty to us. But above that, my lords, I mean to ensure that the Protestant faith remains the religion of this my realm. I realise that my position is not yet as secure as it should be, but I shall pray God daily that, if it be His will, He will preserve me to carry out His work on Earth, so that the wicked superstitions practised by the Lady Mary may never again blight this land.'

I have said too much, I know; one day soon, my brave words, intended to keep these men with me and accountable, might well be regarded as treasonable. But what else could I do?

There is some polite applause. 'Amen!' says one councillor, and a few others echo him, yet I realise that I have failed to touch their hearts. Admire me they might, but they can never forget for a moment that I may be deposed at any time. Until they are certain that I am secure on my throne, I cannot count on their support.

The Tower of London, 15th July 1553

London, Mrs Ellen tells me, is in a ferment. A messenger arriving at the Tower has brought the news that the Lady Mary is advancing on the capital at the head of thirty thousand men. Many towns have declared for her, and there is widespread support for her in the countryside.

My parents hasten to my chamber, their faces tense with anxiety and fear.

'We must issue a proclamation,' my father says, 'stressing the justness of your title and demanding that the kingdom be preserved from papists.'

'Then let it be done,' I say calmly. I have already resigned myself to God's will. If my reign is going to be brief, so be it.

'I don't trust Winchester,' mutters my lady.

'Nor Pembroke,' adds my father. 'And I suspect that Arundel is already in touch with the Lady Mary.'

'Winchester has gone back to his house in the City,' my mother informs me. 'Think you he'll come back? He has his skin to save after all.'

'He'll come back,' growls my lord. 'He'll not dare ignore the Queen's command. And once he's here, we'll have the Tower gates locked early for the night.'

I am surprised to learn that Winchester *has* returned in response to my summons. The gates are duly locked. It is only afterwards that we learn Pembroke is missing.

'What did you expect?' says Arundel nastily. 'He got out while he could. You do realise, my lord of Suffolk, that if your daughter is toppled – yes, and let's make no bones about it, she may well be – we shall all face a traitor's death. And I don't need to spell out what they do to traitors, do I?'

I shiver, and see my father shudder. Perhaps he is imagining the agony of having the disembowelling knife rip into his guts.

'Peers of the realm,' my mother puts in briskly, 'are customarily spared the worst horrors of a traitor's death. For them, the sentence is invariably commuted to beheading.'

'That's bad enough,' mutters my father.

'But the innocent also will suffer,' I say, thinking not only of myself, but, with sorrow, of my poor sister, married to Pembroke's son, whom she loves well. Without a doubt she will pay the price of the Earl's defection. 'I pity Katherine. She has done nothing wrong, but they will hate her for my sake, and have her marriage dissolved.'

'Nonsense!' barks my father, with more bravado than conviction. 'Let's hear no more of this maudlin talk. Instead of mewling like a sick puppy, Madam, I suggest you order your guards to bring Pembroke back, and then deal with him firmly.'

I summon the Captain of the Guard.

'I command you to send some men to Baynard's Castle to apprehend my lord of Pembroke,' I say. 'Bring him here to me, and do not let him give you the slip. And I order you also to bring me the keys to the Tower each evening at eight o'clock without fail.'

The Tower of London, 18th July 1553

The privy councillors are assembled before the throne. My father stands behind it.

'Your Grace,' says Arundel, 'we have grave news. The Duke of Northumberland's forces have mutinied, and he has been forced to take refuge with his few remaining supporters in Cambridge.'

'The French ambassador has hinted that he might be able to summon aid from France,' says Winchester. 'The French fear that, if the Lady Mary becomes Queen, she will make an alliance with their enemy, the Emperor.'

'We need to see the ambassador urgently,' insists Pembroke, still grim-faced after the blistering reprimand I delivered to him the other night.

'It's worth a try, Madam,' says Winchester.

Master William Cecil, secretary to the council, speaks. 'Your Grace, the truth is that the privy council is required to attend the ambassador at the French embassy to discuss the matter in secrecy. The lords will therefore require your permission to leave the Tower.'

'Very well,' I tell them. I am under no delusions as to their real purpose. The days of my reign are numbered, no doubt about that, and rats, it is said, always desert a sinking ship. For the loss of my title and status I care nothing. In fact, I am relieved that I will not be Queen for much longer. As for the consequences of my actions, I put my faith in God. Maybe it will go better for me if I am found alone and abandoned in the Tower.

But my father has no intention of letting them abscond so easily.

'I insist upon accompanying you, my lords,' he declares, with what passes as a friendly smile.

'There is no need, my lord,' Arundel assures him.

'By God, I shall go with you!' my father roars, but Pembroke is ready for him.

'If you abandon the Queen, my lord,' he says smoothly, 'we shall have no choice but to order your summary execution.'

My father splutters with rage. 'How dare you occupy the

moral high ground and accuse *me* of abandoning the Queen? I'm the only loyal one among you. But you have me in a corner, and I'll not be accused of treason where none is intended. Yet I warn you, if you do not return here promptly, you will all suffer such a fate as you threaten me with.'

'I think not, my lord,' says Winchester. 'But never fear. We will return anon.'

Frances Brandon, Duchess of Suffolk

The Tower of London, 18th July 1553

In the evening, Henry comes to my bedchamber. He is close to tears. This truly startles me, for I have never seen him so over-come, even when our little son died.

'What is wrong?' I ask, alarmed.

'The traitors, the bloody, bloody traitors!' he cries.

'What traitors?' My fear is evident in my voice.

'The privy councillors, my dear. They never went to the French embassy. Any fool could have seen that that was a bluff. But what did they do instead? They gathered at Baynard's Castle for some secret conclave, and then, would you believe it, they went to St Paul's to give thanks for the kingdom's deliverance from treachery. Whose treachery, you may well ask?'

'Did they declare for Mary?' Icy tremors are shooting down my spine.

'Not in so many words, but – may God forgive them – they had the bare-faced temerity to order the Catholic Mass to be celebrated in the Cathedral. Can you credit it?'

'Oh, God!' I wail. It is as if the world is about to come crashing down around us.

Henry draws me urgently into his arms.

'Whatever happens, you must accept that I did it all for the best, for us, and for Jane, and for Katherine too,' he whispers. 'I never dreamed it would end like this. Northumberland seemed invincible, his plan flawless.'

'I believe you,' I say flatly. Then my pragmatic streak comes to the fore. 'We should leave the Tower now, while we can, and take Jane with us.'

'No. Best to see what happens first. If the Londoners are set on declaring for Mary, we might be safer in the Tower. You know how volatile the London mob can be.'

'We should at least tell Jane what is happening.'

'Not just now. Leave her in peace for the moment. It cannot be long now. She has borne up well so far, but this latest news might prove altogether too much for her. Her best defence is her youth and innocence.'

'Surely Mary will take that into account?' For the first time it is dawning on me that there might be serious consequences for our daughter as well as for the rest of us.

'I do not believe she will be unmerciful to one of her own flesh and blood,' Henry replies.

'I pray God you are right,' I say fervently. Our eyes lock in concern and trepidation.

Queen Jane

The Tower of London, 19th July 1553

'Mrs Underhill went into labour during the night,' announces Mrs Ellen. Mrs Underhill is the wife of one of the yeomen warders of the Tower. I look up from my book.

'Perhaps she is delivered by now,' I say. 'Please, would you go and find out?' The anticipated birth of this child is a beacon of light in a gloomy world. I could not admit it to anyone, but the prospect of seeing, and possibly holding, a new-born baby is suddenly a very enticing one.

Mrs Ellen misses little. She looks at me thoughtfully, then leaves the room.

She is soon back with a proud and slightly bashful Mr Underhill.

'It's a fine boy!' she tells me.

I smile, and give the warder my hand to kiss.

'Many congratulations, Mr Underhill. When your wife has rested, I should like to visit her and the child.'

'I thank ye, your Grace,' the man stammers. 'I, er, that is, we was wondering, would your Majesty consent to the boy being christened Guilford, in honour of your lord husband?'

'Of course,' I say warmly, although it occurs to me that the Underhills might not have much cause to rejoice in that name in the years to come.

Mr Underhill is still standing there, fiddling with his cap.

'Is there anything else?' I ask.

'Um, your Grace, begging your pardon,' he goes on, 'but I have another favour to ask. Would you do us the great honour of standing sponsor at the christening? It's to be this evening, in the Chapel of St Peter ad Vincula in the Tower.'

'I shall be delighted,' I beam.

When he has gone, Mrs Ellen is pensive.

'What troubles you?' I ask.

'Oh, probably nothing,' she says. 'It just struck me, when I went to the Underhills, how quiet it is in the royal apartments. Do you know, in the White Tower, the state rooms are all but deserted. Where is everybody?'

'You saw no one at all?'

'I did pass Archbishop Cranmer and his chaplain on the stairs. I suppose, if he is here, the rest of the council must be also.'

'Yes, I suppose they must,' I say, but with little conviction.

Dinner is a muted affair, served in my privy chamber. No one arrives to keep me company at meat. Mrs Ellen goes out again afterwards, and reports, on her return, that everywhere still seems to be deserted.

The tense hours of the afternoon drag on interminably in the stifling heat. Then suddenly, soon after five o'clock, the bells of the City churches begin to peal joyously and there are distant shouts. Through my open window I can see drifts of smoke rising above the rooftops, and the river packed with craft.

The steward appears and announces that supper is served. As I seat myself under the canopy of estate in the empty presence chamber, I wonder tremulously if I will soon be informed of the cause of the afternoon's commotion. I think I can guess it, though.

I am right, on both counts. My father, followed by three yeomen warders, bursts into the room and, without paying his respects to me, begins tearing down the cloth of estate above my head. Clumps of displaced dust fall into my food.

I stare at him, half-comprehending.

'Jane, you are no longer Queen,' he tells me bluntly. 'London has declared for the Lady Mary. Go to your chamber and stay there. You must put off your royal robes and be content to live henceforth as a private person.'

'That is all I ever wanted,' I say. 'Nothing could please me better.'

He regards me with some surprise.

'I wonder at your calm acceptance of this calamity,' he says. Then, as I just sit here, unmoving, he repeats more urgently, 'You must take off your royal robes now!'

'I much more willingly put them off than I put them on,' I tell him. Then the precariousness of my situation begins to dawn on me, and I look on this man, my hitherto all-powerful father, who did so much to place me in it. It is his ambition that has brought me to this.

'Out of obedience to you and my mother, I have grievously sinned,' I say bitterly. He stares at me, startled, for my voice betrays the depths of my resentment. 'I willingly relinquish the crown,' I declare. 'I never wanted it.'

He nods. The canopy is down, lying in a heap on the floor. For nine days it has signified my sovereignty. That is over now, finished.

'May I not go home?' I ask. It sounds childish, and perhaps it is, but this is what I long for. My father looks as if he is about to cry. I am shocked to my core. I have never seen him this way in my life.

'No, Jane, you must stay here,' he answers in a choked voice. 'I am going now to Tower Hill to proclaim the Lady Mary

Queen of England. I hope you understand why I am doing this. I am trying to save us all.' And he hastens from the room. I know with certainty that he is going to run for his life and lie low, waiting to see what the new Queen will do. He will leave me to my fate. He must think that Mary will spare me on account of my youth and inexperience – otherwise, surely, he would not have left me here. Of course, I reason, he, a mature adult, can expect no such mercy. He has committed high treason.

My mother does not even come to say goodbye. Later I learn that they have gone to Sheen.

Alone in the chamber of presence, I sit unmoving. What will happen to me now? I cannot believe that Mary will cut off *my* head for what I have done. She will appreciate that I was forced to it, that all this was against my will. Somehow I must convince her that I am no danger to her, and that I wish her nothing but good, even though she is a Catholic. But how to go about that? Should I crave an audience? Will she even consent to see me?

The door opens and I catch my breath, but it is only Guilford who stands there. One glance tells me he has been crying. His eyes are red.

'So you know,' he says. I nod. There is an awkward silence. Even at the best of times we have had little to say to one another.

'What if you are with child?' he ventures.

'Let us pray that is not the case. There are too many Dudleys already in this world.'

His eyes brim again with tears. 'My father,' he whispers. 'What will they do to my father?'

If I were not so numb, and he had not been so brutish to me, I might try to comfort him. I understand that, for him, this is a very personal tragedy. But I have no words to say to him.

He sniffs.

'I will leave you now,' he says. 'I must comfort my lady mother.' He walks out, shoulders heaving.

With dragging feet, I make my way to my bedchamber, trying to assume a cheerful countenance for the sake of Mrs Ellen and Mrs Tilney. But when I tell them what has happened, Mrs Tilney falls to weeping pitifully. Mrs Ellen remains dry-eyed; I realise she is too full of fear to cry. Instead, she busies herself with practicalities, helping me to change into one of my plain black gowns. Life, after all, has to go on.

'It is near six o'clock, Madam,' she reminds me.

I had forgotten. I have promised to attend the Underhill christening.

'We must make haste,' I say, taking my prayer book. But when I open the door to my chamber, I find the way barred by guards.

I am a prisoner.

Lady Jane Dudley

The Tower of London, 20th July 1553

The Marquess of Winchester stands before me.

'Madam, you are required by Queen Mary to surrender to me the crown of England, also the crown jewels and other regalia, as well as other property in this Tower rightfully belonging to our lawful sovereign, such as furs, clocks and portraits.'

'Sir, they are at your disposal,' I tell him. 'I never wanted them.'

He ignores this.

'The Lieutenant of the Tower, Sir John Bridges, will inform you of the arrangements that have been made for your confinement,' he concludes, then gives me a curt nod and withdraws from the room with a speed that is only just this side of dignified.

The Lieutenant, a kindly, avuncular man in his fifties, comes to me soon afterwards. Clearly he does not relish the duty imposed on him in keeping a fifteen-year-old girl in custody, and is sympathetic towards me personally. But, as Winchester explained earlier, I am being imprisoned not so much for what I have done – since the Queen, in her mercy, realises that I have been led astray by wicked men – as for who I am.

'Her Majesty fears,' he explained, 'that you might be the focus of Protestant plots to overthrow her, once this present rejoicing over her accession has died down. Hence you are to be kept in the Tower for the time being.'

Mrs Ellen

The Tower of London, 20th July 1553

The Lieutenant has come again to see Jane. She looks so small and vulnerable, standing before her desk in her plain black gown and hood, clenching those tiny, immature hands. Not for the first time, I wonder how anyone could ever look upon this child as a criminal.

'Good day, Madam,' says Sir John. He's a big bear of a man, but he looks friendly enough. He may sometimes have to carry out the grimmest of duties, but he has a kindly face.

'Good day, Sir John,' Jane answers in a small voice. 'Shall I go to a dungeon?'

Someone, some other time, uttered those words. I cannot for the life of me think who it was, but I am disturbed by them. Never mind that now. It can wait. Please God the Lieutenant will give my poor child some reassurance.

'Of course not, Madam,' he tells her. 'You will be lodged with Master Partridge, the Gentleman Gaoler of the Tower, and Mrs Partridge. They have a comfortable house adjoining my own lodging, overlooking the Green and the Chapel of St Peter ad Vincula. And you may have your lady here in attendance.'

Jane's relief is plain on her face. It is far better than we had both feared.

Tower Green. Of course. It was Anne Boleyn who asked if she were to go to a dungeon. She met her death there, on Tower Green, and her headless body lies in an unmarked grave in the chapel.

The Lieutenant ushers me out of the room with him.

'Mistress, there are times when I do not like my office,' he says when we are outside and the door is shut. 'She's just a child. So small and thin. Learned, too, I've heard − not that I hold with that much myself. It gives girls ideas. Still, by all reports, she's godly and virtuous in her conduct.'

'Indeed, Sir John,' I reply. 'She's a good girl, through and through, and has been evilly used by wicked men.'

'Well, I cannot comment on that,' he says, evasive. 'It's not my job to judge those in my care.' His face softens suddenly, and in a lower voice he murmurs, 'I pride myself on being a decent family man, and I am appalled at the cowardly way in which the Lady Jane's parents have abandoned her. And no, I do not believe that girl ever intended any treason. I doubt she was in any way responsible for what they made her do. I wanted to assure you that I am determined to treat her kindly while she is in my care, so never fear. But remember − not a word of this to anyone. I never said it.'

I am near to tears when I return to Jane. I pray God the Queen has as much perception and compassion as her lieutenant.

Lady Jane Dudley

The Tower of London, 20th July 1553

St Peter ad Vincula. St Peter in Chains. I am as good as in chains in here, even though they are invisible ones. Will I ever taste freedom again?

I am being escorted by Sir John Bridges to the Gentleman Gaoler's house. As we walk past Tower Green, I remember that on this spot Anne Boleyn and Katherine Howard were beheaded. Their bodies now lie in the chapel yonder. It is not a view I would have chosen.

Yet my fate could have been worse. I could be locked in a dark, dank dungeon.

'Am I permitted to have my servants with me?' I inquire.

'You are to be attended by Lady Throckmorton as lady-in-waiting when necessary, and at all times by Mrs Ellen, Mrs Tilney and a page. I'm afraid the rest of your household have been dismissed. Because of your rank, you will be accorded a position of honour within the Partridge household, and will enjoy every comfort.'

'The Queen is most kind. I do not deserve such grace at her hands,' I say humbly. 'Tell me, Sir John, may I have books and writing materials so that I can continue my studies?'

'That I will arrange. Your ladies may fetch your clothes and other personal belongings from the palace.'

'I require very little,' I tell him. 'This is all that any mortal really needs.'

I show him the prayer book I am carrying, a gift from Guilford. It is bound in black velvet.

'Sir John, can you tell me what will happen to me?' I ask. I desperately need to know.

The Lieutenant looks distressed.

'Madam, I cannot,' he answers sadly. 'I honestly do not know, and if I did, I would not be at liberty to tell you without authorisation from the council. My advice is to take each day as it comes, one at a time, and to trust in God. Give matters time to settle down. Then things may become clearer.'

It is as much reassurance as I am going to get, I realise. I ask him what has become of Guilford and his mother.

'They are both in custody, and the traitor Dudley is expected to join them here in the Tower shortly.'

'May I know where my husband is being held?'

'In the Beauchamp Tower, over there.' He points to a grim medieval edifice of grey stone, forbidding in aspect and doubtless freezing in winter. Imprisonment there would be punishment indeed, even without the threat of execution. For that will surely be Northumberland's fate, if not Guilford's. Yet was not he, like me, a mere tool used by ambitious and unscrupulous men?

I have been wondering fearfully – naturally enough, I suppose – whether I myself will be sent to the block for my undoubted treason. Reason compels me to think otherwise, but my terror kept me awake last night, for it was in the hours of darkness that the full horror of my situation impacted upon me.

Yet now that Sir John has informed me of the very generous

terms of my confinement, compared with that of the Dudleys, I am somewhat reassured and cheered. The new Queen is known to be a merciful princess. Sir John told Mrs Ellen that she has already received into her favour several lords who were Northumberland's creatures. Mayhap what he said to me is true, and she does only mean to keep me in the Tower until the country is calm again, and then quietly release me into blessed obscurity.

God, I pray it will be so.

Master Partridge is aptly named: he's a rotund little man of about forty, ruddy-cheeked and jovial – too jovial by far for his calling. He bows at my approach, then quickly remembers himself and straightens.

'This way, my lady,' he says. He conducts me to the best bedchamber, which his wife has sweetened with herb-strewn rushes on the floor and fresh bleached linen sheets on the bed. There is a cream embroidered coverlet, turned back, a chest for the few items of clothing that are suitable for me to wear now – all plain gowns, and nothing to hint that for nine brief days I was Queen of England – and a desk and chair under the latticed window, on which is set a jug of wine and a pewter goblet.

'I hope it suits, my lady,' says Mrs Partridge anxiously, bobbing a curtsey.

'I need nothing more,' I tell her. 'You have been most kind and thoughtful.'

'Supper is at six,' she informs me. 'I hope you will grace our humble table.'

'It will be my pleasure,' I reply, as Mrs Ellen bustles in with a large sack from which she begins to unpack my belongings. Mrs Partridge leaves us to ourselves.

'Well, this is a pleasant room,' says Mrs Ellen.

'Indeed it is.' I feel almost light-hearted. Prison is not going to be so terrible after all. It's certainly far better than my days of greatness in the palace here. Indeed, I shall be quite content to stay with these kind and well-disposed people for a time, without having to rub shoulders with those who have brought me to ruin. The loss of my freedom and privileges is as nothing compared to the huge relief I feel at having been given so light a punishment.

My spirits lift further an hour later when Sir John Bridges

personally delivers my books and writing materials. I realise I now have leisure to read and study. Never, I suspect, will the Queen's Majesty have a happier prisoner!

The Tower of London, July 1553

Master Partridge is a dutiful servant of the Crown, and while he never fails in his simple courtesy towards me, he makes it his business never to discuss with me the events taking place beyond the four walls of his house. Mrs Partridge, on the other hand, relishes a good gossip and, unknown to her husband – who would deplore her lack of discretion – lets slip a great deal of information to Mrs Ellen and Mrs Tilney, with whom she has quickly struck up companionable friendships.

And so I learn of Northumberland's arrest at Cambridge and his subsequent shameful return to London and committal to the Beauchamp Tower. His four sons, Warwick, Robert, Ambrose and Guilford, are imprisoned there with him. I heard the commotion on the day of his arrival – now I know what it signified.

A day or so later, Mrs Partridge reveals that the Duchess of Northumberland has been freed, and has gone to Newhall to plead with the Queen for her husband's life. Later we learn that Mary refused to see her. She has, however, agreed to grant my mother an audience.

Frances Brandon, Duchess of Suffolk

Newhall, Essex, July 1553

It was impossible for me to remain quietly at Sheen, waiting for the knock on the door, the armed guards, the warrant. I was never a passive spirit, and felt compelled to do something to ward off the approaching danger. Unable to bear the suspense any longer, and impervious to Henry's warnings, I saddled my horse and rode off with just one man-at-arms and one lady in attendance, into Essex, to beg my cousin the Queen to show mercy to my family.

On my knees before my purple-clad, bejewelled stony-faced sovereign, I do not try to hide my panic.

'I beseech your Majesty,' I plead, 'of your great charity and mercy, spare my lord husband and my innocent daughter.'

Mary looks at me severely.

'They have committed treason,' she says in her gruff man's voice. 'If they had had their way, I should not be sitting here now.'

'They had no choice, Madam!' I cry. Let Northumberland take all the blame for this. He is going to die for it anyway. It was he who brought us to this pass, and it is he who should pay the price.

'Your Majesty,' I continue urgently, 'we suspected that the traitor Northumberland was poisoning your late brother the King, and we greatly feared he would poison us too – my lord, my daughters and myself – if we did not comply with his schemes.'

Mary looks startled.

'You have proof of this?' she asks sharply.

I decide to take a gamble. This time the stakes are higher than I have ever played for.

'My daughter Jane has twice suffered symptoms that suggest poisoning, symptoms that were similar to those manifested by his late Majesty. It is a fact that the apothecary who gave the poison to the King has just taken his own life, so full of remorse was he for what he had done.' (May God forgive the lie, I pray inwardly. Yet perchance, if rumour is to be believed, it is closer to the truth than any one of us knows.) 'Were his late Majesty's body to be opened, the traces would be there, I swear to it.'

'I do not think that will be necessary,' says the Queen, evidently shaken by these revelations. 'But if it was as you say, you were indeed in grave danger. Northumberland is a ruthless and evil man. I fear he is beyond redemption.' She pauses, thoughtful, fingering the ornate crucifix at her throat. How Jane would hate that crucifix, I think irrelevantly.

The Queen rises, indicating that I should get up off my knees.

'I can see you were in an impossible position, Frances,' she says. 'Rest assured I will not harm your husband and daughter. You may go home to Sheen without fear. An order has been issued for your lord's arrest, but if he pleads for mercy, we will set him at liberty. God knows, most of my councillors were in this with him, and I can't very well proceed against the greater part of the peerage. As for the Lady Jane, I intend for her to remain in the Tower for the present. She is being well cared for. For obvious reasons, I do not wish her to communicate with her friends and former supporters, and I want your undertaking now that neither you nor the Duke will attempt to have letters or messages smuggled in to her. When things settle down, I will consider sending her home.'

'Madam, you have it,' I say firmly.

Thank God, we are all safe. I have managed rather well, I reflect. Now we can abide our time in patience until the Queen gives the order for Jane's release. All in all, it's a miracle we've come out of this business so unscathed.

Mary is as good as her word. My lord spends a mere three days in the Tower before being granted his freedom. Surely now it won't be long before Jane is allowed hers too.

Lady Jane Dudley

The Tower of London, 3rd August 1553

Since before dawn people have been crowding into the Tower precincts. I can see them from my upstairs window: ordinary citizens, Tower officials and warders, Yeomen of the Guard and, later on, courtiers, lords and ladies, many of them known to me. All have come to see the new Queen, who is today making her state entry into London. Tonight she will take up residence in the Tower. Even the normally reticent Master Partridge has told me this much, adding that her Majesty will be lodging in the palace for the next fortnight.

She will probably sleep in the very room I myself occupied,

I realise, and wonder if it will put the Queen in remembrance of my being held a prisoner here, although more likely it will remind her that I slept there under false pretences.

Mrs Ellen has had word from Mrs Partridge of several Catholic prisoners who spent King Edward's reign in the Tower; recently they narrowly avoided Northumberland's axe, because in his haste to make me a queen, the Duke neglected to sign their death warrants. Among them are the old Duke of Norfolk and Bishop Gardiner of Winchester, and all are to be freed today by the Queen in person. I entertain the wild notion that I myself might be numbered among them, but as the hours tick by and no summons comes, it becomes obvious that I will not. Resolutely setting aside my disappointment – it is too soon, of course, what am I thinking of? – I try to settle down to translating a Latin poem, but the sounds from outside are too distracting. When, late in the afternoon, I hear distant trumpets and the deafening noise of the guns saluting on Tower Wharf, I give up writing and hasten to the window, leaning over the stone sill and straining to see if I can catch a glimpse of the Queen through the vast crowds. But it is a vain hope. Too many obstacles block my view, and the press of people is too thick.

An agitated movement below catches my eye. It is Master Partridge, signalling to me to stand away from the window. My appearance is clearly exciting curiosity among the people, some of whom must have realised who I am. Reluctantly I step back, closing the casement and turning again to my books. Soon the cheers start dying away; the pageant must be over.

Presently Mrs Ellen and Mrs Tilney, who went with Mrs Partridge to watch the procession, return with an account of what they have seen.

'Truly, the Queen is a most merciful princess,' enthuses Mrs Ellen, with a significant glance at me. 'When the Duke of Norfolk and the rest were brought out, and knelt before her on the cobbles, she wept with emotion. "These are *my* prisoners," she said, and set them at liberty. Believe me, Jane, you have nothing to fear from her.'

I smile, but I am not entirely reassured. Those who have been released are all Catholics, but I do not like to dampen my nurse's elation by pointing this out. Mary has not said when she will release me, and with a jolt I realise that I could be here for many years, perhaps my whole life. I pray God, therefore, that the Queen's famed mercy will extend to one who is of the wrong religion and the wrong blood.

Queen Mary

The Tower of London, August 1553

Today is my first audience with Simon Renard, the new ambassador sent by my beloved cousin, the Emperor. I know well it is Charles's wish to support me in the great tasks that lie before me, and God knows I need such support. Early this month the privy council made its formal submission to me, smugly secure in the knowledge that, while I might formally refuse to pardon those who supported the usurper Jane, I dare not alienate all my lords because I need them. Of course, I made a token display of displeasure, but in the end I extended my hand for every single one of them to kiss, much to their evident gratification. Some were weeping with emotion and relief.

Even Winchester and Pembroke, whom I briefly imprisoned, are now back at the council table. Pembroke has hastened to have his son's marriage to the usurper's sister annulled, and has, I hear, turned the girl out of his house. She is now with her parents at Sheen, disgraced and dejected.

There is one notable absentee from the council: Thomas Cranmer, whom I will not dignify with the title Archbishop of Canterbury. It is he whom I hold responsible for the breaking of my father's marriage to my sainted mother, and he who was one of the chief instruments in establishing the heretical Protestant faith in England. He has been dismissed and imprisoned.

Renard now stands before me, a dapper little man with Italianate colouring and a large nose. His bearing is respectful, as becomes a diplomat, but I have heard that he is a person of forceful views and great moral courage. Charles has chosen well.

'Ambassador, you are most welcome,' I say smiling, 'and I declare to you most frankly that I intend to place all my trust in you, not only because you are a link with my beloved mother's country, but also because I know you will be faithful to me and to the Catholic cause.'

'Your Majesty is most kind,' he replies. 'Rest assured I will do my very best for you, even if it will not always mean following the easiest path.'

I take the hint.

'Please speak freely,' I say.

Renard's face is suddenly sorrowful.

'Madam, I am deeply troubled. Forgive me for speaking plainly, but I feel that your Grace has been, if anything, too merciful in these past weeks. Mercy is a commendable quality in princes, but it is sometimes more productive for a sovereign to be ruthless in punishing traitors. There are those who pose a serious threat to your security – I am sure your Grace does not need me to name them . . .'

'I asked you to be frank, your Excellency,' I interrupt. 'You know I value your advice, and that anything said to me in this room can remain confidential.'

'I refer, then, Madam, to Northumberland, Suffolk, Guilford Dudley and, above all, the Lady Jane. They should all be made an example of, and put to death.'

An uncomfortable silence ensues. I had hoped he would not ask this of me.

'Ambassador, I cannot authorise the Lady Jane's execution. She has been the innocent tool of ruthless men.'

'Madam!' he cries with feeling. 'You are displaying a weakness that could have fatal results! Innocent she may be, but while that young lady lives, she will always be a lodestar for Protestant rebels, or for those with any imagined grudge against your Grace.'

'I cannot credit that. By all accounts, she never wanted the crown. It was forced on her. She would never incite rebellion against us, of that I am certain.'

'No, *she* would perhaps not. But others might, in her name. Her very blood should condemn her.'

'I hardly think so. Remember, the people were scarcely ecstatic at the news of her accession. Who would support her now?'

'Anyone who is disaffected, Madam. You have mounted the throne to great acclaim, but this present euphoria must come to an end. Contentious issues face your Grace. Be assured that the restoration of the true faith will not meet with universal approval in this godforsaken land.'

'I think you worry over-much, Ambassador. My subjects were well aware of my religious convictions when they rallied to my support. They knew what my accession would mean. And I sincerely believe that that shows how, in their hearts, most of them desire to return to the true faith. But I will take your advice in part. To put your mind at rest, I will send the traitor Northumberland to the block. Suffolk I have already pardoned, and I cannot go back on my word. Guilford Dudley is young, and as much a creature of his father as the Lady Jane. They will remain safely in the Tower. But execute them I cannot.'

'Your Grace is over-merciful,' Renard says again, in a despairing tone.

'Ambassador,' I answer good-naturedly, 'if I were to execute all those involved in this late treason, I would have very few subjects left.'

'My point exactly,' he says. 'That is why you cannot permit the Lady Jane to live.'

'We must agree to differ on that point.' I rise. 'I am sorry to disappoint you, but I cannot agree to the shedding of innocent blood. And, on that, my word is final.'

Lady Jane Dudley

The Tower of London, August 1553

The Queen left the Tower for Richmond in the middle of August; I knew she had gone because it was suddenly so quiet here. Some days later Northumberland was tried in Westminster

Hall and sentenced to death. They tell me he knelt abjectly, sobbing piteously, and confessed his crimes, begging for mercy. His pleas were ignored.

In a final bid to soften the Queen's heart, the craven Dudley publicly announced himself a convert to the Catholic faith. This, too, proved in vain. Today, he went to the block. I watch from my window as the cart bearing his mutilated body, hidden under sacking, trundles back from Tower Hill to the Chapel of St Peter ad Vincula, where the Duke will be laid to rest beside Anne Boleyn, Katherine Howard and his old enemy, Protector Somerset.

'I will pray for him,' I tell Mrs Ellen. 'He was a traitor, not only to his country, but also to God, and he brought me to ruin, but his soul is in dire need of salvation. I fear even now that he is suffering the torments of Hell.'

'He has paid a just price for his crimes,' she answers. 'I find it hard to forgive him for what he did to you. But I too will pray for him, all the same.'

We sink to our knees, as the empty cart clatters away on the cobbles below the open casement.

Later, Sir John Bridges visits me.

'Madam,' he says, 'I bring you good tidings. The Queen's Grace has decreed that the conditions of your imprisonment are to be relaxed. From now on, you may take the air along the wall walks, and may meet with your husband there, although you may not, for obvious reasons, entertain him indoors.' I smile grimly to myself: as if I would wish Guilford to come near enough to get me pregnant. I have no wish to complicate my own affairs, let alone the Queen's!

'Please convey my humble and grateful thanks to her Majesty,' I say meekly.

Sir John does not answer. Ever vigilant in his duties, he is looking at the papers on my desk. He picks one up, frowning.

'What is this?' he asks.

'It is an expostulation against the Bishop of Rome,' I tell him, with a hint of defiance. Northumberland might have proved himself a man of straw, but I will never compromise my principles.

'Madam, I am sure you do not need me to tell you that such writings are not only unwise, but could put you in danger at this present time, when the Queen is carrying out her intention of restoring the Catholic faith. There are those, I must tell you, who wish you ill. This kind of thing, if it were discovered, would be a gift to your enemies, and might tip the scales against you. In the circumstances, you would be wise to keep your opinions to yourself.'

'Whatever were you thinking of, child?' bursts out Mrs Ellen, glancing fearfully at the Lieutenant.

'Calm yourself, Mistress,' he tells her. 'The young are prone to rash outspokenness. I know: I have children of my own, much of an age with this lady. They think they know all, and that they will change the world. It is up to us, who are older and wiser, to drum some sense into their silly heads. Now I assure you, this matter will not go beyond these walls, but my advice to you, my Lady Jane, is to dissociate yourself from such controversies and apply yourself to your needle, like any other girl of noble birth. That will keep you out of trouble.'

My face must betray my indignation, for Mrs Ellen frowns fiercely at me. But it is all so very unfair: I have little with which to occupy myself – is it strange that I should wish to use the brain God gave me? And I will do everything the Queen desires of me, save for one thing: I will not convert to the Catholic faith, so God grant she never asks it of me.

Of course, Sir John is right: I must learn to hold my tongue and keep my opinions to myself. I am sure he means well by me, and it would be folly to risk losing his goodwill by arguing with him, or failing to take his kindly meant advice. He could have reported me to the authorities, I remind myself. Oh, but if only he did not have such old-fashioned, conservative ideas!

The walks along the parapet turn out to be a mixed blessing. It is wonderful to be out in the fresh air and sunshine once more, and to feel the warm summer breeze on my face, but I find that Guilford's melancholy company depresses me. The old awkwardness and resentment still lie between us, not to mention my remembrance of what he did to me, while his obvious grief for his father makes me feel even more uncomfortable with him. He wants, he needs, to talk about Northumberland, but I, try as I might out of human charity, am no sympathetic listener. I can conjure up no words of comfort to offer; his misery repels me. Ordinarily, faced

360

with someone bereaved of a loved one, I would put my arms around them, pat their shoulders, wipe their eyes. But the thought of physical contact with Guilford is now unbearable − I cringe at the remembrance that I have been naked and defiled in his bed − and so I cannot do these things, sorry as I am for him.

It does not help that his imprisonment is more rigorous than mine. As the sons of an executed traitor, he and his brothers are consigned to cheerless stone chambers and permitted few comforts.

'Like some who were held in there before us, we pass our time carving inscriptions and our heraldic device on the walls,' Guilford tells me. 'I have carved your name.'

I am astonished. These days my husband displays none of his former arrogance. He is a diminished figure, deprived of his powerful father, his status, wealth and liberty, and he is pathetic in his increasing reliance on me for affection and solace. Alas, I have none to give. He has hurt and humiliated me too deeply. Yet now he has made this poignant gesture − he has carved my name.

'Thank you,' I say lamely.

'You are my wife,' he plaintively replies.

'Yes.'

'They cannot dissolve our marriage as they did your sister's,' he says. 'Unlike them, we have lain together.'

I say nothing.

'I am sorry for the way I treated you,' Guilford says quietly. 'I was unkind.'

The words of forgiveness stick in my throat. I cannot say them. The memory of what happened between us is still raw.

'Couldn't − couldn't we be friends?' he asks. 'We are in the same predicament. We neither of us knows what the future holds for us. If we indeed have a fu . . .' He breaks off, unable to speak for the tears that are choking him.

I cannot answer him. I do not know how to. To my relief, the guard comes and tells Guilford it is time to return indoors. He goes, not looking back, obviously not wanting me to see him unmanned by his distress.

It is evening, and I sit at supper with the Partridges, occupying my usual place of honour at the head of the table. The talk is all of the Queen's marriage. It is rumoured in London that she means to wed young Edward Courtenay, a descendant of the Plantagenets and one of those whom she released from the Tower. He had been imprisoned here from his boyhood for no other crime than that of being too close in blood to the throne.

'He is very well lettered,' says Mrs Partridge. 'He spent most of his time here studying.'

'Yes, my dear, but he can't even sit a horse,' answers her husband. 'He has a lot to learn before he can conduct himself with any confidence at court. And when the Queen finds that he's been making up for lost time by visiting every brothel in Southwark – saving your presence, my Lady Jane – we'll hear no more talk of this marriage.'

After the meal, Sir John Bridges is announced. He regards me gravely.

'Madam, prepare yourself for ill news. I am commanded by the Queen's Majesty to inform you that you and Lord Guilford Dudley will shortly stand trial. However,' he adds quickly, seeing me pale in horror, and hearing Mrs Ellen's frightened gasp, 'I am also particularly instructed to inform you that, while it is expected that the court will certainly condemn you, you will afterwards receive a royal pardon. The trial will merely be a formality, to satisfy the Imperial ambassador.'

I have quickly recovered myself. That was a nasty moment, and my heart is still pounding.

'When is the trial to be, Sir John?' I ask.

'There is no date set for it yet, Madam, but I will inform you as soon as I hear of it.'

I force a smile. He will never know what it costs me to do so.

'God be praised that we have so merciful a Queen!' I declare, with heartfelt feeling.

The Tower and the Guildhall, London,
14th November 1553

I have dressed myself with care. Black velvet is appropriate for the occasion, and a black satin hood trimmed with jet. Sober and demure, I am the image of innocence. The Queen, they tell me, has insisted upon a fair trial: every witness is to speak freely, without fear or favour, and Lord Chief Justice Morgan has been commanded to administer the law impartially.

'It is her Majesty's pleasure,' the Lieutenant told me, 'that whatever evidence can be produced in your favour shall be heard.'

Guilford and I are not the only ones being tried today. Archbishop Cranmer is also accused of high treason, and is to accompany us to the Guildhall. I feel sorry for him, poor old man; he has been the champion of the Protestant faith in England for two decades now; it was his hand that wrote the beautiful, but now banned, Book of Common Prayer, his heart that guided the reformed Church of England through its formative years.

I cannot bear the thought of all Cranmer's good work being undone, yet there is now no doubt that Queen Mary has every intention of returning England to the Roman fold. She might have proclaimed freedom of worship for all, but many Protestants have fled abroad and the signs of a Catholic revival are everywhere. There are crucifixes once more on all the altars of England, they tell me, and Mass is again being celebrated in the churches.

At the beginning of this month, the Queen was betrothed to the Emperor's son and heir, Don Philip of Spain. Not only is he a foreigner to this land, but he is also the most fanatical Catholic prince in Europe, and has presided over the terrible Acts of Faith, as they call them, during which scores of staunch Protestants and lapsed Catholics have been burned alive at the stake. I am not the only one dismayed at the prospect of this marriage.

'Most people, even some great lords, are objecting strongly and publicly to the match,' says Mrs Ellen, who goes out most days and is aware of what is happening abroad. Many believe that the Inquisition could be introduced into England, and fear that this kingdom will become a mere appendage of the Spanish Empire. There was an angry demonstration in London today, and even some of the councillors, Mrs Ellen heard, have expressed their concerns, but it is said that the Queen has fallen madly in love with Philip's portrait and with the idea of marrying her mother's kinsman. For too long, Mary has been denied those things for which she yearns – marriage and motherhood – so I believe there is little hope of her heeding these objections. Her mind, they say, is already made up.

*

I step into the barge, clutching Sir John Bridges's steadying hand. Behind me comes Guilford, then the Archbishop, who looks aged and drawn in the November mist. Mrs Ellen and Mrs Tilney are already seated in the cabin, ready to attend me. The oarsmen pull away and row upstream, expertly shooting the rapids beneath London Bridge. This is my first foray out of the Tower in four months. I am four weeks past my sixteenth birthday.

Within minutes, the barge glides to its mooring place at Temple Stairs. On the quayside is drawn up a force of halberdiers, who are to escort us prisoners along Fleet Street, up Ludgate Hill and through Cheapside to the Guildhall. More halberdiers line the route, pressing back the crowds who, to my surprise, have come to watch me pass. Their mood is not hostile, as I had feared; although they watch me in silence, I can sense some sympathy radiating towards me.

Escorted by Sir John, I walk with bowed head, keeping my eyes on the little book of devotions that I hold open in front of me. Another prayer book is attached to my girdle by a small chain. I wear no chopines today to increase my height, and my head barely reaches the Lieutenant's shoulder. My gentlewomen follow me, ahead of Guilford, who is also clad in black and looks wan and fearful, and the Archbishop.

Outside the Guildhall there are more guards. The Lord High Executioner waits also, his ceremonial axe held over his shoulder. As I proceed into the building, its blade is turned away from me.

In the huge vaulted hall, with its beautiful stained-glass windows and soaring arches, we three stand at the bar, facing a jury of our peers – the privilege of the nobly born – and Lord Chief Justice Morgan, seated in his high place beneath the arms of England. The indictments are read out, and witnesses called. No one has anything to add to the facts that are known already, although there are many to attest to my reluctance to accept the crown; nor, in accordance with the law, are any of us accused permitted to speak in our defence.

It is all over rather quickly. Although I had been warned to expect it, I listen in alarm as the peers deliver their unanimous verdict of guilty, and the Lord Chief Justice addresses us sternly.

'Lord Guilford Dudley, you have been found guilty of high treason. The sentence of this court is that you be hanged, drawn and quartered at the Queen's pleasure. May the Lord have mercy on your soul.'

Guilford's already pale face blenches and he starts to shake. I put a steadying hand on his arm, but the Lord Chief Justice sees it and frowns at me.

'Lady Jane Dudley,' he pronounces, 'you have also been found guilty of high treason. The sentence of this court is that you be burned alive on Tower Hill or beheaded, as the Queen pleases. And may the Lord have mercy on your soul.'

His words strike such terror into that soul that I barely hear him sentencing poor Cranmer to be burned at the stake. By an immense effort of will, I maintain my outward composure, curtsey to the judges and peers and allow myself to be led away. The executioner's axe now has its blade turned towards me, to signify to the waiting crowds that I have been condemned to death.

The journey back to the Tower passes in a blur. I am impervious to Guilford's tears, the quiet resignation of Cranmer, for whom there is no promised reprieve, and the silent preoccupation of my ladies. I am overwhelmed by the horrifying realisation that I am under sentence of death − and a particularly horrible death at that − and that all that stands between me and a gruesome end is the Queen's word. Desperately I tell myself again and again that I must hang on to that promise, for her Majesty is an honourable woman. All my dealings with her so far have proved that her intentions are just and merciful. I must keep that in mind, I tell myself. I must not dwell on what would happen if Queen Mary were ever to change her mind.

Once back in the Tower, however, I give way to my fears. I cannot forget the words of the Lord Chief Justice, consigning me to be burned or beheaded, and I sit on my bed trembling and weeping. Mrs Ellen is frantic, unable to make me see reason, so she summons the Lieutenant urgently.

'Madam, you must have faith in the Queen's word,' he says firmly. 'Your trial was but a necessary formality. Her Majesty has no intention of proceeding further against you. I know for a fact that she is very kindly disposed towards you, so take heart. Your fears are groundless.'

His smile is sincere and reassuring. Already I am calmer and moving towards a more cheerful and optimistic frame of mind.

'You are innocent, Jane,' Mrs Ellen soothes. 'You did nothing to merit this sentence.'

'I should not have accepted the crown,' I say.

'The Queen knows you were forced to it,' Sir John tells me. 'She has promised you a pardon. You have only to be patient and wait a while for it.'

Queen Mary

Whitehall Palace, December 1553

Renard stands before me, his face set with concern.

'I am still resolved to be merciful,' I declare. 'The Lady Jane and her husband will remain in the Tower for the present, but when the time is right – that is, when I have heirs of my own body' – I can feel my cheeks reddening at the thought of what that will entail – 'I will consider releasing them.'

'Then, Madam, I am to inform my master the Emperor that the Lady Jane will not be put to death?'

'You may, Excellency. Her life is safe, even though there are several persons who would have it otherwise. Common humanity requires no less of me.'

He is looking at me as if I am mad. I hope he will appreciate that I have made up my mind and that the matter is closed.

'Madam, forgive my plain speaking, but this is sheer folly,' he declares, to my surprise. 'The Emperor is of the opinion that, to make all safe in England, you should rid the land of these traitors. Do not be too tender of their youth. They are a threat to your throne.'

'I have spoken, Ambassador, and I will not go back on my word once given,' I say sharply. 'Besides, I am of the opinion that my sister Elizabeth poses the greater threat. Yes, she has been at my side since I was proclaimed, and none showed greater joy when I was crowned, but she excuses herself from attending Mass on the lightest pretext, and I fear she is secretly plotting to marry Edward Courtenay. I need not remind you that Courtenay himself has a claim to the throne. No, Elizabeth is far more dangerous than Jane Dudley will ever be.'

'Madam, that is madness!' Renard splutters. 'Forgive my plain speaking, but I have heard from my spies that the Duke of Suffolk, whom you have rashly allowed to go free and unpunished, is rumoured to be plotting a rebellion. I have also learned that recently, out of your great clemency, you have given permission for the Lady Jane, condemned traitor though she is, to go out of the Tower for walks on Tower Hill. Madam, that is ill-advised. It would be very easy for her father to abduct her and set her up once again as a rival queen.'

'She is well guarded,' I insist, 'and I doubt the Duke could command enough support for a rebellion.'

'Do not make the mistake of underestimating the strength of the opposition to your Majesty's proposed marriage to Prince Philip,' Renard warns. 'Many of your subjects are already disaffected, I am saddened to say.'

'That is as may be, but my mind is made up,' I declare firmly. 'I will not have the blood of an innocent child on my hands.'

I dismiss Renard forthwith. My head is aching and I cannot face more arguments. He is doing his best to wear me down, but I am resolved to stand firm. If what he says about Suffolk proves to be true – I will order the Duke to be watched – then I will double the guards on the Tower. But it is not in my nature to be cruel, and until that happens I will allow the Lady Jane what freedom I can. Perhaps Renard is right and Tower Hill is too accessible. It might be wiser not to take any risks.

Lady Jane Dudley

The Tower of London, December 1553

The air is bitingly cold, but I am enjoying myself. It is exhilarating to wander at will about Tower Hill, browsing among the stalls of the street-vendors, or watching the constant traffic along the Thames. My guards stand a little way off, chatting and laughing.

Guilford, they tell me, is allowed similar outings, but we are no longer allowed to meet. The government will not run the risk of two convicted traitors, husband and wife, plotting an escape. Being unable to see Guilford does not bother me, although I do feel some spark of pity for him, shut up in the freezing Beauchamp Tower in the depths of winter. Mrs Partridge reports him broken in heart and spirit by the thought of the death sentence hanging over him.

The promised pardons have not yet been granted, but it is surely too soon to expect them. There is much unrest at the prospect of the Queen's marriage to Prince Philip, and on Tower Hill I hear rumours that the people will rebel against it. I pray God they do not do so in my name.

When I return to my lodgings, I find Sir John Bridges waiting for me. He bows courteously, but his kindly face is grave.

'Madam, I regret that these walks outdoors must cease,' he says without preamble. 'The council wishes you kept out of the public eye just now. There are good reasons for this, but, as I am sure you can appreciate, I am not at liberty to discuss them.'

I am crestfallen. My little outings were such a joy to me, an unexpected favour. Now I am to be cooped up in my prison again, and the prospect is hardly bearable. I fear that this is a bad sign, a step backwards in the direction of more rigorous incarceration, not forwards towards my promised liberty; and it may betoken that my pardon could be rescinded as easily. As I gaze miserably at Sir John, there is a pounding in my head, and the world shifts. To my horror, I realise that I cannot see him properly: it is as if part of my vision is blocked off. Shocked and shaking, I sink into a chair, blinking and trying to focus my eyes. But the blind spot stays there still.

'Madam, are you ill?' he inquires, plainly concerned at my distress.

'I cannot see properly!' I wail. Mrs Ellen and Mrs Partridge hasten over and peer into my eyes.

'There is nothing to see,' says Mrs Ellen, shaking her head. They are all crowding around me now, solicitous and comforting, but my terror deepens as the blind spot explodes in a pattern of brilliant, zigzagged lines, which dance and flicker across my vision. I feel sick and dizzy, and cannot face sipping the ale they are offering me.

I am made to lie on my bed. The cold winter light hurts my eyes, so Mrs Ellen draws the curtains. It is half an hour before the frightening disturbances fade, leaving me tremulous and drained. No one can offer any explanation for them until Mrs Tilney returns from visiting Mrs Underhill.

'Why, it's a megrim you've got, my lady,' she tells me. 'I suffer from them myself. They're unpleasant, but harmless. My mother had them on and off for years, but lived till she was sixty. You'll probably get a nasty headache, but it'll soon go.'

I only half-believe her, and lie here weeping. She is right about the headache, which comes on soon afterwards. It is the worst I have ever had, and I feel utterly wretched. Nothing exists beyond the pain, and several times I vomit into a pail held by Mrs Ellen, who never leaves my side, but sits patiently wiping my brow with a cool, damp cloth.

In the morning, I am restored miraculously to health, much to my amazement, but two days later I suffer another megrim, and then two more in the space of a week. Sir John, out of concern, summons a physician, who confirms Mrs Tilney's diagnosis, but admits there is little he can do.

'These things sometimes seem to coincide with the female courses,' he explains. 'Are you menstruating at present?'

'I am not.' In fact, I have not seen my courses since I came to this house a prisoner.

The doctor looks at me with pity.

'It is also a fact that megrims occur when a patient is inordinately troubled, or of an anxious disposition.'

All of us know the heavy sentence I am under. 'I suffered the first megrim immediately after being told that my outings had been curtailed,' I say quietly.

He shakes his head sadly and summons the Lieutenant. 'My professional opinion, Sir, is that this young lady is under immense strain and that it is making her ill. She needs good food, fresh air and peace of mind. Of course, it is not my place to advise you, but if I were in your shoes, I would see my duty clear.'

'I will write to the council at once,' Sir John promises.

*

The megrims have ceased, and I thank God for it. And I have Him and the Queen's Grace to thank for once again being able to breathe in the open air and walk on the crisp, frosty grass of the Lieutenant's garden. I can stay out of doors here until my fingers are blue, if I please, before reluctantly returning to warm myself before Mrs Partridge's great fire.

My circumstances have improved, but I remain somewhat dejected. I am sixteen, and shut away from normal life. I have my books, but I have now read them all several times, and have not the means to order more. I am listless, in need of something I cannot put a name to. It might be freedom that I desire, but it feels as if there is something else lacking, something more fundamental. One day, when this is all over, I should like to go and live in the country, perhaps at Bradgate, which seems now to belong to another life, a life I took so much for granted. How strange it would feel to go back now.

I wonder what it would be like to be married to a good man who could love me, cherish me and protect me from all the misfortunes that life can bring. Someone who would be willing to encourage my intellectual interests, and be a kind father to my children. It occurs to me suddenly that I would like to have children one day.

It is all a fantasy, of course. I am married to Guilford, and he too has been promised a pardon. He has no part in my dreams, yet I am tied to him for life and there is no way out. I expect that, after our release, we may learn to rub along together, both softened by this great ordeal. At least he is no longer as arrogant and unfeeling as he once was.

But neither of us has yet received our pardons, and I cannot help but wonder if they will ever arrive.

Thinking of Guilford, I call to mind the inscriptions he told me he had carved. In a mood of melancholy and despair, I take example from him and, using my silver paper-knife, chisel one of my own Latin verses into the plaster of my bedchamber wall, for the benefit of posterity:

> To mortals' common fate thy mind resign;
> My lot today tomorrow may be thine.
> I hope for light after the darkness.

I lay down my knife, my arm aching with the effort of carving, slump on my bed and fall to weeping.

Frances Brandon, Duchess of Suffolk

Sheen, Surrey, 22nd December 1553

'What's that letter you are reading?' I inquire of my lord.

'It's from Edward Courtenay, the Earl of Devon that was in the Tower from boyhood, and who was a suitor to the Queen.'

'What does he want?' I ask, surprised.

'It seems he's angry at his rejection by her Majesty. He tells me he has thrown in his lot with Sir Thomas Wyatt.'

Wyatt, a Protestant gentleman of Kent, has already been in touch with my lord; he has set himself up by stealth as the leader of those who oppose the Spanish marriage. Last month he wrote to Henry telling him that he could rally many people to his cause, if need be, and begged my lord to join forces with him. Prudently, Henry refused.

'Courtenay writes that during the past weeks Wyatt has enlisted enough support to convince him and others that a popular rising against the marriage would not only be feasible, but would probably be successful too.'

'For God's sake, don't get involved!' I warn him. But Henry ignores me.

'The Earl says here that their plans are well advanced. There are to be four simultaneous risings on the same day, Palm Sunday, which will fall on the eighteenth of March next year. Wyatt will lead the men of Kent, Sir James Crofts those of Hertfordshire, and Courtenay and Sir Peter Carew the men of Devon.'

'And what of the fourth uprising?' I ask, fearing the answer.

'Courtenay writes that they want me to lead it,' Henry says. 'I am to raise the men of Leicestershire.'

'If you do, you're a bloody fool!' I cry.

'Listen, Frances,' says Henry patiently. 'It's a sound plan . . .'

'Like Northumberland's was?' I interrupt furiously.

'Much sounder. Listen, and hear me out. The four armies will march on London, overthrow the Queen's treacherous advisors, then force her to repudiate the match with Philip of Spain. Courtenay stresses that no harm is intended to her Majesty, and that he and all the other leaders are her most devoted subjects. There is no element of treason in this plan.'

'My lord, are you telling me that you are planning to engage in a rebellion against the Queen, when our daughter is yet languishing in the Tower under sentence of death? You are mad.'

'This is not against the Queen, Frances. It's a demonstration by her loyal subjects against the man she proposes to marry.'

'And you think she'll make the distinction when your armies are converging on London?' I snap. I am beside myself. 'God, Henry, you are a fool. Can't you see that Courtenay's real aim is to marry the Queen himself? And as for Wyatt, I have my own suspicions about him.'

'And what are they, pray?' His voice is cold, faintly patronising.

'I've no proof or evidence to go on. Call it female intuition, or what you like, but I fear that Wyatt has some hidden agenda of his own.'

'Nonsense, Frances. Your imagination is running away with you.' He turns to face me. 'I'm sorry, my dear, but I will not be deterred. I will not bow the knee to the Prince of Spain.'

Sheen, 22nd January 1554

My husband comes storming into our bedchamber, his face working in distress.

'We are betrayed!' he shouts.

I dismiss the maids who have been preparing me for bed, and go to him, trembling.

'Who?' is all I can trust myself to ask.

'That fool Courtenay. Yesterday, he confessed all to Bishop Gardiner and begged the Queen's forgiveness.'

'The bastard!' I spit. 'I always knew he had no backbone.'

'Yes, but I think someone talked long before he did. Four days ago, the council sent a force to occupy Exeter, as if they had wind of the planned rising in the west country. Carew is lying low, by all accounts, and Sir James Crofts has fled to Wales.'

'What news of Wyatt?' I did not want Henry to involve himself in this rebellion, but now that he has, I can only pray it will be successful.

'When last I heard, he was at Allington Castle, raising the men of Kent. The messenger who came to me is on his way there as we speak. I gave him a fresh horse.'

'What will you do now?' I do not trouble to conceal my anxiety. One false move, and we are all finished.

'We act at once. I have asked Wyatt to come here. If the rising is to achieve its aims, we must strike now.'

Sheen, 23rd January 1554

Sir Thomas Wyatt has arrived at Sheen. He is young – too young – and personable, with an open, eager face and a black, pointed beard. There is no mistaking his sincere zeal for his cause: he is a driven man, committed to seeing the thing through to the bitter end.

Yet I fear it will be an end more bitter than I imagined, for I have just discovered, to my horror and disbelief, that my lord still cherishes dreams of establishing Jane on the throne. And she but lately sentenced to death!

Although I had heard with my own ears the Queen's assurance that Jane would be safe, the news of that sentencing hit me like a cannonball. My own daughter, my very flesh and blood – sentenced to death. God knows, I am not a sentimental woman, and I have not loved her as I should, often finding fault with her, when perhaps there was none to find. I could not help myself. But when I heard those dread words, that were spoken to my poor child, something awoke within me, the mother's instinct to protect that has lain dormant all these years beneath layers of bitterness and frustration. And there it was, staring me in the face, the realisation that my own daughter is in the Tower, a condemned traitor who might face death at any moment. My daughter, that I bore of my body, not just a pawn in a political or dynastic game, whom we could use to our own advantage. And ever since then, I have hated myself for blighting her short life – which may soon be cruelly cut short – with my disappointment and my ambition. As God is my witness, I have wept for her, poor innocent; me, who has ever prided myself on my disdain for those who give way to such displays of emotion. And I have resolved that, if it be in my power, none shall do further harm to her.

'But making the Lady Jane Queen was never under discussion,' points out Wyatt.

'Nor should it be!' I insist hotly. 'It is unfair and unjust to involve Jane. Has she not suffered enough? Is she not in sufficient peril?'

'So you would prefer to see this Catholic queen married to the fanatical Prince of Spain, and the Inquisition burning heretics in England?' Henry shouts. 'Because, I tell you, my dear, that is what will happen if we do not act now to prevent it.'

'So you would risk our daughter's life?' I persist in alarm. 'Have you forgotten that she lies in the Queen's custody under sentence of death? And that she knows nothing of what you are plotting? My lord, this is folly of the worst sort – can you not see it?'

Wyatt intervenes.

'I should say,' he explains, 'that my own preferred plan is to depose the Queen and replace her with the Lady Elizabeth, who is said to be committed to the reformed faith. That alone would justify Mary's removal.'

'My daughter is utterly committed to the reformed faith,' butts in my lord. 'She has never hidden the fact, unlike the Lady Elizabeth, whose beliefs are a matter for conjecture. I tell you both that our best hope for the future lies in Jane.'

'No!' I cry. 'You have no idea of what you are doing. *You* did not face the Queen – I did. Make no mistake, she will not be as well disposed to mercy a second time.'

'There will not be a second time!' my husband snaps. 'Now, my lady, I suggest you hold your tongue. These are fears for children. This time our plan is watertight, and within weeks, mark you, our daughter will be back where she should be, and we will be the power behind the throne.'

'Within weeks we might all be lacking our heads!' I retort, bursting with anger and frustration.

'Your lady wife perhaps has a point,' says Wyatt.

'My lady wife is a woman and, like all women, she has to make unnecessary difficulties,' observes my husband.

I catch my breath – this is intolerable.

'She has more wisdom than you credit her with,' Wyatt contends. 'It would be wiser and safer for all concerned if we back the Lady Elizabeth. Her claim is the stronger anyway.'

'And if I will not support her?'

Wyatt looks unhappy. 'Then – then, my lord, we must abandon our plans. We have already lost much of our support, and without your help, I can do nothing.'

'Aren't you forgetting that overthrowing Catholic Mary is the whole point of the exercise?' Henry reminds him. 'Are we not committed to that? And is it not preferable to replace her by one who is known to be a committed Protestant, rather than by one who is merely thought to be? Come now, Sir Thomas, face the truth. It is my daughter who should become Queen, and it is only on that understanding that I will give you my backing. Without which, to be plain, you will surely fail.'

Wyatt struggles visibly with his better self, and wins.

'Alright, my lord, I agree,' he says. 'But I warn you now, I have more misgivings about this plan than the other. The Lady Elizabeth has the better claim, and your daughter, as my lady here has pointed out, is in a highly vulnerable position. But, as you have made clear, the choice is really yours to make. Therefore, it shall be the Lady Jane. I will be content so long as this land is ruled by a Protestant monarch.'

'Good,' my lord smiles. 'I will send to the Earl of Huntingdon. He has already agreed to raise his tenants in Leicestershire.'

'Then I will return to Kent to muster my forces,' says Wyatt.

'I shall look forward to meeting up with you in London, after our victory.' My husband extends his hand. I look away in disgust.

Later, we learn that the Earl of Huntingdon, having received Henry's message, took it straight to the council.

Mrs Ellen

London, 25th January 1554

There are no restrictions on my movements. I come and go as I please, in and out of the Tower, so I am often out shopping, or visiting my sister in Smithfield. Thus I am in a position to keep abreast of what is going on in the world outside.

The news is not good. The mood in London is tense, and rumour has it that the Kentish rebel, Sir Thomas Wyatt, is approaching the capital with five thousand men. People everywhere are apprehensive, and I have even seen panicked citizens packing up and leaving the City.

I mingle with the crowd at Cheapside Cross as a herald reads out a proclamation by the privy council. My blood freezes as I hear the Duke of Suffolk's name among those of the traitors who have been raising ill-disposed persons to her Majesty's destruction, and who have plotted to advance the Lady Jane and Guilford Dudley to the throne once more.

How could he? How could he be so rash and foolish? I am in a passion of anxiety. I cannot believe my ears.

'If any man brings the traitor Wyatt to justice,' cries the herald, 'he will be granted a fine estate, to be held by him and his heirs in perpetuity.'

This is terrible, I think, as the people disperse. How could the Duke even contemplate involving himself in another plot to set poor Jane on the throne? The man must be mad! And how can I protect that dear child from the knowledge of what he has done – or the consequences? Dear God, what will they be? I cannot bear to contemplate them.

I hurry back to the Tower, agonising. I decide that all I can do for the moment is withhold these dreadful tidings from Jane. In her innocence must lie her safety, I pray God.

*

Later, I join the crowds outside Whitehall Palace in the hope of catching a glimpse of the Queen. It is common knowledge that she has refused to leave London for the safety of Windsor, declaring she knows well that she can count upon the loyalty and love of her subjects. Listening to voices in the crowd, I am not so sure – some will save their loyalty for whoever triumphs in this conflict. Plainly, Mary is no longer the darling of the people as she was when she ascended the throne six months ago.

Lady Jane Dudley

The Tower of London, 7th February 1554

From my window, I can see soldiers everywhere.

I know why they are here, although those who have the keeping of me would prefer that I did not. Undoubtedly Sir John Bridges has been expressly forbidden to enlighten me. I have been told only that a traitor called Sir Thomas Wyatt has risen in protest against the Queen's marriage to the Prince of Spain.

Mrs Ellen told me that Wyatt and his army arrived at Southwark four days ago, only to find that the citizens, inspired by a rousing speech made by the Queen at the Guildhall, had destroyed London Bridge to prevent him from entering the capital. In retribution, he sacked the old priory of St Mary Overy, then moved upriver to Kingston, where there is another bridge across the Thames. Now he is advancing again on London, from the south.

The waiting soldiers are drawn up in lines, ready to march when necessary. I watch them, weapons at the ready, tramp in formation out of the Tower to face the rebels. Some time later there comes the very distant sound of gunfire, and it seems to me as if every person left in the Tower is holding his breath, just as I am. Then there is a silence that lasts several hours.

Evening falls. I am lying face down on my bed reading,

propped up on my elbows, when I hear a commotion outside. Leaping up, I peer through the lattice panes. In the darkness, I can just make out Sir John Bridges and a troop of soldiers riding past the White Tower towards the main gate.

Suddenly Mrs Ellen comes in.

'God be praised, my lady! Wyatt is taken. They are bringing him here now. He is to be lodged in the Bell Tower. The rebellion is quelled.'

'God be praised!' I echo. 'Now we are safe.'

Queen Mary

Whitehall Palace, 7th February 1554

At seven o'clock in the evening I at last have the opportunity to grant an audience to Renard. He has been pressing to see me all day.

'Your Majesty!' he says urgently, kissing my hands with unprecedented fervour. 'I rejoice to see you safe! We are all badly shaken by your narrow escape from disaster. Madam, forgive me, but it is as I warned, and I would be failing in my duty and devotion to you if I did not point out that this rebellion was the result of your Majesty being over-lenient when you came to the throne. I beg of you now, Madam, harden your heart against these traitors, and show your subjects that you are not to be intimidated.'

'You sound like my councillors, Ambassador,' I observe. 'You all speak with one voice.' I try not to betray any emotion, for he will take it as a sign of weakness, but whatever it costs me, I am determined to prove to him, and to all the rest, that I can be as resolute and ruthless as my father when necessary. Saving, of course, in matters that touch my conscience.

I conquer my impulse to give in to my kinder instincts.

'You may set your mind at rest, for mine is made up,' I tell him. 'I will never again show clemency to traitors, and I shall not cease to demand the ultimate penalty for them. Nor, from now on, will I tolerate heresy in my realm, since it has been demonstrated most clearly that it leads to seditious plots against me.'

'Your Majesty shows the greatest wisdom,' Renard replies, an expression of relieved satisfaction on his face. 'I know I have hitherto urged you to go cautiously with the heretics, but I agree, it is now plain that you must proceed firmly against those who do not adhere to the doctrines of the true Church.'

'Indeed. I have thought long on this, and prayed for guidance, and I have decided to revive the old statute against heresy, and root it out, for it is like a canker that gnaws away at the very vitals of the Church. Those who do not recant will be burned at the stake. If my people will not come to salvation by gentler means, then they must be constrained to it, for the safety of their souls.'

'That is exactly the view of my master, the Emperor, and Prince Philip,' Renard says. 'They believe that a foretaste of hell-fire on Earth wonderfully concentrates the mind, and can bring about the conversion of the most stubborn heretic.'

'I pray God it will be so,' I reply, crossing myself. Now I pause. I am fearful of telling Renard the other decision I have made, so I am casting about for ways to prove to him that, when it comes to the most crucial issues, I am immovable.

'Returning to this matter of the traitors,' I say, 'I have decided that the leaders of the rebellion must be executed, and that, in case this is not example enough to others who might be tempted to plot treason against us, great numbers of their followers are to be hanged; there will be gibbets placed on every street corner in London, and in places in Kent, as a salutary lesson and a warning to our subjects. They must learn that it is no light thing to rebel against their lawful sovereign.'

'The Emperor will be most gratified to hear it,' Renard says. 'And it will also be a comfort to him to know that you have at last decided to put to death those persons who will always be a focus for rebellion. I mean the Lady Jane and Guilford Dudley. Your Majesty has sensibly recognised that, as long as they live, they will prove to be thorns in your side. I urge you, Madam, to have the sentences on them carried out without further delay.'

'They are to be spared,' I say quietly.

There is a sudden silence. Renard is, for once, speechless.

'I did not say I would execute them,' I remind him. 'Only the leaders of this rebellion and their followers. Believe me, I have suffered much anguish over this issue. I hear what you and my councillors have to say, but in truth the Lady Jane and Guilford Dudley are innocent of any crime. They were not involved in any way in this rebellion . . .'

Renard suddenly finds his voice.

'Madam, for the love of God . . .'

'No, dear friend,' I protest. 'I have promised them mercy. I cannot go back on the word of a prince, nor do I want their deaths on my conscience.'

Renard is relentless.

'Sometimes, Madam, it is necessary for a ruler to be pragmatic and bow to expediency. They may not have deserved death this time, but alive, the Lady Jane and her husband will always be a danger to you, an ever-present threat to the security of your throne and the succession, and to the restoration of the true faith in this realm. Can your conscience permit you to put all that at risk?'

'Do you want me to behead a girl of sixteen for a crime she did not commit?' I cry in agitation. 'I am the fount of justice in this realm, and if I make a virtue of expediency in this case, I would also be making a mockery of justice, and breaking my coronation oath to uphold it.'

'Your royal father would not have been so nice,' he says slyly. 'He would have done what was necessary without a qualm. Madam, I beg of you, harden your heart, set your private conscience aside. Be a queen in truth.'

'I cannot,' I say, sinking into my chair and resting my forehead on my hand so that he shall not see the tears in my eyes. I have spent days putting on a brave front in the face of the rebellion, and gathering all my reserves of courage. I dare not give way now.

Renard ignores my distress. He is implacable.

'Very well, Madam,' he declares. 'You leave me no choice. The Emperor is naturally concerned for the safety of his son and the security of his alliance with your Majesty. He is adamant that, while the Lady Jane and her husband live, Prince Philip will never set foot in England.'

It is blackmail, no less, I see that at once. I feel as if I have been struck. They have me in a corner. I need this alliance to carry through my great reforms, for Philip has behind him all the might of Catholic Christendom. And – dare I admit it? – I need him. His picture haunts my dreams; it inspires strange longings, and makes me catch my breath with desire. He is my champion, a handsome man coming to rescue me from my long spinsterhood. I love him already, and I can never give him up.

It is a cruel choice, crueller than most of those I have had to make in my unhappy life, but I realise that the Emperor, for all the brutality of his methods, is a wise man. He has shown me my duty clear.

I have done it, God forgive me. I have given the order for the executions of the Lady Jane and Guilford Dudley. They are to suffer death on the morning of the ninth of February, just thirty-six hours from now.

I must remain firm in my resolve. I will not waver or succumb to womanish notions of clemency. One day, when I hold my son in my arms – Philip's son, the heir to a Catholic England – my conscience will be justified and set at peace.

They have laid the death warrants before me. I am sitting at my desk, steeling myself to sign them. Even now, I would give much to exercise my prerogative of mercy, but I know it would be madness.

I pick up my quill, dip it in the ink-well and sign my name twice.

Lady Jane Dudley

The Tower of London, 7th February 1554

I am nearly asleep when I hear the knock on the door. It is Mrs Ellen in her nightgown; she carries a candle and, in its flickering light, her face looks very perturbed.

'Is it morning already?' I ask, dazed.

'No, it is near midnight. Come, you must put on your robe quickly. Sir John wishes to see you now. A messenger has come from the Queen.'

'My pardon! At last!' I exclaim, fully awake now and scrambling out of bed. Then I glance at Mrs Ellen's stricken face and realise that it might be something entirely different. Something I do not want to hear.

Gathering all my courage, I brace myself to face the Lieutenant, who is waiting in the downstairs parlour, attended by Master Partridge. Sir John's face is grave, his voice gruff as he greets me. He does not look like a man bearing glad tidings. I begin to understand what he has come to tell me, certain that it is something he must have said to other prisoners far older and far more wicked than I.

'My Lady Jane,' he begins, 'I would for all the world that I did not have to say these words to you. I fear it is my heavy duty to inform you that the Queen's Majesty has given the order for your execution, and that you must prepare to die on Friday morning at nine o'clock. Her Majesty has graciously commuted the sentence to beheading, and it will be carried out in private, on Tower Green.'

Mrs Ellen bursts into heart-wrenching tears, but I stand silent. What did he say? I can hardly take it in. I am to die? On Friday, less than two days hence, my living body, with its breath and blood and warmth, its thoughts, fears, feelings and hopes, will cease to exist. It is a devastating prospect, beyond comprehension. And I have so little time in which to make my peace with God, to enable me to face Him in a state of grace. I am so overwhelmed that I cannot speak.

'The same sentence has been passed on your husband,' Sir John continues gently, after giving me a few moments to understand my fate. 'But as he is not of royal blood, he will be beheaded on Tower Hill.'

I find my voice. It sounds strangled.

'Has he been told?' I quaver.

'He has. He is very distressed. I pray God he calms down and reaches a true state of repentance in the time left to him.'

I muster all my reserves of courage. I remind myself that my religion has taught me how to die, and that death is not the end. I must hold fast to that now. I remember a saying beloved of both my mother and Mrs Ellen: what cannot be avoided must be endured. So I must endure; I have no choice. If I am to die – and it seems that, for all her promises, the Queen is now determined on it – then I will make a good death, so that the world will remember me for my bravery and my sincere faith, and that I may earn favour in Heaven.

In no time at all, I will be with God and His angels in Heaven – I cannot believe that my sins are so great as to bar me from it. And I will see Our Lord, and Jesus on His right hand. All shall be well. There *will* be light after the darkness. No more suffering, no more betrayals. In Heaven, I will not be the helpless tool of greedy, unscrupulous men. I will be free.

I straighten my shoulders.

'I am ready and glad to end my woeful days,' I say simply, then turn to leave the room. Mrs Ellen follows, sobbing as if her heart will break. 'Please – you do not help me by weeping,' I reprove her. 'Please be brave, for my sake.'

She blows her nose loudly and wipes her eyes. All her love for me, and her grief, is in them, naked, exposed. She has loved me, more than my mother ever has, and I have taken it for granted, as children do. But now, in this new awareness brought on by the prospect of my imminent death, I see that I have been truly blessed in my nurse. And I realise that the prospect of losing me is tearing at her very soul. I would go to her, if I could, and comfort her, but I dare not; if I did, I should fall apart in misery and fear.

'I'll get you a hot posset,' she sniffs, and leaves the room.

Much later, in the small hours, when the whole household is abed, I sit wakeful at my desk. I cannot sleep, so turbulent are my thoughts, nor do I want to. Soon, I will be asleep for all eternity. I must not waste these last hours on Earth.

I fall to my knees and pray as I have never prayed before.

'Help me!' I beg. 'Help me! I am a poor, desolate soul, overwhelmed with sorrows, vexed with temptations and grievously tormented by my long imprisonment.'

It dawns on me that I will never again know freedom, never see another summer's day or walk in a garden, never again see my parents or my sisters – at least, not in this life. I pray for them, for God to comfort them when I am taken from them; and I ask Him to forgive my parents for their unkindnesses to me. I confess to Him that I have not always been a dutiful daughter, and crave forgiveness for myself also.

I ask, too, for God to sustain me during my last days.

'O Father, please help me to put away worldly things, and to realise that they have no value. Help me to put my trust in You, so that when the time comes, I shall not falter.'

Steeling myself, I visualise the moment of my death, I kneeling and the axe swiftly descending. Will I feel anything of the heavy blow? Or, worse, after it? I remember Mrs Tilney telling me that, when Anne Boleyn's head was held up by the executioner, her lips and eyes were seen to move. Please God, I pray, let me not know anything about it! Let me be dispatched instantaneously into the next world. Grant that the headsman has a steady hand. And grant me, O Lord, the strength to lay myself down on the block without shrinking. I do not wish to make a public spectacle of myself. I must die well, and not let my House down.

I am tortured by thoughts of what lies ahead for me, but I will not give way to tears. What good would they do me? I must put all my trust in God.

When I have prayed so long that my knees are stiff, I sit in my chair and read my Bible, gaining great comfort from its eternal truths and ancient wisdom. It is four o'clock before I retire to bed, and it is only now, as I lie wakeful, that I begin to wonder what made the Queen change her mind.

The Tower of London, 8th February 1554

In the morning, there is a visitor for me. I am disconcerted to find a Catholic priest waiting in the parlour. The old man smiles as I enter, and his still-handsome face lights up with an uncommon radiance. Against my will, I find myself drawn to him.

'Good day, my daughter,' he says. 'I am Dr Richard Feckenham, Abbot of Westminster. The Queen has sent me here to speak with you.'

'Forgive me, Dr Feckenham,' I reply, 'but I am of the reformed faith. I do not see what we could have to say to each other.'

'Please hear me out,' he asks.

I sit down. 'Out of courtesy I will hear you, Sir, but please remember that I die tomorrow. I have but little time, and many things to do.'

'You could have all the time in the world,' he says.

'What do you mean?' I am startled.

'I mean that you have it in your power to save yourself from execution. That is why I am here.'

'To save myself?' I whisper in awe. 'What must I do?'

'You must convert to the Catholic faith,' Dr Feckenham tells me. 'The Queen offers you a reprieve in return for your soul and the prospect of eternal salvation.'

I cannot speak for a moment. I am fighting desperately with my conscience. I do so long to live!

'This is a most refined form of torture,' I say at length, with some severity. 'To offer me an earthly life in return for depriving me of the means to attain eternal life. I cannot accept.'

'Do not be so hasty to throw your life away,' counsels the priest. 'Think on it – for more than fifteen hundred years countless men and women, many of greater intelligence and understanding than you, have followed the true faith. Were they wrong? Are they damned for all eternity just because one man, Martin Luther, comes along and denies some of the tenets of that faith? You know your Bible, I am sure, and you must know that Our Lord appointed St Peter to be His vicar on Earth. How then can you, a mere child, deny the authority of the Pope, who is St Peter's successor and the ultimate and true authority on matters of religion?'

'I can and do deny it,' I affirm. 'How can *you* accept that a piece of bread and a cup of wine become the actual body and blood of Jesus Christ? It is against all reason.'

'Yet you accept, my lady, that Our Lord rose from the dead, and that too is against all human reasoning. Jesus Christ did not ask us to find rational explanations – He enjoined us to have faith. Those are two very different things.' He sighs. 'I can see us going round and round in circles, and your time is precious. Use it wisely, I beg of you. I accept that you have your own convictions, even though I know you are sadly in error. Would you at least promise to think over what I have said? Death is a very terrible thing at your age – and you have everything to live for. Believe me, God

385

does not need your soul yet. You are young, and youth is dogmatic. An old man such as I has learned to question his convictions. I will go now, but promise me that you will think it over.'

'I will, Dr Feckenham,' I assure him, 'if only because, however misguided, you mean to be kind to me. But I do not think I will change my mind.'

'Then I pray that God will change it for you,' says the Abbot as he rises to take his leave.

Queen Mary

Whitehall Palace, 8th February 1554

Dr Feckenham has come straight to me from the Tower.

'What did the Lady Jane say?' I ask apprehensively.

'She is an obstinate girl, Madam, but a very brave one. I was most impressed with her. Not once did she falter or break down during our conversation, though I could see that the prospect of life was most pleasing to her.'

'Yet she will not abjure her heresy?'

'Not yet, Madam. I need more time, and so does she. If you would, of your clemency, grant a three-day stay of execution, I think I might make some progress with her.'

'I pray God you do,' the Queen says with feeling. 'I do not want to send an innocent child to the scaffold.'

Lady Jane Dudley

The Tower of London, 8th February 1554

I am at my prayers again.

'Deliver me from temptation!' I beg. 'I so desire to live, and my flesh shrinks from the axe, yet I know I could never embrace the Roman religion. I pray that I might not deny Thee, O my God. Be unto me a strong tower of defence. Suffer me not to be tempted above my power. I beseech Thee, let me stand fast!'

I am interrupted by a knocking noise and shouts from outside. I stand up, feeling a little dizzy, for I was unable to face breakfast this morning. Looking out, I can see some workmen unloading timber from a cart, while others are hammering nails into planks laid out on Tower Green.

They are building a scaffold for me, I realise. It is another jolt into reality. I begin trembling, fighting down the rising panic. I must not, I *must* not lose control.

All afternoon the banging and clattering go on. It is impossible to pray or read, so I go downstairs and sit with Mrs Partridge in the kitchen at the back of the house. Where once she would have welcomed me warmly, this good woman is now awkward in my company, but there is something I have to ask her.

'Mrs Partridge,' I say, looking directly into her eyes, 'do you know why the Queen has suddenly ordered my execution?' Mrs Partridge's obvious discomfiture tells me that she does know, so I go on, 'It is bad enough having to die, but far worse not knowing why. The Queen had promised me a pardon. Why did she change her mind?'

Mrs Partridge is reluctant to say anything, but at length I coax from her the truth.

'It was your father,' she says. 'He was one of the leaders in the late rebellion. He meant to make you Queen again.'

Understanding dawns. I see now why the Queen considers me a danger. I, who would not willingly harm a hair on her Majesty's head. It is my own father who has done this, and I who am to pay the price of his folly and treachery. I am appalled, and nothing that Mrs Partridge may say can comfort me. I weep for a very long time.

Presently, when the workmen have laid down their tools and gone home, I go upstairs, not daring to look out of the window. I do not want to see the scaffold they have built. Besides, I have farewell letters to write to my family and friends, and must put myself in the right frame of mind.

'Live to die,' I exhort my sister Katherine.

Deny the world, deny the Devil, and despise the flesh. Rejoice at my death, as I do, for I shall be delivered from corruption and will put on the mantle of incorruption. Farewell, dear sister. Put your sole trust in God, Who only must uphold you.

Your loving sister, Jane.

Early in the evening, Dr Feckenham returns with the news that my execution has been postponed until Monday.

'Her Majesty desires that you have more time in which to consider your conversion. Again, she promises you mercy if you will agree to it,' he tells me, and looks surprised to see me so dismayed.

'Alas, Sir,' I say, 'it was not my desire to prolong my days. I was prepared to die tomorrow. As for death itself, I utterly despise it, and her Majesty's pleasure being such, I willingly undergo it. I assure you, my time on Earth has been so odious to me that I long for death.'

The Abbot looks deeply moved. Surely he cannot feel so distressed at the prospect of someone dying? After all, a Christian is supposed to rejoice when a soul goes home to God, as I am trying to do myself. Yet he looks as if he is on the verge of weeping.

'I have another suggestion to make,' he says. 'Believe me, I understand your doubts . . .'

'I have no doubts!' I interrupt.

'My lady, I am doing my very best to help you save your life, and your soul. Will you not hear me out?'

'I beg your pardon,' I say, suddenly humbled. 'Pray go on.'

Dr Feckenham smiles at me.

'It has occurred to me that it might be helpful to set up a debate between yourself and some Catholic scholars and churchmen, here, in the Chapel of St Peter ad Vincula. You could hear their arguments, make answer yourself and, with God's grace, you might even be persuaded to change your mind.'

'I doubt that,' I tell him. 'Dr Feckenham, it would be a waste of my valuable time. Such a disputation might be fit for the living, but not for the dying. Please leave me alone to make my peace with God.'

The Abbot takes my hands in his and looks deep into my

eyes. In his, in this moment, I see a compassion and under-standing rare in a human being, and my resolve weakens.

'I beg of you, give yourself this last chance,' he urges me. 'I beseech you. You have everything to lose – and all to gain. Just think, if you were wrong in your beliefs, would it not be a terrible thing to die for them, and to die in error?'

'Alright, Dr Feckenham,' I agree, capitulating. 'Set up your debate. I will attend, if it pleases you.'

The Tower of London, 9th February 1554

Under guard, I walk back from the chapel with Dr Feckenham, averting my eyes from the scaffold on which I will certainly die on Monday. Inside, I am rejoicing that I have remained true to myself and strong in my beliefs. It was a trial I could have done without at this time, for I was calm in my faith and needed no tempests to disturb me. They tried to put doubts in my mind and break my resolve, and every time I refuted their arguments, I was aware I was being an advocate of my own death. But I was given the strength to hold fast to the truth, and for that I am truly thankful.

The old priest's face is infinitely sad. Alone of my inquisi-tors, he was gentle with me. But he failed to move me, and he looks as if that failure will haunt him for the rest of his life.

It is I who break the silence as we near the Gentleman Gaoler's house, where the Abbot must take his leave of me for ever. There are tears in my eyes once more. 'I weep, Sir, because we shall never meet again,' I tell him. 'Not on this Earth, nor even in Heaven, unless God turns your heart.'

Choked with grief, he lays his hand on mine.

'I have one request, my lady. Might I accompany you to the scaffold?'

I am immediately suspicious. 'Has the Queen commanded it?' I want no last-minute attempts at conversion, not at that time.

'No, Madam. I myself humbly request it. I cannot go with you all the way on your journey, but I would go as far as I might.'

Such kindness disarms me: it is almost too much to bear. He is a truly good man, for all his wrong-headed religious convictions.

'Of course you may,' I say warmly.

He is suddenly brisk again, clearly desperate that I shall not see how moved he is and give way myself.

'You must go in, my daughter. I am sure you have much to do.'

'Yes, indeed,' I agree, blinking back the tears. 'I have not finished my farewell letters, and I must dispose of my few poor possessions. Then there is the matter of a gown for − for Monday. It should be black, but mine are somewhat worn.'

'My lady, for your virtue and goodness, God would receive you in rags,' Dr Feckenham blurts out. 'Farewell.'

He turns abruptly and walks away. Shortly afterwards, in the privacy of my room, I give way to my terrible distress. Then, when I can cry no more, I force myself to get up and attend to practical matters.

The Tower of London, 10th February 1554

'Your father is here in the Tower!' cries Mrs Ellen, coming into my chamber. 'He has been discovered and brought here under arrest.'

'What happened?' I ask, catching my breath.

'After the rebellion, your father fled to Bradgate, where he snatched up a few possessions before going to ground. But the hue and cry was out, and it was not long before the Earl of Huntingdon . . .'

'Who was once his friend,' I interrupt.

'Yes,' she says simply. 'Not any more, evidently. The Earl discovered him hiding in a hollow tree trunk at Astley Park in Warwickshire. He was very dishevelled, frozen stiff and ravenous with hunger. Then the soldiers came.'

'Where is he being held?' I ask.

'Mrs Partridge wouldn't say.'

'Perhaps it is as well. They will not let me see him, and anyway, it would be painful to both of us. He will not escape the Queen's justice this time. He is doomed, just as I am.'

'*He* has deserved it,' Mrs Ellen cries bitterly.

My feelings for my father are ambivalent. I owe him the duty of a daughter, but it is his actions that have brought me to this extremity, and I am struggling to suppress my anger and pain at his reckless stupidity and his callous indifference to its consequences for me. But I cannot go to my death with hatred and resentment in my heart, so I am constraining myself to forgiveness.

I have mixed feelings, therefore, when my father sends me a message expressing his remorse for what he has done, and craving my absolution. Sir John Bridges has authorised this letter, and tells me that I might send a reply if I so wish, although it must not be sealed.

Remembering my Christian duty, I take pity on my father, who also faces death and must die with such dreadful sins on his conscience. To bring him to an awareness of the health of his soul, I cannot help reminding him, in charity, of why I am to die. I write:

> *Father,*
> *Although it has pleased God to hasten my death by your means, by whom my life should have been lengthened, yet I can so patiently take it that I yield God thanks for shortening my woeful days. I count myself blessed that, washing my hands with my innocence, my guiltless blood may cry before Almighty God.*

Reading this over, I think it sounds a little harsh, so I end on a gentler note:

> *The Lord continue to keep you, that at the last we may meet in Heaven. Your obedient daughter till death, Jane.*

After Sir John has taken this letter, I am overcome with remorse: I should be comforting my father, not castigating him. The hours left to us on Earth are too short for recriminations, and I must go to God with a heart cleansed of bitterness. Therefore, in my old prayer book, which once belonged to my grandmother, Mary Tudor, and which I have decided to carry with me to the scaffold, I write a second message to my father:

> *The Lord comfort your Grace. Though it has pleased God to take away two of your children, think not that you have lost them, but trust that we, by losing this mortal life, have won an immortal*

life. I, for my part, as I have honoured your Grace in this life, will pray for you in another life.

When the Lieutenant next visits me, which he does twice a day now to see if I have all I need, I ask him to ensure that my prayer book is delivered to my father after my death.

He looks at what I have written.

'Very proper, very fitting,' he says, then clears his throat. 'Madam, I wonder – might I also crave some small remembrance of you?' he asks. His eyes convey far more than he is able to say.

I cast around, then pick up the velvet-bound prayer book given to me by Guilford.

'You may have this, Sir John,' I say. 'I will inscribe it for you.' And I write:

There is a time to be born and a time to die, and the day of our death is better than the day of our birth.
Yours, as the Lord knows, a true friend.

Sir John reads my words. He cannot speak. He nods his thanks, and leaves me.

Fighting back the ever-ready tears, I sit down to compose the speech that I must make from the scaffold. It must not be too long, for it will be a cold morning and I must not be seen to be delaying the execution. Nor must I appear to criticise the Queen or the sentence against me in any way: to do so might lead to the confiscation of my family's property – if there is any left of it, I think grimly. My father will surely be attainted and deprived of his life, titles and possessions, and the last will all be forfeit to the Crown, leaving my mother and sisters facing penury. So I will say nothing against the Queen. Indeed, I have no cause to.

I am writing out a fair copy of my finished speech when Sir John Bridges returns.

'Madam, I have received a message from the council. Your husband, Guilford Dudley, has petitioned the Queen for permission to say farewell to you in person, and her Majesty has granted his request, if you are agreeable.'

I am already shrinking inside. I cannot cope with Guilford now. He belongs to a part of my life that I have put firmly behind me.

'How is my husband?' I inquire.

Sir John shakes his head.

'Very distressed, I fear. His gaolers believe he is on the verge of collapse; he never ceases railing against what he perceives to be an unkind fate. He does not have your courage, my lady. Perhaps if you were to see him, it would calm him.'

'No, I prefer not to. I am sorry for him, but to be truthful, I could not face it. Yet I will send him a message. Tell him I desire him, for the love of God, to omit these moments of grief, for we shall shortly behold each other in a better place. Tell him also that I shall watch from my window as he leaves for Tower Hill on Monday.'

'I will pass on your message, Madam,' the Lieutenant promises.

After he has gone, I sink down at my desk.

This waiting is sheer hell. It seems that every last refinement of suffering is to be my lot in these final days. Truly, I think that death, when it comes, will be very welcome to me. At least I will then be at peace.

Mrs Ellen

The Tower of London, 11th February 1554

Distraught, I weep into my pillow, as I have done every night since last Wednesday. The pillow is sodden with my grief, and I am ragged from lack of sleep. It is all I can do to restrain myself from crying aloud my agony. Instead, I toss from side to side, whimpering in torment.

My charge, my darling child, whom I have carefully nurtured from birth as if she were my own flesh and blood, is to be butchered to death in the morning, just a few short hours from now. All that care, all that love – and I can do nothing to help her now. That she should be brought to this, to die so untimely in the most beautiful bloom of her youth – the prospect is unbearable.

It is against Nature, this taking of a young life. At sixteen, Jane should be occupied, like most girls of her age, with domestic things; she should be mistress of her own household with at least one infant in the nursery, and a lusty husband in her bed. She should be doing all the normal things that young women of her rank do: ordering the servants, stitching her lord's shirts, making infusions in the still room, supervising the nurses. Instead, her life is to come abruptly to a bloody end.

It has been torture these past days to watch her, so slender and pretty, with her burnished red hair and the soft bloom on her freckled skin. Those childish hands with their thin fingers holding the pen that writes such adult words. The grace of her movements, the carriage of her head, the curve of her cheek. All the things I love about my young lady, who is at an age when a girl's looks are at their finest, when youth is urgent with the zest for life and the future stretches endlessly ahead. Yet by this time tomorrow, my child will be in her grave.

Was ever condemned prisoner as innocent as this? She has not deserved this punishment. She is as good and honest as the day. It was that wicked Northumberland, and her unspeakable parents, who brought her to this. May God forgive them, for I never can. If I had my way, they would burn in Hell for all eternity. My hatred for them is like a canker, consuming me. Along with my grief and my pain, it is tearing me apart.

So far, I have managed – just, and only by a supreme effort of will – to maintain my outward composure for Jane's sake. My prayer now is that I will not fail her on the morrow. If I can just be strong for a few more short hours . . . It will be the last comfort I can offer her.

Frances Brandon, Duchess of Suffolk

Sheen, 11th February 1554

I am in my lodging at court, lying in the arms of my young master of horse, Adrian Stokes, and crying bitter tears for my daughter, whom I am to lose for ever tomorrow.

Until last Thursday, when I heard the terrible news, my affair with Adrian, which I admit has been based purely upon lust, served as an antidote to my wild rage at my husband for his rash incrimination of Jane in his madcap schemes. But now Adrian barely exists for me. My innocent Jane is to pay the price of my husband's treason, and he in turn will follow her to the block. Yet only one of them deserves to die. And if I could get my hands on Henry, I would kill him myself.

I no longer care that I am to be left widowed and destitute. Henry means less than nothing to me now. He forfeited all rights to my love and loyalty on the day he issued an ultimatum to Wyatt. At thirty-seven, I am still a handsome woman, and a lusty one at that, and I did not hesitate to inveigle my young master of horse into my bed. It was my way of having my revenge on Henry, but it also provided me with the comfort of another human body, and a means to ward off the night terrors that have beset me these past weeks.

Adrian came willingly enough, and has proved a considerate and inventive lover. But tonight, as on the past three nights, his presence in my bed hardly registers.

Instead of turning to him hot with desire, as I did before last Thursday, I lie here punishing myself with remorse. I have been a harsh mother, when I could have been kinder and more understanding. I can see it now, with the benefit of hindsight and the clarity that follows misfortune and grief. What crucifies me especially is the knowledge that there is no way in which I can make reparation to my daughter, no way that she will ever be able to extend to me the forgiveness that I crave. I can only pray for God's mercy.

The young man beside me is now asleep. He is distressed by the tragedy that is overtaking me, but blessedly distanced from it. I envy him his oblivion.

I know there are those who are criticising me for having returned to court, and perhaps it does look as if I am thinking only of my own future. But the Queen is my cousin, my own flesh and blood, and I had thought to soften her heart by my presence, which I hoped would call to her remembrance the plight of my poor child. But she has not condescended to notice me. I have waited hours, jostled by hosts of petitioners, for her to come forth from her apartments, bound for chapel or presence chamber, only to have her pass by me unseeing. I have tried to send messages begging for an audience, but none of my erstwhile friends will deliver them. I have even thought of throwing myself on my knees in the Queen's path, but I know it would do me no good. The bitter truth is that I understand why Jane has to die.

I know that sleep will elude me tonight. Carefully I slide out of bed, put on my nightgown, take the candle and make my way to the chapel. Here, on my knees before the altar, where a flickering lamp bears witness to the ever-constant presence of God, I immerse myself in prayer as never before, beseeching the Almighty to pardon my grievous faults and sins of omission, and to give me the strength to return to Him with a good and ungrudging heart the daughter that He gave me.

Queen Mary

Whitehall Palace, 11th February 1554

It is quiet in the palace tonight, as if the world is holding its breath until the morning. I lie wakeful, my thoughts in a turmoil. It goes against all my convictions to send Jane to her death. If

I could issue a reprieve, I would. But too much is at stake, I fear: the respect of my advisors, who suspect me of harbouring womanish scruples when it comes to punishing traitors; the scorn of Renard, who would never trust my word again; the obedience of my subjects, who might attempt further liberties if I do not assert my authority; and, above all, my marriage to Prince Philip, for which I am longing with all my heart and soul, and which will bring so many benefits to England.

I am discovering that it is no easy thing to be a queen, and not for the first time I find myself wishing that I were a simple country goodwife with a houseful of children instead.

But there is no point in wishing. I must go on my knees and ask God if He will work yet another miracle for me, and turn Jane, at the last, to the true faith. Then I will be able to spare her, and will do so gladly, for, converted to the Catholic religion, she could no longer be a figurehead for my enemies.

Dr Feckenham has his instructions.

Lady Jane Dudley

The Tower of London, 11th February 1554

In my bedchamber in the Tower, I am sitting in my nightgown, writing my last testament:

If justice is done with my body, my soul will find mercy with God. Death will give pain to my body for its sins, but my soul will be justified before God. If my faults deserve punishment, my youth at least, and my imprudence, were worthy of excuse. God and posterity will show me more favour.

Wearily I lay down my pen. There is silence all around me. I climb into bed, expecting to lie awake for hours, as I have done these past nights. Why should I sleep? There will be sleep enough for me after tomorrow.

My belongings lie parcelled up and stacked in the corner by the desk. Mrs Ellen knows the names of those to whom she must distribute them, and has promised to do so faithfully. My clothes for tomorrow, and my prayer book, are all that are left of my worldly possessions.

How strange to think that, nine hours from now, I will leave this world and cease to exist. So little time. I cannot lie here any longer. I must use these remaining hours for my devotions. Then I can rest for all eternity.

The Tower of London, 12th February 1554

I fell asleep at my prayers, but not for long. Dawn is just breaking when I awaken, stiff and disorientated, with a vague sense that something is badly wrong. The notion is fleeting, for grim reality intervenes. My execution is less than four hours away. The knowledge fills me with dread. Everything seems unreal, as if I am dreaming it.

Mrs Ellen arrives, her face taut with sadness and fatigue. Clearly she has not slept much either. We bid each other a quiet good morning, knowing that there is nothing that is good about it. Then, with trembling fingers, Mrs Ellen pulls on my lawn chemise, and helps me to dress in the black kirtle with the low, square neckline, and the high-collared velvet gown that goes over it, the clothes I wore for my trial. She then plaits my hair and coils it high on my head before securing the black veil and hood.

We kneel together to pray.

An unexpected knock on the door signals the arrival of Sir John Bridges. I am alarmed: it is not yet seven o'clock. Surely it is not time yet?

Sir John looks embarrassed.

'Madam, I regret to tell you that the Queen has sent an order requiring you to submit yourself to examination by a panel of matrons, to ensure that you are not with child. If you are found to be, your life will be spared, since her Majesty cannot sanction the killing of an innocent babe.'

I look at him in astonishment.

'Sir John, I have not seen my husband since November,

and then not alone. I know I am not with child.'

'I am sorry, but the Queen's command must be obeyed. If there is even the possibility of a pregnancy, you would be spared the axe. Her Majesty is giving you every last chance of life.'

'Then I must submit,' I say dejectedly. 'But it will be a waste of time.'

I lie on my bed, skirts pulled up, legs splayed, unable to believe that this last indignity is being forced on me almost at the hour of trial. Around me stand four sober and discreet matrons, all experienced mothers and grandmothers. They probe gently inside me and press my stomach. They ask me questions. When did I last lie with my husband? When were my last courses? Are my breasts tender? They are kind with me, and conscientious in their duty, but this is an invasion I could well do without at this time, and, as I predicted, it is all for nothing. I am not with child.

Having smoothed down my skirts and tidied myself, I ask to see the Lieutenant.

'Have they taken Guilford yet?'

'No, Madam, but they will soon.'

I take up my place at the window, as I promised I would do, and presently see some men emerge from the Beauchamp Tower. It is Guilford, under guard. With a tear-streaked face, he looks up at me and lifts his hand in a forlorn salute. I smile wanly at him.

'Go with God,' I mouth. Whether or not he understands, I cannot tell, but he seems to be making an effort to control himself. Waiting for him near the White Tower is a group of young men, amongst whom I recognise several of his friends. Not so long ago he was roistering with them in the taverns of London, an immature youth with no cares in the world, eager to prove himself a man. Now they are come to support him in his last hour. I watch the sad little procession as it makes its way on foot towards Tower Hill and out of sight. Inwardly I am begging God to give Guilford the courage to make a good end.

It is now that I force myself to look across to the scaffold on Tower Green. It has been draped with black material and strewn with straw, but there is no sign of the block. As yet, the green is deserted. Sir John has told me that, as my execution is to be held in private, attendance is by invitation only, and that the numbers have been strictly limited. They are probably all at Tower Hill just now, watching Guilford being beheaded, I expect. And when that is over – which cannot be long now, I pray – it will be my turn. It is the waiting that is so hard.

Two men come into view, hastening towards Tower Green. They are wearing black velvet gowns, long white aprons and black masks with slits for their eyes. The one in front carries an axe. I know that he is the executioner, and that my hour is upon me.

My eyes widen in horror, for they are bringing back the cart bearing Guilford's body. I can see his torso wrapped in a bloody sheet, and beside it a round object swathed in a red-stained cloth. As the cart passes, I cannot restrain my tears. He was a shallow youth, but there was some good in him, and he did not deserve this.

'Oh, Guilford! Guilford!' I sob. 'Oh, the bitterness of death!'

A crowd of people is advancing on Tower Green. There is little time left. I pick up my prayer book and try to concentrate on the passages I have marked for my final devotions. But as the words dance before my eyes, I hear footsteps on the stairs, and the door swings open.

'It is time, my lady,' says Sir John Bridges gently. Behind him stands Dr Feckenham, who is gazing at me with deep compassion. Holding tightly onto the Lieutenant's arm, for my legs suddenly feel weak, I descend the stairs and walk out of the Gentleman Gaoler's house, followed by Mrs Ellen and Mrs Tilney, both weeping silently into their kerchiefs. But my eyes, thankfully, are dry, and I progress slowly and, I hope, with dignity, towards the scaffold. I am determined that the onlookers – amongst whom I recognise privy councillors and noblemen who once sat at table with me – will be impressed by my composure.

At the foot of the scaffold steps I catch sight of the waiting coffin, lying on the grass, and falter for a moment. Dr Feckenham whispers, 'Have no fear, Jane. I will be with you to the end, and God is with you for ever.' This gives me the courage to mount the steps, leaning on Sir John's arm, and then stand alone, grasping the rail, facing the crowd. There is a respectful silence as I speak.

'Good people, I am come hither to die, for by law I am condemned to the same,' I say, in a voice that sounds clear and steady in the crisp air. 'My offence against the Queen's Highness was unlawful, and my consent to it; but touching the procuring and desiring of it by me, I wash my hands in innocence before God, and in the face of you, good Christian people.'

I pause. My heart is pounding so fast that I can barely catch my breath, and my head is swimming. With an involuntary shudder, I wring my hands and continue, 'I pray you all to bear me witness that I die a good Christian woman.' I look at Dr Feckenham as I say this, knowing he will understand the significance of my words. He smiles sadly back.

'And now, good people,' I conclude, 'while I am alive, I pray you assist me with your prayers.'

I turn again to the Abbot, pointing to a marked page in my prayer book.

'Shall I say this psalm?' I ask him, then wish I had not, for he is clearly too distressed to answer me. I wait awkwardly for a few moments, then hear him whisper, 'Yes, Jane.' At this, I kneel and recite in English the nineteen verses of the *Miserere mei Deus*. When I have finished, I rise and put my arms around the priest, kissing him on the cheek, marvelling that my last comfort in this world should come from a Catholic.

'I beseech God that He will abundantly reward you for your kindness towards me,' I say fervently, then add, with my usual tactless honesty, 'although I must needs say that it was more unwelcome to me than my instant death is terrible.'

His old eyes are full of love. We understand each other very well.

The formalities are almost completed. It is time to prepare myself.

The Executioner

Tower Green, 12th February 1554

It never fails to get to me, every time I officiate at an execution, how it starts out dignified, with all these ceremonies and protocols, as they like to call them, and then quickly turns into a gory bloodbath. Happens every time, although I pride myself I'm that good at my job that the poor buggers don't suffer in the way they do under some ham-fisted headsmen. Worst case I ever heard of was poor Lady Salisbury, back in the old King's time. The chief executioner was off sick, and his stand-in hadn't had no experience. Chased the old girl round the block, he did, chopping this way and that. Made a bloody mess of her.

It don't do to get too sentimental about this job, though. It is, after all, just a job. Well, no, of course, it's more than that. Hanging's easy, and I'm handy and quick with a disembowelling knife, but there's an art to beheading people, and I'm a master, if I say it myself. I've topped a good few in my time, and done it well. And I've seen all sorts go to the scaffold, from great ones like the Dukes of Somerset and Northumberland, to humble folks as have got themselves caught up in lost causes, such as this rebellion that they've just put a stop to. God, we've been rushed off our feet with hangings these past few days.

And now this. Two of them to dispatch this morning. That poor lad who couldn't speak for blubbering. A sorry end he made. But this execution is different. I ain't never had any like it. This one's nothing but a slip of a girl, just a little kid. Gave me a jolt when I saw her; all sweet and demure, walking along in her black dress. Couldn't say boo to a goose, let alone commit treason. And to hear the Lieutenant talk – although naturally, he don't give too much away – he thinks she's innocent too. Seemed quite upset about it, actually, and told me to make it quick. Well, if there's anyone who can do that for her, it's me.

You've got to admire her courage. I see all sorts face death, and for one so young, she's pretty calm and brave. No howling or struggling. I suppose it's because she's very religious, so Sir John says, and believes she's going straight to Heaven. I wish there were more like her. A lot of them go out crying and screaming for mercy.

The Lady Jane takes off her gloves and hands them to her women. She turns to the Lieutenant and gives him her prayer book. He looks stricken, poor sod, and he's having to struggle to control himself. I've never seen him like this before: he's usually a tough one, is Sir John. Does his duty proper, even if he might not like it.

The two women are now beginning to unlace the girl's outer gown. I step forward and ask if she needs any help with undressing.

'No, Sir,' she says. Her voice is surprisingly steady. 'I desire you to let me alone for now.' And she stands there while they take the gown off, and the hood, and the veil. When she's left in her kirtle and bodice, she starts shivering, poor kid. It won't be for long, though: soon, she'll be past feeling the cold.

One of the women steps forward with a kerchief to bind round the Lady Jane's eyes. They throw their arms around each other and the woman starts kissing her and sobbing. If she goes on like this, we'll have to prise the girl away. But no. The Lady Jane gives her a last kiss, and steps back. This is too much for the poor woman, who has to turn her back to hide her distress.

Scaffold procedure requires me, at this point, to kneel down before the prisoner and ask her forgiveness for what I am duty-bound to do.

'I give it most willingly,' the Lady Jane tells me, and hands me a purse that the Lieutenant gave her containing part of my fee. The other part is my usual perquisite, the prisoner's clothing. It's a good gown, the one she took off, and will fetch a fair bit of money, like the kirtle she's wearing. When everyone's gone, we'll strip it off her.

My assistant, young Will, has been standing in front of the block, which his long apron has hidden from the prisoner's view. He always does this, as we've found that the sight of it often makes the condemned more jittery. But now it's time for the lad to stand aside. The block is low, only ten inches high, and it has a scooped-out hollow for the chin. The girl stares at it.

'Please to stand there on the straw, my lady,' I direct, pointing to the space in front of the block. The Lady Jane steps into position, and kneels at my nod. She's shaking uncontrollably, poor little soul, and I think to myself, dear God, are we all to be accomplices in butchering a child? Christ, I'm not comfortable with this. But where's the choice? What can I do about it? I'm not the one who makes the decisions. I've just got a job to do and a reputation to maintain.

'I pray you dispatch me quickly,' the girl says fearfully in a low voice. 'Will you take it off before I lay me down?'

'No, Madam,' I answer. 'When you are ready, stretch out your arms.'

It's time. The people watching fall to their knees on the grass, out of respect for the passing of a soul. For a long moment the Lady Jane looks her last on the world, then takes the kerchief from her attendant, who has stopped crying now, and ties it round her eyes. Thus blindfolded, she holds out her hands to grasp the block.

She's too far away from it. She's groping wildly.

'Where is it? Where is it? What shall I do?' she cries, panicking. The poor child is leaning forward, flailing her arms in desperation. 'What shall I do?' she sobs. 'Where is it?'

I move forward quickly, but the priest is there before me. He takes her hands and gently guides them to the block. Breathing heavily, she lays herself down as best she can, pressing her chin into the rough wood and arching her shoulders to support herself.

Sir John gives me the nod. I am startled by the pain in his eyes – I've never seen him looking like that. Then he stares straight ahead.

The Lady Jane is lying there, finishing her prayers. She ends, like many do, with the words that Jesus spoke on the Cross.

'Lord, into Thy hands I commend my spirit!' she cries, and stretches out her arms.

I raise the great axe and bring it down swiftly, slicing expertly and cleanly through flesh, bone and artery; the slender body jerks violently, and the little head drops like a stone in the straw, which is soon soaked crimson by the torrent of blood spouting from the severed neck. Even I, with all my experience, have never seen so much blood at a beheading.

Now I've one more thing to do before we strip and chest the corpse and clear up. I bend down, then brandish my trophy aloft.

'So perish all the Queen's enemies!' I cry. 'Behold the head of a traitor!'

Author's Note

This novel has been based on a true story. Lady Jane Grey is an intriguing and tragic figure, and readers of my historical works will know that I have already written about her in two previous books: her childhood is documented in *The Six Wives of Henry VIII*, and her nine-day reign – the shortest in English history – and its horrific sequel in *Children of England*.

Most of the characters in this novel really existed, and most of the events actually happened. However, where the evidence is scanty or missing, I have used my imagination. For example, we do not know the identity of the female quack who was called in by Northumberland to administer arsenic to Edward VI, but I have spun a tale around her. There is no evidence that Jane witnessed the burning of Anne Askew in 1546, but I have used it as the catalyst for her conversion to the Protestant faith.

Some parts of the book may seem far-fetched: they are the parts most likely to be based on fact, such as the discovery, by one of Katherine Parr's ladies, of the death warrant that had been dropped in a corridor. This story is related by John Foxe in his *Book of Martyrs*, and most historians now accept it as the truth. However, there is no historical evidence that it was Jane who found the warrant, although she was in Katherine Parr's household at the time. And my account of the fate of Edward VI's body is not as incredible as it sounds, for what happened to that body is described in a letter written by the Earl of Warwick, Northumberland's son.

Above all, I have tried to penetrate the minds of my characters, which is something that serious historians attempt only at their peril. Writing this book has therefore been something of a venture into the realms of psychology, as well as a foray into the past, because history does not often record people's motives, emotions and reactions, and I have had to make some educated

– and occasionally wild – guesses, in order to ensure that they sound credible within the context of the known facts.

After having published ten historical non-fiction books, writing this novel filled me with a heady sense of freedom. No longer was I focusing only on the available source material and the strict disciplines of historical interpretation, but I could allow my imagination free rein. It has been wonderful to be this creative, and even provocative, whilst at the same time striving for historical accuracy.

Lady Jane Grey's story is compelling and shocking. Although she was the product of her age and its prejudices against women, within the constraints of her time she remained true to herself and her ideals and beliefs. Precocious, highly gifted and intelligent, she was educated to an unusually advanced standard for a girl, and realised that there was more to a woman's life than just marrying, having children and running a household. Never one to compromise, she was outspoken, feisty and unafraid to challenge the received wisdom of her day. In these respects, she could be considered a very modern heroine. In telling her story, I have used as many of her own words as possible, although in places these have been slightly modernised so as not to appear incongruous in a twenty-first-century text.

The Tudor period continues to exert a perennial fascination over the imagination of vast numbers of people, and this novel deals with one of its most dramatic episodes. It is my sincere hope that the story that has unfolded in these pages has both enthralled and appalled you, the reader.